JEOPARDY

Also by this author

Trilogy
Mistaken Obsession
White Roses for My Love
A Mistaken Angel

Gray and Armstrong Private Investigations series
The Passport Mystery
Missing
Innocent

JEOPARDY

Book 4—Gray and Armstrong
Private Investigations

Eve Grafton

Library of Congress Control Number:		2019904608
ISBN:	Hardcover	978-1-7960-0094-8
	Softcover	978-1-7960-0093-1
	eBook	978-1-7960-0092-4

Print information available on the last page.

Rev. date: 04/18/2019

To order additional copies of this book, contact:
Xlibris
1-800-455-039
www.Xlibris.com.au
Orders@Xlibris.com.au
792323

This is book 4 in the Gray and Armstrong Private Investigations series, featuring Alicia and James Armstrong; business partner Percy Gray; and Alicia's grandmother, Valerie Newton.

CHAPTER ONE

The young woman was running along the pavement in the well-lit streets. She had finished her shift at the hospital where she was a nurse. Having not run in a while, too scared someone was following her as on a previous occasion, stopping when she stopped and starting up again when she did. She wondered at times whether her imagination had taken over her. This scare had put her off her favourite pastime. She had been thinking of joining a club for marathon running where they ran with a group, but it did not seem to her to be the same as the enjoyment she felt from running after a day at work, winding down from a busy day, getting some fresh air instead of the air conditioning in the wards where she worked.

She listened now for any running sounds behind her and was sure she heard the pad of feet coming towards her. She stopped in a doorway, pretending to knock, as the runner came up to her. Deciding to find out who the runner was instead of panicking each time she heard someone running behind her, as the man came up to her position in the doorway, she said, 'Excuse me, are you following me?'

The man turned his head, stopped, and looked at her. 'I am not actually following you. I am out for an after-work run, and you happened to be going my way in front of me. Technically, I was following you, but it could have been anyone ahead of me down the street. I could only see an outline of someone moving ahead. Did I scare you?'

'Yes. I have had another follower who has tried to attack me in the street where I live, so I have changed to this area, which is well lit. Since the attack, I have not run, and this is my first run in months.'

'I am sorry for your scare. However, I am not going to attack you or anyone else. I only wanted some exercise after sitting in my office all day, and I need to keep fit and clear my head, hence the run. Do you have far to go and want company beside you?'

She looked at him suspiciously. 'Have you proof of who you are?'

The man felt in his shirt pocket and came up with two cards. 'This is my business card. I am the Armstrong in the title of the business, James Armstrong. This other card is for Harry Burton's keep-fit classes. He can vouch for me. In fact, if you want exercise, you could join his keep-fit classes for ladies on Tuesday evening, at 8 p.m. Harry is an ex–army sergeant who runs a business in his father's barn. Men on Monday and Wednesday, and ladies on Tuesday. It is really worth the five-pound fee to join in for two hours of fairly gruelling drilling. It builds up your strength and gives you confidence.'

'I am sorry I have delayed you, Mr Armstrong. It is just such a copy of the other fellow who followed me. He attacked one dark evening. I was lucky a householder heard me scream and came out to find out what was going on. The runner took off before he was apprehended. That is why I stopped here. The householder has a light on, and I could knock at the door if you appeared to be an attacker.'

'It sounds as if you need those self-defence classes. My wife attends and thinks they are great, and it has given her a quiet confidence that she can handle anyone who tries anything on her.'

'I will give it some thought. Thank you.'

'Do you want me to accompany you to your street now?'

'Thank you, Mr Armstrong. I am sure it will be okay now. I have not heard any further footsteps.'

'Do you mind telling me your name now that we have met?'

'I am sorry, of course. I am Julie Norris. I am a nurse at the general hospital.'

'If you are sure you will be okay, I will be off to my dinner. Can I suggest you carry a high-pitched whistle, to use in case of any future attack? Good luck, Julie. Cheerio.'

James sprinted off. He was going to be late for dinner now. He always timed his runs so that he arrived back home as Alicia, his wife, was ready to serve dinner to her grandmother; Percy Gray, his business partner; and himself. He did not want to upset Alicia; she was so warm and loving and uncomplaining. He looked at his watch. It was okay; he was still within his time allowance. It was only six thirty. He laughed to himself. He felt it was later because it was so dark that wintry late February evening.

It was his first run since arriving home from their excellent holiday in India with their friends Jameel and Indira, and his first week back at work was hectic as he got back into the swing of things. He felt he had not been out of the office for a week, catching up with outstanding chores, and had needed the run to clear his mind.

His partner, Percy, and the other staff—Ken Johnson, currently on loan from the London police, and Kate Langford, an ex-policewoman—had kept the home fires going while he and Alicia were holidaying in India, and he had come home enthusiastic from the trip, vowing to go again at some time.

Within ten minutes, he was back at the bookshop apartment, where he lived with Alicia, and went directly to shower, which was needed after the run. Then he went into the house next door, which was Alicia's grandmother's house, where they ate the evening meal so that Alicia could help her grandmother out.

He was greeted by each of them heartily, and Percy said, 'I have a job you may wish to discuss after dinner, James. It is a Saturday job, and as my Saturdays have been spent in the bookshop while you were on holiday, I have been saving it up for you. It came in a week ago, and I rang the people concerned and explained that you were away at the time and would be back to work this week. I left a few days for you to get back into the swing of things before I mentioned it.'

'Okay, Percy, we will get down to it once we have cleared the table.' He turned to Alicia. 'This looks nice, Alicia. Have you been experimenting?'

She smiled. 'Yes, I was intrigued when we had that lesson on how to make samosas while we were in India, and this is my contribution to tonight's dinner. Granny did the rest, as it took me longer than I expected to work out my handwriting while we were watching in the marketplace where we enjoyed them. I have tasted one, and they seem the same. I will appreciate any comments you have about them. I am intent on getting them right, as I enjoyed them so much. I suppose that if I have to, I can always resort to Mrs Sharma at our weekend market when they start up again next month, although samosas are not really Indian—more Asian, I think.'

James took one and tentatively tasted it and smiled. 'You have it right, Alicia. This is delicious. Try one, Percy, and see what you think.'

Percy and Granny also tried one and agreed they were good. Alicia said, 'These are our entrée, not the main meal, but I wanted to try them out before I forgot the lesson. Now that I have done it, they will be easier to produce in future. I can make extra and freeze them next time as well. These are the vegetarian ones. Next time I will try the lamb mince type.'

'Well done, Alicia. They are great, and you have the right amount of chilli in them, not too hot.'

'I know Granny does not like the hot chilli, so I made them mild. If you want heat, you can always add chilli sauce. I bought some and will keep it in the fridge for future samoses.

'I am sure they will be our favourite for a while. They would be great for party food as well.'

'I will keep that in mind for the next party we have and add them to the menu.'

After they had eaten and tidied up, James said, 'Okay, Percy, what have you got?'

'It is about someone following and watching girls when they are exercising, He seems to turn up at all the netball games. They called the police, and they came to the game in uniform, of course. The man saw them and wandered off, but he was back next week for the next games.

'The lady who runs these events is an old friend of my daughter-in-law and asked her how I could be contacted. Jenny told her that investigations are now my business, so there would be a fee attached. Barbara Talbot said she would be willing to pay to rid her teams of the embarrassment each time the fellow shows up. One or two of the parents have asked the man to leave, but other than a bemused expression on his face, there was no reaction from him. He keeps coming.

'Barbara said that some of the girls are fascinated with him, but these girls are twelve to seventeen in age. Their parents do not think it funny at all that a grown man is watching the girls so intently.'

'It does sound off, Percy, but he is not doing anything criminal. Just watching breaks no laws. What does Barbara want us to do with the man?'

'Chat him up and ask him not to return, I suppose. Let him know that watching young girls display their legs while playing sport is not a suitable thing to do.'

'Does the man pay to get into the netball court area?'

'Yes, I believe it is only a nominal amount. These are schoolgirls. Usually the only people watching are family members, so the amount is low and used for maintenance of the courts.'

'I could go along on Saturday and have a look at the situation. They should just deny the man entrance. That would stop him. I will suggest it to save them our fee, Percy, if you will help out in the bookshop with Granny. You are getting pretty adept at selling books, I am told.'

'I actually enjoy it, James. It also gives the mind a big shake-up, recognising the customers as well as trying to remember where each book is situated, but Valerie has them all worked out and has told me the formula to make it quicker.'

James told the story of the runner who had wondered if he had been following her. He said she had sounded sincerely frightened, and he mentioned how he had suggested Harry's keep-fit classes to her. He turned to Alicia. 'Keep an eye out for her, Alicia, will you? Her name is Julie Norris. Medium height, dark hair, and quite pretty. She is a nurse at the general hospital. We will not butt in unless she asks, but if she has a predator chasing after her, she should try to find out who it is and stop them in their tracks. If she turns up at Harry's barn on Tuesday evening for the keep-fit class, it will be a plus for her. No one should be scared to go out to get exercise if running is their choice, and Harry will be able to teach her how to retaliate if she is attacked again.'

'I will, James. This Tuesday evening is my first lesson this year. Harry closed down over the really cold weather.'

*   *   *

Tuesday evening came around quickly. Alicia looked forward to going to the keep-fit classes with Kate, who worked in the business with them. They had agreed it was a good thing to keep up; each of them felt more confident that they could protect themselves if the time arrived for them to need it.

After greeting Harry, Alicia looked around for any new members of the group and spotted a new face. She asked Harry if the new person was Julie Norris, and he said, 'I believe so. I have not spoken to her yet tonight, although I received a phone call this afternoon asking if I was open for a new customer. Let's go and ask her, shall we?'

'Good idea, Harry. This is one of James's pickups. He met her while out on a run last week and recommended your services to her. She was attacked once while out running and was saved by a householder who heard her screams, and she has only now taken up running again in our area, where the lighting is better, although she is still nervous.'

They walked over to the young woman, who looked a little tentative in joining the group, and Alicia said, 'Hello, are you Julie Norris? My husband, James Armstrong, asked me to keep an eye out for you and explain your problem to Harry here.' She turned towards Harry, who gave a grin and said, 'I know you, Julie. You were my cousin's bridesmaid at her wedding two years ago.'

'Is your cousin Amanda?'

'Yes. You were kind to a poor soldier in a wheelchair, chatting with me to make me feel better because I could not join in the dancing and the music was so good. It is the thing I miss most after losing my leg. I used to love to dance.'

'You were that soldier? Harry Burton, now I remember you. I remember you looked so forlorn. I felt I had to cheer you up. I am sorry I did not recognise you. You do not look so forlorn now.'

'My leg had just been amputated at that time, and I was feeling very sorry for myself. But I have come to terms with it now. The army chaplain made me understand that I should accept the things I cannot change, and I have moved on.'

Alicia had been listening to the conversation and said to Julie, 'I can confirm that he is no longer forlorn. He is teaching the young and forlorn how to look after themselves. He is an ace, and every person in the barn admires him greatly.'

'I am hoping you can teach me how to defend myself if someone attacks me while I am out running.'

'Well, I will get this show on the road, and you can tell me at the end if anything seems like it may work for you. If not, we can work around it.'

Alicia said, 'Come, Julie. We will join the line over here.' She moved over to stand beside Kate and introduced them.

*   *   *

At the end of the lesson, Harry came over and asked Julie if anything suited her particular attack.

Julie said, 'Yes and no. The man I am afraid of is bigger than me by far, taller and bulkier. Do you think I can overcome somebody like that?'

'Probably not yet. With a bit of practice, I think we can overcome the fact that he is bigger, but it depends on whether the bulk is fat or muscle. It would be good to know who your assailant is. Is that possible?'

'I have no idea. The assault happened in twilight and was so quick I had no chance to look at him properly. He was wearing a balaclava at the time. When he was interrupted, he dropped me and ran off. The only clue I can think of is that he put his hands over my mouth, and his hands smelt like the hospital lotion they use for sanitising. I look at everybody in the hospital, trying to see him, and so far, nothing. I suppose that lotion can be used in any place they want to sanitise, not just the hospital, but it was such a familiar scent.'

'You need to employ James Armstrong to find that bloke for you. He is good at his job. Alicia too is very clever, and James often uses her in the business to help out.'

Julie looked at Alicia. 'What do you think, Alicia? Can you help me find him? This man is ruining my life. Running is my way of coping with a heavy workload. It calms me down and freshens me up to be able to continue.'

'Investigations are our business. There is a payment, but if I come to the hospital alone and work with you, it will be less than the usual cost, which is for two people. I will have to ask James and Percy to agree to it.'

'I am prepared to pay the full price, Alicia. As I said, this man is ruining my life. When can you begin?'

'I will ask James and Percy in the morning, and I will give you a call. What is your phone number?'

Harry smiled. 'You should know where to find that fellow soon, with Alicia on the job for you. Anything I can do to help, just give me a call.'

'Goodnight, Harry. You are a gem. See you next week,' said Alicia and Julie together.

Alicia drove Kate home to where she was living with Ken Johnson in Percy's house and went on to the bookshop. She was excited to think that she had a job to do for Julie Norris—finding the man who attacked her—and could not wait to tell James about it. This would be her first solo job for the business, outside of working in the office, but she was sure she could handle it.

James was doing some research on his computer when she went upstairs, so she waited until he had completed that assignment before interrupting him. She made a cup of tea while she was waiting. It was thirsty work that Harry handed out for them to do in the barn, but she always felt so good about herself after completing the exercises.

When James was told of what she was planning, he grinned his cheeky grin and said, 'Doing me out of a job, are you, Alicia?'

Alicia was flustered. 'Do not think of it like that, James. I have been thinking about it all the way home and have a plan of action in mind for finding this man. Julie seems sure the offender works in the hospital, but as the staff is large, she has not spotted any one person yet who looks like the person who attacked her. I believe it will be easier for me to see if I follow her around for a day, looking at the men's reaction to her. Someone is sure to give himself away to me. She said the only clue she had was the scent of the hospital sanitiser on his hands when he grabbed her, so the possibility of it being someone who works near her is great. She is just so busy with her work she has not picked out who it is.'

'It sounds like you have it all worked out, Alicia. Do not approach this person without me being there. Go tomorrow and do as you say: follow Julie around, watching the reaction of the men. If possible, get a full-length photo of the person you think is the one you are looking for, but do not accuse him yet. I will come in with you the next day and have a look at the chap and, if necessary, get a search warrant to see if we can find the balaclava he wore. I will tee up Tony Walton, our favourite policeman, to search his property in that case.'

'Yes, James, I agree to all that. I will be circumspect and not put myself or Julie in danger. Would you believe that Harry and Julie have met before? She was his cousin's bridesmaid at her wedding two years ago. Harry had recently had his leg amputated and was in a wheelchair, and Julie sat talking to him for a while because she felt sorry for him. I think I noticed sparks between them. I do not think a romance with Sharon will go far, because she lives in Winchester and it is too far to travel to see each other often. Maybe Julie will be the one for him. She is going back for the exercises next week.'

'Whoa, Alicia, do not jump to conclusions on one meeting.'

'I know it sounds mad at this stage, but he really seemed interested in her.'

'We will wait and see on that one. You want everybody married because we are happily married. Some people prefer to take it a little slower to make up their minds.'

'Well, if there is something happening there, remember, you heard it first from me.'

*　*　*

James drove Alicia to the general hospital next morning and stopped the car when they saw Julie waiting on the steps at the front entrance. She was in her nurse's uniform. Alicia had anticipated this and wore flat shoes and a neat dress so she would not look outstanding beside Julie.

Julie explained that she was on general duties for the day, as it was nominally her rostered day off, so that she could show Alicia around and meet some of the staff, introducing Alicia as a prospective nurse who wanted to see what duties she would be doing—a work experience day. This was not a normal duty, but she did not think others would be too inquisitive. Everybody was so busy all day they would not have time to stay and chat for long, but it would give both Julie and Alicia time to look for a possible suspect.

'I have checked everyone out over the last few months, although I am so busy myself, I have no time to reflect on whether each person is capable of such a dirty trick,' Julie said. 'I am pleased to have this time with someone else's opinion as well to go by. I know it must be someone from here. I still remember the smell of the sanitiser the guy had on the hand he had over my mouth. It is similar to the one we use in the wards.'

'Where are we going to start, Julie? It is such a big hospital.'

'Yes, it is. But I reasoned that it had to be someone close to where I work, with my ward duties, so I thought we would start from there. We have several male nurses, and then there are the doctors. But I cannot see them resorting to chasing women in the streets. There are enough nurses here that would be happy for a doctor to chat them up. Anyway, we will start there and then go out from that ward and follow up on any male we find.'

'That sounds like we have quite a lot of choices. Okay, let's start. I am going to photograph some of them for a comparison, all those who are taller than you. Do you think they will mind that?'

'It seems to be the thing nowadays, and I cannot see anyone objecting. If they do, we shall have to delete it.'

They went from wards to corridors and work stations, until Julie said, 'Let us go to the coffee shop and observe the crowd while we have coffee. We have not seen anyone that is a suspect yet, have we?'

'No, it is a bit disappointing so far. Not one of them has appeared to be a suspect yet, but the day is still early. The coffee shop looks like a good place to spot our quarry. There seems to be several males here,' Alicia commented, looking around at passing staff members.

Julie explained, 'Everyone comes in for coffee as soon as they get a break. It is a tradition, or perhaps it is more like an addiction. It is a great pick-me-up after a heavy session with the patients. Most patients are amenable to being looked after, but it can be hard sometimes when you get one that does not want a jab and will put up quite a fight to get away. Some of them can get quite aggressive, especially in the emergency ward. I have done a couple of stints in there and have had to grapple with patients—some on drink or drugs—to get them to quieten down enough to allow a doctor to examine them. Harry Burton's lessons are going to come in handy for that in the future. While I was doing the exercises on Tuesday evening, I was thinking, all nurses need to do those lessons.'

'So you will be back to continue them on Tuesdays?' asked Alicia.

'Definitely. I came away feeling a bit sore, but I can see how they are going to benefit me. Firstly, it will prevent patients from hurting me, and secondly, it will benefit my running because it is using all the muscles, not just the legs and breathing.'

'Good for you, Julie. Kate and I are sure we can look after ourselves. We have been having Harry's lessons for several months now. We both feel as if it gives you more confidence in yourself, although I have not had to try the moves out on the general public yet. Mainly because James looks after me in a crowd.' Alicia laughed at the thought.

Someone caught Alicia's eye—a young man wearing a white pharmacist outfit. She could see him looking at Julie intently. She watched him for a few minutes, and he did not take his eyes off Julie. He then came over and asked if he could join them.

Julie looked up at him and smiled. 'Sure, Adrian, pull up a chair. This is my friend, Alicia. I am showing her over the hospital. She is thinking of joining our staff, and I have not put her off yet.' She turned to Alicia and said, 'Adrian is the pharmacist here. We have not reached his rooms yet this morning, but we will call in and have a look around before the day is out.'

Adrian pulled himself away from looking at Julie and glanced at Alicia. 'Nice to meet you, Alicia. Yes, come in and have a look around any time.' His eyes went back to Julie.

Alicia made up her mind almost at once. He was taller than Julie by several inches. He was obviously entranced by her. He was not chubby or heavy, but warm clothing could have made him look like he was. So far, he was the only one she suspected of all the men she had seen that morning. She must get a photo of him standing next to Julie, to show her. Perhaps she could colour the photo later to show him in dark clothing. That white coat was certainly misleading if you were looking for a predator; he looked more angelic, if anything. She had a sudden thought: Julie was not going to like the thought of this friendly person as a predator; she obviously liked him. It would be better not to say anything to her until they had seen more of the staff, even leaving it until the next day, after she had drawn a picture of a different Adrian from the photo.

It was all going through her head while the other two were chatting, and then Adrian suddenly got up. 'Sorry, I have to get back to the pharmacy. I am already late. Call in after your coffee, girls.' And he was gone.

'How long have you known Adrian, Julie?'

'From about the first day I started work here. We both graduated the same year from university and met the first day when we both turned up to start work for the first time. I often go down and have a chat with him when I want to get away from a fretful patient for a rest. He is busy in the pharmacy every day, but I think he enjoys our almost daily chats as much as I do, even if they are only for a few minutes each day.

'Okay, we have finished our coffee. There are no suspects hanging around, so we need to search further,' said Julie. They left the coffee shop and went down another corridor and tried out several different wards, winding back until the pharmacy came into view.

'We will visit Adrian's domain, and I will show you the different sanitisers we use here. Some are for hands, and some for wiping the furniture and walls. It is a constant occupation trying to keep bugs at bay. It becomes a habit after a while that you sanitise your hands each time you enter a ward,' explained Julie.

'I have noticed you using them, Julie, and have followed your action. I have been thinking. It would be a good thing to have in our office and even in the bookshop, before we get into another influenza season. I imagine especially in the bookshop, with everyone coming in and handling the books. I will ask Adrian for his recommendations and may take some home with me.'

'That sounds like a good idea. At least if you purchase it here, you will know it is a good product.'

Adrian was serving a customer but quickly finalised it when he saw Julie appear. Alicia had her phone out and snapped a picture of Adrian looking at Julie. He did not notice, and when she asked if she could take a photo of them side by side, he came out from behind the counter and stood beside Julie, looking into her eyes. To Alicia, it was easy to read that he was in love with Julie, although she did not appear to know it.

Alicia snapped two more photos of them together, and Adrian did not notice. Alicia asked about the sanitisers, explaining the surfaces she wanted to cover, and he produced a spray for her to try out and also a hand lotion to put by the doorways. She thanked him for his help and purchased one of each, and the two young women left the pharmacy. Alicia was even more convinced they had found who they were looking for, but she still said nothing to Julie. She thought it would need some convincing; Julie was very friendly with the fellow and would think a suggestion that he was the culprit could be denied out of hand. Tomorrow would be soon enough.

When it was time for a lunch break, Alicia suggested that she come back the next morning to have another briefing. By that time, she would have a picture to show Julie to see if she would accept Alicia's suspect. There had been several other men the same size as Adrian, but those men had shown no interest in the two women. Surely if someone had tried to grab a girl while she was running, they would show some interest in her. Julie was disappointed; she had hoped Alicia would find the suspect, and now she was leaving without producing the rabbit out of the hat.

She drove Alicia back to the investigations office and promised she would see Alicia at coffee time the next day at the hospital. Her shift would start at mid-day the next day, so it fitted in nicely.

When Alicia entered the office, James asked how she did, and she answered, 'I have a photo I want to draw of the chap I believe is the suspect. Julie is going to be very upset when she sees it. The man is a friend she thinks well of, but he is the only person I came up with. I will do that this afternoon and go home with you later. It will give me time to come up with a good likeness of the person who attacked her. I will present it to her tomorrow, if you have time to come with me, but I believe we do not need the backup in this case. What do you think?'

'I will come with you all the same, Alicia. It sounds as if you will not be long convincing Julie, and I would like to be there to give a warning to the person. It will be stronger coming from me.'

'All right, James. I do not think it will be a problem except to convince Julie. I am going to work on this photo for a while, putting dark clothes and a balaclava on him to show her. May I sit at your desk for a while, to draw my pictures?'

'Certainly, Alicia. I would love for you to sit opposite me. I have missed your smiling face in the office this week.'

'It was only a few days, James, and we have just spent ten days with each other on our holiday.'

'Nevertheless, I miss you in the office, and I am sure the others do as well. Nobody is as chirpy as we were when you were here full-time.'

Alicia looked at him and decided not to say any more. She had enjoyed her time off the previous week, catching up on all the jobs she normally had no time for when she spent the week working full-time in the office. She picked up her drawing pencils and sat down with her sketch pad. She changed the clothes in the first picture she drew, and in the second, she drew a balaclava over the face of Adrian, the pharmacist.

She flicked through the other photos she had taken during the morning visit to the hospital. There was one other fellow who was the same size as Adrian. She had dismissed him at the time but decided to give him the same treatment, as Julie might need some convincing. So she added the dark clothes and balaclava to him as well. She was satisfied that she had done a good job and asked James to have a look and give his opinion.

'You have done a good job, Alicia. Your drawing of Adrian is very like him, and the next one with the balaclava could be him. It is up to Julie now to look at these pictures, as she is the only one who saw the man who attacked her.'

'Yes, I think Adrian is in love with her, and she genuinely likes him too. She is going to be upset when I show her these drawings.'

'We will go softly, Alicia, and try to work something out for them. Julie may not want to charge him if he is her friend, but she will be very disappointed and will want to know why he did it.'

*   *   *

The next morning, Alicia looked again at her drawings and gathered them into a file cover, ready to take. She walked to the office to meet up with James, and they set off for the hospital together, in time to meet Julie in the coffee shop, where they found her waiting for them.

Alicia handed the file to Julie, who took it, wondering what she would find inside. After she pulled out each drawing, she looked mystified for a few minutes and then said, 'This is Adrian? No, Adrian would not do that to me!'

Alicia put her hand on the shaking arm of her new friend and said, 'Julie, I have also experienced something in my past and jumped to conclusions before hearing the full story. It nearly ruined my whole life. Please do not jump to conclusions quickly, but show these pictures to Adrian and see what he has to say about them, before you speak and show your concern. There may be a reason behind the story, as there was in my case, so just present them to Adrian and do not say anything. Just listen to what he has to say.'

Julie looked at James and said, 'You believe the pictures too, James?'

'Alicia's drawings are very lifelike, Julie. He can only dispute them if he is not guilty. That is why Alicia's advice to listen and not accuse him right off is such good advice. We will take it from there if he denies everything.'

'What will you do in that case?'

'We will bring in a policeman with a warrant to search his apartment and car to try and find his balaclava. Not a lot of people wear balaclavas, and it would show his guilt if we find it.'

Julie sat for a few minutes, looking ready to burst into tears, and then pulled herself together and said, 'Okay, let's go and visit Adrian.'

The three of them went to the pharmacy and saw Adrian putting up in the doorway a sign, 'Back in ten minutes', obviously because it was coffee time for him. When he saw Julie striding towards him, his expression was of love, as Alicia had seen the previous day.

Julie did not say anything as the group approached, except 'Come back into the shop, Adrian. I have something to show you.'

The four of them went into the pharmacy, closing the door behind them, leaving the sign in place. Julie handed the file of drawings to Adrian without another word.

He opened the file and drew out the pile of drawings and photographs taken the day before. As he went through them, no one said a word. He looked as if he was going to faint, and he looked at Julie and said, 'Can I explain, Julie, the day this happened?'

'That is why we are here, Adrian. I have been advised by my friends here that I should listen and not accuse you of accosting me, until you finish speaking. So go ahead. I would like to hear your explanation.'

'This occurred the day I received notice that I was going to receive an upgrade of my duties here. I was to become the senior consultant, with a good raise in salary. I was so excited I had achieved this in such a short period and wanted to share my day with you, to take you out to dinner to celebrate. I had missed you that day in the coffee shop. I had been very busy all day. I rang your home number to invite you out to dinner, and your mother told me you were out running.

'I was still so excited and did not think things through and decided to go and catch up with you. If I left it too long, it would have been too late for dinner. You had explained to me which route you usually took for your runs, so I went to my apartment and changed into my running clothes, which included a balaclava because I had been advised by my medical specialist I should wear it to stop the car fumes from giving me asthma-like conditions. The fumes from the vehicles at that time of night in cool weather hang around so low, causing the problem. Running can give me excessive coughing and nausea because of the fumes. I had asthma as a child, and it soon became second nature to me to wear the balaclava. I have had no problems with the fumes since I took to wearing it.

'I saw you ahead of me and called out two or three times, but you did not hear me. I then realised it was because you had earphones on and were listening to the radio or music, so I ran up to you to grab your arm. You had not heard me coming, and you screamed. I put my hand over your mouth to stop the screams, then a man came out of an adjacent house, holding a baseball bat.

'I quickly realised that I had messed up, and I gave up and went home. In my mind, I have gone over and over what I had done. I knew I had blown it. Any chance I had with you would now be negated by my actions. I am so sorry, Julie. I love you and have wanted to tell you many times, but I knew if I owned up to the fact that I was the one following you that day, you would never forgive me. I am so sorry to be the one who caused so much distress. I curse myself every day.'

Julie was staring at Adrian. 'Oh my god, Adrian, this has been so much of a mess-up. I have often wondered why you did not ask me out. We are such good friends. I never dreamt it was you that night, and I know that I have talked too much about it and that no real harm was done to me. It was mainly the shock that caused me to be petrified each time I wanted to go out running.' She turned and looked at Alicia. 'Thank you, Alicia, for telling me to handle it like this. It was a story about misunderstandings. You were right!'

James said, 'I gather you will not want to take this further, Julie. We will be off to the office now and leave you two to work things out together.'

Alicia said, 'I will see you at Harry's barn on Tuesday evening, Julie.'

As they walked to their car, James said, 'That was a good job, Alicia. All your own work. Congratulations. A great result.'

Alicia was pleased with the remark; she was a person who liked to study human nature and the way people cope with life. It had been a good experience for her.

CHAPTER TWO

Two days later, Alicia was helping Granny in her bookshop, sorting out some books to put into the baskets of discounted books, when her friend Sacha came in to see her. Sacha was a building and construction engineer from Poland, and he was contracted to a building site in the old town area. This time he had a younger version of himself accompanying him; he introduced his brother, Pieter, saying he was visiting from a ship. Pieter had signed on as a sailor especially because the ship was coming to this port, so that he could visit his brother, Sacha. He had finished his schooling and wanted to go to sea, but first he wanted to try it out before starting studies; it was a once-only return trip for him. His English was limited, so they spoke Russian with Alicia, who had studied it during her airline period, when she had gone to Russia on a monthly basis.

Sacha said, 'My brother is undecided on what to do. This was the first time for him on a ship. When he went on board for the first time, he met a nice young woman passenger—although it was not a regular passenger ship, mainly cargo—and they chatted. It was the first time for the girl too. She had answered an advertisement in her newspaper about a Doctor Roland Cooke wanting an au pair to look after two children. Marta was on a three-month break from her university studies and answered the advertisement and got the job, with paid fare to come to this port to work for the duration of her three-month study break, with the idea of improving her English.

'My brother is here for five days while the cargo is being unloaded, so he decided to visit Marta at her workplace. Marta had given him the address, so he took a cab to the house and knocked on the door. The lady who opened the door said she did not know what he was talking about. Her children were grown-up and did not need a maid to look after them, and she had no domestic help.

'Pieter was dismayed. Marta had disappeared. He knows it is the correct address, because Marta had shown him the letter confirming the position in the household and he had captured it with his phone camera at the time. He had taken a photo of Marta holding the letter. He had also taken a photo of the four girls who were passengers, at the lunch table. He asked the lady if Dr Cooke lived there, and she confirmed that he did and that his office is in the city.

'He thanked the lady and came and talked it over with me, and we have decided it is a mystery. Perhaps the lady did not understand Pieter's English. We do not know what to do. Should we report it to the police? We are afraid they will not understand our English either. Could you come with us to tell them the story?'

Alicia said, 'I think we will have to go and talk with my husband and his partner at their office, Sacha. Percy is an ex–police detective, so he may have some answers about what you should do. I will help with translating when it is needed, but your English has greatly improved, Sacha. Wait until I change my shoes and get a coat, and I will take you to the office.'

*   *   *

James and Percy were both in the office when they arrived. Alicia asked if they could use the conference room; she wanted both Sacha and Pieter to feel comfortable when telling their story.

She asked if Ken and Kate were available, and James said they were due in shortly; they were following up on surveillance for an insurance company, which was almost complete. Alicia said, 'I thought they would like to hear the story of Sacha and Pieter so they could keep their eyes out for anything that may come up unexpectedly. Anyway, we will get the story going, and we can fill the others in later.' She gestured to Sacha to tell the story he had told her.

When he finished talking, Alicia said to James, 'Did you understand? Sacha's English has vastly improved, but Pieter has minimal knowledge of English at the moment. We were able to speak in Russian to fill the gaps.'

'Yes, I got the gist of it. Marta did not turn up at the doctor's house, nor was she expected there. There is something wrong, as both chaps have indicated, but where to start? What do you think, Percy?'

'Like you, James, I agree there is something amiss. She has not been missing long enough to be reported as missing to the police. As she was a stranger to the country, there could have been a misunderstanding about where she was to go. But if the letter clearly indicated that she was to go to Dr Cooke's house, there appears to be something wrong, as Mrs Cooke says she was not expected and Mrs Cooke knew nothing about it. It needs investigation for sure. Girls do not just disappear into thin air. You have checked the ship, Pieter, to see if she was still there?'

'Yes, sir,' said Pieter after looking at Alicia and having the question translated. 'That was the first thing I did when she was not located at the doctor's house. I went straight back to the ship and was told she had left earlier than I did. I checked the security list to see if she had passed the door to exit the ship. Everybody is given a card, to monitor comings and goings on the ship. She left with an older woman who had also travelled on the same journey, I was told when I asked. The four young women all left at the same time.'

'Did you know the name of the older woman, Pieter?' asked Percy.

'No, sir, we called her Madam when we addressed her, because we were not given her name.'

James asked, 'What were your duties on board the ship, Pieter?'

'I was the steward who had to bring the meals from the kitchen and serve them. That is how I came to talk to Marta. She had a friendly manner and asked where I came from and what I was doing on the ship and if it was permanent. It was not a long journey, so I did not have much chance to talk to her, although she showed me the letter from

Dr Cooke. She was so excited to be an au pair for the three months of her vacation.'

'Did she seem to be friendly with the older woman, Pieter?'

'Not that I saw. The older lady had her meals with the captain of the ship. Marta sat with three other girls travelling. They usually sat apart from the other crew members. It is not a big passenger ship, so we only had ten passengers total. They shared two to a cabin. There were four male passengers and then Madam, of course. Marta was in a cabin with another girl called Misha, who is a Russian, I think. We did not have much opportunity to chat. I was kept busy serving and had my own meals after I cleaned up after the passengers and crew.'

'Do you think Marta may have gone with the other girls, Pieter?'

'I am sorry, I do not know for sure, nor do I know where the other girls were going. When I looked at the security check, I did notice that they all signed off at the same time, so they may have gone together. I could be thinking wrongly, except I saw the letter written to Marta by Dr Cooke and Mrs Cooke does not know anything about her.'

'I will telephone a police detective we know quite well and ask him if this sort of thing has happened previously.'

'Could you telephone him now, sir? I am due to go back to my duty on the ship in two days, and I would like to think Marta is safe.'

James smiled at the young man's earnest voice. 'Okay, Pieter, I will see if he is available.' He rang the number for Detective Inspector Paul Morris. 'Hello, Paul, we have only just come up with a curly one.' He went on to describe Pieter's story of Marta. When he finished, he asked, 'Have you heard of anything like this before, Paul?'

'Not personally, James, but occasionally you hear about unknown females being pulled out of the water who appear to have been strangled. Besides looking as if they are of European origin, they are usually not recognisable after they have been in the water for a while. We usually have to transfer this type of crime to Interpol because we have no records to go by here.'

'If I were to contact the immigration department, they should have a record of Marta landing at least. I will try that. With the free borders in Europe, it is harder to keep up with the moving population. It seems strange that the letter was from an actual doctor in the town. Do you have anything on this Dr Cooke, Paul?'

'Not that I am aware of, James, but I will ask around and get back to you on it.'

'Thanks, Paul. If I cannot get any answers, I may have to contact your chief on this one. Young Pieter is only a few weeks from being a schoolboy and would not be able to manage our fee. Also, he is going back on the ship in two days, but he has got us all wondering what happened to this girl. It does not add up.'

'I can almost hear that great jigsaw puzzle in your mind grinding out, James. I will ask around to see what comes up. Good luck with this one.'

James turned to Sacha and Pieter. 'My police detective has not heard of anything like this happening. I am sorry, chaps. I made some notes as you were talking. You did not tell us Marta's surname, Sacha. Do you know it?'

'It is Marta Nowak. I noticed it on the letter she showed me,' said Pieter after this was translated for him.

'And the Russian girl was Misha. Do you know her surname?'

Sacha repeated the question to Pieter, and the shake of his head answered all of them.

Pieter spoke again, and Sacha translated: 'I am sorry, I do not know any more about this strange occurrence. I had not expected any irregularities, and I am positive that Marta thought she was going to the home of Doctor Roland Cooke.'

'What is the name of your ship, Pieter?'

Sacha answered for him. 'The *Balbir*. This is Russian for *brave—courageous* and *strong*.'

'Is there a coffee house or lunch restaurant near where the ship is docked?' asked Alicia.

Sacha answered, 'Yes, there is both. I sometimes wander down there when a ship comes in, to hear my language being spoken. I do not really talk to anyone, but I listen to other people speaking. It is good to hear your own language sometimes. It makes you feel closer to home.'

'When does your contract finish, Sacha? That building looks almost complete,' said James.

'It is almost finished. Maybe a month to go to get all the details finalised.'

'Are you going home when it is finished?' asked Alicia.

'I have another contract if I want it. I am not sure yet. I would like to go home to visit my parents before I make up my mind.'

Alicia, after being quiet for a few minutes, turned to her husband and said, 'James, I have been thinking while we have been sitting here. It sounds like Marta arrived and was whisked away to an address other than the one she expected. Can I suggest that Kate and I go to the eatery with Sacha and Pieter today, before the ship sails and Pieter will have to join it? Pieter may see someone he recognises from the ship and may be able to ask questions about the girls who landed and where they have gone. Meanwhile, Kate and I will have a look around to see if there is anything suspicious going on. The last time Marta was seen was when she was leaving the ship, and there has been no word of her since.

'We could see if anyone recalls the girls getting into a car, for a start. I have a suspicion they are still in the ship area. I wonder if there is any CCTV in the area? To bring a girl all this way with a false promise of employment is highly suspicious to me, and I think the ship is involved, possibly with kidnap. You will say I have been watching too much television and that not all girls are brought in for sex trade, but you have to admit that it does sound a little like it. Why else would someone give her false information?'

The three men looked at her as Sacha interpreted Alicia's comment for Pieter.

Sacha said to James and Alicia, 'This has been my thought as well. Since Marta was not expected at Dr Cooke's home, I cannot think of any other answer. It has been well known in Poland that some girls are picked up against their will for sex trade in various parts of Europe. These girls are usually poor and looking for work and, until they arrive at their destinations, are not aware what their lives will be like. Some are returned home as drug addicts, and some just disappear, never to be seen again. There are many pictures in the newspapers for missing girls. Marta is different. She is a university student from a good family, I believe. This is not the usual type of girl to go missing like this. She wanted the job to improve her English, to help her get a good job when she graduates.'

'I have seen reports of it here also, Sacha,' said James, 'but it is in the early stages yet. We may find that it is all a big mistake.'

Sacha said, 'That is true, James, but we cannot leave it until it is too late for Marta and the other girls. It is our duty to try and find them—and quickly.'

James thought for a minute. There was going to be a problem with language if he went looking, but he was wary of sending Alicia into the lion's den to look for the girls. He thought it was a problem that the police would have to work out. He said, 'Because of the language difficulty, I believe we will have to ask for police department backup for this. I am uncertain of sending Alicia and Kate into a situation that could turn nasty if they are suspected. I will ring the police chief and take the problem to them to see what they think about it.'

'The reason I did not go to the police, James, is the language barrier. However, I will be happy if you would come with us to ask about this conundrum.' Sacha looked at Pieter and repeated his statement to his younger brother. Pieter responded with a smile and nodded. That was what he wanted to do—to find out where Marta had gone.

'Right,' said James. He looked up the police number in his phone and dialled it. He explained the story to the chief, who said, 'It sounds like this needs a little more thought, James. Come in at four o'clock this afternoon, and I will scout around for a few people on the beat to meet you here. Bring in your Polish friends. We might get to the bottom of the story quicker that way if your wife can interpret for us.'

'I have already called Detective Morris, asking if he has heard of Doctor Roland Cooke, so perhaps he could be included in the meeting,' said James.

'Okay, James, if he is available. I will see you at four.' He put the phone down.

James turned to the others. 'It is lunchtime now, and the meeting is at four o'clock. I suggest we go to the wharf and find this restaurant and have a meal and a quick look around to see what is there, for a start. I have never been down to the wharf area, so it will be good if you can tell us where to go, Sacha.'

Sacha and Pieter smiled; they were happy that there was going to be some action on this problem.

Alicia had been trying to find Doctor Roland Cooke on the Internet, and she came up with a picture of a tall graceful-looking man and his history. He was a doctor, a general practitioner, forty-five years of age. His interest was opera, and he had a seat reserved permanently for shows. He had travelled extensively throughout Europe.

Alicia showed the picture of the man, and Pieter said, 'I saw that man at the ship when I was leaving. He was talking to the captain.'

Sacha said, 'I have seen that man in the restaurant. He caught my interest because he was friendly with the staff, who are mainly Russian or Polish. I could not hear if he was speaking English though. I was on the other side of the room.'

'Okay, we will go to the restaurant, Alicia, but remember, this is only a preliminary look around. Do not go snooping on your own, or you may join the missing girls.' James turned to Sacha and asked, 'Have you heard anything about prostitution anywhere in the dock area from any of your workmates?'

'I am not interested in visiting a prostitute, James, so I have not paid attention when the boys talked about anything not connected to work. My team usually has more time off than me. I have to study the next part of the work while they are out on the town, because I am the supervisor on the job.'

'I can understand that, Sacha. When you go back to work, perhaps you can throw a few questions at your team. These girls will be able to talk to your men in their own language. You may be able to find out more about the girls that way.'

Pieter looked gloomy and said to his brother, 'Does James think Marta and the other girls have been coerced into prostitution?'

Sacha did not look happy either and translated Pieter's question.

'I am sorry, boys. I have no real reason to think it except that it is a very strange set of circumstances. The girls' English may be very rudimentary and it could only be that the girls have gone elsewhere of their own volition, but it is very strange that Dr Cooke's wife was not expecting Marta. On the way back from the restaurant, I will call in and quiz Mrs Cooke about it.'

'No, James. I think I should do that,' said Alicia. 'I think I should say we are friends of Marta's family and have been asked to look out for her, as she is visiting a strange country for the first time and is still a schoolgirl. We have promised to visit her to see if she has settled in okay so we can report back to Mrs Nowak, who is worried about her being away from home. I will copy that photo that Pieter has on his phone.'

'That is a good idea, Alicia,' said Percy. 'Play it softly at first. If you do that on the way to the police meeting, you will be able to report on the answers you get. She may have been putting Sacha and Pieter off because the girl is supposed to be working, not playing around.'

'I bow to your superior knowledge of women's behaviour, Alicia and Percy,' said James. 'It is a good idea. As you say, she may have been putting the young men in their place. Okay, we will do it like that. Kate hasn't come back yet from the surveillance job with Ken. I will come with you to the lunch, Alicia. It will look as if we are friends being taken to lunch.'

James handed Sacha some money to pay for their lunch, saying, 'It will look better if you are paying for our meal, Sacha, to introduce Polish dishes to us. So you check the menu and order for us, and we can be discussing the food when the waiter comes to take the order. That will make us less conspicuous. Meanwhile, we can check the other people around us and the surroundings.'

He thought for a minute and asked, 'Is this all right with you, Percy? We will bring you something back for your lunch, seeing as you are holding the fort. Kate can take over for you when she comes in, while you come to police headquarters with us.'

'I understand, James. I shall hold the fort until Ken and Kate return.'

'Okay, it is starting to get a little late, so we had better move now. We should only be an hour or so, Percy.' James stood up and looked at the other three and said, 'Are you all okay with this suggestion?'

Alicia and the two young men stood up, and they each said yes.

Alicia was a little apprehensive; she had no idea where they were going or what they were looking for. It did not sound good for the four young women. She had copied Pieter's photo of Marta and the letter to her phone so she could refer to it if someone looked like Marta, along with the photo of the four girls together at the table, all smiling at the camera.

The four of them went in Sacha's car; it was better to keep up the appearance that the Polish boys were taking them to lunch. He was a good driver, but Alicia found herself hanging on tight around the corners—he cut them quite quickly. She laughed at herself. *I must be getting staid in my old age.* She would be thirty next year, and it had been a while since she had gone out in a car with a young man.

She looked over at James and laughed again when she saw him also hanging on tight around the corners. They were growing old together.

James was very interested in the part of the wharf that they entered. He had not been in this area previously. All the ships in this area were cargo ships; the cruise ships came into port closer to the town, near where they lived. He was amazed by the shipping and the containers lined up, having not realised until now that the port was so busy, and he was amazed by how big the area was.

Pieter pointed out the ship he had arrived on, the *Balbir*. It appeared to be unloaded. James wondered why it was not going out for two more days. He asked Pieter, who said via Sacha that they had to wait for a customs clearance and the tide, and they would sail early the day after next.

They arrived at the restaurant, which was set back behind all the loading areas, in a street of old houses; it had obviously been there before the port had grown so big. The restaurant was an old house that had been done over as a restaurant, and it was quite attractive.

As they walked in, they noticed that the food was in containers at the counter, with a woman taking the money; everything was self-service. They lined up to help themselves, with Sacha telling them what the dishes were. Alicia recognised the borscht soup; it had been her favourite when she was in Russia. Sacha pointed out the Russian dishes and the Polish dishes, explaining the ingredients in each.

They took a table at the rear of the room, and James and Alicia looked around the room. Alicia said, 'You would think we are in Russia. Most of the other customers are Russian or Polish.'

James said, 'I have seen nothing like it. It is as if we are in a foreign country.'

Sacha said, 'You can see why I come here to get a taste of home. I do not miss my mother's cooking so much when I come here. The food is very good.'

Alicia said, 'I thought the girls might have been given jobs as waitresses, but they do not have any. So we can rule that one out.'

Sacha said, 'I thought that too, but it was always this way. Maybe they are helping in the kitchen.'

'I have enjoyed my borscht so much. Maybe I can con my way into the kitchen to see if they are there. I can chat up the cook,' said Alicia, getting up from the table and going to the counter. She spoke to the woman at the desk in Russian, and the others watched in admiration as Alicia was shown into the kitchen.

When she returned to the table, she explained that there was no sign of the girls, but she had an invitation to return the next day, in the morning, to have a lesson on how to make borscht.

James laughed heartily and said, 'Good one, Alicia. So you can ask questions while you are cooking, clever girl.'

'That is what it is for, of course, although I would also like to learn how to make borscht, to add to my list of dishes to make. So it is twice as good as you think,' Alicia answered with a grin.

'Will you come alone, Alicia?' asked Sacha.

'I cannot see any reason not to. Everybody is very friendly, and they are amazed I can speak Russian so well. Of course, I will not get tangled up in long words and will stay with my basic Russian. I like to practise it when I can.' Alicia smiled at the others. 'When I learn to make the borscht, Sacha, you will have to come to dinner and try it out with us.'

'I would love to, Alicia. I admire you for the way you have arranged things,' said Sacha. He turned to Pieter to explain what was going on. Alicia was rewarded with a big smile from the boy.

They decided there was no reason to stay any longer and returned to the office, with Alicia and James hanging on to the straps again around corners. Alicia explained to the two young men where the police headquarters was and said they would meet them there outside at 3.45 for their appointment at four in the afternoon. Meanwhile, she would visit Mrs Cooke to see if the woman had fooled Pieter and had only pretended she could not understand him. This would also give Sacha time to talk with his workmates about prostitution in the area of the wharf.

James turned to her. 'You intend to visit Mrs Cooke alone, Alicia.'

'Yes, James. I want to see if I can get onside with her. Maybe she is ignorant of her husband's affairs. It is a possibility. I am going to present myself as following up on a query from Marta's family, and I will show her the photo of Marta and the letter from her husband. They are indisputable. I want to present her with a friendly face. She does not know I got it all from Pieter. I should get some feedback from her, and if she holds back, we can then go together and face up to Dr Cooke himself.'

James thought for a few minutes and said, 'Yes, I can see that working. Having some time off seems to have heightened your investigation skills, Alicia. Well done this morning at the restaurant and with this chat you will have with Mrs Cooke. You might solve the mystery before the police get on it. Come back into the office to pick me up before the police appointment. I do not want them to think you are cleverer than me.' He laughed and kissed her cheek and watched as she drove away in the office car.

Alicia felt exalted; she had thought James might want to come with her, and she knew that in this case, it was better for her to go alone. Mrs Cooke was more likely to be relaxed with her rather than feel like she is being bullied by two people appearing. This was better done by one-to-one, two women in a friendly chat. She knew she could make it appear like that. The husband, Dr Cooke, was a different situation altogether. Pieter had seen him on the ship, talking to the captain, and he often appeared in the restaurant, according to Sacha. There was something afoot; their team only had to find out what it was. Alicia felt she had time to think over all the different situations, whereas James was catching up from his time away from the office after their lovely holiday in India and had a backlog of work to contend with. She felt fresh and ready to go.

The doctor's house was an impressive two-storey building in a lane of other impressive houses, with nicely laid-out gardens and parking for two or three cars and a driveway on which to dispense passengers at the front door. Alicia did not park in the driveway; she parked in the street outside the house and walked up the path to the front door and rang the bell. After a short wait, the door opened, and an attractive woman of about forty years old appeared. She looked as if she was ready to go out, so Alicia introduced herself.

'Good morning. Are you Mrs Cooke? My name is Alicia Armstrong. May I come in for a few minutes to explain my sudden appearance at your door?'

Mrs Cooke looked at the neatly dressed Alicia, in a black mid-calf skirt and a jacket of beige, with a colourful scarf around her neck. She did not hesitate and stepped back, allowing Alicia in. She showed her into a sitting room, beautifully arranged, with flowers on a piano and elegant furnishings in the rest of the room.

She sat down and invited Alicia to sit opposite her. Alicia decided she was a beautiful woman, but she had a dissatisfied look on her face; she looked as if she welcomed having someone to talk to, even if it was a stranger.

Alicia started to tell her story. 'I have been asked to look into a situation for my husband's business, which is Gray and Armstrong Private Investigations. However, this is more a private proceeding, because I have been asked personally to make sure a friend's daughter arrived safely and is comfortable with you in her job as au pair.'

Mrs Cooke looked cross. 'This is the second time someone has called about this subject this week. I do not have a girl as an au pair. I have a woman come in once a week to clean the bathrooms and do the washing and ironing. Otherwise, I do not have any house help. My husband is away several nights for his clinics in other towns, and my children are grown-up and in university and live away and spend little time at home, even when they are here. Most of the time, I am here alone, so I do not feel as if I need any more help, even though the house is large. I do not know where you got the idea of an au pair. I have never had one, even when the children were small, although I would have welcomed one at that time.'

Alicia believed her but said, 'Can I show you a photo of the girl I am looking for and her work details? I have been sent them on my phone.' She opened her mobile phone and brought up the picture of Marta and showed it to Mrs Cooke. Then she switched to the letter of Marta's appointment as au pair at this address.

Alicia could see that Mrs Cooke looked baffled, and she went on. 'May I send a copy of this to your phone so you can show your husband when he arrives home? Perhaps he knows more about it. You can imagine that there will be consternation when I get back to our office and report it. The police may have to be involved. This is a missing girl. It is no small matter. We have proof that she arrived on the ship *Balbir* two days ago. With this photo and the copy of the letter, there will be more explaining to do for them to try and find her.'

Alicia sat back in her chair and looked to be thinking. The woman did appear as if she knew nothing about the missing girl, but was she fudging it? The letter clearly stated that the girl would be employed at this address.

'What time does your husband arrive home, Mrs Cooke? If we are to interview him.'

'There is no definite time for him to come home. Sometimes his clinic runs over, and if he is in another town, he does not come home until the next day. Quite frankly, I think he is having an affair with the nurse there. I am not positive, but he has been staying over more and more lately.' She looked very sad at this revelation. 'I suppose that with the children being at university and boarding and only me at home, he is looking for more excitement. But this does not explain this letter you have shown me,' she said, pulling herself together. 'I am sorry I cannot help in any way. I will speak to my husband when he eventually arrives home, and I will have him call you.'

Alicia saw that she looked ashamed at letting her guard down and talking of her problems to a stranger, and Alicia decided to ignore her speech about her husband having an affair. She said, 'I will leave you our office card so that your husband can ring. Ask for me or my husband, James Armstrong. As I said, it is a private matter at the moment, but if we cannot find Marta very quickly, we must take it to the police. We cannot have young women disappearing as soon as they land on our shores. Something has happened to her, and we will have to find out quickly. Has anything like this happened to you before?'

Mrs Cooke sat thinking for a moment and said, 'Strangely, it did once before. About six months ago, someone came looking for a girl she said was my au pair. I showed her through the house to show that I had no one living here with me. I had forgotten that for the moment. I thought she had a problem with speaking the language and had the wrong end of the stick and came to the wrong address—merely a language mix-up. It slipped my mind until now. That is strange, isn't it? That it should happen twice.'

Alicia was excited. So it had happened before; she was on to something here. 'Do you mind if I get a written statement from you, Mrs Cooke, about these two incidents? It is a strange thing, as you have said. I will have to have it written down and signed by you so that I can look further into the coincidence. Something is strange here. I can see you are not involved, except that someone is using your good name to enlist these girls in working in this country, but they disappear before you learn about them.'

'I am puzzled about all this. For one thing, I do not speak these girls' languages. And how would I get their names to contact them in their own country to invite them here? It is strange altogether. Do you think I need a lawyer?'

'Not at the moment, Mrs Cooke. I am sure if we look harder, we will find Marta. It does not explain the letter with your details on it, but if we can catch up with her soon, perhaps it will become clearer.'

'I do not mind telling my side of it. After all, I am innocent in this strange happening. Do you want to write up something now? Or should I come into your office?'

'If you could come into our office, it would be appreciated, and I can bring James up to date with the story. Do you want me to drive you in, Mrs Cooke?'

'Yes, that would be nice. I woke up this morning with a headache and do not trust myself to drive. I was going to shop but decided not to go. After hearing about this strange story, I feel quite wobbly. It is not usual for me to get headaches, but I have been having them for two weeks now. It is no use for me to ask my husband to give me a prescription for them. He would just say "Go and see your GP", as he usually does when I feel unwell. He knows that I will not and that I will just rest until I am better again.'

'That does not seem very sympathetic. Are you well enough to come with me?' asked Alicia.

'The trip will do me good. To get out of the house for a while sounds like a good idea.' She looked very pale.

'Okay, we will go now. A cup of tea or coffee in our office is available to help with the headache. You do understand we are not blaming Marta's disappearance on you, don't you?'

'I am not sure of anything right now. I feel totally confused as to why my address is on that letter. I know, despite my headaches, that I have nothing to do with inviting young foreign women to come and work for me.'

Mrs Cooke did not look very well by now, and Alicia was worried she was asking too much. She decided to make it a quick trip to the office and back again. If Mrs Cooke continued to look ill by then, Alicia might ask if she could take her to a doctor.

Mrs Cooke picked up her handbag and checked her appearance in a mirror in the hall and walked out to Alicia's car. She said, 'Just the thought of getting out of the house seems good to me. It stops me from thinking of my husband and wondering what he is up to.'

'I am glad I called to see you, Mrs Cooke. I must say, you have been looking even more ill by the minute since I have been with you. I would like to take you to a doctor, who can have a look at you and prescribe something to perk you up a bit.'

'May I call you Alicia?' Mrs Cooke said, looking over at her and receiving a nod. 'My name is Susan. Please drop the *Mrs Cooke*. I have a feeling that is not going to be my name much longer. I was a nurse when I met Roland, and he was very attentive to me at first. There has been an endless supply of nurses since then, and I am sure that we stay married because it gives Roland an excuse for the affairs not to be too messy for him. This time I believe he is attached to a nurse at one of his clinics. It has gone on longer than all the others, so I expect to get my marching orders soon.'

Alicia glanced over at the woman. 'My impression of you, Susan, is that you are very much in control of the situation. Why not pull the pin before he does and give him something to think about? Go to a lawyer first, I suggest. Not his lawyer. We have a very good chap whom we do a lot of work for. Go and see him and get a bit of advice before Roland is aware of what you are planning. Get one up on him if he is treating you so badly.'

'That sounds like good advice, Alicia. I will do that. I am certainly not happy with the way things are going, and I could get myself a job where I do not meet him daily, perhaps in a smaller hospital. It will be better to make a move before he realises what I am doing, and I feel now it is the right thing to do, before I get too old to find a position. Nursing is a good career to have, because we can get a placing somewhere even if we are a little older. I have had too much time on my hands since the children left home. I need the stimulus of a job to stop things that go over and over in my head and the loneliness of an empty house.'

Alicia felt sorry for the woman being put in that position by an uncaring husband, and she said, 'It sounds as if this is giving you a direction to move and to do it in your own time rather than wait for your husband to make the call. Well done, Susan.'

Susan smiled. 'It is always easier to talk to strangers. My friends would say "Stay where you are. You have a nice house and enough money." But they are not the ones feeling lonely, and I am aware that

I am getting older and need to think of myself now that the children and Roland are not there for me any more.'

'If you have brought the children up right, you will not lose them. They will still be there for you, but their focus is now on their studies,' assured Alicia.

Alicia parked the car and showed Susan Cooke into the office. She introduced her to Percy and James, explaining the circumstances of why she was there. They sat in the conference room, and Alicia wrote up the statement for her to sign, stating that she would still be interviewing Roland Cooke the next day when he became available.

James looked very approving as Alicia went on to give Mrs Cooke a card for their business and for Alex Overington, the lawyer, if she decided she needed to contact him. Percy volunteered to drive Susan Cooke home again while Alicia discussed the case with James. Susan looked much better now; it seemed as if saying her intent out loud to someone had cleared her mind, and her headache was receding. Alicia saw them to the car and said, 'I will keep in touch, Susan, and will let you know when we have found Marta, the missing girl.'

Later in the office James said 'I received a call from the police chief saying that he would like to have a discussion with both of us after he speaks to Sacha and Pieter this afternoon. Do you have time for that?'

'It seems strange, but yes, I have time. I am up to date with my home duties for the moment. Have you any idea what it is all about?'

'He seemed to have had a couple of people in his office when he rang, so he did not disclose the subject. I guess we will learn what it is about when we get there.'

'It is almost time to leave now.' She turned to Percy. 'Sorry, Percy, to leave you in charge again by yourself. Where are Kate and Ken?'

Percy smiled at Alicia. 'Out on a small job. They should be back soon. I will not be lonely.'

She hugged him. 'I know how it is to be left in the office, wondering what everyone else is doing.'

'We always hurried back when we knew you were alone, Alicia,' said James.

'Do not take it wrong, you two. I do miss not being here every day. I needed a break to catch up at home. We will hurry back, Percy.' She picked up her handbag and, looking at James, said, 'Come on, James. There is work to be done. Sacha and Pieter will arrive any time soon, and we are to meet the boys at the police headquarters. Let's go.'

James and Percy looked at each other, and James said, 'Meet our new investigator, Percy. This the second job she has done by herself this week. It looks as if we have a new talent rising.'

They all laughed as Alicia went out the door with her husband, smiling broadly.

*　*　*

The two brothers were waiting as the investigators arrived at police headquarters, and the four of them went up in the lift to the police chief's office.

Detective Inspector Paul Morris, James's friend from earlier cases, was in the chief's office, and the two shook hands. Pieter was asked to give his summary of events first, which he did in Russian; Alicia translated for him. James could see that the other men were captivated by Alicia's abilities.

Alicia asked Sacha if there were any further remarks gleaned from the men on the building site which he managed. He stated that some of the men had been to visit the house next door to the restaurant they had been to there were a number of girls of Russian or Polish nationality as prostitutes, all very young and good-looking. Most of them did not speak English. They did not get much time to talk, as they were half-hour visits, so the men did not learn how the girls came to be there.

James asked, 'Do you know of this place, Paul?'

'I have heard rumours, but we have not had reason to call there. I believe it is a licensed business. I asked around after you rang.'

James explained that, after lunch, Alicia had visited Mrs Cooke, who did not know that her address was on Pieter's cell phone. 'Alicia merely stated to her that Marta's family is curious about her time in her au pair job and that Marta is missing. It appears Mrs Cooke was unaware of Marta's expected arrival, and she has signed a statement on that in our office.'

Alicia would go the next day to have a cooking lesson at the restaurant which was next to the house they suspected was being used for prostitution, so that she could ask more questions and have a look around. She had arranged that herself.

Pieter explained that he needed to join his ship by 4 p.m. the next day, as it would sail early the next morning. He did not want to make it look like he was looking for Marta, in case of repercussions to him on the ship, which he believed was a part of bringing the young women to this country and taking them away when they completed their time here. He explained that he had seen Dr Cooke on the ship, talking to the captain. Also, Sacha had seen the same fellow in the restaurant several times.

The police chief looked very interested in the whole conversation and turned to James and said, 'We will sponsor you on this one, James. It is apparent that this Dr Cooke is managing this deal. We will have to have a look at his movements. As DI Morris has said, it is a licensed business, but it is not licensed to take unknowing girls into the business by luring them into this country on false promises.'

Sacha and Pieter looked very pleased with the outcome of the meeting and stood up to leave as the chief said to James, 'I need a word or two, James. Would you mind staying for a while?'

Paul Morris showed the two young men out and came back into the office and sat down. The chief shuffled a bunch of files on his desk that had been there when they had come into the room.

He started to speak, looking at James. 'I spent the weekend in London at police headquarters, attending an official meeting held every six months to discuss budgets and staffing. On the completion of the meeting, I was asked to stay and have a few words with Harold Griffiths, whom you know. He asked me how you were doing, and when I told him of your completion of the customs saga and other dealings you have had, he was very interested in what I had to say. I think you have a friend there, James, who is aware of your capabilities.

'What came out of this conversation is, he suggested we offer you more work that you can fit into your schedule and he suggested you try some cold cases that a fresh eye could perhaps find a few clues to work with. I have thought it over, and with DI Morris's help, we have picked out a bundle which have had us stumped. You do not have to agree, but I would like to say that I admire the way your cases have been completed so quickly and accurately, including DI Morris's house fire, which he never gave up on and which you solved. That had been an outstanding case for years. You never lose the fixation. It becomes a nightmare when you cannot see the clues but know there was a crime. We have all been through that at some time.

'If you decide to try it, log the hours spent and the expenses, and I will see that you are paid on time, including all staff members. I can see that your wife's experience will be handy for a couple of the cases. I know that until now, she has been your receptionist and is not licensed along with the rest of your crew, but I suggest that we produce a licence for her. She could have her own cards to hand out. She has been an immense help to you in some of your jobs—indeed, as she already has been in your new missing-girl job. Also, her language skills will come in very handy for a couple of them.

'I have been speaking to your partner. I called your office earlier and Percy was the only one there, so I asked a few questions. I hope you will forgive me for that. I only wanted to confirm Alicia's part in the business.'

Alicia and James looked at each other. 'What about your retirement plans?' James asked.

She laughed. 'I was getting a little bored after the initial flurry, and I thought I did well with Julie's job and with Susan Cooke, so yes, I will be in it.'

James turned again to the chief and said, 'We have allowances for our usual jobs, and these cold cases will fit in as we deem fit? Is that correct?'

'Yes. Also, you have DI Morris as backup to confer with, and he can arrange anything you need, such as DNA testing. You two seem to get along well together.'

'Yes, we do, and it is always good to know that someone has your back. I think we have a deal here. It will be good to know that if things slow down in the business, we have a fallback with the cold cases.' The more James thought about it, the more he liked the idea. They could afford to offer Ken full-time employment with this to back up expenses.

He stood up and shook the chief's hand, and also the hand of Paul Morris. Alicia did the same, saying, 'A promotion, eh? How could anyone knock that back?'

*   *   *

Alicia's cooking lesson took place the next morning. Other than how to make borscht, she learnt that the girls from the next house came in for meals early in the evening. Some meals were delivered to the house, but mostly the girls were keen to have a break and come in and help themselves. The tab was given to Madam, the woman in charge of the house. Alicia asked who the meals were delivered to, and the answer was 'Always the madam'. So she decided it was not worth trying to gain entry by delivering meals herself. Another thought she had: should she return in the early evening to see if Marta would come for a meal?

The cook, Nancy, did not appear to be wary of Alicia's questions. She thought it was natural for someone to be curious about the house next door; she herself was, she admitted, but she had never been able to get into the house, even though she had been a cook for the restaurant for two years.

She had always been met at the door and the meals taken from her, or the bouncer would come in to pick them up. When the girls came into the restaurant, they had obviously been told not to talk to anyone, so they only talked amongst themselves. They seemed happy enough, and they changed several times a year, mostly only staying about three or four months and then getting replaced by newcomers, always Russian or Polish. Nancy had wondered why only those nationalities. Listening to the girls' conversations as they went around the room, she realised that the girls were brought by ship, and it appeared to be the same ship each time, on its regular run.

Alicia was amazed to learn so much so quickly and asked Nancy how she understood the girls' conversations, because she appeared to be English.

Nancy laughed. 'My grandfather was a Polish flying officer in World War II. My mother learnt the language at his knee and passed it on to me. They were very proud of their Polish aristocratic roots and wanted us children to understand. Everything they owned in their homeland was devastated, and then the Russians took over after the war. So they never returned. We had a small clan of these officers here in England during and after the war, but they have spread out over the years. The only Polish thing about me, except my heritage, is that I learnt from my grandparents how to cook their food, not knowing I would eventually wind up being a cook next to a brothel. I speak Polish, of course, and get by on Russian because I hear it so often.'

'You had me wondering, Nancy. You seemed to be English, but I have heard you speaking both of the other languages. You are so fluent. Have you ever visited Poland, now that it is part of the European landscape and easy to enter?'

Nancy's rueful answer made Alicia feel sad for her. 'I went with my brother several years ago now, and we followed the map our grandfather had left for us in case we were ever able to return. We found our villa, or what was left of it—just a few partial walls still standing. Even the bricks had been carried away. The land itself had been taken over by the Bolsheviks. We enquired about the chance of having the land returned to us, but it was all too hard. It has been divided between many families, all making their living from their plots. Our home is here now anyway. We do not have the sense that Poland is our home, like my grandfather and even my mother and her brother did all their lives.'

'Do you have a family of your own to take and to show where you came from?' asked Alicia.

'I have a daughter. She is twenty-eight and a lawyer. We went together to Warsaw for her twenty-first birthday present, with my husband, whose family came from there originally. We did not know anyone, so we stayed at a hotel in the centre of the city. It was a first-class place in its heyday, one of the few still remaining after the war.

The decor was original, by the looks of the staircase and carpets and beautiful crystal chandeliers, probably because the Nazis stayed there. It seemed very old and cared for by the staff, showing how things were done when the gentry of the city went dining, before the war turned everything around it to rubble. In the corner of the room were a grand piano and violinists playing waltzes. You could imagine what life had been like for my grandfather's generation—so beautiful even though it is old and threadbare now. Hitler stormed in and spoilt so many lives. My grandfather was the only survivor of his family. We visited all there was to see at the time and decided we had a good life here, and we were anxious to come back to good old UK.

Alicia smiled at Nancy and asked, 'Does having a daughter make you more interested in the girls next door?'

Nancy looked at her quizzically. 'You are very observant about people, aren't you? Yes, it does worry me. Some of the girls look very unhappy when they first arrive. I have often wondered if they are here by their own choice. I have never asked questions, because the girls are accompanied by a bouncer-type man called Bruce. One look from him is enough for me to close my mouth.'

Alicia decided that it was time to leave; her lesson on borscht was done, and she had gleaned everything possible at the moment. It might take a police raid to learn more about the house next door. She returned to the office and told the others all she had learnt.

James said he would ring DI Morris and follow Alicia's story through; perhaps a raid could be carried out. As he said that, there was a phone call for Alicia from Susan Cooke, saying that Roland Cooke had turned up at their house that morning, accompanied by Marta, who was to be her au pair, Susan was told. Susan had called him the previous evening and relayed the story of the missing girl to him and how it was being turned over to the police today, and lo and behold, the girl had appeared, looking dazed but very much alive. Her husband's story was, he had advertised for an au pair to help out in the house and to provide company now that their children had left home. Susan did not believe him. And where had the girl been since the ship she arrived on landed four days ago? Susan was going ahead with her visit to the lawyer, Alec, the next day to discuss divorce plans; her appointment was for ten in the morning.

The staff at the investigation office were also disbelieving of Dr Cooke's story, and James said he would mention it to the police after he interviewed Marta. Alicia turned to him and objected; she claimed it was her case and that she should be the one to talk to Marta. Everybody laughed, and the others agreed with her, which in turn made Alicia laugh, seeing the look on James's face.

He drew back, raising his hands in front of him and saying, 'Sorry, Alicia. Yes, this is your case. We always travel in pairs. May I be your companion on this one?'

Alicia laughed and said, 'Yes, James, I look forward to your interrogation of Roland Cooke while I interview Marta. It sounds as if he could be a slimy creature. I want to do a background check on him before we go, to see what comes out of the woodwork. My previous check was a very quick one, just to establish who he is. By the way, dinner tonight is a Russian menu that Nancy gave me before I left the restaurant. It includes the borscht I made. I have put it in the refrigerator here. Please remind me to take it home.'

Kate and Alicia went to their computers to see what they could find, and after twenty minutes, they looked up at each other and said, 'What have you found?'

Alicia said, 'He received honours for his medical degree from university. He must be a very intelligent man. He was employed first at the hospital here and went on to specialise in sexual diseases.'

Kate laughed. 'It seems as if he is using that knowledge to run brothels. He is the owner of an escort agency, running about ten women at a time. He is also the owner of the brothel on the docks, next to the restaurant. Quite a boy is our doctor Cooke. He also runs clinics in the area between this town and other coastal towns. That would explain his staying away from home so much.'

'I wonder how much of this Susan, his wife, knows?' Alicia had been taking notes as Kate talked through his history. 'He sounds like a busy man. No wonder he is not home often. Right, I think we have enough to go on for the minute. I will fill James in while we are in the car. The good doctor is at home, waiting for us, according to Susan.'

James came into the office and said, 'Ready, Alicia? Kate, if you have a few minutes, can you go through some of these files and take a pick of any that you want to have a go at? Record the time you spend on it. We will talk a little more about it when we get back.'

Kate was interested when she saw the files, which were definitely police records from where she had been employed previously. 'Percy will be interested in these,' she said to James, who was going out of the door.

James paused at the doorway. 'I thought of him and you when I picked them up from the chief, and I thought you would be interested. Call him in to have a look when he is not busy. We should not be more than an hour. This is a preliminary interrogation at best. It is Marta's story we want to hear.'

*   *   *

During the drive to the Cookes' home, Alicia read out to James the notes she had written down from the computers. 'And this is only ten minutes' worth of looking into the man. There must be more to find.'

'I agree, he seems to get around. We will leave Marta to you, Alicia. It sounds as if her English is only minimal.'

They arrived at the Cooke home and walked up the driveway to the front door. Susan Cooke had been watching out for them; she opened the door and led them into the sitting room, where her husband was sitting and using a computer. After the greetings, Alicia looked around for Marta, not seeing her there. Susan took Alicia's arm and showed her to Marta, who was sitting on a chair in the kitchen, where she had a cup of coffee and magazines to look through. James stayed to talk to Roland Cooke.

Alicia greeted the girl in Russian and asked if she spoke English, knowing from Pieter that her reason for coming from her home was to perfect her English to help her job prospects. The girl answered that her knowledge was minimal, but she would like to speak it to further her vocabulary; she could speak in Russian if Alicia did not understand.

The girl had a lovely presence, and Alicia could see why she had
been chosen for a job. She was not cheap-looking at all, so Alicia knew
she would not be the type to work at a brothel on her own choice,
although Alicia thought, *I do not know anyone who works in a brothel.*
In fact, Marta looked like any girl attending university—from well-
to-do parents, well dressed, and polite. Alicia felt cross that this girl had
gone through the experience of entering the brothel, and she was glad
she had pressed on with enquiring about her. It was obvious that it had
rattled the doctor's cage. She wondered just how many had fallen for his
advertisement. There was at least one other that Susan had been made
aware of but had not understood at the time.

Alicia asked Marta in English, 'Can you tell me where you have
been since departing from the ship you arrived to this country on?'

Marta smiled. 'Yes, I understand you. This is good, my first
opportunity to speak your language. When I left the ship, the doctor
was not there to greet me. Madam suggested I go with the other girls
to a house near the docks to await his arrival. He did not come until
this morning, and I thought I was stranded with the other girls. I had
no money to take a taxi to this house and was not allowed to go out the
door of the house by the docks. The other girls had the same problem.
No one came to pick them up, and Madam was saying they could stay
and service the men who came calling. This would pay their board and
lodging until they earned enough money to go home again. I did not
like to do this. I am not a prostitute, which is what Madam was talking
about. She said it would take a three-month period to earn enough to
pay for our food and until we had the fare to go home on the ship again.

'The other girls were not as horrified as me. One of the girls said,
"We may as well get paid for sex. We give it away to our boyfriends
for free." I did not like that thought. My mother and father would be
angry with me if I did this, so I was very happy to see Dr Cooke this
morning. He told me he had been away from the city, so he was unable
to pick me up until today.'

'What was Madam like to you, Marta? Was she pressing you to
have sex with the men?'

'Not the first day. We were shown to bedrooms, and we were allowed to sleep until the evening. It had been very rough on the ship on the last day and night before we landed, and we were all quite seasick. We got up from our beds in the evening when a meal was delivered from the restaurant next door. It was then we realised we were in a brothel, as several other girls came out of their rooms for the meal and quite candidly told us we should expect men that evening.

'For me, it was a nightmare, and I refused to entertain the men. I locked myself in the bedroom I was allocated, and refused to open the door. Madam called a meeting the next morning and laid out the conditions if we stayed there. All of us were in the same position. We had no money. Some of the girls did not speak any English, the Russian ones particularly. So where would we go? How would we get back home? Our phones had been taken off us when we arrived, and we could not contact anyone. It was as if they had done their homework very well and chose poor girls to come to their brothel, and we had no choice but to say yes to them. This day was to be the last day to think about it. Tomorrow those who do not cooperate will be put out the door to fend for themselves. I was so happy to hear that Dr Cooke was looking for me, and he has brought me here to meet his delightful wife.'

Alicia was amazed that it had all been so easy; she had expected threats from Dr Cooke. Having spoken to Susan first seemed to have made all the difference. It was as if Marta could not stop talking, as she went on and on, describing what had happened; she believed it had all been a mistake. Alicia had other thoughts on that but said nothing to the young woman.

She held out her hand to Marta and said, 'Good luck, Marta. I am sure you will get on well with Mrs Cooke, and your English is very good already and only needs a little polishing up to get rid of the accent.'

Susan Cooke and Alicia went back to the sitting room. James looked up. Alicia nodded, so he got up to leave with her. They knew they had caught Cooke out in his scam, and a raid could collect a number of girls not there by their own choice. Marta was the lucky one to escape.

After leaving the house, Alicia rang Pieter's phone, and he answered almost immediately. When he heard the news of Marta's escape from the brothel, he gave a sigh of relief and thanked Alicia for all she had done. He was on his way to join his ship. He had to be aboard by four o'clock, ready to serve meals. Alicia wished him a happy trip and a safe arrival back home.

When they arrived at the office, James decided to ring Paul Morris and report the contact that Alicia had set up at the Cooke home with Marta, the girl missing until now, and Roland Cooke. He told him about how Marta thought of Dr Cooke as her saviour, and Roland had described to James that it had all been a mistake of mistiming and that everything had been sorted out now. However, both the Armstrongs strongly believed that it was the practice for the scam to get young women to the brothel and that it had been operating for some time. The turnover time was three months, when the ship would come on its regular runs, or the girls would stay on another three months to earn extra money, as the first three months was to pay for their board and lodging for the period and for the boat fare back home.

Marta boarded the ship in Gdańsk in Poland, and the other girls had boarded in Vladivostok in Russia; this appeared to be a regular three-month run, with girls going both ways on the same ship. James suggested that the police department or the vice squad follow this up. Most of the girls were unaware that they would be going to a brothel and thought they were going to have jobs in the region for short-term stays. James also said that Cooke owned an escort agency with mostly English young women and also owned the brothel in the docks. He told Paul Morris this and said he would write it in a report for the vice squad.

Once again, Paul was amazed by how quickly James and Alicia had solved the problem, and he asked if James had looked into any of the files he was given by the chief of police.

James laughed and said, 'I am not usually in two places at once and have just now returned to the office, as we were interviewing at the Cooke home. I will look at the files this evening and let you know tomorrow.'

CHAPTER THREE

James saw Kate hanging around his doorway and called to her to come in and sit down. She excitedly mentioned that she had worked on one of the cold case files in her earlier career with the police.

'It was the presumed murder of an Indian girl who was pushed through a plate-glass window of a dress shop, where she was employed as a salesperson, in a shopping mall. She fell from the balcony and died at the scene. No witnesses come forward, and the other shopping staff had been in another part of the shop when the accident or murder took place, as it was lunchtime and some of the staff were off duty at the time.

'The girl's family—her father and two brothers, as the mother was away in India at the time it happened—were all bereft at the girl's death, but basically no one came up with a reason it happened. Each person claimed it must have been an accident. I was of the opinion that it was an honour killing, but I could not find anyone to give an opinion. All possible witnesses were silent, and it became frustrating coming up against a brick wall each time they were asked questions. It was the last assignment for me before I left the force, and I still have not got over the frustration I felt when each potential witness was questioned.'

Kate took a long breath and went on to say, 'The incident seemed unbelievable. The girl was pushed through a plate-glass window and over the balcony outside the window. For an accident, the general opinion in the force at the time was that there was too much distance between the window and the edge of the two-metre balcony of the second storey of the centre. We were sure she was pushed, but no one saw anything. For something like that and the noise it would have made, it seemed unlikely to us that no one saw anything, but nobody came forward. Several people saw the girl hit the ground, but nothing else.

'This is the job that caused the break-up of my marriage. I spent so much time at work and became cranky, I suppose, and tired when I would eventually come home to my husband and the children. But I kept thinking of this young woman and her terror at being attacked. I could not leave it alone. It is not seen to be the sort of crime a stranger would do. It had to be her family or someone hired by her family, although the father and two brothers had alibis, all work-related. Actually, the two boys were at school. They were fourteen and eleven years old and were unlikely to take part in any sort of killing at that age, but we could not get through the line-up of closed faces to make any sense of anything. Seemingly, people were afraid to come forward.'

James thought about it. 'I have heard of honour killings, but I have not come across it previously. It seems we have been given Indian-related crimes because of our previous Indian connections with Sahib. Yes, Kate, this is a strange case, especially if there was a hired killer brought in to do the deed on behalf of the family. It is strange also that the mother of the girl was not available. If the family brought in a hired killer, it would make sense to make sure she was not around to answer questions. A woman would get very emotional about a loving daughter being done away with, so the men of the family possibly chose to send her away, out of the line of sight. Check to see if the mother is available now. It has been some time since this happened, a year now. The family likely think they are in the clear. The Indian community must have some opinions on the death of one of their number. Now that the hubbub about it has diminished, there may be a few whispers that we can reconstruct and connect. We will have to invite Mrs Sharma to dinner to ask her some questions on Indian customs and tell her about our holiday trip in the Maharajah's train.'

When James rang Mrs Sharma, he did not tell her the purpose of the invitation; he only said he wanted to tell her how enjoyable the trip

Alicia and he had on the Maharajah's train was, and he also wanted to ask her about a few Indian customs.

Kate nodded. 'That was well done, James. I have read through the file and find that I still feel frustrated that we could not close it.'

'I will take it home tonight and read it with Alicia and Percy to see if we can come up with some questions. Sometimes a new face on the scene can see some different things.' James closed the file and put it in his briefcase. He called out to Percy as he organised to go home. 'Anything catch your attention in those files, Percy?'

'One or two that I remember, James. Most of them are more recent, since I left the department. Shall we take them all home, James, or do you want to leave them here?'

'We do not get the distraction at home, Percy. Pick them all up. Granny may be interested in reading through them. Remember how keen she was in the Whittall case.'

'We could not have done it without her, James. That is a good idea. Between the four of us, we may see something missing.'

Kate said, 'It sounds as if you have an interesting time at home, discussing cases. I have not had that benefit in the past. Now that Ken and I have teamed up, perhaps we will have the same rapport you have with your family group.'

'You are young still, Kate. Plenty of time for you to discuss cases at home once the children have their own lives. Enjoy the children while you can,' said Alicia as she joined James, ready to go home.

*   *   *

On the walk back to the bookshop and home, James filled Alicia in on Kate's cold case, mentioning that they were all going to meet up with the Sharma family over dinner on Friday evening, at their favourite Indian restaurant, to discuss honour killings amongst other topics.

Percy had gone through all the cold case files quickly during the day and came up with two that he thought James might be interested in. The first was a young girl, aged ten, disappearing from her bedroom at her parents' house during one evening six months previously. The bedroom door had been locked from the inside, and the window had been open, even though it had been a cool weather period. There had been posters of the missing girl in newspapers and on walls at the railway station and bus stations, but there had been no sightings of her mentioned. Those posters were still currently in position at access points to the town.

Percy said, 'This sounds right up your alley, James. You have previously found missing persons quickly with Alicia's help. The second is the one that Kate brought up. As you think, Mrs Sharma will be interested in helping you solve that one. There is another one regarding the death of a pair of gay boys, and incidentally, they were also of Indian extraction. That happened shortly after the girl falling in the mall. Do you think there could be a possibility that Kate's case and that one are linked? There were less than two months between them, and the boys' case is later than the girl's, so it may be easier to pick up.'

'You could be right, Percy. We will have a look at it tonight. There may be something to connect the two of them. I am not sure how far the honour thing goes. Does it include men and women? I will have to write out a list to ask Mrs Sharma on Friday evening. We may have to pay her as a consultant because we have so many questions.'

Alicia said, 'I could see how it would be handy, paying her for her time when we need to consult her. Despite the people migrating to England, they still bring with them their customs, which are against our laws. They want our benefits but do not like to change their customs to be English. It is amazing to me that it happens. If they do not adapt to our ways, there is not much point in coming.'

'That's it in a nutshell, Alicia. We have had so many Indian-related problems, and it is a good idea to ask Mrs Sharma to be our consultant. We may not make her rich, but we will help her make her dream of a trip on the Maharajah's train possible.' James grinned at the memory of the look on Mrs Sharma's face when they had told her they were going on a trip on the luxury train.

'I am sure your grandmother will be interested in these files, Alicia,' said Percy with a grin. 'Perhaps we will have to pay her as a consultant too.'

'You guys have got her interested in the business now. Nothing will stop her. She calls it "mind stretching".' Alicia smiled.

* * *

Granny was interested, as they thought she would be, and she read through what they were now calling 'Kate's cold case' quickly while Alicia was preparing the evening meal.

Her first comment was 'I think this killing was done by a woman'.

This immediately caught the attention of the other three in the kitchen.

Percy said, 'Why do you think that, Valerie? Would a woman be strong enough to push the girl over the balcony? The whole investigation was done on the premise that it was a man they were looking for, because it would need considerable strength to shove someone through a heavy glass window and over the balcony two metres away.'

'I think that a man in a ladies' dress shop would have caught someone's attention. Women usually prefer to try on clothes when they are alone, or the man waits outside the shop for them to come out,' said Granny. 'Some supply seats in the shop for men waiting for their partners, but there was no mention of anyone seeing a man at the time. With the loud crash of glass, eyes would have turned in the direction of the noise, yet no one mentioned any men in the area.'

Alicia turned from the stove and said, 'You may have something there, Granny. I believe that in the majority of cases, that is true, and as this girl was a salesperson, it would have seemed wrong to the other staff for her to be talking to a man and would have captured their attention. Nowhere is it mentioned in the file that a man was seen in the shop or in the vicinity.'

'That seems to rule out a hired killer doing the dirty work,' said James. 'That leaves family members, but they all had alibis that were confirmed by other people.'

Granny said, 'We will have to learn more about this girl to find if there was any reason for her being killed. Something must have led up to it. She was nineteen and had been working in the dress shop since leaving school. The other staff members were happy with her employment. In fact, it seems one of the girls was very upset about the whole thing and took a week off work. Perhaps she had a special relationship with the murdered girl. That is not mentioned at all in the file but would be worth pursuing.'

'Keep it up, Granny,' said James. 'You are on a roll here. That is all good sense. There must be a list of her closest friends there somewhere. Is that particular girl mentioned?'

'Yes, James, she is Aisha Choudhury. I have just found her interview details. They shared a flat since leaving school and being employed. They had been friends at school.'

Alicia turned again. 'She should be the first one we interview to find out about the life—what was the dead girl's name? We cannot keep on saying "the dead girl".'

'She was Anaya Patel,' answered Granny, who held the file.

'Shall I make an appointment to visit this girl, Aisha, tomorrow?' asked Alicia. 'Now that time has passed, she may feel more comfortable talking about it. I imagine she must have been really upset when her friend died, and she was unable to talk about the case to anyone.'

'I believe you are right, Alicia, and your gentle persuasion may be just the thing to bring her story out,' said James. 'But will Kate want to talk to her? It was her case in the first place.'

'It was her case, which is why I think it would come better from me. As soon as the girl sees Kate, she will remember her and the murder of her friend, and she will clam up. I will be a new face, without the terrible memories of the time it happened, and I may be able to get her talking by going gently.'

Percy voiced his opinion 'Yes, James, I can see Alicia's point. We could set Kate to look up the family and talk to the mother about Anaya. She was away at the time of the death and would not recognise Kate. The mother can also give a background on the girl, which no one else seemed willing to discuss at the time. I am sure a mother would like to talk about her missing daughter.'

'All right, we will do it that way. Do you think Ken should go with Kate?' asked James.

Alicia demurred. 'No. Like when I spoke to Susan Cooke, women trust women and get a little shy around men and are less likely to talk. We are able to get them onside generally. In both of these cases, I do not believe there is any danger yet. We are just going to stir up buried memories, and we do not suspect either of these two women, so we will not seem out of line questioning them. It may take a little longer to get them to speak, but to be able to talk to strangers about their story one-to-one helps clear their souls.'

Granny joined in. 'I think Alicia is seeing it correctly, James and Percy. Men get a bit off-putting, looking officious, and in this case, women interviewers would get more out of them if they approach it softly, saying that it is a follow-up and asking the right questions in a friendly manner.'

'Exactly, Granny,' Alicia said with a smile at her grandmother.

*   *   *

After reading through the file of the murder of the young gay men, Alicia said, 'Despite the possibility of it being an honour killing, I cannot see any resemblance to Anaya Patel's murder. This was done quite differently. The boys were killed in their bed in an apartment they were renting just out of the old town. We will have to ask Mrs Sharma about this one to see if it is likely an honour killing or just a gay bashing that went wrong.'

Percy said, 'I remember that one. It stirred up a lot of angst in the community, and the newspapers loved it. It stayed in the headlines for some time. I did not work on the case, as it was well after I retired, but the chaps in the department said it was a gruesome killing, blood everywhere. So it may have been a blood thing. Shall we do that after we solve the girl's murder? Valerie's views on that one have opened up new avenues worth looking into.'

James had been looking at the file with the two young men in their bed, covered in blood, and said, grimacing, 'Ugh, I have not done any gruesome, bloody killings yet, Percy. The customs murders are the only murders I have seen, and they were more "wham, bam, " type and we already knew who the culprit was. Looking at those bloody scenes in the file makes me want to throw up. They are so bad. I think this is for our male members to work on, don't you?'

Percy had to agree. 'Yes, James, I have to go along with that. They look really bad, but at least you do not have to see the real thing. The hard part is over. Maybe Ken would have some ideas on that one.'

'I think that will be enough for tonight. Tomorrow Alicia will go and see Aisha, the murdered girl's young friend, and Kate will go and see Mrs Patel, the girl's mother. I like Alicia's idea of "softly, softly", so I will have a word with Kate before she goes,' said James. 'If work is slow, we can go over some of these other files together, Percy. It is a little hard to absorb them all in one sitting.'

Granny said, 'You have not mentioned the missing ten-year-old. It seems rather urgent to discuss that one.'

'She has been missing for six months already, Granny. She will have to wait another few days,' said James. 'We do not have the resources to cover all these files in one go. We will leave that one for you to mull over for the present, while we will have a go at these three young Indian people. It could be a serial killer attacking specific races. We need to find an answer for them first.'

*   *   *

As Alicia and James went into the bookshop and upstairs to their apartment, Alicia said, 'Wow, we do have Granny helping out in the investigations now. That was an insight that nobody else came up with in the original investigation, and it seems to me to be spot on. She was very quick in redefining the file.'

'She was like that in the Ross Whittall case last year too. She had answers before we could ask the questions. She is a very canny lady.' James smiled and gave her a hug. 'A bit like you in that, Alicia.'

*   *   *

In the office next morning, Kate and Alicia made phone calls to make appointments with the women they wanted to interview. Kate's was arranged with Mrs Patel for ten o'clock, and Alicia's for twelve with Aisha, for a lunchtime interview; she would be met at the coffee shop on the ground floor of the mall.

At the last minute, James asked Percy if he would go with Kate, just in case the men of the family decided to attend. He did not want Kate overpowered by the husband if he turned up. He wanted a low-key interview and thought that Mrs Patel may be more comfortable with Percy, as he was older.

Kate and Percy set off for their appointment and found a very attractive-looking woman of perhaps forty-five, wearing Western clothes, with her long dark hair tied back with a ribbon. She was, in Percy's opinion, a beautiful but sad woman, with an Indian accent, and was welcoming to her guests, offering tea for refreshment, which they accepted.

Mrs Patel's opening statement was 'I wondered why nobody came to ask me about my daughter since I arrived back in this country from India five days after my daughter's death. I have thought about it many times in the year since it happened. I wanted to go to the police office and ask what they were doing about her murder. My husband has held me back, saying that we do not know what happened to have someone kill Anaya and that by stirring things up, we may be the next target for the killer. It has been a thorny barb in my brain all this time. What do you want me to tell you?'

'We know that your daughter was three years old when you arrived in the UK, and your sons were born here,' Percy said.

'As you said, our daughter was three years old, and when we arrived, we were met by Bharat Kumah, who had offered my husband a job in his tailoring business. The men had been employed together in India and had become friends, so Bharat asked my husband to join him. We have kept up with these people since we arrived here. My husband still works in the same business with them, although we do not live near them because, quite frankly, I do not like the woman, his wife, Iris Kumah. Although the men got along with each other, I kept clear of the family, except at parties and social occasions.

'There had been some talk between the men about arranging a marriage between Anaya and the son of my husband's friend, but I honestly could not like the idea of his wife as my daughter's mother-in-law. She was not of our caste, and anyway, I believe in the way you find your own husbands and wives here in the UK. It seems so much nicer than being married to someone that someone else chose for you. Actually, the evening I went to India, as we were waiting for the flight, Anaya told me she thought she had found someone nice for a husband. It was the first time she spoke of it, and we have no idea who it was. I did not ask, because at that moment, my flight was called. I thought we would have a lot of time to discuss it when I got home from India.

'My daughter went to the local school and was not a star pupil. She preferred reading and drawing, and she said she wanted to be an artist. She was quite artistic but dropped it as she got older. She did not go to university. She was too excited about getting a job and having some money to spend "for a change" and said she might continue her studies after a year-long break. She was not sure what she wanted to study and thought that with time, she would come to see her way.'

Kate asked, 'Did she have any particular friends, Mrs Patel?'

'She had one particular girl friend, the same companion all through her schooldays. This is the girl who talked my daughter into a year-long break from her studies. The two of them rented a flat near the shopping area, and they both got jobs in the same dress shop. My husband was not happy about our daughter leaving home, but the girls talked him round. He said one year was the limit, and then Anaya must return home and join the family again. Anaya loved her father and could twist him around her little finger and get anything she wanted. She could be quite persistent in getting her own way.'

'Did Anaya have any boyfriends previously, with the possibility that someone may have got jealous of her new acquaintance?' Percy asked.

'No, Mr Gray, there was never anyone serious. She was more interested in living life as it came, and she was not interested in settling down. She was barely nineteen years old, and her friendship with Aisha was more important to her. I do not believe they were lovers, as some nasty people have talked about—just friends. Both intended to go to university and study before making any plans. They just wanted to have fun. Her father and I could see that, and we were happy to go along with it. There was time enough for getting serious about things—or so we believed anyway. We heard on the grapevine that the girls were lovers, but it was not true. Some people seem to get off on other people's misery and will tell all sorts of stories. They do not realise how hard it is to have your daughter's name dishonoured for the sake of sensation. It has been a hard cross to bear in these last months.'

'Is it true, Mrs Patel, that girls of eighteen in your home country tend to marry by arranged marriage?' asked Kate.

'Yes, it is common, but we are in England now. We do not have to do things in that way. We believed that Anaya had enough sense and beauty and that she would get married in time, to someone of her own choice.'

Percy asked, 'Why did you go to India at the time we are asking about, Mrs Patel?'

'My mother was dying and asked me to come. She wanted to see me one last time, as it had been several years since I had been to see her. I arrived only two days before her death, for which I was grateful, as I was with her at her end. It was the same day I heard of Anaya's death, and apparently it was the same time for both deaths. That is very strange, isn't it? I want to believe my mother heard Anaya calling to her as she fell, and joined with her. I know I am strange to think that and have not told anyone else, but the feeling is strong within me and gives me a little comfort. The two people in the world I loved the most were gone from me at the same moment.'

At this moment, they saw a calm come across Mrs Patel's face, so Percy felt it was time he asked the most important question. 'Did Anaya have any enemies, or do you know anyone who might have harmed her?'

'I have thought over this question every night when I could not sleep, and the only person I have come up with is Iris Kumah, because Anaya refused to marry her son. But this is always followed with, is this a reason to kill someone? No, it must have been a case of mistaken identity, of Anaya being in the wrong place at the wrong time when someone got the urge to kill someone.

'I felt no animosity towards the police department for not finding the killer, just curiosity to find out if the case is still open. For me, it will always be open. I thank you for coming today to talk to me. To keep memories bottled up within and not be able to talk about it because my husband was so distraught and would break down in tears on hearing her name and my sons were so bewildered by what happened to their beloved sister—it has left me feeling like there is a desert in my heart with the loss of her.'

'Then, Mrs Patel, we can dismiss the motive of an honour killing?'

Mrs Patel looked startled and hurriedly said, 'Definitely not an honour killing. Not in a million years. She was the flower of our hearts, especially of her father's. He was the example. She was going to find someone like him to marry. The boys are too young, and quite frankly, we had no reason to want her dead. We have each mourned her every day, in our own ways. We loved her, all of us.'

Kate could see her disbelief. 'That is how I read it, Mrs Patel, but we have to ask the questions, no matter if we do not like to. I spoke to your husband at the time of the interrogations and could see he was in deep shock. We also spoke to your sons, but we could see that they did not know of any reason for someone to kill her. They were also in shock. I was deeply sorry for them at the time. However, if we do not ask questions, we may never find the answers we are looking for. The only other question I have is that everyone appeared to be cautious about answering questions—almost afraid, as if they thought there could be personal danger to them if they said anything. This caution virtually closed down the case, as it stopped us in our tracks, with nothing to go on. Can you have any reasons for what caused that attitude?'

'Once again, it is a mystery to me, unless those around had seen the offender and were frightened by them. Perhaps strangers thought it may have been an honour killing. My husband did mention that people looked at him oddly for some time after it happened, but I can assure you, he had nothing to do with it. I know fully in my heart that he would not harm Anaya, and he had no reason to at all. She was his little girl, and the first child always stays longer in your heart.'

Kate asked, 'Please, Mrs Patel, could you describe your daughter for us? Was she moody, happy-go-lucky, a good sharer? Did she make friends easily? Any characteristics at all to describe her. You, after all, were the closest person to her.'

Mrs Patel looked at her daughter's photograph that stood on the mantelpiece. It showed her daughter receiving an honour certificate for art at school on the final year she attended.

'The words I would use for her are: she was happy when she got her own way. She could be persistent until she convinced us of what she wanted. She could be secretive but would laugh when I found her out. She was always cheery, even cheeky when she was smaller. Like all children, she believed she was always right. This made her annoying sometimes. Yes, she made friends easily, although Aisha remained her closest friend.'

Kate and Percy stood up, and Percy said, 'Thank you, Mrs Patel, for being so gracious to us. Sometimes our jobs are hard to carry out, and you have made this easy for us. Your daughter's case has been taken over by our team of private investigators, Gray and Armstrong, and Kate is now outside of the police force and working with us. We promise to find the person involved, and we will make an arrest sooner or later.' He handed a business card to her. 'At any time, if you remember anything relevant or want to have a chat, give Kate a call on this number. There is someone, if not Kate, on the line for you, night or day, and we are all involved now in Anaya's story. Or if you discover something untoward, let us know. The difference between us and the police department is our total involvement. We never sleep, or it seems like it sometimes.

'Talk it over with your husband. Who knows? He may think the same as you but is trying to be careful not to upset you. Talking is a great leveller. You might come up with what seems like an innocent thought, and it will expand if said out loud. So let us know. One thought before I leave: ask your husband about his friend's wife and what he thinks of her. Every little thing needs a follow-up, and we might call on her and confirm that your nocturnal thoughts are just that and have nothing to back them up.'

Kate and Percy shook her hand and went out to their vehicle. In the car, Kate said, 'What do you think, Percy?'

'I think an honour killing is out of the question, by her parents at least, and we have already ruled out a hired killer. So it is a matter of either being in the wrong place at the wrong time or Mrs Kumah really not liking Anaya refusing her son. I have not heard of that as a reason to kill anyone yet, but I suppose there is always a first time,' said Percy.

'Do you think we should visit Mrs Kumah on the strength of that conversation?' Kate enquired.

'Yes. She is the only person that is in anyone's mind at the moment, so we will have to see if we can rule her out. But what of the son? Did he want to marry Anaya, and was he disappointed? I would go for the son myself, but first we will have to check them out. I did not want to ask for the address from Mrs Patel, as it would leave her wondering. We can look it up in the office and see what Alicia has come up with from her visit to Aisha today. She should be back in the office by the time we get there.'

'Thanks, Percy, for coming with me today. I think having an older person and also a woman put her at ease. I think Alicia is right that you need to have the right gender for interrogations, especially as we are no longer police officials, to put the person more at ease to answer questions. Mrs Patel seemed at ease with us. It's different from police procedures, where you have to do everything by the book, and I am still getting used to it. I have not had many of these interview-type jobs. I have mostly done the more mundane things in the office, but it is good to get out and hone my skills of observation.'

'Yes, Kate, she did, and I think all her answers were honest. You did well,' agreed Percy.

CHAPTER FOUR

Alicia met Aisha Choudhury at the coffee shop, as agreed. The young woman appeared to be suspicious of the people drinking their coffees and having lunch, and she was looking around at everyone in the coffee house. She was a pretty young woman, with very long dark hair tied back into a ponytail, and she spoke quietly so Alicia could see her hesitation to talk to her. She suggested that Aisha go with her to her office, where there was privacy and no chance of anyone except the team overhearing the conversation. The relief on the young woman's face showed Alicia that that was what she wanted. Alicia was curious now. What did the girl have on her mind to make her hesitant to speak, a year down the line from her friend's death?

Aisha said, 'I will ring my boss and say I will be a little late back.' She brought out her mobile phone and dialled.

Alicia finished her coffee and stood up and walked out of the shopping centre with the uneasy girl beside her. When they reached the office, Alicia took her into the conference room and asked James if he would join them. She was sure by now that Aisha had something to say that she had not told anyone previously, by the way she was acting—very twitchy and breathless. Something had surely had this girl wound up for some time, and she was afraid of telling what she alone knew.

James brought tea and Danish pastries into the conference room and said pleasantly, 'We are happy to make your acquaintance, Aisha. Kate and Percy, the other members of our team, have just now returned from speaking to Mrs Patel, who said you had a wonderful friendship with her daughter. Could you tell us of this relationship, Aisha?'

'Yes, James. Anaya and I were friends from the day we started school together. I suppose it was because we were the only two brown girls in our class, but it was more than that: we felt like sisters. Anaya only had brothers and so did I, so it seemed as if we were meant to be friends. We could tell each other anything and knew it would be kept a secret. You know how little girls can go away from a group and whisper to each other. Of course, there was not really anything much to whisper about until we were almost grown-up, but we were bound together then by our friendship.'

Alicia said, 'I understand that. I was an only child and had my friendships at school, which have grown up with me and are still close by. Was there a particular happening in the last year of your friend's life, Aisha?'

'Yes. It happened when Mrs Kumah kept asking her to come to her house to talk about marrying her son, Jamal. Anaya said she did not like Mrs Kumah, and the thought of living with her for the rest of her life was decidedly not her idea of heaven. We would laugh about it, and she would say she felt sorry for Jamal. His mother still treated him as if he was a child, and he hated it, although he would never complain. He still goes to school. He is in university now. He is quite bright and is enrolled in computer science. He was in the same class as us at school, and he was okay as a friend, just not as a prospective husband. I suppose it was because he was the same age as us. We thought of him as too young. Girls always seem older than boys at school.

'One day, towards the end, Mrs Kumah called Anaya's phone and asked her to come to her house. Anaya did not want to go. She dreaded another argument about marrying Jamal. She said she was not going to be bullied into it, so she said I should go with her. We would say we were lesbians, so there was no chance of grandchildren for her. That would put her off and stop her scheming. We did this, and you should have seen Mrs Kumah's face. She went red and practically pushed us out of the house. She was so angry. Anaya said on the way back to our flat, "Well, that is sorted. That has got rid of that terrible woman and her poor son." I thought at the time that Anaya was cruel in the way she said that. Jamal is a nice person, and we always got on well with him at school. He is a very bright person and was always ready to help us with our homework if we had a problem understanding things.'

At this stage, she started to cry. James and Alicia waited until she had herself under control, and then James asked, 'What happened next, Aisha? Mrs Kumah did not finish it there, did she?'

Aisha wiped her eyes and blew her nose on a tissue and hiccupped. 'The day Anaya died, we were not really happy. Anaya, the artistic one of us, was arranging a window display, moving models backwards and forwards until she thought she had it right, and I was helping her. I explained to Anaya that she had the colours wrong. It turned into a small argument. Our boss, Mrs Turner, must have heard us and called to me to go out and pick up the lunches. I had taken the orders earlier on, so I left to pick them up at the coffee shop where we met today. As I came out of the coffee shop, I heard an almighty crash and then a bang, and I looked over to see someone lying on the floor of the mall and a crowd moving over to the spot.

'I was in a hurry to get the lunches back warm and made my way to the escalator, and it was then that I saw the woman, Mrs Kumah. As she passed me, she put her fingers to her lips. And she walked on out of the centre.'

Aisha was shaking as she said this, and Alicia moved to put her arms around her. When she had quietened, James asked, 'When did you realise it was Anaya you saw lying on the floor under the balcony?'

'Not until I went back into the dress shop and saw the window smashed and glass all over the place. At that stage, Mrs Turner, who had been the only one there, thought that Anaya had fallen and smashed the window and fallen over the balcony. I did not say anything about seeing Mrs Kumah. I was too frightened.

'The manager of the mall called the police, and they were there very quickly. They also called an ambulance, but the paramedics said Anaya was dead. We were all questioned, and I was so shaken that they let me go quickly. I asked if I could have a few days off and I rushed home to our—my flat and started packing up. I called my mother and told her what happened, although again I did not mention Mrs Kumah. I said I was too upset to stay there alone any longer and I wanted to come home. They believed me because I was an emotional mess by then and could not stop crying. My mother and brother came to help me pack up our things and clean the flat, and they took me home. I have been with my parents since then.'

'You went back to work at the shop, Aisha? Were you not too frightened to do that?' asked Alicia.

'The man who owns the shop is a friend of my father. That is how Anaya and I got the jobs after we left school. His son helps out on the buying side of the business, although it is part-time because he is still at university. The son, Derek, comes each morning to pick me up and takes me home in the afternoon or evening, depending on what shift I am on. Derek and I are engaged to be married now. I do not have to worry any more. He will look after me.' Aisha gave a timid smile, as if she hoped this was true.

'Congratulations, Aisha. Is this why you have told us this story?'

'Yes and no. When you rang me to make an appointment, I went to Derek and asked him, should I speak up now? It has been a year, and I have only recently started to put the whole story behind me. He said that you should know the truth and that something should be done about it or I would have it in the back of my mind forever, upsetting me. I thought about it, and the realisation came to me that he was correct. It still worries me a lot, and I find myself checking around to see if Mrs Kumah is there. So that is why I agreed to talk to you.'

James said, 'I am glad Derek said you should. You have put an entirely new light on the case. Mrs Kumah's name has not come up as the perpetrator so far. In fact, no name came up at all. It was a case where nobody knew anything, and it has been a frustrating case for everyone concerned. Now that we have this information, we can go back over the file with a fine-tooth comb to see if there is any reason to call on the woman. It is not only you who has spoken of her nastiness. Mrs Patel is not too fond of her either. We had some other staff chatting with her this morning. So I think our next interview will be with Mrs

Kumah. Are you happy to go back to your office now? Alicia can drive you back.'

'I shall ring Derek, and he will pick me up. He told me so when I rang him earlier to ask to have extra time with you.'

'All right, Aisha. I will make a cup of coffee for you while we wait for him,' said Alicia.

A tall, dark, and handsome young man came in ten minutes later to collect Aisha. She introduced the man as her fiancé, and she proudly took his arm. As they left, Aisha turned around and smiled at Alicia.

*   *   *

All the staff sat over their lunches, talking about the interviews they had done and what they thought had come out of it. Alicia mentioned the triumphant smile Aisha had given her as she went out of the office on the arm of Derek, saying, 'At first I thought it was because she was on Derek's arm, but the more I think about it, I do not know why she looked at me directly like that.'

James looked at her, knowing how intuitive his wife was, and said, 'Let's go over her visit again. Do you feel as if something did not quite add up, Alicia?'

'I had the disturbing thought that Aisha did not like her friend, Anaya. I will have to think about it a little, but something in the interview was not right. It may have been the look on her face when she spoke of Anaya. I still have to pinpoint it.'

Kate spoke up. 'It may be that each time she speaks of her friend, she remembers that they had been arguing a short time before what happened, and she is still upset.'

Alicia looked at Kate. 'You could be right, Kate, if it was a nasty accident, but I for one do not believe it was an accident.'

Percy said, 'I think it is time we look into Mrs Kumah. What do you think, James?'

'Yes, but I would like to interview her son first in our office, away from his mother,' James said thoughtfully, once more flicking through the file on the desk, going over the details.

'I will ring and ask him to come in at his convenience. We do not want to upset him so early in the case,' offered Percy.

'Make it for tomorrow if he cannot come today. We understand he is at university and may have lectures which we will have to plan around,' said James.

When Percy rang the home number they had picked up from the Internet, Jamal answered immediately and agreed to come in right away for an interview, as he would be in lectures the next day.

Percy was pleased. They were all in the office and would hear the interview, except for Ken, who was on a surveillance job. It would give them an opportunity to hear what Jamal had to say, and they would be able to discuss it together afterwards.

Ten minutes later, a young man walked into the office and introduced himself as Jamal Kumah. James and Alicia were both in the reception area when he walked in. They saw him and looked at each other. Jamal laughed and said, 'I often get that reaction when people see me for the first time when they are expecting me. I have got used to it and indeed look for the reaction nowadays.'

Alicia said, 'Come in, Jamal, and explain yourself to us.'

They sat down in the conference room, and Jamal's first words were 'I was not stolen from strangers when I was small. My mother is as white as me. We seem to have left the coloured strain behind us. It has caused us many a dark moment over the years amongst the local community, believe me, but we cannot help the way we were born.'

'How do you mean? How has it brought you dark moments?' asked James.

'Not everyone in a continent of brown faces wants to be white, and many names have been hurled at my mother, who does not deserve the angst it causes.'

'Can you explain more about your parents, Jamal? To put us in the picture, as we know nothing about you. Your name came up with a witness, and we wanted to follow everything up about the death of Anaya Patel. We have been given the cold case from the police department on the off-chance we can come up with some new clues,' said James by way of introduction to the young man.

'Okay, I will start with the white gene we inherited. My mother was an orphan, left as a newborn on the steps of the Catholic church in the area where they lived in Mumbai. The church also ran an orphanage, and Sister Angeline was the nun in charge. We went back to visit her before she died five years ago, and she explained to me, a fourteen-year-old at the time, how she found the new-born baby in a cardboard box on the steps of the church. She took the baby into the orphanage and asked around if anyone could point to the mother, who must have still been having postnatal symptoms, because the baby was definitely only a day or two old. However, no one ever came forward. It was a shame because caste is a big thing with Indians, with nothing known of my mother's parents, no caste could be written down for the child. The baby eventually had brown eyes and brown hair, but her skin was white. She passed that on to me, obviously, to the disgust of my father, who decided one child was enough if that was the pattern set,' Jamal said, laughing.

'How did your parents meet and marry if he felt that way, Jamal?' asked Alicia.

'You have to see my mother, and you will understand. She is very beautiful, is intelligent, and does not play on her beauty. There were no mirrors in the orphanage, so Mother was completely unaware of how beautiful she was. Her parents would have been proud of her, but of course, they will never know. However, my mother's looks and intelligence have been something she has had to battle against. With her white skin, she has many people putting her down at every opportunity, and she has withdrawn considerably so that she rarely goes out. The other thing she now has to battle with is her diagnosis of lung cancer. She was diagnosed shortly before Anaya's death. She knew she did not have long, as the cancer was spreading. That is why she asked for Anaya to come and visit, and asked her to marry me—to get me settled before she got too sick. This is the way things are done in our community. The mothers usually get together to discuss their children's marriage.

'Mother knew that Mrs Patel did not like her, so she went straight to Anaya. It seemed that her mother's dislike of my mother had influenced the girl, and she was very rude to Mother. I was listening from my room and heard the whole thing. I would not have wanted to marry Anaya after hearing her be so rude. She even boasted that she was going to be married to someone else. No one knew about it yet because her mother needed to go see her own mother in India, and the engagement would be announced when her mother returned home and when the period of mourning for her grandmother was over. I must admit, we were disturbed by Anaya's dismissal of my Mother. It showed how selfish the girl was, to speak to her the way she did. What else do you want to know?'

'Do you know who she was to marry, Jamal?' asked Alicia.

'She did not say, and she and Aisha left straight after that. I could tell my mother was disgusted with Anaya by then.'

'Can you remember what you and your mother were doing the day Anaya died?' asked James.

'I had an early lecture that day, I remember. I had taken my mother to the mall medical centre at ten o'clock for an appointment with her oncologist and left her there, and she was to get a taxi home. When I saw her later when I got home, she was shaken by Anaya's death. She had been there just before it happened. She had heard it on the taxi's news from his radio on the way home.'

Alicia asked, 'Why do you think Mrs Patel does not like your mother, Jamal?'

Jamal thought about it for a few minutes and said, 'Basically it is because we are Christians, and the Patels are Hindu. Secondly, because my mother was an orphan, she has no caste, and they think she is a chichi, a half-caste, because of her pale skin. It is all tied to beliefs. It is now updated in the modern world, but in the world they left behind, it is very much still adhered to. The Brits are very class conscious, but they have nothing like the classes in India. It works well for them at home, but we have moved on and should leave all that thinking behind us.'

'I can see your point, Jamal, especially the way it has affected your life,' said Alicia. 'How did your parents meet? Is your father a Christian also?'

'Yes, my father turned to Christianity when he was in his late teens, after his parents died tragically, and he met Mother during social events at the church. Sister Angeline welcomed him into the church congregation with a plan in mind. Mother was still in the orphanage although she was soon turning eighteen, because nobody wanted to adopt her, and because she was such an attractive girl, women did not want her in their households, in case their husbands or sons strayed— this is the story Sister Angeline told me. She said that Mother, Iris, had been in the orphanage for so long, the whole church congregation took an interest in her. When Father spoke about wanting to immigrate to the UK, they thought it would be a good idea to push the two young people together. Eventually they blackmailed my father into marrying Iris. The church people all put in enough money for the fares and enough to set them up when they arrived here. The first earnings of the tailor shop that Father opened were sent back to those kind people who had helped them, with his thanks. We also send a quarterly stipend to the orphanage. Mother has never forgotten her roots and the care and love she received from the nuns there.

'I think that is a part of the Patels' looking down on Mother as well. Mum and Dad had enough money when they arrived here, so they had no worries about setting themselves up. Meanwhile, most new arrivals had only the basics at the beginning. Dad took Mr Patel into the shop, as they had worked together in India. Mr Patel has never looked down on us. It is only his wife who does. Just plain jealousy, I think.'

James said, 'Well, Jamal, you have given us a good rundown on your family and the mixed reasons for the Patels' dislike of your mother. What of your father?'

'Dad goes along with the flow. He is friendly with Mr Patel. They have worked together in my father's tailoring business for years. They both go along with no talking about religion and politics, and it keeps them friendly. We do not socialise with them often except for events like school concerts or other things like that. I think that because Mother was given a death sentence by her oncologist, she suddenly decided to invite Anaya to our house to have a word with her. I am glad she did, because I know now that there is no use pursuing someone else in the same position. I will eventually find someone who does not have prejudices.'

'We wish you well, Jamal, in every way for the future. You seem like a level-headed young man, very articulate, and you should do well,' said James.

'Thank you, Mr and Mrs Armstrong. Are you going to interview my mother?'

'Is she well enough for us to call around and visit with her? There are a few questions we would like to ask her,' said James.

'She is going through a good patch right now. The oncologists think it is the calm before the storm. She has lasted longer than they expected, and they put it down to her ability to pray. There is something to say for a life of prayer such as there was in her upbringing.' Jamal smiled.

'If we call at your house at ten in the morning, do you think that would suit her?' asked Alicia.

'I am sure it will. If she is not well, I will ring you in the morning, but I think she will welcome your visit. She does not get many visitors.'

'Thank you, Jamal,' they both said as he walked towards the door.

After he had left the office, Alicia said, 'What a nice young man.'

James concurred. 'You are right, Alicia. I am looking forward to meeting his mother in the morning.'

*   *   *

Next morning, Percy was consulted on whether he would go with Kate to visit Mrs Kumah. He said that in his opinion, Alicia and James should be the two to go, as Alicia could read the condition of the lady and see if she was able to understand and was well enough to be questioned.

James said, 'Good, I was hoping you would say that. After meeting the son, I must say, I am looking forward to meeting his mother. The young man impressed me with how articulate he is.'

'I was really impressed also, James. I think he is a caring son and not the "poor son" that Aisha described. It has made me wonder what Mrs Patel did not like about his mother. Could it have been jealousy, as Jamal commented?' said Alicia.

'Let's go now, Alicia. We will tread carefully with our enquiries at the beginning,' said James.

When they arrived in the street where the Kumahs lived, the pair were impressed with the neighbourhood that the home was located in. As they drew closer to the house, Alicia said, 'Well, this shows that it is not poor Jamal. To purchase one of these stately homes, you would have to be in the top pay bracket. It is very nice. The tailoring business must be very successful.'

When they knocked on the door, Jamal was ready to let them in, and he showed them into a living area with wide windows overlooking a manicured lawn with flowers in the borders and a type of jasmine spilling from earthenware pots and climbing over lattice. A birdbath sat in the centre of the lawn on a pedestal, obviously the place to go for the birds of the district as they flew in and out. They found Mrs Kumah sitting in an armchair, watching the birds, and she rose to greet them. She was indeed the beautiful woman Jamal had described, stately and upright and not showing any sign of her illness.

Jamal went off to the kitchen and reappeared with a silver tray with a teapot, teacups, and biscuits for them. He then excused himself, saying, 'I have a lecture at eleven. I should be back in an hour and a half, if you are still here and want to know anything more.'

His mother said, 'You do not have to hurry home, Jamal. We will be fine together, and I promise I will not do anything you do not approve of.'

As Jamal left the room, Mrs Kumah said, 'My son worries about me, but I am doing better than anyone expected. I am fine unless I try to do too much, then I get very tired and cannot concentrate. What can I help you with?'

James spoke first. 'Aisha Choudhury has told us of her visit to you prior to Anaya's death, regarding a wedding agreement and the subsequent anger you felt as she belittled you and Jamal. Could you tell us your version of events, please? Before you start, do you mind if we record our conversation?'

'No, I do not mind. I have nothing to hide. I will only tell you what I have heard and seen. There is nothing secret there. Yes, that was a strange visit I had with the girls, Anaya and her friend Aisha. I had instigated the visit. I asked Anaya to come for a friendly visit to discuss a marriage between her and my son, but she was very rude to me from the moment she appeared with Aisha. I could see Aisha cringing at the things Anaya said, such as that they were lesbians. I knew this could not be true. Anaya had always been a boy-chaser while she was at school. At the age of thirteen, she would show up here at our home, looking for Jamal to help her with her homework, but all I ever heard from Jamal's room were giggles. No homework was done. This went on for some time until I mentioned it to her mother at one of the school meetings, and after that, she was no longer allowed to go out after school—or to come here anyway.

'When I realised that Anaya was not interested in a marriage between Jamal and her, to be polite I tried asking her what her future was to be. At that stage, she said she was getting married, and her family was waiting to announce it after the mourning period for her grandmother, because she was on her deathbed. She had only mentioned that she and Aisha were lesbians as a let-down for me. I personally think it was rude of her.

'Aisha looked as if she wanted to be anywhere else but here. The strange looks she was giving Anaya showed first of all with the lesbian bit of the conversation and then when Anaya said she was getting married. Aisha looked stricken. It seemed it was the first she had heard of either story. I did not ask who Anaya was to be married to. By that stage, I'd had enough of the girl. Her rudeness and way of talking to me showed that she had no respect. I was not well at the time, so I showed her out quite abruptly. I needed to have some tablets because I was not feeling well. That was all there was to that, really. Is there anything else you want to know?'

'Aisha mentioned to us that she saw you in the mall on the morning that Anaya died. Is that true?' asked Alicia.

Mrs Kumah looked interested. 'Ah, did she? Covering all bases, I presume, in case you spoke to me. Yes, we did meet. I had been to see my oncologist that morning. I was quite ill that whole week. I suppose the upset with Anaya had triggered it, so I had made an appointment with the doctor to get a prescription for stronger tablets to relieve the pain. When I came out of the doctor's office and had been to the pharmacy, I was feeling very tired, so I went to the coffee shop to sit for a while and nurse my cup of coffee until I felt better. When I entered the coffee shop, I met two young men who were friends with Jamal. They played football together, usually after school hours so the field was clear. They came and sat with me at the table and chairs outside the shop after I bought them a coffee and a sandwich each, and we chatted for a while about what they had been doing since the end of the school year.'

She stopped for a moment, sitting back in her chair, remembering. 'We had finished our snack, and I stood up before moving off. The two boys and I looked up at the window on the second floor, where we could see Anaya standing on a ladder inside the window of a shop, decorating with some clothes and models. As we were looking up there, we thought she was doing some sort of dance on the top of the ladder. I was feeling very shaky and ill, and I turned to walk out of the mall for a taxi to take me home.

'As I turned away, Aisha came running down the escalator and stopped when she saw me. I was too ill to talk with her at that moment, so I waved my hand and walked away. No, that is not right. I did not wave. I was holding my hand over my mouth because I thought I was going to vomit. It had all been such an awful morning, and I did give a small wave with my other hand, because I was concentrating on getting to the lavatory quickly and then getting a taxi to go home before anything else happened. I did not want to collapse in front of the crowd, although I felt as if it was a possibility, as I felt so bad.'

James was very interested in what had been said, and he asked, 'Did you actually see the girls in the shop window and see Anaya fall?'

'No, not me. I did see Anaya in the window for a few moments, but I left before Anaya fell. The two boys had a perfect view of everything for that short period. My eyesight has not been good lately. I think I am of the age when I should have my eyes tested, as I could not see properly what was going on.

'I was not asked about Anaya's fall by anyone, because I was ill and left the building to go home. I was taken to the hospital that evening and remained there for a while after that. The boys, with their young eyesight, would have had a perfect view of it all. I did not put myself forward for questioning. I had gone home before the authorities arrived. I do not know if the boys spoke to the police.'

She sat quietly for a few minutes. James and Alicia could see she was still thinking of what happened the previous year, so they did not disturb her.

'Those two boys were murdered themselves a month later. It was a terrible thing that happened. They were stabbed to death in their flat while they were in bed. They were homosexuals, I have been told, so I think their deaths were put down to "gay bashing gone too far". I was still in hospital at the time, and it was a dreadful time for me when I read it in the newspaper, thinking of them and how happy they had been the day I saw them in the mall before Anaya fell.'

Alicia and James looked at each other, and James asked, 'I have not seen anything in the files about a ladder being at the scene of Anaya's fall. Are you sure about that point?'

Mrs Kumah nodded. 'Absolutely. Anaya was standing at the top of the ladder, and Aisha was holding it at the bottom. The boys remarked, "It is just as well they are wearing jeans, or they would have a crowd of men here watching." I watched for a short time and then stood up to leave. Anaya had the fall after I left, so I did not see it happen.'

James looked very thoughtful and turned again to Mrs Kumah. 'I think you have come up with several points that no one else has mentioned. Would you be prepared to make a statement for us, saying what you have told us? I would like you to include the boys in the statement as well. It could be pertinent to the story. I can copy it down from the recording we have taken, to save you time, if that is okay with you. You could read through it and say it is correct and sign it.'

'If it will help, I will do so. Come and sit at the table, and it will be more comfortable for you, James.'

Alicia was worried. 'Are you still feeling all right at the moment, Mrs Kumah? We do not want you to get ill by doing too much.'

'May I call you Alicia and James?'

'Certainly. I am sorry we did not say so earlier,' said James.

'My given name is Iris. Please call me that. I feel good for the moment. It must be the stimulus of your company.'

Alicia looked interested and said, 'That does not sound like an Indian name. How did you cone to be called Iris?'

'My son told me that he spoke to you of our history. When I was baptised by the Catholic priest, there was a cluster of white iris flowers in a bowl near the font, and when he asked the nuns for a name for the baby, they all said, "Why not Iris? They suit her." So that is how I came by that name. My last name became John because we were the John the Baptist church. Therefore, I was Iris Angelina John. The second name was for the nun who found me on the doorstep of the church.'

James asked, 'Were you a cigarette smoker, Iris?'

'No, never. Nor were the nuns in the orphanage. The oncologists say the lung cancer may have been helped along because I worked for several years in the tailoring shop, and the fine wool from cutting the fabrics may be the cause. It is hard to say, really, but we did make hundreds of woollen suits and coats. Then again, there were periods in my early days when we did not have very much to eat at the orphanage, because we relied on handouts from the church congregation. Sometimes they too would go through hard times, so we did not eat much. At least, we were all slim. Those periods may have left me with a weakness. There is not one reason for it. There may have been something passed on to me at birth. We will never know. We will have to put our trust in the Lord, and he will call me when he is ready.'

'That is a great attitude. I congratulate you,' said Alicia. 'Were you happy in the orphanage, Iris?'

'I loved the nuns and tried to help them when I was old enough. I knew no other kind of life. I used to wonder why no one came to claim me to be their little girl when I was small—a lot of the younger children were adopted—but I grew out of that as I got older. I felt the nuns could not do without me to look after the new little children who came. I tried so hard to be like the nuns. I did not want to go anywhere else. It was the nuns who organised my marriage for me to try something else other than the orphanage. They said if I was unhappy in my new life,

I could always go back, but I would have to join the nunnery. As you can see, I never went back except to visit.'

'You sound very content with your lot, Iris. Not many have the peacefulness you exude. Life is such a rush nowadays for everybody,' said Alicia.

'Sister Angelina always said, "Life is what you make it. It is better to be happy than sad." She said this often because the orphans were always saying they missed their families. It did not worry me, because I only had the nuns as a family. Since I married, I have had the pleasure of living and working with a contented man and a wonderful son. I have been lucky in my life.'

James had been typing out on his computer the conversation from the recording since they arrived, and the statement was almost complete when he asked if there was a printer in the house.

Iris laughed. 'My son has almost everything the computer world has invented. His office is like a computer store. I am sure he must have a printer you can connect with. He will be home within the next few minutes, and he will arrange it for you.'

James looked at his watch and was amazed. She was correct. The time had flown so quickly because the conversation had been so interesting.

Alicia asked, 'Iris, did you ever contact Mrs Patel after she returned home from India?'

Iris thought about it and said, 'No, I was still in hospital when she arrived back. When I eventually came out of hospital—I was in hospital for a month—I tried to ring her, but she never answered my phone call. I sent her a condolence card but never received an answer. Of course, I was unable to attend Anaya's funeral. My husband and I spoke about it, and he said she was aware I was ill. He had told his friend about the lung cancer and its advancement, and he presumed he had passed that information on to his wife. I have not spoken to her since Anaya died, and I have not heard from her. We have never been friends, acquaintances only, really. I do not think she approved of me working in the tailoring business, and as my husband is her husband's boss, she felt I would belittle her, I suppose. Nothing further from the truth, but I have not allowed her attitude to worry me. It is her problem, not mine.'

'Do you think Anaya's attitude may have come from her mother?' James asked.

'Probably, although I still believe Anaya was trying to show me up for her friend Aisha. I did not have much to do with Aisha previously. She was a quiet girl, and I do not recall her taking part in any school activities, like plays and concerts or sports, although Anaya was into most of those activities and liked to put herself forward. I could be wrong. It was just that Aisha never pushed her way forward as Anaya was wont to do, so Anaya overshadowed her somewhat. That showed also on the day the girls were here. Aisha looked absolutely stricken when Anaya announced that she had chosen her prospective husband. I suppose she would have presumed to hear the news first, seeing as they were such good friends.'

'They were sharing a flat,' said Alicia. 'Perhaps the friendship was in danger of floundering. Living with someone is different from just meeting them from time to time or even day by day. Such closeness can cause upsets. Anaya sounds as if she was the bossy type. That can be annoying in close quarters.'

James looked from one woman to the other. They were chatting to pass the time, but to him, it was all making sense. Both women were right in their assumptions, and it was a big possibility that the relationship between the two younger women had changed since they had spoken to Iris in her home before Anaya died. He made up his mind to seek out Derek, Aisha's fiancé, and ask a few questions. Perhaps a visit to Aisha's mother may bring something to the surface. Sometimes young women resort to their mother for advice. It was worth a try. He would make the appointments when he returned to the office.

Jamal came in the front door and, after one look at his mother, turned to James and Alicia. 'You have done my mother good. She looks happy and relaxed. I have been worried since I left that it would be too much for her, but I have been proved wrong.'

Iris laughed at her son. 'I have not thought of pain since you have been gone, Jamal. The company has livened me up. Can you show

James to a printer so he can have a copy of my statement to sign and another copy for me in case I need it in the future?'

'Certainly, Mother. Come into my office, James. It will only take a few moments to make the connection to your computer.'

The two men went from the room, and Alicia said, 'You are lucky to have a son like Jamal. He obviously cares for you a lot, Iris.'

'I have been lucky in my son, Alicia. I had the care of a lot of unhappy children when I was growing up myself. I suppose I picked up some good points on how to manage a child, but he has always been a happy boy. It has made me aware of how important a loving family is and what I missed out on. I did also see what a family can do to a child if the parents are cruel. Many of the children in the orphanage came from parents like that, and the children were taken from their parents and put in the orphanage to keep them safe. Strangely, some of those children used to cry for their parents when they first arrived. When I saw the wounds some of the children had, inflicted by their mother or father or sometimes an older brother, I could not understand it.'

Just then, Jamal and James returned with the statement ready for Iris to sign. She took a chair at the table and read through the statement and said, 'This is fine, James. Do you want me to sign it at the bottom?'

'Yes, please, Iris, and an initial on each page if you would.'

'No problem. There you are,' Iris said as she laid down the pen.

Alicia said, 'I have enjoyed your company, Iris. Would you mind if I call in from time to time to see how you are? I can bring you up to date on our investigation. I am sure you will want to know now what we come up with.'

'I would greatly appreciate a visit, Alicia. I too have enjoyed your company, and you have certainly stirred my imagination. If I can come up with anything at all that I think you may be interested in, I will give you a call.'

Jamal said, 'I have not seen Mother so animated in a long time. Thank you, Alicia and James. You have given her something to think about. We have not spoken about Anaya's death or the how and why of it, because it caused Mother to have a breakdown after she had almost seen it happen. We did not want her to relive the event, which was something she could not banish from her mind, and it is good to be able to talk it over with someone.'

Iris looked at her son. 'You amaze me sometimes with your intuition, Jamal. That is exactly how it feels—relief that I am able to say these things out loud to interested people. I thank you all.'

James and Alicia shook hands with the couple and left. Alicia remarked, 'It is good timing on our part. Iris was starting to look tired.'

James said, 'Yes, I could see that. There were some differences in Aisha's statement of events and Iris's version—about the timing of the encounter in the mall. Of course, there is the year-long gap in their memories. I did not want to interrupt the flow of memories, but we will go through them when we get back to the office, and compare the two statements.'

Alicia said, 'Twice Iris spoke of the look on Aisha's face when her best friend announced her forthcoming engagement. It made me wonder if Derek was the proposed bridegroom. Aisha may have believed that Derek was her property and that he had been stolen from her. That would have been enough to cause anger—enough to push her bossy, secretive friend off the ladder.'

'Wow, Alicia, you have solved the case already. Now all we need is proof,' James said, laughing.

'Don't laugh at me, James. It is feasible. Murders have been done for lesser reasons than that. If it is so that the fellow was Derek, I can see how it would have made Aisha very angry. It also answers why she smiled at me the way she did on the way out of our office. She was saying "See, I got Derek after all".'

'Mmm, I understand what you are saying, Alicia, but we do not yet have tangible proof that we can take to a court of law.'

'I know that, James. But we have a theory, and now we need to go after the proof. Find the ladder in question. Interview Derek and see if he knew Anaya. We cannot interview the other two witnesses who saw the whole thing, because they are dead. *Wow.* They are dead, and they witnessed the crime. Do you think there is a connection there?'

'You know, Alicia, while Iris was telling us about the three of them viewing the crime scene before it happened, I thought the two boys would have better eyesight than Iris, because she is older and not well. But there is no mention of them being interrogated at the shopping centre or anywhere else in the file, or I missed it if it is there. What if they decided it was a good opportunity to make some money, and they faded away before the police arrived? And this is a big statement, but what if they were blackmailing Aisha, and she decided to do away with them?'

'That could solve the two murders, James, and to me, it sounds about right. We just have to find the connection after the fall, which Iris almost witnessed as well. She could not be interviewed, because she was taken to hospital that day and was very ill. She was not brought in as a witness, so no one knows what she saw. I think that once this comes out, she will have to be careful to stay with her family for a while or have someone to care for her, in case of repercussions, or she may become the fourth victim. She may not have been thought of as a threat, because she was so ill. It was thought that she was going to die soon. Also, she had not told anyone what she saw in the mall.'

'We are doing well here, Alicia. We are almost at the office. I suggest we lay all the statements out on the conference table, including the file details of both murder scenes, and see if the others find what we believe happened. Perhaps we are too close to it to see the connecting points, and we are biased because we believe Iris's version. There must be some obvious clues somewhere. To be truthful, I only skimmed the boys' murder scene. I was put off because of all the blood. I did not read the forensic results. Sometimes it is not the thing to do, taking the files home after a full day at work. We are tired by the time we arrive home, and we need to relax to wake up fresh the next morning.'

'James, I am now worried about Iris and even Jamal. We told Aisha we would be interviewing the Kumahs. Now it could put them in line as the next group of murders.'

'Yes, I can see what you mean. I think we had better advise the police straight away, and they can arrange for a policeperson to guard them until we make an arrest. I will call Paul Morris as soon as we arrive at the office. They may already be in danger.'

Alicia felt worried; she knew it was her fault for mentioning that Mrs Kumah was to be interviewed. She sat up straight and said, 'I think we should warn Jamal. He might have some friends who can come to stay with them. Someone living in the house would be better protection than a policeperson standing outside.'

'That is a good idea, Alicia.'

Alicia called Jamal on his mobile. When he answered and was told that they could be in danger from Aisha, he laughed. 'Little Aisha? She is only a handful. There is no need to be worried about her.'

'Truly, Jamal, we may be wrong, but at the moment, both James and I believe the possibility that she has already carried out three murders. We do not yet have proof and will be working hard in the next few days to change that, but we think your mother could be in danger—and possibly you as well—no matter who the murderer is, because she saw something. Do you have any heavyweight friends that can stay over for a while? Remember that you leave your mother alone while you go to university lectures. Aisha is aware of that. She told us that you are studying computer science. So do you know anyone at all available, or shall I get a policeperson to guard?'

'No, to the police guard thank you. How would it look to the neighbours? I can ring a couple of my uni mates to stay over for a while. Some of them are always looking for freebies, so I am sure they will jump at the idea. We have plenty of room here, and there could be one or two at home with Mother at all times until we do not need them any more. I will ring them right away. You have me worried now. I will let you know what I have organised. The boys will not be any trouble to Mother, as we have a housekeeper, and when Mother got ill, we took on a cook. So the fellows will think of it as a luxury break.'

'Do it now, Jamal. We might be jumping to conclusions so early in the case, but it is better to be safe than sorry.'

'On it, Alicia. Thanks for the warning. I am not sure what Mother will say about it, but I will do my best to set it in motion.'

'Thanks, Jamal. It will stop us from worrying. If things change—because we do not have proof of anything yet—we will let you know, but it is always better to err on the side of caution.'

After she finished the call, Alicia turned to James. 'At least we tried. I do not think Aisha would be so brazen as to take on another person now that the case is so old, but you never know.'

'It cannot do any harm for a couple of Jamal's friends to stay for a week or two. Here we are, at the office. I hope the crew are all in at the moment,' said James as he manoeuvred the vehicle into a parking bay.

CHAPTER FIVE

J ames took out the statement he had in his briefcase and the rest of the file—Mrs Patel's statement and also Aisha's—and placed them on the conference table. Then he asked the other staff to have a look, and when they had done so, they would have a round-table conference on what their thoughts were after reading it all. Alicia said she would look after the front office and take any calls while they were occupied, to save from breaking off and losing the flow of things.

While sitting at the front desk, Alicia went over things in her mind and thought, *We haven't spoken to any of the men in the families, except Jamal. What of Mr Patel and even Mr Kumah? They must have some thoughts on the accident/murder. They were both in town when it happened, and they were both close to the dead girl. Chatting with them might bring something forward. Mr Patel was interviewed by the police, and they said he was too stunned to comment. Mr Kumah was probably not available because his wife had to be taken to the hospital. It may be worthwhile to interview them, to see what they think may have happened.*

James came into the reception area to tell her to come in so they could have a conference now, and Alicia followed to hear what the others thought. Now she was an investigator. *Yay!* She smiled. Kate was invited to go first, as she had attended to the original case.

She began. 'First of all, there was no mention of a ladder in the shop or anywhere else. There was no sign of a ladder at the scene. This is new evidence. From what I remember, when we—that is, our crew who attended the call—arrived at the premises, there was a small crowd around the girl on the floor. Many of them were upset, although none had actually observed the fall. They were virtually following the crowd to see what had happened when they heard the crash from various corners of the mall. In fact, we found no one who saw the girl fall, or no one who admitted to it. I suppose it was the old thing: "I do not want to get involved". I do not recall the two young men mentioned in Mrs Kumah's statement. I checked to see if any other officer had interviewed these persons, and there is no mention of them.

'After we cleared the crowd, we went on to interview the dress shop personnel and also the coffee shop personnel. As we looked around, we saw that anyone sitting in there may have seen something. But the coffee shop vendors had no idea, and the staff had been in other areas of the shop when they heard the crash. They said that the customers were usually chatting with each other and would have only heard the bang and looked after the event, and they could not remember who had been in the shop at that time.

'The dress shop where the girl had fallen from was obviously littered with broken glass,. The forensic people called them shards of glass. There was no ladder there that we could see. We questioned the manager, Mrs Turner, who said the girl had been completing a window display that she had started the previous day, and she said, looking around, that it looked as if she had finished it, except that the window was broken now. We asked if any other assistants were available to be interviewed, and she pointed to Aisha, who was crying like her heart was broken and who could not do much more than hiccup. She seemed no more than a schoolgirl. We did not think she was a likely suspect, and when she asked if she could go home, we took her details down and agreed that she could go.

'It was the quiet period of the day, and the other staff member had been at lunch and did not know about it until she came in half an hour later. That only left Mrs Turner, the shop manager, who said she had been talking on the telephone in her office when she heard the crash. She completed her call and rushed out to see what the noise was all about, and she discovered a hole in the window. At that stage, she had not realised Anaya was lying on the floor below. She also appeared to be at a loss as to how it happened and was, of course, very upset when we told her, although two of us who were interviewing said afterwards that she seemed more worried for her own job and how she was going to get the window repaired than for anything that had happened to her shop assistant.'

'Can you remember, Kate, if you asked her who she had been talking to on the phone when it happened?' asked Percy.

'Yes, it's mentioned here. She had been talking to Mr Kumah. He was to deliver some coats that day and was apologising because they would be late the next day, as he had to go to the hospital with his wife to have some tests done. She usually organised the delivery but was very ill at the time and had not been able to finish the order in time. That is the only time the Kumahs' name was mentioned in the investigation.'

'Yes, here it is in the file an officer called to verify the call the next day,' said Percy.

'Did the forensics come up with anything, Kate?' asked James.

'Very little, James. It baffled them too. The glass had broken quite high from the top to the floor, but there was no blood until the girl had hit the tiled floor—it was the impact that killed her, as if a push had forced her through the glass, which carried her over the balcony. They considered it a high chance that it was an accident, but they could not work out how the glass had broken, as it appeared to them that something tall had caused it.'

'Yes,' said James, 'like a ladder perhaps.'

Alicia promoted her view. 'What if she had been on the ladder, and it had toppled over and fallen through the window, taking her with it? Would you need someone to push it, or could it have happened if she had missed her step and the ladder had been unstable?'

Percy moved forward and remarked, 'It wouldn't be the first time that has happened. Elderly men often go to emergency wards at the hospital because they fall off ladders. They do not need someone to push it. Maybe the girl had been flailing, and the momentum carried her through the window and over the balcony. There is a possibility it was an accident after all.'

Kate remarked, 'I would really like it to have been an accident. I spent so much energy trying to pin it on someone, but there seemed no obvious perpetrator. If it was an accident, that is probably why I could not pick any one person to blame.'

'The only thing wrong with that solution is, what happened to the ladder? It was not at the scene,' said James.

'No, James, it was definitely not at the scene.' Kate was emphatic on the subject. 'We need to find who removed it and why.'

Percy said, 'We cannot write this one off yet. We will have to speak with Mrs Turner and also Aisha again. They were the only two in the shop with Anaya at the time. The other staff member had gone to lunch and was not around to see it happen.'

James said, 'We agree then. We will interview the manager of the store and Aisha. I would also like to speak to Derek. He might have something to say about Anaya. And if we are going that far, I think we should also interview Mr Patel and Mr Kumah.'

Kate said, 'I would like to interview Aisha's mother and get some details about the girl. Aisha seems to have had a long association with Anaya which she did not disclose in her first interviews, and I would like to follow up to find out why.'

Alicia volunteered. 'I would like to speak with Mr Patel. His interview in the file seems to be very short and emotional—as it would be, I suppose, if your daughter had just died—but it still seems minimal.'

'Have you any questions, Ken?' asked Percy.

'After listening to you all and reading the statements, it does appear to be an accident, but it is not clear yet. What of the two young men who were front and centre to see everything? There is no mention of them in the file. Something sounds fishy there. I agree that there needs to be further interviews to clear the file. We do not have anything except Mrs Kumah's statement that the boys saw everything, yet they cannot be asked because they are now dead—which also seems curious in its timing by itself.'

James said, 'We all seem to agree on this then. Alicia, you and Kate interview Mrs Choudhury, and then go on and talk to Mrs Turner and Aisha in the shop, and other shop people as well. If you do that this afternoon, ask about a ladder while you are there. Have a look in the storerooms at the shop to see if you can spot it. Ken and I will make appointments to see Mr Kumah and Mr Patel in the tailor shop in the morning. Meanwhile, I will tee up an interview to fit Derek in. Doing it in that order, we should have the full picture before speaking to Mr Patel, and we may by then be able to tell Mr Patel it was one big accident if nothing else comes up to upset our story. Meanwhile, Kate, ask Mrs Choudhury what Derek's surname is—no one has mentioned it—and what the address of his workplace is. Aisha did say that her parents and the parents of Derek are friends.'

Ken said, 'I am sorry, I have a job at the council house to clear up—something about fencing. I must do that tomorrow. It's half-done. The council assistants are looking out the plans for me to view. I do not want it to wait, because it concerns two people fighting physically to solve their problem, and their wives asked me to clear it up before it all goes wrong. Can Alicia go with you to interview the tailors tomorrow, and possibly you can take Percy with you to talk to Derek?'

'Okay, Ken, we will do it that way. I want to finish this off as quickly as we can, to get on with our own work or move on to another cold case. It seems to me that we should be able to work on these quite quickly because of the previous work done by the police. It is just a matter of juggling interviews so we have someone here in the office to take calls at all times.'

Percy said, 'The plan you have mentioned sounds good, James. It is good to have Alicia filling in. She is doing well and deserves the action while I man the desk. I am happy about that.'

Alicia hugged Percy. 'Thank you, Percy. If you need to get out of the office for a while, I can always switch with you.'

Kate was on the phone, asking Mrs Choudhury for an appointment. When she completed the call, she turned to Alicia. 'We are on in half an hour. Mrs Choudhury prefers it early, as she needs to do some food shopping. I have looked up the address, and it will take about fifteen to twenty minutes to get there. So are you ready?'

'Ready. We will see you all later,' said Alicia, moving towards the door.

After they went out of the door, Percy remarked, 'Alicia is so keen, and she has been proving her worth in the interviews and jobs she has done lately.'

James concurred. 'Yes, Percy, she is good with people, and she is very keen at the moment. She seems to have forgotten about having time off. I believe she is enjoying things.

James rang the tailoring business and made an appointment first with Mr Kumah and then with Mr Patel for the next morning.

*   *   *

When Kate and Alicia arrived to talk to Mrs Choudhury, they saw a small woman in a sari waiting for them.

Alicia started the conversation 'Kate and I are employed with Gray and Armstrong Private Investigations, and we have been asked by the police department to carry on with the case of the death of Anaya Patel. Our mission with you is to find out a little about your daughter, Aisha, and her friendship with Anaya. We understand, from what Aisha has told us, that they were friends at school and throughout the years. Could you tell us about those years?'

Mrs Choudhury spoke with a strong Indian accent. 'Aisha was a shy little girl, and we were pleased when Anaya took her under her wing at first. However, over the years, we have not been as happy with that friendship, as Anaya had a very strong personality and completely overshadowed Aisha. My perception of the friendship was that Aisha was the mouse and her friend was the cat. Many times, I wished they would break up, to allow Aisha to stand on her own two feet instead of being ordered around by Anaya all the time. It became very bad for us to see once they decided to move into a flat together. We thought that Aisha had become a servant at the beck and call of Anaya. At least when they were at school, my daughter could come home to get some relief from being put down all the time. We considered refusing to allow Aisha to move out of our home but she was already eighteen and was lawfully able to make her own choices.

'We, my husband and I, talked it over and decided that once Aisha was available to do Anaya's wishes all the time, she would soon tire of it and come back home. Towards the time of the accident, it was becoming clear that she would return very soon. Aisha came to see me that week and told me of how rude Anaya was to Mrs Kumah, who looked quite ill at the time, and Aisha was ashamed of her part in the meeting. Part of Aisha's reticence is her good manners. She does not like to upset people, and she told me that Anaya was dreadful. I felt happy, as I could see that her perception of her friend was changing. After so many years of obeying that girl, it was as if she was having her eyes opened.'

Alicia asked, 'Aisha has told us she is engaged to marry Derek. Is that correct?'

'Yes. Derek is the son of my husband's second cousin. They are intended to marry at twenty-one, according to our family's conditions. The family has a book that all of us refer to, with family births and deaths. It dates back over one hundred years, perhaps longer. I have not actually seen it, as it is held by an elder of our branch of the Choudhury hierarchy, and if we marry or want our children to marry, it is all written down.

'When Derek's father decided to immigrate to the UK, he arranged the marriage of Derek and Aisha. That was many years ago. He then arranged for my husband and I with Aisha, to come here as well. My husband works in the clerical department of his workshop. It works well both ways. Our future is assured, along with theirs. Aisha will not change names, as Derek is a Choudhury as well.'

'Can you give us Derek's phone number, please? We would like to interview him as we are doing now with you. We are confirming details about all the people who were close to the Patel girl, and I believe she was appointed by Derek in the dress shop alongside Aisha,' said Kate.

'Is there anything else that you can think of, Mrs Choudhury, that you feel we should know?' asked Alicia.

The woman thought for a few minutes. 'There was a comment by Aisha at the time of the accident, when she was so very upset, which has niggled at me ever since, but as Aisha has not said anything again,

I have tried to repress the thought,' said Mrs Choudhury. 'I am not sure I should repeat it. It may have been because she was so emotional at the time.'

'Is it because she saw something? Or someone? It may help if we could exonerate that person or deed,' said Alicia.

'Well, it was only a comment while she was so terribly troubled. It was a whisper, really. As she was sitting down, thinking of the day, she murmured, "I cannot believe he was there." She was not talking to me but said it very quietly to herself. She looked concerned and was shaking her head, and I barely heard the words. I did not question her about it, thinking it was better to try and get her mind off the happenings of that day. Anyway, I do not think she knew I heard her words.'

Kate and Alicia were scribbling in their notebooks, and Alicia said, 'It probably does not mean anything, Mrs Choudhury. She did not say anything to us when we interviewed her. But we will keep the comment in mind in case it has to be justified. She may have been talking about something or somewhere else, but we will check it out quietly.'

The two younger women stood up, and Kate said, 'Thank you for your time, Mrs Choudhury. It is so good to get other people's views. At the time of the accident, we could not find anyone to comment. It made our investigation very difficult.'

Alicia phoned the office to give James the phone number of Derek Choudhury and said that she and Kate were now on their way to the dress shop in the mall.

*　*　*

At the mall, the two young women looked at the scene on the lower level where Anaya had landed when she fell from the upper level. Alicia suggested they have a cup of coffee in the opposite coffee shop to review the position of Iris Kumah and the boys. They sat outside, from where Mrs Kumah stated she had seen the girls in the window, so they could assess things before they went into the dress shop.

Kate said, 'That is a really good idea. We can assess her statement that she saw everything except the actual fall. It could make a big difference to her statement if we see that she was not able to see the window.'

Alicia agreed and said, 'We may as well have some lunch while we are doing so. Let's order first and sit in those seats outside, the way Mrs Kumah did.'

As they sat facing the shops on the next floor, the girls realised they would be able to see into the shop at certain times of the day when the shadows did not fall on the window. At that time, Alicia checked her watch. It was right around midday, and they could see clearly into the shop and see people moving around. It was about the time Mrs Kumah and the two young men had sat there. The file had the time of death of Anaya Patel as 12.15 p.m.

After they had finished their sandwiches and coffee, they went into the shop, returned their cups and plates, and asked the man behind the counter if he had been working there a year previous, on the day of the fall from the dress shop window. He looked amused and said he had the lease on the lunch bar/coffee shop. He had been in the shop at the time but had not seen anything of the fall, only the aftermath, as the shop had filled up with customers and they had been run off their feet. He and the waiters had been busy in the small room where they made lunch orders for several of the shops, including the dress shop; there had been one person at the counter taking orders, but they had not seen anything either, as the shop had started to get busy with the lunch trade. People came and went all the time; it was hard to keep a tab on the comings and goings.

Kate said as they came out of the coffee shop, 'Well, they have not changed any of their testimony at all. That is all in the file.'

They went up the escalator, trying to picture Mrs Kumah walking towards the lavatories and Aisha coming down on the escalator. It appeared to check out as Mrs Kumah had described it.

When they reached the doors of the dress shop, they could clearly see Aisha talking to a customer; another woman was hanging dresses up on hangers and arranging them on stands. When Aisha saw Alicia, she took a long breath. Then she finished with the customer and came over to greet her interviewer and asked, 'What can I do for you, Alicia?'

Alicia could see that Aisha did not recognise Kate from the previous year, so she introduced her and went on to say, 'We are going to have a look around where the accident happened, Aisha. If we need you to answer any questions, we will catch up with you in a little while. Is Mrs Turner in her office?'

'Yes, she is. I ordered her lunch and was about to collect it for her and any staff that wanted lunch. I phoned an order through a few minutes ago.'

'That is fine, Aisha. We will just puddle around, trying to get the picture and the layout of the shop, and perhaps knock on Mrs Turner's door to say hello before we go.'

When Alicia saw Aisha go out of the shop and head for the escalator, she said to Kate, 'I noticed two storerooms. We are looking for a ladder. You go to that one.' She pointed to one at the rear of the shop. 'I will look in this one for anything suspicious.'

They went their different ways, and Alicia went to the storeroom closest to the window that had been broken. This seemed to be the cleaner's department. There were brooms, dusters, brushes, buckets, and cleaning materials, and at the rear of this conglomeration of cleaning things, pushed to the wall, was a ladder with cloths draped over it, as if left to dry. There were a few models of young women at one end of the small room, but no clothing, so it was the cleaner's department. They probably used the ladder for cleaning the long, high windows. Alicia snapped some photos with her iPhone camera and walked back out to go in search of Kate.

Kate was entranced by all the different models that looked so lifelike, which she found in the storeroom, and she gazed around at the layers of clothing on shelves and racks. It was a wonderland of women's clothing. She was sure it was every woman's dream to be let loose in some place like this. Taking out her iPhone, she took photographs in all directions and met Alicia in the doorway and said, 'Look at this. With this for choice, you should find something to wear for any occasion.'

Alicia poked her head in, laughed, and agreed. Then she asked, 'Any ladders?'

Kate replied truthfully, 'I got caught up in the wonder of the clothing and the lifelike models, and quite frankly, I forgot about ladders. But I have not seen one, because if I had, it would have brought me down to earth for the subject at hand.'

They both scrutinised the walls and floors, and they decided there was no ladder there. Then Alicia smiled and said, 'Never mind, I found one in the cleaner's room.' She showed Kate her photo.

Kate was impressed with Alicia's find and said, 'What next?'

'We will go and knock on Mrs Turner's door and ask a few questions.'

Mrs Turner was a bustling middle-aged woman who did not like to waste time, it seemed. She hurried the two young women into her office to sit down and returned to her place behind the desk and said, 'How can I help you?'

Kate introduced the two of them and started. 'I was part of the police force investigation a year previous, and now I am contracted to Gray and Armstrong Private Investigations.' She handed a business card over the desk and went on. 'Our business has been asked by the police force to continue looking for an answer for the death of Anaya Patel, as they were not satisfied with the results they got at the time of the girl's death. We are interviewing the same people as previous to find out if there is something that has come to mind after the distress of the accident that everyone must have felt at the time. Sometimes something triggers the memory after the event.'

Mrs Turner looked annoyed but answered in her brusque way, 'I answered all the questions to the best of my ability at the time. I have nothing to add to that.'

Alicia looked at her curiously and said, 'Could you explain who was in or near the dress shop when you went out to see what the noise was about, Mrs Turner?'

'There was nobody around who should not have been there. In fact, the shop was empty of customers at that time of day. Lunchtime is always a slow period for us, for which we are thankful, because it can get very busy at times, and I have to go into the shop to help out. Aisha I had sent downstairs to get the lunches, and the other assistant was at home for her lunch break. She had a sick child at the time, and she had gone to check up on them at home.'

'And what about Derek? Was he here?' asked Alicia.

'Only for an instant. He is our owner's son and brings things from the workshop for us. He was just leaving the storeroom as I went into the showroom, and he asked me what the noise was about. We looked at the broken window together, and he said he had to get going, as he had an appointment he could not miss. At that moment, we were not aware that Anaya had gone through the window. We thought the ladder had caused the crash by sliding.'

'So did you see a ladder in the showroom at that time, Mrs Turner?' asked Kate.

'Anaya had been using a ladder earlier, but she was not there when I went out to find out what the noise was about. The display appeared to have been finalised, so I presumed that Anaya had finished the display and that Derek had put the ladder away for me.'

'What did Derek say about the broken window?'

'He asked me to ring the insurance company to have the window fixed. It was a business decision, and he mentioned to make sure we got toughened glass, as the old glass had been there many years and may not have been tough enough to stop ladders from breaking it. We were unaware at that moment that Anaya lay dead on the tiled floor of the mall. Both of the girls were out of the showroom. I knew Aisha had gone to pick up our lunches, and I presumed Anaya had gone to the bathroom, as she had been very busy doing the display all morning. It was not until Aisha returned upstairs and the police arrived that I was told that Anaya had gone through the window, and by that time, Derek had left.'

'You made a statement at the time, Mrs Turner, but left out Derek Choudhury's name and the comment that he had been coming out of the storeroom when you saw him. Will you sign this statement now, Mrs Turner? I was writing it out as you were speaking. This is to complete our records,' said Kate.

'Certainly, but I do not know what adding Derek's name could do. He was only delivering clothes from the workshop. He does that once or twice a week.'

'We are confirming the facts, Mrs Turner. It may have nothing at all to do with the accident, but we need the facts,' said Kate.

'All right, I will sign the statement. It is true after all, but it was just a moment in time. I do not see Derek often, so I was surprised to see him. He usually comes in and delivers the clothing, puts it in the storeroom, and gets one of the girls to check and sign the order. There is no need for me to see him. I presumed Aisha had signed the form. In fact, because of the commotion in the shop and the police being there, I never did check the order.'

Alicia took a photo of Mrs Turner signing the statement, and when the lady looked up and saw the camera, she asked again, 'Is that necessary?'

'Only proof that you signed this handwritten statement, Mrs Turner.' Kate smiled at her. 'Just getting the facts, Mrs Turner.'

The woman looked very annoyed, and Alicia asked, 'Do you mind if we have a quick word with Aisha? We have one question we forgot to ask when she made her statement to us.'

'It all seems to be out of my hands. You may ask your question. Aisha has gone to pick up our lunch order. She may be back by now.'

'Thank you, Mrs Turner.'

Aisha had returned with the lunch order and was waiting for them to finish speaking with her boss. Alicia waited until the girl came out of Mrs Turner's office, and she said, 'We do not want to spoil your lunch, but there are a few questions we would like to ask you, Aisha.'

She sighed and said, 'Come and sit in the staffroom. I will hear the doorbell if someone comes in to be served. It is the usual way I have lunch. Someone has to serve. I am the junior staff member, so it usually falls to me. What is it you want to know?'

Alicia looked at the girl and thought, *I do not want to rain on her parade, but it looks to me as if the storm clouds are hovering.* 'First of all, Aisha, at the time of Anaya's death, what was your relationship with Derek?'

'Derek and I have been promised in marriage since we were two years old, by our families.'

Alicia noticed the girl's hesitation in answering. 'Did Anaya try to come between you?'

'Yes. Anaya was ambitious, and when she met Derek here in the shop, she would not listen to me when I told her of the family agreement. She said that was nonsense now that we are in England and that sort of agreement was behind us and we should be allowed to make our own choice of who we marry. This caused disagreement between us. When she took me to see Mrs Kumah and told her she was to be married soon, I asked her if the prospective bridegroom was Derek, and she said it was. I was stunned. It was what we were arguing about in the shop before she had her fall. I was very angry at her. She was standing on the ladder, looking down at me, looking as if I was the crazy one, not her. We do not flout our parents' wishes and do what we wish. She was ruining my life. I believed in following my parents' agreement, and I looked forward to my marriage with Derek in time.'

'Did you see Derek in the showroom that morning, Aisha?' asked Kate.

'No. I caught a glimpse of someone who looked like him as I was going down the escalator from the upper level, but I could have been wrong. I stopped for a moment to look behind me and could not see him.'

'Was he alone at the time, Aisha?' asked Alicia.

'I thought at first that I caught a glimpse of him following a group of people. But when I looked back at the group, he was no longer there, so I thought I was imagining things. I picked up the lunches, and my attention was then taken up after I heard it was Anaya who had died on the ground floor of the mall. I never thought any more about it.'

'Thank you, Aisha. That is all for now. We have taken a few photos of the window intact. We have several photos of it when it was broken, on file. If we need to know any more, we will get back to you. Oh, there is one more question. Did you put the ladder Anaya had been using back into the storeroom?'

Aisha looked dismayed. 'No, I do not remember what happened to the ladder. Anaya had just been finishing up as I left the showroom to go for the lunches. She had still been standing on it as I walked out.'

Alicia looked at Kate and said to Aisha, 'Thanks, Aisha. We will move on now.' They both stood up and moved out of the lunchroom. They inspected the window and its surrounds once more before moving out of the shop and heading down the escalator and back to the office.

*   *   *

When Alicia and Kate told the others of their findings, Percy said, 'It could not have been an accident if the ladder was missing, unless we find who put the ladder away and they had a reason for it. Did Derek really put it away? The manager, Mrs Turner, changed her statement from the original one given to the police.'

James turned to Percy. 'I would like you with me in the morning, Percy. Mr Derek Choudhury has been brought up to look up to his elders, and you may make an impression on him. It seems to me that considerable force would have been made to push a ladder hard enough to break the glass window and catapult the girl over the balcony. I do not think it was an accident.'

'I would like to sit in, James, to hear what he has to say. Alicia and Kate can listen outside the door. We will leave it open for that purpose. If they come up with any thoughts, they can convey them to us either on the phone, which we can turn to vibrate mode, or by passing a note.' Percy gave the two young women a smile. 'They may like to make a list of questions for us to take in for the interview.'

James gave a chuckle. 'This case has been a communal affair for all of us. It is good to see. The only thing is, Kate, unfortunately we will not be able to let you make an arrest. We will have to get Ken to do that. He is still licensed. If he is not available, we will have to call in Paul Morris.'

Kate smiled. 'At least I will see the case signed off. It is amazing how it niggles at you when you cannot make an arrest or finalise a case.'

CHAPTER SIX

D erek Choudhury arrived on time at the office, and the staff saw a well-built young man, neatly dressed, with polished shoes, standing on the doorstep when they arrived. James apologised for being late, and Derek gave a charming smile. 'No, sir, I am early. My father would rather drive around the block than arrive early at the destination, and I have followed his guide. I arrive at the designated time. It is now only 9 a.m.'

James and Percy laughed, and James said, 'Come on in.' He led him to the boardroom. 'Take a seat. I will bring in the file and a pen and paper. I will only be a few seconds. Percy and I will be chatting with you. Two heads are better than one. We will be recording our chat in case anything comes up about it in the future.' He disappeared to bring the file from his office, and he followed Percy back into the interview room.

Percy started the 'chat' by asking where Derek had been on the day of Anaya's death.

Derek said, 'I was actually in the showroom when the accident happened, but I was unaware of it until two weeks later. I went to the showroom that morning to deliver some goods made at our workshop. I usually deliver them with one of the shop assistants checking them off the list as I open them. It was an unscheduled delivery. I was going in that direction, so I was asked to take the delivery on my way. This particular time, I arrived at 11 a.m. Anaya was standing on a ladder, doing a display. Aisha was holding the ladder, and the girls were arguing.

I heard my name mentioned, so I did not tell them I was there. I went to the room where stocks are held, and I put the parcels down. I went back towards the window where the girls were working, meaning to ask Aisha to come and check the arrival goods with me, and once more heard my name mentioned, so I stopped and listened. They say you never hear well of yourself if you listen in on another's conversation. It was true of this one. What I heard Anaya say shocked me.' He stopped and sat looking at his hands for a few minutes.

Percy waited for a few seconds and then prompted, 'What was it you heard, Derek?'

The young man looked up and went on. 'Anaya had been stalking me for several weeks. I play in a jazz band each Friday evening, from 8 to 11 p.m., and also on Sunday afternoons, between 3 and 5 p.m. Anaya had started turning up at each session and sitting close to where we played. This was annoying to the waiters delivering drinks, as she would order a lemonade and sit there for the whole time with her full glass, but I think they thought she was with me. At the conclusion of the gig, she would come over to me and ask if I would drive her home. When I asked how she got there, she said she had come by bus, but they stopped going to her area at that time of night.

'The last thing I wanted to do after playing the piano for three hours was take a young woman home and have to go in a different direction from where I lived with my parents. I felt sorry for her the first time it happened, but she turned up for several weeks and the same thing happened each time. I was quite annoyed with the situation but did not know how to politely say "buzz off", which I wanted to do. When I heard what Anaya was saying to Aisha, I was very distressed.'

He stopped again, and James said softly, 'What was Anaya saying, Derek?'

He looked very distressed and went on. 'Anaya told Aisha that we were dating. She said we had not discussed marriage yet, but we would as soon as her mother arrived home from India. I could hear that Aisha was upset. She told her friend that she no longer considered her a friend—she had betrayed her. This whole thing was untruthful. I was not dating Anaya. She just turned up at the jazz show each evening we were playing.

'At that stage, I went back to the storage room. I had a coach to catch, and I would have been late for it if I did not get on with the job. I usually have one of the assistants with me, but the girls were busy and Julia, the other assistant, had gone home to see how her sick child was. This was told to me by Mrs Turner when I enquired where everybody was, after we heard the crash of the ladder hitting the window.

'As I said, I had a coach to catch, so I hurried out of the shop. Because I had a trolley that I had brought the clothes in on, I had to go down in the lift and straight out to the car park. I did not speak to Aisha or Anaya. I believe that they were unaware that I was there, and I did not want them to know I had heard their argument. I have never discussed this with Aisha. When Anaya's death is brought up, she always gets upset. I believed it better to leave things and go on and change the subject.'

Percy asked, 'Why were you catching a coach, Derek? Where were you going?'

'I attend the local university and am completing the business management course, but I am also enrolled in the math course, as I am good with figures. That particular day, I was catching a coach to take a group of math students for a cramming week. I was asked to go along, as I was ahead of the other students and the professor thought I could help out. I felt highly honoured to be asked, so I agreed. We went to a beach house in Bournemouth. The weather was fine, so we had lots of sunshine and fresh air, which always helps the brain work.

'After that week, I joined a walking tour. This group comes from around here, and I do many walks with them when I am able to fit them in. So I teed up with them in Bournemouth, and the four of us walked the beaches and cliffs along the coast.'

Percy asked, 'When did you hear about Anaya's death?'

'When I arrived home two weeks later. We had our mobile phones taken off us while we were cramming, and no television was allowed. We were there to cram in as many of the math questions as we could, and we did not want diversions—we may as well have stayed at home if that was allowed. Although I got my phone back at the end of the week, all I did was contact the friends I was to walk with. There is usually no signal where we walked, and we are used to that when we get away from civilisation. It is part of the pleasure of it.'

James looked at the young man; he did sound sincere. 'Did you attempt to see a police officer and tell them what you knew?'

'No, I did not believe I knew anything. I had put the broken window down to the ladder breaking the glass as it fell.'

'Why did you pick the ladder up, Derek? Surely the insurance investigation team would have wanted to know what happened?' said Percy.

Derek looked at Percy with a bewildered look on his face. 'I am sorry, I did not think of it. At the time, all I thought of was that it was blocking the balcony and stopping anyone from passing. I thought I was doing the right thing. Mrs Turner was there with me and could tell the insurance people what they wanted to know. I thought it was an accident with the ladder slipping off the wall, and I was so intent about catching my coach I did not give it another thought. I did not know of Anaya's death at the time.'

Percy asked, 'Did you tell anyone about the showroom window being broken?'

'I did not have time. I did not even tell my father. Mrs Turner was to have the window replaced. She is in charge of the showroom. I confess that I thought no more about it. It must sound selfish, and in hindsight, it is. At the time, I had the next two weeks planned out, and I was kept occupied—first with the students, and then with walking the coastline. Frankly, I thought no more about it until my father told me about Anaya when I arrived home. I admit I was dreadfully shocked when he told me. To think I was unaware of it after it happened. I was there while it was all going down, really. I had no idea. When you are in the stockroom with the door shut, it is shut off from the rest of the showroom, and after I returned to it after I heard the girls talking, I did not hear another thing. I was hanging the clothes up, until the smash of the window awakened me from my own thoughts. All I could think was, I needed to hurry to catch my coach, which was leaving at one o'clock, and it was time for me to go.'

James asked, 'You are engaged to marry Aisha. Are you happy with that?'

'It is our way of keeping the bloodlines clean, according to our faith. I have been brought up to think of Aisha as my future wife, and I have never contradicted my parents about the arrangement. My mother has told me that if I like the girl, love and passion will come later. They chose Aisha, I suppose, because it was convenient. We are from the same family, and there are no major defects in our kin. It suited my parents, when they decided to immigrate to Britain, to bring Aisha's parents with them, and her father has worked in our workshop, in the accounts department. We also have a small shop where we sell saris, and Aisha's mother helps out there. It is all kept in the family, and we are all happy about it.'

'It sounds very well organised,' said Percy. 'Have you ever thought of bucking the system?'

Derek laughed. 'I get that question all the time. I have looked around at my friends falling in love and considered everything in my own life, but I am happy with the system. It also allows me to do what I want, such as my walking trips and my music, without anyone saying I am not taking enough notice of them, like some of my band chaps get from their girlfriends. I am selfish in that, but it is the system, as you call it. I go along with it.'

Percy now laughed. 'It must improve the chance of your marriage succeeding, I suppose, if you and your wife are happy with the system.'

'It has succeeded for many hundreds of years. Some have bad luck in their partner, and things go wrong. I suppose that is why my parents decided to choose someone from our own family.'

'When are you to be married, Derek?' asked James.

'Aisha will have her twenty-first birthday soon, and it will be at that time. She is younger than me. I am already twenty-three. We are no longer considered children, but we still have to obey our parents' wishes.'

James had left Percy to do most of the interview and now said, 'When you were leaving the showroom, did you see anyone else around that you knew?'

'It was such a long time ago, and I was in a hurry to get the trolley back into the vehicle without snagging women's stockings or ankles. It is a tricky business, pushing a trolley with a crowd of people around. I seemed to be pushed by the crowd. Now I know why. They were all heading down to the first floor as I was, but coming out of the lift, I went in the other direction, to the car park. I did not question the crowd. Sometimes they have attractions on the first floor that draw a crowd. At that stage, I did not know they were rushing to see Anaya lying on the floor. I suppose it was like that in the olden days, when crowds gathered to watch a hanging. Sorry, the question was, did I see anyone I knew? Not that I can recall.'

'We seem to have exhausted the questions for now, Derek,' said James. 'If we want to know any more, we will give you a call and have you come back in. We have a statement for you to sign for us. We keep a record of everybody we interview. It is easier than asking you the same thing over and over, and it jogs our memory of the discussion.' He handed the statement that Kate had been typing in the next office to the young man, with a pen to sign with.

As they showed Derek to the door, James showed him a photo of the two young men who had died shortly after Anaya. 'Do you know these young men, Derek?'

Derek took the photo and looked keenly at it. 'I have seen them at our jazz shows, but I do not actually know them. Now I remember why they look familiar. Didn't they get murdered about the time Anaya died? I remember seeing it in the paper and saying they turned up quite often at the evening shows.'

'Did you ever speak to them?' asked James.

'No, they were just part of the audience. We do wander around during our breaks and talk to members of the audience. I may have stopped and had a word with them, but I do not recall it. I could ask around about them if you like. One of the other boys may know them, or one of the waiters. It has been a year since they were killed. Haven't their murders been solved?'

'I might come and see one of your jazz shows. I have always been keen on jazz, and perhaps you could introduce me to your players and the waiters at that time. I will turn up soon and bring my wife. She enjoys jazz as well.' James smiled at the young man.

'I will look forward to seeing you, James. Bye for now.' And the young man left the office.

The four detectives looked at each other, and James said, 'What do you make of that interview?'

Percy said, 'He sounds sincere. His story after he left the showroom is easy to check up on. It is only the part when he was in the showroom that is questionable.'

Alicia said, 'I agree with Percy. His story of the time in the showroom could be queried. Nobody saw him until after Anaya had fallen. It does sound a little thin about then.'

Kate said, 'Could all that be going on around you and you do not take any notice? It seems doubtful to me.'

James said, 'We will have to speak to some glass people to verify that a ladder can fall and break a window on its own. If not, it puts Derek right in the picture. The timing is right. He had a motive. Aisha also had a motive. In fact, her motive is stronger. Could they have done it together? What do you think of him as a person, Alicia? Your insights into people are usually accurate.'

Alicia sat thinking for a while before answering. 'I could not see his face because I was listening from outside the office, but his voice went from "What, me?" in little boy style when describing being in the showroom, to being quite arrogant when he spoke of his music and his math capabilities. To me, he sounded like the sort of person that has been overindulged because he is clever, and he likes things to go his way. He said it is his music group. Perhaps he arranges the performances, but to me, he sounded like he is in charge and if you do not like it, move on. I believe the story he told, with reservations. It was all too pat. He has had time to organise it in his mind, and it came out sounding like that. I think he is very clever, but I do not know if I would trust him.'

'Wow, Alicia, I think you have him sorted out okay. I think because you could not see him, his charm was lost on you. What do the rest of you think about Alicia's description?' James said to the group.

Ken had come in halfway through the interview and had listened with Alicia and Kate outside of the office, with the door open, and he said, 'I think Alicia is right. This is not a man who likes being second. He wants to be in charge. I can see him as the person who pushed the ladder. Aisha is too small to have achieved such a spectacular fall. The photos of those marks on the glass show me that a bigger person pushed from higher up.'

Percy said, 'My thoughts exactly. I like the way Alicia described him. I think she is right on the button.'

James asked, 'Kate? What do you think?'

'As Alicia said, this is a man who likes to be in charge. I agree he is very clever. I think it is a real possibility that he is the pusher. His math skills would have come into action for him to work out the trajectory of the window and balcony to the mall floor. I think he is quite capable of the deed. What are his motives? Just the rumour of him dating Anaya is not enough for him to want to kill her, and if he did kill her, it would have been a moment of madness, not something he planned.'

Kate was more inclined towards Aisha, James could see. But he agreed with Ken. Aisha did not have the height or the strength. Whoever had pushed the ladder was taller and stronger. Glass was not that easy to break the way that one had been broken.

'Friday evening is the night we are taking the Sharma family to dinner. I suggest we go to the jazz show after dinner and have a look around and ask some questions,' said James.

'That is a good idea, James,' said Ken. 'Waiters are always good for questioning. They tend to blend into the background, and no one takes any notice of them, except when they want a drink. All sorts of conversations are overheard by them, and no one is aware of the fountain of information they carry in their heads. I always make a beeline to the waiters when they are available.'

'Good, this is what we will do then. You and Kate sit at a different table than us, somewhere at the back of the customers, and chat with the waiters. Percy, Granny—if she wants to come—and Alicia and I will sit up front so we can see the expression on Derek's face when he sees us. He will possibly be so busy looking at us, he will miss Ken and Kate in the background,' said James.

Alicia said, 'We must not forget to question the waiters about the two young men who were murdered. Remember, Mrs Kumah said those two boys had been looking up at the window the moment Anaya fell. What if they had seen something—like Derek pushing the ladder? Perhaps when they saw Derek, they knew him from the jazz shows, and they thought it was a good ploy to blackmail him. Ask the waiters if they have ever seen the boys in conversation with Derek. If he is cold-blooded enough to push his shop girl through a window, he might have tried to clean up his act by killing the boys who had seen it all and who had possibly filmed it to blackmail him.'

'True, Alicia,' said Kate. 'We will make sure we take the photo James showed Derek, to show around to the waiters.'

James picked up the file to take back to his office and said, 'This file is getting thicker by the day. I can see how you felt when you could not find anyone to question when the deed happened, Kate. Everyone was in denial and disappeared, so you could not find any witnesses. It must have been very frustrating. I cannot see those young fellows taking off as they did without saying they had seen it happen, except for blackmail purposes. Most people, when they are witnesses of such a terrible thing as a girl falling from above them, would come forward to tell their story. I am next to sure that it is all entwined.'

Each of them nodded, and Percy said, 'I think you are right, James. Surely though, the boys would have been wary about approaching someone they had seen murder a girl? They must have felt very confidant about getting away with it. Perhaps they knew something else about Derek to have made them think like that?'

'That is a good comment, Percy. We will have to work on it that way.'

*   *   *

The next morning, James and Percy went to interview Bharat Kumah and Vivaan Patel at the tailor shop. It was an imposing warehouse building and they were impressed when they went inside. There were two tables the length of the main hall, with cutters working, and at the side of each cutter was a desk with a sewing machine. Everybody looked very busy. It was a bright atmosphere, with chatting going on, light background music playing, and people moving around. The light that came from windows high up in the hall added to the lights over the tables and machines. It did not look like the pictures the men had seen of earlier-century mills and workshops.

Mr Kumah had an office at the rear of the hall, beside what looked like lunchrooms and toilet facilities, although his office faced out to the main hall. On the other side of the lunch area were drawers of patterns and shelves of material of all kinds. This looked like a very successful tailoring business. Mr Kumar's office space was a large area with four desks, with seating behind partitions, making each desk appear private. Each area had a name printed on a timber bracket, and his own office and Patel's were larger areas at the front of the others. Everything was very neat and looked successful, with workers in place.

James and Percy were shown into the main office and were greeted by a tall, handsome man in his late forties or early fifties, with large brown eyes and dark curly hair, standing to shake their hands. After greeting them and pointing to the chairs for them to sit down, Bharat Kumah looked inquisitively at them and said, 'Iris said you were polite, and she was happy to have seen you, to clear her mind of the day Anaya went to see her and also of Anaya's death. She had worried that she had been unable to tell anyone what she saw at the time.'

Percy was the first to speak, and he asked, 'Did she tell you, sir, what she saw and heard?'

'Yes, although at the time I was more worried about my wife's illness. Anaya's visit had upset her terribly and made her most unwell. She could not get over the fact that Anaya could be so rude to her. She had offered the girl marriage with our only son. As you can see, we are well off compared to the average person, and we all came from a very poor background. We thought we were helping the girl settle down, because her father was upset with the direction she was going. She did not want to be helped. She wanted to make her own decisions, but her father thought some of her decisions were wrong. She was a headstrong girl. In my opinion I am glad not to have such a person in our family. She appeared to me nothing but trouble.

'Vivaan and I have been friends for many years. We started as apprentices at the same time. We had come up to Mumbai from the country to start as apprentices at the age of fifteen. It was a very hard period for us. Our master tailor was a hard man to satisfy, but he did teach us good tailoring, of which I am very proud now. However, at the time, I was resentful that he did not feed us enough and did not allow us to go out to enjoy ourselves occasionally. To him, we were there with him to work, and work we did, from early morning to dark, seven days of the week.'

'When did you decide to immigrate, sir?' asked James.

'Our five-year apprenticeship was ending, both Vivaan and I were turning twenty, and we would be leaving the tailor's business to find work for ourselves. Then my parents were killed in an accident when their horse and cart turned over in our village. The only ones that went to help them were the Christian minister and his wife. Everybody else was too happy at the Holi ceremony that was being held, and they ignored the broken cart and its dying passengers. When I returned to Mumbai after their funeral, I went to the Catholic church which stood at the end of our street, on a hill. I was received with much kindness, so I kept going to the services and any events they held. I was able to attend whenever my work commitment allowed.

'Over a few months, I got very friendly with Sister Angeline. She was the type of person who saw goodness in everyone, and because I seemed sad, she showed special interest in me. Iris was part of the church, and I think the sisters expected her to become a nun as well. It was the impression I got from their attitude to her. She would have made a good nun, but she had never been far from the orphanage since her arrival there shortly after her birth. So Sister Angeline thought Iris should try the outside world for a while. One afternoon, at a tea party, a group of us started talking about immigration to the UK. Someone's brother had immigrated and was doing well. I listened, and Sister Angeline, sitting beside me, asked if I would be interested.

'I think my answer was "I want to get away from here, from the people who ignored my parents lying dead in the gutter, from bosses who do not feed us enough, from hard work from morning to night. The only nice thing is coming here to the church. You are the only people I see, and you are so kind to me." Sister Angeline looked at me and said, "Would you be prepared to take a wife with you?"

'I remember saying "A wife? I do not know any person willing to be my wife. I would be an unemployed tailor who knows nothing of the world. I would be useless as a husband."

'Sister Angeline did not give up and said, "I know a girl who knows nothing about the world except what goes on in the orphanage. She would make a good wife, and you could learn about the world together. It is easier when you have someone to back you up rather than going through it alone." I still did not know who she was talking about until she moved to the next group and brought Iris to our group. She was this stunning-looking white girl, and I fell in love with her immediately. I knew who she was, because I had asked around when I first saw her, but I had never spoken to her. We asked if we could talk to each other for a while, we spoke, and I was even more smitten. I did not worry that she was white. If we were going to England, wouldn't everyone be white? Because she was admitted to the church society as a fellow Catholic, it never dawned on me how hard it was for her in our community because she was white. She never complained about people's rudeness to her.

'The church community paid our fares, and Sister Angeline asked her parents to help set us up in business. We worked hard, and I have never used my old boss's method of starving the staff to get them to work harder.' He said this with a smile. 'We have paid back the money we owed, with interest, and we send money to the orphanage every quarter. Despite that, we are still doing well. I paid for Vivaan Patel and his wife to come over and join us once we were established. We paid their rent until they were settled in, and we helped them when necessary, to give them a good life. We even paid for Anaya's mother to visit her dying mother in India. This is why I was angry that Anaya snubbed my wife. It was the manner of the snubbing that made me most cross. As I said, Iris was snubbed all the time when we were in India, and now this Indian girl whom we had been so good to, a chit of a girl, looked down on my wife. Yes, I was angry.'

'Did you kill Anaya, Bharat? Were you angry enough to do that?' asked Percy.

Bharat Kumah looked at them sadly. 'I was angry enough, but Anaya was my friend's daughter. I am a Christian these days, and I try to keep to the Ten Commandments. No, I did not kill Anaya, but I have said many prayers for her soul. Come,' Bharat said. 'I will introduce you to Anaya's father.' He rose from his chair and showed them to another office, similar to his own, and introduced them to his friend.

Vivaan Patel was a lean, shy man. When he spoke, it was with a quiet accented voice. 'Good morning, sirs, please sit down. I have cleared a space for you. I usually have a jumble of patterns and fabrics strewn around the place, so I did a long-due clean-up this morning to make some room for you. How can I be of help to you?'

Percy explained who they were and what they were doing, and he ended with 'We now believe there is a possibility your daughter was pushed through the window and fell to her death. We are following through by talking to all those who were interviewed at the time, hoping we can pick up some clues that people may have thought of after the event. This is often when things come to light, as memories of the initial onslaught are thought over. Nobody can forget a happening like Anaya's. It stays in the mind for years to come, and we hope to wake up those memories to see if we can find out what actually happened.'

James said, 'Can you tell us your opinion of what happened to your daughter, and can you tell us more about her to help us in this line of enquiry?'

Mr Patel looked as if he was about to cry. 'I am still grieved at my daughter's death. It is as if it was just yesterday. The sadness of it has not faded for me. I was angry at my daughter at the time. She had snubbed our benefactor, a lovely lady that had only ever been good to us. If not for her, we would still be struggling in the streets of Mumbai, earning a living. Iris has never done anything nasty in her life. She was brought up by the nuns in her church, and her main aim in her life was to help people. My wife and daughter did not like her, because I did. Yes, I loved Iris—like a sister. My wife was aware of it and made my life miserable because of her jealousy. She had no need to be jealous. Iris loves Bharat and is loved by her husband, so she never was anything but kind and friendly to me.

'I admit that my wife did most of the bringing up of our children. She would not allow me to interfere when it came to Anaya. They were both strong-minded women, mother and daughter. Anaya had reached the age of eighteen and thought it was wonderful that she no longer had to obey her parents. When she moved out of our home to rent a flat with Aisha, I was afraid she would get into bad company. She was an outgoing girl and thought that she was always right and that her parents were only here to supply her with food and clothing. While she was under our roof, we could monitor her hours, and we did not allow her to drink or smoke. As soon as she moved out, we heard that she was doing both and running around with men. We loved our daughter, but we would not kill her for sowing her wild oats. We prayed for her future, and when Bharat told me about how she had spoken to Iris, I was almost ready to give up on her. But your daughter is always your daughter. I went to see her that last day to let her know how displeased I was with her. She refused to talk me, so I went away, angered by her manner. My wife had gone to India for her mother's funeral, so I was bargaining with Anaya alone. But she would not listen. I am sorry I did not try harder. She was a silly girl, I thought, and my failure will stay with me for the rest of my life. I could see Anaya was treating Aisha like a servant, and I wondered how long that would go on without Aisha bailing out of the friendship that had lasted through their school years. I was ashamed of my daughter at that stage.'

'Anaya claimed she was going to get engaged to marry as soon as your wife returned from her bereavement trip,' James said. 'Have you any idea who the man was that she claimed to be close to an engagement with?'

'I did not get close enough to Anaya in the last few months of her life for her to tell me of it. She avoided me and hung up on my phone calls when I rang. If I tried to question her on her private life, she explained to me that it was her own business now that she was eighteen. As I said earlier, I was ashamed of my daughter at that stage, the way her life was turning.'

'All right, sir, we will keep you informed if we come to a conclusion. One way or another, we will try our hardest to solve the mystery,' said James, feeling sorry for the man.

As James and Percy left the building, Percy remarked, 'You have to admire these men, bringing themselves to a strange land and building up such a successful business. I wish them all the best, but they have the same problems we have with our children when they reach their teens.'

James agreed. 'I do not think either of these men guilty of killing Anaya, even though they thought of her as a pain. Well, we will keep looking at Derek. He is not of the usual mould and seems to think of himself as someone a cut above others. We will have to find out if he is right.'

CHAPTER SEVEN

The dinner with the Sharma family was scheduled for that evening, and the party at the Indian restaurant was a merry one as Alicia and James told of the journey on the Maharajah's train and how magnificent they thought it. Mrs Sharma was especially interested, vowing that she and her husband would do that trip sometime in the future.

After they finished eating, James broached his idea of Mrs Sharma helping them out by telling them of Indian customs and the local Indian community in general, with a payment for her time. The usually business-like Indian woman looked so happy to be asked; her reply was 'Mr and Mrs A, I owe you so much for allowing Sammy off the hook for the petrol bombing of your office. I am eternally grateful for the way you have treated our son. Any information I can help you with does not need to be paid for. What do you want to know?'

James said, 'We have been asked to look into the murders of three young Indian people. At first, we believed the Patel girl was an honour killing, but we have ruled that out and feel that her parents are not guilty of doing it themselves or of ordering it. We now believe it was a murder, not an accident, which it initially appeared to be. There is also the murders of the two young gay men. We have a few ideas there, but nothing has been proved yet. I think what we want to know is, what does the local Indian community think of it? All three murders were so close together. Have there been any expressions of interest? How did they react at the time? That sort of thing. We know how people talk about these things when they happen.

'We do not want you to ask questions of people. That is too dangerous for you. Just perhaps bring the questions up to see how people react. We have to advise you that open questioning could put you in danger. The person who killed the three young people is a very dangerous person and is likely to repeat their actions if someone popped up asking questions and got too close to the bone. Have I made myself clear, Mrs S?'

'Perfectly, Mr A. Do you want my personal opinion on the time it all happened?'

James laughed. *This woman is not a dismissive type of woman. She knows what is what,* he thought. 'Yes, Mrs Sharma, I know everyone would have been very concerned at the time about who in the community could have done these terrible murders. So what do you believe, Mrs S?'

'I believe that the general Indian community here was disturbed that there was a vindictive killer on the loose, perhaps a racial radical,' Mrs Sharma explained. 'For months, people locked their windows and doors, and some even went to the extreme and bought bolts for their doors. We were all scared for some time. But nothing else happened, so we started to talk about the reason for the men's killings. The girl, well, we all thought that it was probably an accident.

'In our general conversations about the murders, someone said they heard that those two guys had been selling drugs. Their sons had been approached at school by them, and some said the selling point seemed to be at musical events more than any other place after they finished school, but definitely done by the same two young men. The conversations petered out, with most people believing it was drug-related or was done by a gay hater. In India, until quite recently, it was a criminal offence to be gay. That has changed recently, by law. But some of our people here are stuck between being British and being Indian, and the Indian side of them is also stuck, back in the time they left home. It is a strange thing, being an immigrant and starting a new life. Some of the old life is still retained.'

James exclaimed, 'Mrs Sharma, you are a miracle walking! This is exactly what we wanted to know. There is no need now for you to send shock waves through your community by asking questions. You have it all here. There is one more question for you. Do you know a Derek Choudhury—university student, plays piano with a jazz group on Friday nights and Sunday afternoons, a good-looking young man, very assertive, son of a self-made, well-to-do local businessman?'

'I know his parents, very nice people. I have been told the son is very clever, indulged by his parents. He is their only son. I have had nothing to do with the son, Derek.' You could tell Mrs Sharma was trying to recall if she had heard any more about Derek Choudhury. She was quiet for a minute.

'There is gossip in every community. I dismiss a lot of what I hear, but I do recall he got a girl in trouble. Either because she had an abortion and nearly died and named Derek as the father of her child, or some other reason I cannot recall, because it was some time ago. There was a bit of commotion at the time, and Derek's father paid the girl a large sum of money for whatever it was. Oh yes, now I remember. It was not an abortion. The girl involved blamed Derek for drugging her drink, and she was unconscious at the time he raped her.'

James and the team looked at each other, and James said, 'Wow, Mrs Sharma, you have come up with the goods. There is no need to ask anyone else. We were concerned about asking you because we thought it could put you in danger, so do not question anyone at all. We have enough information. I remind you, the killer is still at large.'

Mrs Sharma smiled at the group. 'I am pleased to be of service, Mr A. I hope you catch this person who killed the two young men and Anaya Patel. They were too young to die.'

The dinner party finished, and the Gray and Armstrong group took off in their two cars to go to the jazz show. They parked in separate directions and entered the building as they arrived. Percy, Valerie, Alicia, and James sat by the front of the large area, quite near the band. Kate and Ken sat at the rear, where they could see Percy and James; they did not appear to be part of their group. The room filled up around ten o'clock, and the drink waiters were kept busy. As one waiter placed drinks on the table for Kate and Ken, Ken placed a business card on the table and asked if the man knew of any drug dealers in the room. The waiter turned his back to the band and answered, 'My name is Jerry Jones. I work for the drug squad, and I will call into your offices first thing in the morning to have a chat if that is okay with you.'

'Yes,' said Ken, surprised. 'I will be there, although I am not sure if the others will be.'

'I am sure you can pass the message on,' said Jerry, hurrying away to serve more drinks.

Ken looked towards James, waiting for him to glance their way. When he did, Ken gave a nod, then stood up and walked to the door. He saw James talking to Percy, and Percy and Valerie stood up and followed them out of the hall. James and Alicia stayed in place until an interval was announced, and they waited for Derek to acknowledge them. They did not have long to wait. Derek said something to the drummer and walked off the platform and came to the table where James and Alicia sat.

'A very impressive performance, Derek. You and your group make good music. We both enjoy jazz, but we must be off now. We have a very busy morning tomorrow. We will come back and enjoy the music another evening, or perhaps even on your Sunday gig. I am glad we came. It was very good,' said James pleasantly.

'Thanks, James and Alicia. It was nice of you to come. Goodnight,' said the impressive young man.

'Goodnight, Derek. Now that we know where to come, we will be back. We enjoyed the music so much,' said Alicia.

Ken was waiting by the car when James appeared. On the journey home in the car, Ken told him of Jerry Jones and of him coming to the office in the morning to have a chat.

James said, 'Well done, Ken. I will be there to meet with him. Percy is good nowadays in the bookshop, so I can leave him and Alicia to help Granny with the sales. It is always very busy in the bookshop on Saturdays. Do you want to come to the office? It is your day off, so I can manage if you have other things to do.'

'I would like to hear what the fellow has to say, James. I admit I am caught up in the web now with this Derek fellow. I do not trust him at all. It seems everything is about him—or so he thinks. He does not appear remorseful about Anaya at all, as he should be, since it is his family business the girl fell from.'

'That is true, Ken. Looking at things that way, it did seem like an ordinary day's experience to him, and he dismissed it. That in itself is not a normal reaction. Okay, I will see you in the morning at 9 a.m.'

*   *   *

James and Ken were in the office at nine, and Jerry Jones showed up only minutes later. They took a seat in the interview room, and Jerry explained that he knew of James and Percy's job the previous year, catching a murderer who had taken off with a million pounds' worth of cocaine from the customs house. 'I must tell you that your name is held in high esteem back at headquarters in London. It was a job very well done. I meant to look you up when I arrived, but as usual, work got in the way. I never made it. There has been quite a lot of speculation in this town because sales of cocaine escalated locally after the arrest of the two ringleaders of that job. We know it cannot be those guys selling cocaine, because they are in jail and are likely to stay there for quite a while. What or who are you chasing now that brought you to the jazz show?'

James said, 'I would like a few more answers from you first, Jerry. Can we see your identification before we go any further?'

Jerry smiled. 'They did tell me you were meticulous in your reporting. Here is my card and identification from those above.'

'Why are you serving as a waiter on the job, Jerry? Obviously plain clothes. Is it any drug, or is it only cocaine?' asked James.

'I will start from the beginning,' said Jerry. 'Sometime before I arrived, there was a new case concerning drugs, but it was not cocaine. It was a young woman who visited the jazz show on a Friday evening and who was given the rape drug by, at that time, an unknown source. She was raped by someone we believed was a novice at it, because far too much of the drug had been given to her at a house not far from where the jazz show is held. At two o'clock in the morning, after being at the show, the girl was delivered to the hospital and left on the steps of the entrance. She was unconscious, and her breathing was almost non-existent. She was in a very bad way. She was placed in a coma, and it was two weeks before she recovered enough to tell who had administered the drug.

'When we questioned her eventually, she said it was Derek Choudhury who had raped her. He had taken her to the house he was renting, on the pretence of finding some music for her so she could practise the songs and be a singer for some of the shows. We arrested Choudhury, who said, of course, that he was not guilty. But when we interviewed his father, who was devastated by the girl's story, Derek finally threw up his hands and confessed. The girl was discharged from hospital, and a deal was done between Choudhury senior and her. For an unknown sum of money, she would not make a charge against Derek.

'He got away with that one, but it did make a rift between father and son. Derek moved out of the family home and bought his own apartment. It was about that time I was brought into town to see what else was going on. It had been whispered that drugs were being sold at the jazz shows, and I was put in place to see what I could find. As a new man in town, it was most unlikely that I would be recognised. I have been there each Friday evening for the last six months, and I have to admit, I have not found very much with which to make an accusation. Something is going on, I can feel it, but they are very practised in what they do. It is hard to find. So what were you looking for?'

'We suspect Derek in a murder. Once again, there is not a lot of proof, and we are going quietly on it for the moment until we find more evidence. Do you remember seeing an Indian girl with Derek at all? No, it would have been before you came here. We also suspect him in the murder of two young gay Indian men. They were murdered in their beds shortly after the girl was pushed through a window, so perhaps that rape drug was used on the young men to enable that to happen while they were asleep. That sounds probable. As you said, Derek was known to have that drug. It was wondered why they just lay there and allowed someone to knife them. It was a very bloody murder. I have the photos of it here. I will go and get them to show you. These two boys were suspected of dealing drugs, by the local community. Somewhere there has to be an answer to bring it all together. There is a link missing, and we only have to find it.' James got up to pick up the files from his desk.

When he returned, he said, 'We have only had this file for a few days. It is a cold case, and we have been asked to have a go at it by the local police department. We have interviewed every person interviewed at the time. Derek Choudhury had been missed and had not been thought of as a possibility. However, when we interviewed him, it was after a woman said she saw him at the site. This was taken up by us, and we now believe he is guilty. We think him guilty of killing the two young men, because another source saw the young men photographing someone pushing the girl through the window. We now believe the young men were trying to blackmail Derek, and that caused their deaths. Other than the two women's testimony, both were virtually at the scene when the girl fell to her death, but we have no proof. It is all conjecture by us at the moment. We are still in the initial stages of the investigation, so things may change. We thought following up on the drug story may give us some insight and prove something to us which will hold up in a court of law.'

Jerry Jones said, 'If you have only had the case for a few days, you have certainly gone from woe to go very quickly.'

James answered, 'We heard from another reliable source that those two boys had been trafficking drugs since they were at school. My question is, where did they get the drugs to sell? When we were working on the customs case, one of the suspects there was stealing cocaine on an almost daily basis, and we wondered at the time whom he was selling it to. Perhaps he had been using the two young men to move it for him. If it was cocaine they were selling, then that is our missing link. The only thing wrong with that assumption is, the man has been in jail over a year now. You did say at one stage that it was after the customs deal that you were brought in to find out who is selling cocaine. I wonder if the man's wife has continued selling it, on the word of the man in prison, whom she must visit on a regular basis.'

Ken looked interested in this theory and said, 'We cannot give a description of her but we know where she lived at the time the customs deal went down. What if I start up surveillance and get Kate to help me? She could knock on the door with some sort of excuse, and I can take a photo when the door opens. Then we can send it to you to see if you recognise her as being a person who appears at the jazz show. That would be much better than us attending the show each time it is on and bringing suspicion on us, when you are a Johnny-on-the-spot—or I should have said "Jerry-on-the-spot".'

James said, 'Good one, Ken. That would sort it out for us. Perhaps her husband is telling her to pass on the cocaine. If she was using the two boys, she must now be dealing directly with Derek, and he is the one selling it. I do know that her house was searched after Gerald's arrest, and they found nothing. But what if Gerald got to her first and told her where the cocaine was hidden and to move it away from the house before the police arrived? If that is the case, perhaps the boys had been holding it.'

Jerry looked pleased at the way things were going, and he said, 'It all sounds right somehow. Get the photo, and I'll see if I have spotted her. Then we can organise a warrant to search Derek's apartment.'

James asked, 'Do you know where Derek lives, Jerry? He told us he lived with his family.'

'He moved out of his parents' house and purchased a penthouse in a deluxe area. He must have used his cocaine earnings to purchase that. They are very swanky apartments, and he has the penthouse. I followed him home one night to confirm it.' Jerry smirked. 'I can almost imagine him in handcuffs.'

'We will arrange the warrant to search Derek's property if we are able confirm that Gerald Norman's wife visits him. What do you think, Ken? Is it too early in the investigation? We may find evidence of the boys' killing if we find the cocaine he has hidden.' James turned to Ken and went on. 'I cannot see us getting much more on Derek without a search of his property and even a search of his parents' house. Perhaps he visits his parents once a week, like most sons, and while he is there, he picks up some of the booty he hid there after taking it from the two young men when he killed them. He would think it safer in his parents' house. They are less likely to bring suspicion on themselves that would cause us to go hunting in their house.'

'I think there is good cause to search their house, although it may be harder to get a warrant, seeing as they have done nothing wrong,' Ken said.

'Mmm.' James pondered this. 'I might have to call in the big guns on this one. Okay, Ken, you and Kate go for the photo of Gerald's wife. Send it to Jerry. We will ring you, Jerry, when it is ready. If it is confirmed that she knows Derek, we will get the warrants. I for one want to search Derek's apartment and meet his parents. This young man has me very interested in him.'

Ken nodded. 'Count me in. I am also interested to see what made a young man who has everything go off the rails so dramatically.'

Jerry said, 'Drugs will do it every time. I have seen it over and over. It touches everyone the same way, no matter who they are. You see that, after a while, having drugs will bring them down. It would be better that I do not appear at the house and apartment if I want to stay incognito for further investigations. I do most of my work going underground and blending in.'

'Thanks, Jerry, for the information you have given us. This is a triple sentence awaiting Derek if we can find the proof. Three murders and drug dealing, and the man is only twenty-three. If we do not find something to prove it, he can move on to be a crime boss in the future with the way he is going,' said James.

*   *   *

Ken and Kate went to take the photograph on Sunday, as they had suggested, and returned to the office on Monday morning looking triumphant. They had a very clear photo of a woman standing in a doorway, with the morning light showing an almost perfect picture. They had taken it to get developed and had an A4 picture for the board.

Alicia arrived at ten o'clock in the office, and when she saw the photo pinned to the whiteboard, she said, 'I have seen that face before.' She went into James's office and brought out the Anaya Patel file and took it into the conference room. She laid out the papers side by side until she got to the photos of the viewers around Anaya's body, and she pinpointed a face in the crowd. 'There, I knew I had seen her before. Not in person, but here she is, looking around her. The police photographer caught her as she was looking towards the lifts. She must have seen Derek leaving with his trolley. I think I will do some research on her. Did you find out her first name, Kate?'

'I have it written down here. I was pretending to do a survey of children's activities in the area. She was quite voluble on what she thought was required. She is Fiona Norman, and she has two young daughters. She loves the area where she lives, and the girls go to the local schools.'

James came and looked at the photos, and he saw Fiona staring towards the lift area. 'She reminds me of someone. Percy!' he called. 'Who does this woman look similar to? You are good with faces.'

Percy looked at the two photographs, and after a few minutes, he said, 'I would bet Ian Haskell is her brother.'

'Yes!' exclaimed James. 'The same foxy face, but on her, it looks exotic. And her hair is dark, and his was mousy. Perhaps she colours it. They could even be twins. They look so much alike. We have all the details on Haskell in the customs file, and it should be easy to line them up. So that is why Ian Haskell and Gerald Norman were so matey. They were family.'

Kate said, 'I thought she was a nice-looking woman, sexy somehow with that long dark hair and, as James said, somehow exotic. She looked too young to have a twelve-year-old, so she must look after herself.'

James laughed. 'It is amazing that what makes a woman look exotic makes a man look weaselly. I would never have described Haskell as exotic.'

'Well, James, Ian Haskell probably did not wear make-up, and this woman was well done up, even though it was early morning yesterday when we called at her home.'

'She was probably going to the jazz concert in the park to meet up with Derek Choudhury,' said Percy.

Alicia came back into the room and said, 'I have looked Fiona Norman up, and her maiden name was Haskell. This certainly puts her in the picture now for the drug sales. What if she was the one who killed the two boys? She has the family history of killing people. After all, her brother's total is four dead. She may have learnt about the boys blackmailing Derek, and she intervened. That could leave Derek in the clear, or with only Anaya Patel to account for.'

'This certainly changes the picture,' said James. 'I will send a copy to Jerry Jones to see if she has appeared with Derek at any time. We should have a call back within a few minutes.'

Ten minutes later, James's phone rang, and they all stood closer to hear the call on speakerphone. Jerry's voice came through loud and clear. 'Yes, I have seen that woman at the Friday night shows on several occasions. I do not go to the Sunday shows in the park. I leave that to the university students to serve drinks. Derek organises them. He seems well up in their estimation. A couple of them turn up for the Friday shows, and they speak of him as a great role model.'

'What time do you pack up on Friday nights, Jerry? Does Derek leave at the same time, and does the woman go with him?'

'That is three questions, James. Number one, we close up at 11 p.m., although it takes us a good half hour to clean up after the crowd has left. Two, Derek does leave about the same time as us. He has the band area to clear. Give or take a minute or two, we do leave about the same time. That is why I was able to follow him to his apartment building. Three, he does leave alone usually, but lately the only one he seems interested in is the woman in the photograph. What do you want me to do?'

'Just watch them, Jerry. We would be pleased to have a report, but I think they have a private conversation after they leave the show. If they are going to the apartment together, it must now be an affair, not a one-night stand. We might do surveillance to see when she leaves. She is the sister of the customs staff killer, Ian Haskell, the man who tried to take off with a million pounds' worth of cocaine, and she is the wife of the daily-drug-snatches fellow, Gerald Norman, so she must have a cache of cocaine somewhere. Her house was gone over with a fine-tooth comb after her husband and brother went to jail, but nothing was found. So she has moved it off site somewhere. We are hoping to find it at Derek's apartment, but we still haven't moved on a warrant until we have more information.'

'Still looking good and moving along. Thanks for keeping me in the loop. I will get back to you if I find out any more.' And Jerry was gone.

James said, 'Wow, he certainly does not stay around too long. I think it is about time we organised some warrants, one for Derek's apartment and one for his parents' house. If we poke around too much, we may get sprung and miss out on the asvantage to take them by surprise. If we are not careful, we may warn them into changing their timetable, and we may not find what we want.

'We have to organise a surveillance. It appears Friday night and Sunday afternoon are the times. Percy and I can do those, and you will have to leave your phone on, Ken, at those times, in case we want to go into the properties. The other surveillance time is when Derek goes to his parents' house. It looks like we will have to cover that on rotation, as we do not know when to expect the visit. We do know he goes to the university five days a week, and he does math tutoring after his own lectures. We will be able to pick up his trail from there or wait outside his family home—actually, that will be easier. We will start the family home stake-out today and go on till the weekend.

'Percy, you and I will start the stake-out this afternoon after we have been in to see the chief of police to talk to him about the warrants. I will phone him now for an appointment. It only needs one person for the stake-out, as it is only surveillance, so the girls can go about their usual business. Ken and Percy and I can take turns after today when we check the area out for a good position. Are you all okay with that arrangement?'

Ken said, 'It is fair. I am not sure whether you will be given a warrant to search the parents' home, unless you have more proof. They are not under suspicion for anything but being loving parents. To us, it makes sense that that is where any drugs would be stored, but you will have to convince the magistrate. I think they will give you a warrant for Derek's apartment, and if we come up clean, we may have to try harder for the older Choudhurys' home.'

James and the others looked at Ken, and James said, 'There goes the voice of reason. Of course, you are right, Ken. I was getting a bit carried away. I still think the stake-out to see if Derek goes to visit is worthwhile. We are being paid for our time spent, so we will not lose anything and may win something. Do you agree with that?'

'Yes, James. It is only because I know how hard it is to get a warrant that I reminded you.'

'We will try the argument with the police chief anyway,' said James. 'He can only say no, and we can come again from a different angle if the apartment does not give up its secrets. I will still bet on the parents' house though. We will just have to wait and, if necessary, put a hand on Derek's shoulder when he leaves his parents' house.'

Ken apologised. 'I am sorry to put a spanner in the works. I think your thinking is on the button. Magistrates are wary about warrants, though, if we cannot prove things, and the parents are not guilty of anything that we can put a finger on yet. Have you thought of going to the senior Mr Choudhury directly?'

Percy said, 'James and I discussed it last night and decided that it is too early yet. We do not want to lose the element of surprise. We agreed that Derek's father would go straight to his son and ask him questions. That could startle Derek out of his fantasy of a love nest and independent means by selling cocaine and could send him away to hide. We do not want that to happen. We want to find out if he is guilty of all we believe of him and his lady friend. It is too much of a coincidence that Fiona has fixed him in her sight.'

'I agree with all that,' said Ken. 'He may only be a lovelorn young man, and Fiona is the monster, as Alicia has put forward. Looking at that photo of Fiona Norman, she does look like a Mata Hari type, the World War I spy.'

Alicia said, 'You make good sense, all of you. Just do not judge a book by its cover. Who knows what is between the pages?'

Everybody laughed, and James said, 'That is a comment I would have expected from a bookseller. Those words are ones Granny would have used on us.

'I have the appointment with the police chief now, so Percy and I will be out for a while. With luck, after we have completed our stakeout, we will be back in time for the workout at Harry's barn. If I do not turn up at all, Ken, would you apologise for me? Harry is aware that work gets in the way sometimes, and he knows I try my best to make it to the barn each Monday and Wednesday.'

'Sure, James. I am sure you will not go flabby by missing one evening,' said Ken.

'No, that is not what concerns me. I helped him start up his business, and I feel obligated to go as often as I am able. I do not want to let him down. He does such a fabulous job with all the men who go along, and the women as well on Tuesday nights. It is a courtesy only, to let him know when I cannot make it,' explained James. He waved to the group as he and Percy went out the office door.

*   *   *

After laying all the details and photos out for the chief policeman to listen to and look at, he agreed to ask the magistrate for a warrant for Derek Choudhury's apartment. However, as Ken warned, he balked at the parents' home, saying he would ask, but not to count on it.

James shrugged and said, 'Nothing lost. We expected that, but we felt we had to tell you all the facts. We are all convinced of our argument that Derek would hide the cocaine in a safe place, and what is safer than an innocent location that he has access to any time he wants it? We will try the apartment first, but we do not expect to find anything. However, it will give us insight into how the young man lives. He has told some lies and some truth, and we want to know the difference.'

The policeman looked admiringly at James and Percy, and he said, 'Your ideas on the case are way more asvanced than what was discovered at the time, and to me, it looks as if you will solve two cases at once. That is admirable. I look forward to seeing this finish as you have laid it out, although sometimes things get a little slippery at the conclusion, so you may have to expect some hiccups. I will try for both warrants, but I wanted to warn you that magistrates are hard to convince sometimes if proof is not clear.'

Percy said, 'Once the woman, Fiona Norman, was recognised as the lover or follower of Derek Choudhury, we felt we had the connection. Her husband must have squirrelled away a lot of cocaine over the time he was in the customs department, and now she has it to dispose of. We do not know if she is being led by her husband from prison or is doing her own thing. But somehow she is deeply guilty of something. Even if it is only selling cocaine, we believe there is more than that, and the death of the three young people could possibly be put on her door as well.'

'It is amazing', said the chief, 'that the customs job has come back to bite you. We did not see that when we handed the case over to you. We thought both cases were just murders. The possibility of the girl being an accident was always there, but we thought the young men might have been a racial or gay killing.'

'It is hard to believe what comes out of the woodwork when you have a new group look at the evidence from a different angle. With this job, I can see that the lack of witnesses coming forward at the time must have been very frustrating.' James looked at the chief and went on. 'I would like to thank you for giving us this case. It is stretching our minds somewhat, but I believe we are getting there. We knew that Gerald Norman, the manager of the customs container group, had stashed away cocaine, and we are pleased we can chase it up. We are concentrating on that first. After we have more information, we are going after Fiona Norman.'

'I like your attitude and hard work, James and Percy. Keep it up. I will let you know what the magistrate says and get back to you as soon as I can.'

'Thanks, Chief,' said Percy and James, and they went off to do their stake-out of the senior Choudhury's home.

James had looked up the address earlier, and they were able to find the home in a suburban area. This was not the home of people as well off as the Kumahs were, or they were living below their potential. The house was around the corner from a shopping area, with a school down the end of the street, and it looked family-friendly, much like the house next door to it and the one next to that. It was a nice area, unchanged over the years. As the house they were to watch was only two houses down the street, around the corner from shops, it was easy to find a parking area where they would not be noticed and where they could see anyone approaching the house.

James got out of the car and said to Percy, 'I will bring us snacks and drinks, as we did not come prepared this time.' He disappeared into a delicatessen.

When he returned, Percy said, 'No action yet. We could be here all day.'

'We are being paid for it, Percy. I gave the chief a list of the hours we have done so far, and he did not blink or look concerned. We can have a rest here for a while. You can have a snooze after you finish your snack, and I will watch and carry on thinking, like I usually do when on surveillance. It is good to have a break between running around, interviewing, and doing office duties.'

Percy answered, 'It is good to know we are on the same wavelength, James. It does get a bit tiring sometimes.'

*   *   *

James's phone rang an hour later. It was the chief of police, saying the warrant for the apartment was ready to be picked up. James told him they were on surveillance at the senior Choudhury home and asked if he would mind having a courier take the warrant to the office. They would be back that evening to pick it up.

The phone call woke Percy, and he said, 'That is good news. Well, it is better than nothing. But I personally think we are going to find Derek visiting here at his parents' house. He will have orders for the cocaine from yesterday at the jazz show and will come here to collect it for distribution.'

'My thoughts exactly, Percy. We are on the same wavelength—it must be all your teaching—and we are getting things together. We will wait for a little longer. It is almost afternoon teatime, so perhaps Derek will stop in to see his mother and have a cup of tea.'

They waited another half hour, until James said, 'This looks like his car. There would not be too many BMWs around this area.'

They watched as the car turned the corner and stopped in the Choudhury driveway. Derek got out of the car to enter the house.

Percy said, 'We should stay to see how long he is in there. Shall I get you a cup of coffee from that shop I see across the road?'

'That sounds like a good idea, Percy. I will give Ken a call after Derek leaves, and we can go directly to his apartment to meet Ken with the warrant. We will do our search, and hopefully Derek will have a dozen cocaine swatches in his pocket.'

'I hope that is just not wishful thinking, James. I will be back quickly with our coffee, and I will watch for you to signal so that I do not walk into the man as I come out of the coffee shop.'

All was clear for the coffee to be delivered, and they stayed another hour before Derek came out of the house and got into his car.

James remarked, 'He is leaving in time not to meet his father, it seems. Let's watch a little longer to see when the father comes home. It will be an indication that they are still estranged, I believe.'

Half an hour later, Derek's father came home. Percy turned to James and said, 'Are you a mind reader or something? You are spot on.'

'It makes sense. That is all it is. If Derek was leaving before his father arrived, it would have been timed as such. Therefore, he did not want to see his father,' said James with a grin.

They drove off towards the road where the apartment was situated, and they met Ken, who was waiting on the pavement outside. They went together into the foyer and pressed the button on the wall that denoted *Choudhury*. They waited a short period, then Derek's voice asked who was there. When James gave his name, they were able to enter the building proper and catch a lift to the penthouse.

When Derek opened the door to their knock, the entrance hall gave them a clue of what would be seen inside. It was elegant beyond anything they had seen before. The walls were painted white, and standing in the corner was a shiny tall black pot with a lush palm growing. There was a spotlight highlighting the beautiful leafy palm. Percy said, 'How do you get a palm tree growing in this climate?'

Derek grinned. 'It is centrally heated in here, with the heating at twenty-four degrees on a daily basis, and the palm thrives. I presume that if the central heating was turned off, it would die. I like the exotic appearance it has.'

As they moved into the large living room, they were stunned by the theme carried forward—white walls and black furniture. In the window space was a shiny black grand piano standing on a platform, opened to show the keys, with music sheets awaiting a player. It appeared as if Derek had got up from the piano to open the door. On the shiny white marbled floor were red rugs, strategically placed. The whole room was immaculate, with nothing out of place.

There was nothing Indian in this decor. It looked like something out of a magazine: very upmarket and trendy. James walked over to the window and saw that it overlooked the park across the road, with views of the city. Sitting on the piano seat must have felt like sitting in the gardens below, amongst the trees. It was so dramatic and beautiful. It was a wonderful setting for a musician.

Derek watched as the three men looked around, not saying anything, until James said, 'Wow, this is so beautiful.'

Derek smiled. 'I am so pleased you like it. How can I help you, gentlemen? You are obviously not here just to look at the view.'

'No, Derek, you are right. We are here with a warrant to search your apartment.'

'For what will you be searching, James? I cannot imagine I have anything here that you would want.'

'We are looking for evidence of cocaine, Derek, or any other drug that may be hidden.'

'Search anywhere you wish, James. You will not find any drugs here. I live a very clean life. I eat out a lot or have my meals delivered, but mainly this apartment is so that I can play my piano in peace and quiet without disturbing the neighbours. The walls are insulated, so the music does not leave this room. You are welcome to meet the neighbours if you wish to confirm this and the fact that I have never run amok, out of my head on drugs. They will testify to that as well.'

'All right, Derek, but this is a search to satisfy us that you are not dealing with drugs. We heard a rumour that you have used a drug in the past. We want to satisfy ourselves that that was in the past and that you are no longer dealing or using drugs. We will start by searching your person and move on to search the apartment.'

The three associates were watching Derek's face, but he showed no emotion at all. He shrugged and put his arms out and said, 'I have never used drugs. Get on with it. I reiterate that you are wasting your time.'

At that moment, James was cross with himself. He should have asked Jerry Jones where he could have acquired a sniffer dog. He was still learning how to operate with a search warrant and had not thought of using a dog to sniff out the cocaine. He would have to come back sometime and start again. As he was thinking this, his phone vibrated in his pocket. When he answered, he found himself talking to DI Paul Morris, who said, 'Alicia rang me to ask if I knew where we could get a sniffer dog. I have been out to the airport kennels and am now standing outside on the street, waiting for you to let me in. Am I too late?'

'Perfectly timed, Paul. I will ask Derek to open the door to admit you. His apartment is on the top floor.' He could not stop himself from grinning. What a wife and colleague he had! What timing! It could not have been better.

As Paul Morris walked in the door with the dog on a leash, James watched Derek's face and saw it blanch. He thought, *Aha, so we were not too wrong after all. There is cocaine somewhere in here.*

The dog walked straight over to the piano, and Derek yelled, 'Do not let that dog near the piano! It is a very special instrument, and I do not want it damaged.'

Paul turned to look at Derek and said, 'The dog will not damage the piano. Produce the cocaine you have stored in or around it, and we will leave.'

Derek walked over to the piano and moved a panel on the platform and took out the small parcels of cocaine stored there.

DI Paul Morris turned to Derek and read him his rights and handcuffed him after handing the dog leash to James. As Paul took Derek from the apartment, James asked, 'May I borrow the dog for an hour or two?'

Paul looked with interest at James and said, 'Will you return him to me later? I need to take the animal back to the kennels tonight.'

'I think an hour or two may be enough, perhaps sooner if I cannot make it work. I will keep in touch with you.'

'Okay, James, I know you lot have a lot more leeway than we do in the force, so I will take that into account. Give me a call when you are ready.'

As Detective Morris took Derek away, Percy asked, 'What is your plan, James? Are we going back to Derek's parents' house?'

'I know we do not have a warrant, but talking to Derek's father just might be enough. We do not need a warrant for that. If he lets us in and gives us permission to have a look around, we might find the dog essential to our search to make the man and his wife believe us. I think I should go alone and have you and Ken stand by initially. Is that okay with you two?'

Ken said, 'I am not sure what you are doing, but I will say that just talking to the man is not illegal, and if he is willing to show you around with the dog at your side, that is fair enough. We will wait outside until you call us in or come out.'

'Well, I for one want to see the rest of this apartment before we go. This room and entry hall are magnificent, and I am curious about the rest of it,' said James with a grin.

The other two looked hopeful, and James said, 'Come on, boys. We might find something else. We do have a warrant for this place.'

The kitchen was also done in white walls and cupboards, and the bench tops were black granite. The splashbacks over the sink and hotplates were a soft grey, with red poppies painted on over them. There was a dining setting, adjacent to the kitchen, in the same colours. Once again, it all made a dramatic effect. Down the hall were two bedrooms, the first with the same dramatic white walls, with a red eiderdown on the double bed and fluffy white pillows on either side. The wardrobes were mirrored doors. They looked inside and found women's clothing hanging and women's shoes on the floor. They looked at each other, and James said, 'I do not know what size Fiona Norman wears. Would you have any idea, Ken? You saw her at her house.'

Ken said, 'I am not too sure what sizes are, but she was tall and very slim—almost slinky, I would say. Kate is a medium size, so I think this woman may also be that, but slimmer, so maybe a small.' He held up a dress and said, 'Yes, I think that could be hers.'

There was an en-suite bathroom which had a door to the bedroom and a door to the passageway for visitors. Also, a toilet was just inside the passageway, next to the bedroom. The cabinets held women's make-up and perfume. A stack of fluffy towels were stored under a bench, on a shelf. The bench had a thin waterproof mattress on the top—obviously a massage table—close by. Everything looked very new and untouched.

The master bedroom was again in the black-and-white theme, with a white eiderdown and small red cushions over fluffy white pillows on the bed, but this time the walls were painted stark black. Over the large picture windows was a white blind with red poppies painted on the inside, facing the room. They looked out of the window and could see again the parkland, and as it was getting dark outside, they could see the city lights. It could only be described as magnificent. They looked into the wardrobes, and only men's clothing was inside, and men's shoes. An en-suite bathroom with a double sink and an upright Japanese-Jacuzzi stood next to the shower instead of a bath. Only men's cologne and shaving gear were in the cabinets. They looked around, and they saw a stack of fluffy towels behind a glass cupboard door that was as tall as the bathroom door. A toilet stood further back, behind another door.

James said, 'This is the tidiest and cleanest apartment or house I have ever seen. There is absolutely no clutter on any bench, no eiderdown or cushion askew, no drops of water in the bathroom. It is almost obscenely clean and tidy. Most single men are untidy or messy. This is the opposite. It looks as if it is straight out of a *Homes & Gardens* magazine. I have also noticed that the dog has not pointed to any area, so there are no more packets of cocaine here. I think we are done here, mates. We will move on to the parents' house.'

Percy said as they were going down in the lift after locking the apartment door, 'After seeing where Derek lives, it does make you wonder what sort of man he is. There is nothing about him that I have ever come across previously. He is a "one of" type of person for sure. I have never seen such an apartment and the way it is kept. It is almost like he expected visitors, so he tidied up.'

James said, 'Yes, it does look that way, but I think he is normally a clean and tidy person. He always looks immaculately dressed. We must ask his mother if he has always been like that.'

Ken affirmed the conversation. 'It is most unusual to find a house or flat as clean and unlived in as that. Yes, that is the word—*unlived in*. Don't you think?'

Percy and James both said together, 'Yes, that is a good description.'

Percy drove with James in the car, and Ken followed in the other car to Derek's parents' house. James went to the front door with the dog, and the others sat in the cars, waiting for his word to come in or leave. A knock at the door soon brought Mr Choudhury to answer.

James introduced himself and gave the man a business card and asked if he could come in for a chat. When Mr Choudhury stepped aside to let him in, James asked if he could bring the dog in with him. The affable man looked a little disconcerted and then shrugged and led James and the dog inside.

Mrs Choudhury had evidently just finished in the kitchen after the evening meal; the house smelt of a fragrant curry. She greeted James as if she knew him and sat down and patted the dog, which went to her for the biscuit she held in her hand.

'I suppose you are always greeted with this question, Mr Armstrong, but why are you here?' said the harassed-looking man. 'Is this something to do with our son?'

'Yes, sir. Derek was arrested this evening for having drugs in his possession. Not a small amount. We were following him today on the advice of a drug squad member. We waited outside your house this afternoon when he arrived, and we followed him back to his apartment, where we accosted him with the drugs. We believe he picked it up here from your house.'

Mr Choudhury went red in the face. 'We do not allow drugs in our house, sir. We do not believe in drugging people without cause.' He turned to his wife and said something in another language. She went white and nodded at what must have been the question of 'Did Derek visit with you today?' When asked about drugs, she shook her head.

'How did you come to believe Derek has drugs?' he asked. 'We thought he had only done something once, and he promised he would not be doing it again.'

'I do not believe Derek is taking drugs himself. He seems too rational to me,' said James. 'But we believe he is holding drugs and selling them on behalf of some other person.'

'And you have proof of this?'

'Yes, sir. We met him at his beautiful apartment, and Rosco here'— he pointed at the dog—'found the cocaine in seconds. It was not a large amount, but it was big enough for him to be taken to the police department to be held overnight. If you will allow it, Rosco can prove one way or the other whether Derek has stored the remaining cache in this house.

'It is better to know than to go on wondering if I am speaking the truth. Rosco is an airport entry dog and smells drugs from some distance away, on luggage and passengers, and will let us know when he finds something. Really, we are only jumping the gun a little, because we can ask a magistrate to issue us with a warrant to search your house and grounds. I felt it was better this way, to come quietly to your house to ask for entry and a search. The alternative would have had the neighbours all putting their heads over the fence or walking by to see what is happening. Also, we did not arrive in police cars. We have our own private vehicles.' He went on, looking at Derek's mother, who looked very flustered and upset. 'May I ask, Mrs Choudhury, which areas of the house Derek went to today?'

'My wife is overcome,' said Mr Choudhury. 'We cannot believe our son would put us in this position. I will ask her in our home language. We speak in our own Punjab dialect in the house when we are alone.'

'Thank you, sir,' said James politely. 'I am sorry to bring this to your notice. We believe Derek is under the spell of a dubious woman who had access to cocaine and needed somewhere else to store it when the drug squad came to her house to search it. Perhaps Derek is only helping her out, but it looks bad for him. We need to get to the bottom of it.'

He stopped talking, to allow time for the husband to speak to his wife. When they both stood up, James stood too, holding the leash of Rosco, following them from the sitting room to the kitchen, where they said Derek had sat talking to his mother. They then moved to the toilet and bathroom, and then down the passageway and up the stairs to Derek's former bedroom.

Mrs Choudhury said to James, 'Derek always asks if he can pray before his shrine before he leaves the house. He did have a bag in his hands. I did not question it, because he often brings his old books here and picks up new ones for his coaching at the university.'

As soon as Rosco entered the room, he went and stood beside the shrine, with his head pointing to the back of the box-like base. He did not move, and James said, 'May I have your permission to move the shrine?'

The older couple looked devastated, and Mr Choudhury moved forward and helped James move the idols and candles from the top of the box before turning the box around for them to see bundles of cocaine piled high inside it.

'What a sorry day this is for us,' the father said, while the mother burst into tears.

She said, 'I am very sorry to see this day. All our hopes have been dashed for the sake of a woman who will leave him when he is arrested and not acknowledge him again.'

James felt sympathy towards the crying woman and said, 'I think you have read this right. He is such a brilliant fellow. I am sorry to bring him down. I have a few questions to ask you about his life and what sort of boy he was, but I can call and see you, if you need time, perhaps tomorrow? Rosco needs to be fed and taken back to the kennels. I will call in my men to take this cocaine back to the police station after I make a couple of calls so they know we are coming, or perhaps the policemen can meet us here. If you are feeling upset, I can have a policewoman or such to keep you company. In fact, thinking things over, that is a good idea. We would not like this woman to find out we have her stash yet. There could be repercussions from her. A policewoman standing by to help you through the trauma is a good idea.'

James called Percy and Ken and said, 'We will watch over this lot here until the police squad arrive, so come in. I will open the door for you. I will call Paul Morris to have a crew move the cocaine out, and he can take the dog back to the kennel.' He looked down at the dog and said, 'I would like a dog like this. It saves us a lot of work.'

When he rang Paul Morris, he was asked, 'Doing something illegal, are you? But then you are not a policeman, so you can get around the rules.'

'Wait one minute, Paul. It is not illegal to knock on a door and ask if we can have a chat. That is all we did. I was very polite, and these are charming people who are intelligent and were ready to be helpful when I asked if we could have Rosco have a look around. Nothing to it.'

Paul laughed. 'Do you know what hoops I would have had to jump through if I just "had a chat" and found a pile of cocaine without a warrant?'

James laughed. 'Okay, matey, get the police chappies to bring a van to carry this lot. Good old Gerald was not hanging back when he did his daily scoop of the warehouse at customs.'

He turned to Mr Choudhury. 'As a precaution, we will guard the cocaine until the police arrive, and they will take it away. When the police arrive, I will ask if they can organise for a woman policeperson to stay with you for a few days. The woman Derek has become entangled with is an unknown quantity so far, but not for long. We will go after her now that we know the cocaine has been confirmed. We have had dealings with her brother and her husband—not nice people to know— in the past, so we will be judging our dealings with her as if they are still with her. We believe they are speaking behind her from their jail cells. All the same, I would not like her to turn up here and be belligerent to you. Do you have somewhere else to stay for a while until this is sorted?'

'Yes, we have an apartment attached to our offices, where we put people up occasionally when they arrive in town for business. It is vacant at the moment, so we can go there. I do not think it is a well-known location. It has always been a business secret. I am not sure if Derek is aware of it to pass the news on.'

'That sounds like the place to go. Perhaps we can have our chat about Derek's childhood and teenage years whilst we are awaiting the police van's arrival. Is there anything in his past to show why he is going off the rails? We went to his apartment today, as we said, and we were amazed by how clean and tidy it all was—not a thing out of place. Amazing for a young man to be so tidy. Has he always been like that?'

The mother said, 'Yes, he has always been neat and extra smart compared to other students. He was always the top of his classes. He is our only child, so we do not have anyone to compare him with to gauge his behaviour. He has been absorbed in his piano since an early age, and he was not a child that needed others' company. I thought I was very close to him, and that is why I am so disappointed in him. It seems the only reason he visited was to pick up those terrible drugs, not to see me.' She started to cry again.

'No, he was picking up drugs, but he did come to see you. You must keep that in your heart. He did stay for a chat. We noticed that he left your home before your husband came home. Is that normal for him?'

'Yes, there was a bit of trouble a while back and a big argument between father and son. I did not interfere, because I thought it would blow over in time. I was sorry he moved out of our home. His weekly calls have made up for me not seeing him every day, but I thought of it as a chicken-leaving-the-egg situation. While he kept coming to see me, I was happy.'

Her husband came back into the room and said to her, 'I have packed a few things to take with us. Would you like to do the same? I think we should leave as soon as the police take the cocaine away. I do not like the sound of that woman.' He sat down where his wife had been sitting and said, 'We all have secrets in our past. I would like to tell you mine. It may help with your assessment of Derek.

'We have always been extra careful in our marriage arrangements. It is such a populated country where I came from, and you could get into trouble marrying the wrong person. That is why we choose marriage consultants. They do a full history of the backgrounds of bride and groom. My father fell in love with a beautiful, very intelligent, and gifted girl while he was at university, and he married her, against his parents' wishes. What he was unaware of was that in her lineage, there was a dark secret. Her family was hiding the secret that early dementia was likely to crop up. It did not trap everyone in the generation. It was as if it took the smartest and most talented people in the family, and unfortunately, it chose my mother.

'She was the sweetest and most unlikely person for it to take. She won honours in science. She played the piano like Derek. She was a lovely person, and she was very beautiful.' He got up and took a photograph of his mother from the wall to show James. 'This is my mother and father's wedding photo. They make a handsome couple and were obviously very much in love.

'I have not had any symptoms, but I have been told that it can jump a generation. Of course, that is Derek's generation. We have watched for signs of it, and until this year, we have not had to worry about him. However, he has started to grow secretive. He has turned more towards his music. These are all signs my mother had at first. At times she was normal, and then suddenly she could turn on someone. She had to give up her job as a university science professor because, although she had the science in her head, she started to forget who her students were and what time her lectures were. She would turn up very early in the morning although she had an afternoon lecture to deliver. Things became awkward when she hit a janitor who asked her to move on one morning, and she was asked to resign.

'From that moment, things went from bad to worse, until she strangled a girl who was trying to help her in our house. My father had engaged the young woman to be a watchdog, I suppose you could say, but I like to think she was a nursemaid. Anyway, Mother's reasoning was calmly given by her to the police, who were called. "She was annoying me by spying on me." The police placed her under arrest, and she was taken to a mental division. There she died six months later. She was only fifty years old and looked 100 by that time, as the dementia did not creep up on her—it galloped.

'I was already married, and we had Derek, who was several months old, before my mother started to show any symptoms to us. So we vowed not to have any more children who might also have the dementia gene. As I said, we have watched Derek carefully. He does not seem like other boys of his age. He seems older, and we have worried, in case he shows other patterns.'

'Is it possible that Derek could push a girl through a plate-glass window and show no emotion?' asked James.

Derek's father looked shocked. 'You suspect Derek of the Patel girl's death?' he asked.

'It has crossed my mind, sir, I am sorry to say. He was at the showroom that day and was there at the time of Anaya's fall. He acknowledged that he knew the girl and told us she had been stalking him. Is that reason enough to push her off her ladder for her to fall to her death on the floor of the mall.'

Mr Choudhury was trembling. 'This is the first I have heard this sample of events. I did know that he delivered some clothing to the showroom that morning, but no one mentioned that he was there other than that. If the dementia is starting to come through in Derek, it is a possibility. My mother hit a janitor with a broom handle and injured his head for only being asked to move while he swept the floor. She was a little older than Derek is at the time that happened, perhaps ten years. However, of course, we do not know everything that happened with her. She may have had episodes earlier than that. We only know about that one because the university asked her to resign. She became very secretive, and there is a lot we do not know. I suppose too that the dementia can start at any age. I have researched early dementia, and not everybody that has it is violent.

'My mother was not usually violent. It was as if she was confused some of the time, and something would upset her enough to make the acts of violence when she was particularly confused. She had hidden the moments of dementia for a long time before we realised what was happening. We thought it was an old person's disease. We did not recognise it for a long while. She was still young, we thought, and we put her moments of confusion down to overwork at the university, until it came to our attention that the university had asked her to leave because she was not coping. We were unaware of the janitor incident until the man asked for compensation from my father.

'After leaving the university, she went downhill very quickly. Derek is aware of his grandmother's illness and the reason for her early demise. I wonder if it is playing on his mind. That could be the reason for his compulsive cleaning and tidiness, trying to keep it away through constant movement. He has always played the piano, as she did until the end. The dementia never seemed to make her forget the music. Otherwise, except for him staying away from us, he seems normal. But you have made me wonder about the Patel girl. My mother seemed to be unaware of what she did to the janitor and housemaid, as if it was wiped from her memory as soon as it happened. I do not want to think of Derek having done that.'

Mr Choudhury stopped speaking and stared into space, looking absolutely exhausted. James patted the man's hands and said, 'I will ask the medical team at the police station to have a good look at your son and give him some tests. This conversation has opened up more questions than we have prepared answers for, so we will keep you informed along the way.'

There was a knock on the door, and James got up and opened it for the police team, headed by Paul Morris. James introduced Paul to Mr Choudhury, then led the police team upstairs to Derek's room, where Percy and Ken and Rosco were waiting for them. Paul, along with the others, was amazed by the pile of packets of cocaine stored in the box, and they carried the box out of the room and down the stairs into the police van. Paul came back and asked the exhausted Mr Choudhury to sign some paperwork. He had photographed the cocaine in the bedroom and now took a photo of the man signing its consignment.

The elderly man thanked the policemen and James for their politeness, and he turned to James. 'You have conducted yourself in a very decent manner, James. Thank you for your explanations of our son, and I look forward to seeing and hearing from you in the future. It has lightened my heart somewhat to be able to tell you our story, and I hope it will make the assessment of Derek easier. It is not a subject we share with anyone normally, but this is a different time. I think it needs the explanation.'

'I will certainly keep in touch from time to time, sir. Thank you for your time,' answered James.

Outside the front door, Paul said, 'You seem to have won a heart there, old chap. I continue to be amazed by how you do it, but you certainly get results. Keep up the good work.'

James laughed. 'Do you mind if I hand Rosco over to you now, to return him to the kennel? He is an amazing asset to have around. I have to confess, I am hungry. Percy and I have only had one snack all day, so we will faint with hunger if we do not go home for something to keep us going. Alicia will be pacing the floor, trying to find out where we have been. Even Granny will be pacing. Percy and I left the office around eleven this morning and have not been able to make contact all day.'

'Your wife did well to ring me this afternoon to ask about a sniffer dog, James. Was that your idea?'

'It was all Alicia's idea. Perhaps it was thought transference, because I was standing there in front of Derek, thinking I needed a sniffer dog to help us out, and you rang the doorbell. How good was that for timing? She is an exceptional help in the business,' said James.

'Will I see you in the morning for the interview with Derek, James?' asked Paul.

'Alicia and I can be there at nine in the morning, Paul. We will both want to question him now that we know a little more about him. Although it might make a big difference to what he has to say if we take him to our office and have a quiet "chat" with him. In our office, the others listen in as well, and I leave the door open so they can hear clearly. Then we all know what is happening. It helps with our investigation to be able to chat after an interview, to find out what each person got from the story. Some good ideas come out of it, and it is easier than having everyone read about things from the reports. We are all working the case together, but we do not want him feeling outnumbered by people in the office—hence the open door.'

Paul laughed. 'I am not sure that is legal, James. These interviews are supposed to be confidential, and you could be sued for sharing.'

'It is no more or less confidential than a tape recorder going in the room. I will ask at the beginning if he minds if we record the session. If he says that he objects, then I will not record it and will close the door. I have had no objections so far. I think from watching television shows, everyone expects to be recorded,' said James.

'Yes, your chats tend to work out well. I agree with that. After we have our own chat first with Derek at the station, I will bring him to your office. I would like to listen in to one of your chats. I might learn something.'

James got into his car, laughing at Paul's expression. 'You are welcome, Paul. Nice doing business with you.'

*   *   *

As soon as he entered the street where the bookshop was located on the corner, James gave a great sigh. Percy said, 'I feel that way myself, James. I am looking forward to a nice cup of tea.'

'It is so nice to come home to the bookshop and house here, Percy. I appreciate how close it is to our office, making life very convenient for us,' said James.

CHAPTER EIGHT

The team was excited next morning, waiting to hear what Derek had to say. Kate had her notepad and pen waiting for her on the table in the entrance, to take notes. The others went to their own offices, waiting until Derek arrived, but everyone was too excited to concentrate on anything else. Ken approached James and asked, 'How do you plan to manage the interview, James?'

James grinned and said, 'I will ask any questions as they come to mind. I do not like to be locked in one way or another. I find it closes up conversations. I will ask a few questions to get the client started, and I will follow where he leads me.'

'Ah,' said Percy, 'that is your strategy. I have wondered how you do it. Whatever it is, you always seem to come out on top.'

'I thought you were aware of my little presentations by now, Percy. There really is no strategy. Mostly it is just common sense. You try to get the person onside if you can, and they come out with the things you want to know, with surprising ease.' James laughed.

Ken said, 'It is the one thing about policing I felt I was not good at. Everybody recognises me as a policeman, and by then, they are already sitting ready to say "no comment" to every question I ask.'

'I can see your point, Ken. I had quite a lot of that too in my days. I blame the copper TV shows which all the crims try to copy and which make them say "no comment",' said Percy. 'James here has a different technique altogether, so "listen and learn" is my advice. It works particularly well with juveniles, I have noticed.'

At ten o'clock, the door opened, and Paul Morris came in with Derek. Although Derek had spent the night in a cell, he still looked neat and tidy. James wondered how he did it.

Alicia greeted the two men with a happy smile and said, 'Hullo, Paul and Derek. Just in time for morning tea or coffee, whatever your preference, and I have brought from home my nicest teacake, still hot from the oven. What is your drink preference, Paul?'

'Coffee for me, please, Alicia, and a piece of that cake sounds nice,' said Paul.

'And you, Derek? Do you prefer tea or coffee?' asked Alicia.

'I prefer tea, please, Mrs Armstrong. Black and one sugar, thank you.'

'Coming up, chaps. Take a seat in the boardroom, and I will be right in to sit with you,' said Alicia. 'I am going to be holding your hand, Derek, for the interview today. James never gets rough when interviewing, so you can relax. That is why we had you brought here rather than to a police interview. We have seen grown men break down and cry when they are interviewed by the police. We will not make you go through that.'

'Thank you, Mrs Armstrong, for your assurances. I must admit, when I woke up in the cell this morning, I felt like crying. I think I am over that feeling now,' said Derek with relief.

When the morning tea session was over, James gathered the file on the cases on to his desk and said, 'Do you want to join us, Paul, if Derek does not mind?'

Derek said, 'I do not mind. Detective Morris has been very kind to me so far. Do you think we will be finished by midday? I have a math tutorial at one o'clock. If I am not going to make it, I would like to send a text to my professor, if that is possible.'

James looked at his watch. 'Perhaps, Derek. It really depends on you and your answers to our questions. You can text your professor later if we look like we will be running overtime.'

'Okay, that is fair. What do you want to know? First of all, I would like to say that the stash of cocaine is not mine. I have been asked to hold on to it by an acquaintance until she finds a better place for it. She said this at the time she asked me if I could hold it for her.'

'Your acquaintance, Derek, is Fiona Norman?' asked James.

'How do you know that, James? Fiona said it was a big secret that she is holding for someone else, but because she has to move out of her house within twelve months, she needed a temporary hiding place.' Derek only looked interested, not flustered, at this stage.

'I will tell you a story, Derek. It is a very interesting story. Last year, Fiona's husband, Gerald, called me and asked if I would help him out with a problem in the customs house storage area, where he was manager. Percy and I went along with him, until we decided that something fishy *was* happening and that Gerald was a part of it. He pretended he knew nothing about an intended heist so as to stay in his job, which would have meant that he would be in place for more cocaine to come to the customs department in the future.

'We sat in wait, and with the help of Detective Morris, we were able to hold up the van carrying a million pounds' worth of cocaine. Unfortunately, in the process, we were unable to stop the killing, by Fiona's brother, of two men and the wounding of another man. These men were forced into helping him load the cocaine into the van. All this was aided and abetted by Fiona's husband. Once more, we suspected that Gerald Norman had ferreted away some of the cocaine for himself. That is the cocaine found in your parents' house. Fiona had taken over Gerald's job of selling the cocaine with the help of the two young men who were found murdered. Now we have the cocaine. Incidentally, the reason Fiona had to find a new place for it is that the government has taken her house as proceeds from crime. Because she has two young children, they have allowed her to rent the house back, because of the children's schooling, for a period of twelve months, to allow her time to resettle the family.

'Did you know anything about all this, Derek?'

He could tell by the look on Derek's face that he did not know anything of this story. He appeared to be in shock.

James did not allow him to get over his shock. He pressed on. 'We are now looking for the killers of those two young Indian men. Did you kill them, Derek, so that you could take over their patch to sell the cocaine for Fiona? There must have been a good commission paid for the sales. Your apartment looks very expensive. Did you need the cocaine money to purchase it? We believe that the rape drug was given to the boys to hold them still enough for the stabbing frenzy. You had used that drug before, hadn't you, Derek?'

'Hang on, James, you are totally on the wrong path here.' Derek was unnerved. 'Perhaps I had better go back a bit and explain some details. You are talking about the raping of a young woman found on the hospital steps. Am I right?'

James nodded. 'Yes, I believe your father paid out a large sum of money to keep that young woman from going to the police.'

'James, that was a scam.' Derek spoke earnestly, looking at James. 'When I left school, I rented a flat in the commercial area, where our group could practise our music at night and no one would be bothered by the noise. All sorts of singers and musicians turned up when they heard about it, wanting to have an audition to join our band. One night, someone found a girl unconscious inside the house, near the doorway. We were panic-stricken. Instead of calling an ambulance like we should have, we put her in my car, and I took her to the hospital. It was not my idea to leave her on the steps. The others in the car took her out. I thought they were taking her into the emergency room, but suddenly they were back in the car and saying "drive".

'We were all only eighteen or nineteen and straight out of school, and we were not experienced in drugs and such. It was a disturbing time for us when we found her, not knowing what was wrong. We did not know she was drugged. She was scarcely breathing and unconscious. We thought she was close to death. That is why we panicked. She was a complete stranger to all of us, we agreed at the time.

'When the girl eventually woke up in hospital several days later, she willingly told me that it was a scam to get money. She had taken the drug herself, but she miscalculated the dose and nearly killed herself. She laughed about it to me when I was taken in to see her in the hospital, where she was sitting up in bed, enjoying the luxury of everyone running around her. When she was interviewed by the authorities, she changed her tune and said that it was me who gave her the drug and raped her. I was absolutely flummoxed. I had never seen her before that night.

'My father, of course, was very upset by this information and paid the girl five thousand pounds and made her sign a statement to say she would drop charges against me. I tried to argue with my father that it was not me, that she had done it to herself, but he did not believe me. Everyone I tried to talk about it with seemed against me. Nobody interviewed the members of my band, who could have confirmed I was innocent. I had not left them all night because we were concentrating on some new tunes. I admit that we did not have the door locked and anyone could come in, but we thought it was okay because we knew most of the chaps who called around from school. In the end, I threw my hands up in the air and said, "You believe her over me. Go ahead and pay her if you want, but I know I am innocent."

'If you have spoken at length to my father about me, I am sure you are now aware of the early dementia condition I am likely to inherit. Dad looks at me as if it is going to break out any day. This is so hard to live with. I feel as if I am under a microscope each time I see him. That is why I purchased the apartment when I turned twenty-one, with the inheritance left to me by my grandmother. I do not need to sell cocaine for a living. I inherited a very large sum when I turned twenty-one. My grandmother came from a wealthy family.

'He would have told you of the violence of his mother in the latter stages of her illness. It has not applied to me yet. I have no signs that it will get me. I am completely normal at this stage in my life. I do not know what life has in store for me yet. It could change, but no one can look into the future. I feel that nothing is hanging over me at the present. My father was desperately unhappy about what happened to his mother. He adored her and was stunned to have the dementia take over her so quickly at such a young age, and he does not want it to happen to me. I understand that, but surely I would recognise symptoms if they turned up. So far, there is nothing to worry about that I can see.

'There is another thing I do know. I did not kill Anaya by pushing her through a window, and I did not kill those young men. That's all, folks, believe it or not. Everyone seems to think I am a monster, but I can assure them I am not. I am only a normal young person trying to do the best I can.' Derek sat back in his chair and looked at the others around the table.

They were all astounded by the forthright manner with which he told his story, but there were more questions to be asked. Alicia said to Derek, 'You sound reassuring, but you have not told us yet how you came to have a large amount of cocaine hidden in your parents' home.'

He cocked an eyebrow at her and said, 'I am minding it for an acquaintance. I did say that when James asked, and it is true.'

Alicia had not finished, and Derek was starting to annoy her. 'What kind of friend would ask you to hold that much illegal substance for her? When did you meet Fiona Norman?'

'I am sorry, you are right. Fiona is not a friend. She thinks she knows things about me. She does know things, such as the rape charge and that I was at the shop before Anaya's death and I caused it. They are both untrue. However, she stated that she would think up some more charges and bandy them around the university campus if I did not hold the box of cocaine for her. I believed her. She has a convincing manner about her, and I could imagine how cruel she would be if I did not follow her orders.'

'How did you meet her, Derek, and how long ago?' Alicia persisted.

'She has been coming to my jazz show on and off for about a year. The first time I met her, she told me that Flora McDonald, who was my fake-rape charger, is her youngest sister. Her real name she would not tell me, or I would pursue her now that I am older and can employ a lawyer, for which I was too young at the time of the incident. Flora McDonald is a name obvious to me now, a fake. I thought I may be able to make Fiona break down and tell me the truth on all that, but she is "a canny woman", as she calls herself. I would like to clear my name.'

'And how long have you had the cocaine, Derek?' asked James.

'Since soon after Anaya's death. I did not think of it as curious timing until I heard of the two young men who were murdered about that time, and I wondered if they were linked. I am in a hard place now, James. You have the cocaine. Fiona is going to think I told you where it was, and she will come after me. I suspect she killed the boys. She was very chummy with them when I saw them together at the jazz shows. I think she now thinks of me as their replacement.

'In a way, I am glad it is now out in the open, but I request a bodyguard. I think she is a crazy woman who will stop at nothing. I even suspect that she was the one who pushed Anaya out of the showroom window. I have not been able to work out how she did it, or I would have screamed blue murder by now. I do not know how to get her out of my hair.'

Paul Morris asked, 'How did you get the cocaine, Derek? Did she hand it over to you? It is a little large for her to handle.'

'She had it delivered by post, would you believe? I came home from a two-day walking trip and found it in the foyer of my apartment. When I asked the manager of my building how it got there, he told me the postal delivery people rang his doorbell to let them in to place the delivery inside, out of the weather. It had been a wet week. The manager signed the delivery form on my behalf. That was a Wednesday, end of semester at the university, and I had organised the walk to celebrate because all the students I had helped passed their exams. On Friday evening, Fiona asked me to take her to my apartment after the music finished. She wanted to make sure the package arrived safely. She then told me that if I reported it to the police, she would say that it was my cocaine and that she knew nothing about it. I was to bring her a small quantity, which she would tell me each Sunday, to the Friday night shows to give to her. I was in her clutches. She was blackmailing me with things I had not done, and I was frightened to say no to her.'

'Has Fiona come to your apartment at any time, Derek?' asked James.

'No way!' said Derek explosively. 'I try to have as little to do with her as I can. She gives me the creeps. Even that day, I did not let her past the foyer.'

'When we checked the rest of your apartment with the dog, we noticed women's clothing and cosmetics in the second bedroom. Who do they belong to, Derek?'

'They are Aisha's things. She and I had a discussion about our wedding, to be held in two months' time. I suggested to her that, for her own benefit, before the wedding ceremony gets too close, she should come and spend some time in my apartment to see if we could get on together. I felt it was unfair for her to move into my apartment with my things distributed about, fully knowing about my possible future health and that we should not have children ourselves. I wanted to be as fair as I could for the girl. She has been twice now, for two days at a time, and so far there are no regrets. We seem to get on well together. We will extend to three days soon and then four, and by then, it will be time to send out the invitations, as we should know by then if we are compatible. This is with her parents' permission.'

The group looked at each other, and James asked, 'Does anyone have any more questions?'

They all shook their heads, and James said, 'We are letting you go for now, Derek, but do not disappear on us. We may need more information. We will be in touch daily to make sure you are safe. You will be all right until Friday night, as Fiona does not know yet that we have her stash. You have time for lunch, and you will get to your classes on time today. We have told no one about picking you up with cocaine. Only us and your parents know, so you should be safe for a while. If you can think of anything that could help us, give us a call. Meanwhile, take care. I will ask Percy to drive you back to your apartment to save you from having to explain the police car to your neighbours.'

Percy had gone out on a job, so Kate volunteered to drive Derek home. James agreed. Maybe Derek would break down and tell Kate something he had not mentioned in the office.

It was time to work out how they were going to approach Fiona Norman. It was not going to be an easy interview. There were several ways they could go about it—go to her home, bring her to the office, or the best bet, arrest her and take her to the police station. James asked the team for suggestions. After all, they were all more experienced than he was.

Paul Morris had the first say. 'I think we need a warrant to search her home again. We need to look for some sort of proof. So far it has all been hearsay. We have the cocaine but only Derek's word that it belongs to Fiona, so we need to find where it was stored previously, the postal receipt to prove that she had it delivered to Derek's apartment, any written notes about her customers, things like that. After that, we could interview her.'

James said, 'Good, notable things, Paul. What do you think, Percy?'

Percy looked up; he had just arrived back in the office. 'I have made some notes here.' He held up his notepad. 'I agree, we need to see the postal delivery receipt. We could find that by talking to the apartment manager to find which date it was delivered on and then approach the post office. I would bet though that she gave a false name for her commission of it. As Derek said, she thinks she is a canny lady. We need to catch her out. It would be better for us if we could find the delivery note in her house. The other note I made was about Fiona's boast that it was her younger sister who was the Flora McDonald in Derek's story of drug rape. We have to find her to verify that, and it could be seen to that the sister be arrested for false testimony and theft of money not due to her.'

'Ken, what do you think?' asked James.

'All of the above, James.' He paused to think. 'Have we anything to tie Fiona up with those two young men and Anaya? We seem to have swerved off the path a bit to concentrate on the direction Derek wants us to go, and it is now all about the cocaine. Was that intended by him, do you think?'

'What about you, Alicia? What are your thoughts on it?' asked James.

'I think it is all about timing, James. There were some anomalies between Iris Kumah and Aisha's accounts in the timing when they met in the mall after Anaya fell. We now know that Derek was in the showroom at the time Anaya fell, but he claims he did not know about it. And then we have a photo of Fiona in the mall at the time also. At the moment, we could put their names in a bowl and ask someone to draw one out. We are no closer than we were three days ago, except we have the cocaine. What if it was all about the cocaine? Only Iris has mentioned seeing the two boys, but what if they were in the mall to meet Fiona? They had been selling cocaine for her since we do not know when—again, not proven.

'I want to tell you what I think. I do not mind if you shoot me down, but we are getting in a mess with all these different directions we are going in. Perhaps we should ask Derek to wear a wire when Fiona approaches him on Friday night, and we can listen in and then arrest her rather than go to her house earlier.

'What if Fiona had seen Anaya in the jazz show attendance each time she sat at a table and waited for Derek? She had been going to dismiss the two boys from selling her drugs because they were not selling it fast enough, so she decided to sell it herself. But she needed somewhere to store her cocaine to keep suspicion from herself. Derek seemed the most likely candidate, and she tried to get closer to him. Derek told her he was not interested in an affair and that he was going to be married shortly. She saw Anaya and presumed that Anaya was the person Derek was marrying. Anaya was attending all the shows, and Derek had driven her home after them. This could be presumed quite easily by someone who did not know them well, because they were both Indian.

'Fiona went to the mall to see the two young men, looked up, and saw what they were looking at. She ran up the escalator and pushed Anaya through the window. It would only have taken a few minutes. She did not know Derek was there until she returned again to the ground floor. She saw him come out of the lift, and another opportune moment appeared to her. She could blackmail Derek, saying she had seen him in the showroom. She went back down to see the boys, and they said they saw her in the window, pushing Anaya, and they had taken a photo of her. They asked her to pay them blackmail and possibly asked for more of the cocaine. This sounded their death knell. Fiona came from a violent family. Who knows whether her planning had not been there in the other deaths put down to her brother?

'She knew about the rape drug. Her sister had taken it to perform the charge Derek was supposed to be guilty of, and once again, she obtained it to drug the boys and to kill them and search their flat to remove any drugs they may have hidden and any evidence that she and Gerald were associated with them. After all that, she had enough to blackmail Derek into helping her, and you know the rest.'

She stopped and looked around her. Each man was gazing at her, not open-mouthed but stunned to have it laid out for them like that.

Percy said, 'Valerie said it was a woman we should be looking for, and that story sounds feasible. But how to prove it?'

James said, 'Bravo, Alicia. A good story. What do you think we need to prove it?'

Paul and Ken sat looking pensive, and Ken said, 'Once again, it is all about timing, as Alicia says. What time was that photo of Fiona in the mall taken?'

James went through the photographs and stated, 'Twelve thirty. The fall was twelve fifteen, and the police and paramedics arrived twelve twenty-five. Does anyone remember the time Aisha went down for the lunches?'

Alicia looked up. 'Yes, she left the showroom at twelve ten, it said in the police report, and Aisha confirmed that to me in her interview. Her statement seems to be correct—that she went to the coffee shop, not seeing Mrs Kumah and the boys sitting outside in the mall, and picked up the lunches, coming out of the coffee shop just after she heard the crash of Anaya falling. When it is a busy time such as lunchtime, you can miss seeing people eating outside or even inside if you are in a hurry. She ran into Mrs Kumah near the escalator about then as she left the coffee shop. At that stage, Aisha was unaware that Anaya had fallen and that it was her lying on the floor, because a crowd had gathered around the body. I can imagine the shock for her when she went into the showroom and saw the gaping window and no sign of Anaya. In Kate's report, she was unable to control her tears.'

Paul said, 'I will ring the forensics and see if they have a CCTV and if they have a view of Fiona arriving in the mall. Perhaps we will see what time she arrived and left. They should have those details, but it may take some time to find her, one person in a crowd.'

Percy, sitting quietly, was thinking things over and announced, 'I think we should get a warrant to search her place soon rather than wait for a while. We have nothing to lose and everything to gain by confronting her before she finds out that we arrested Derek. We have more chances of leading her to confess something that will give us a move on her. I know you have her down as canny, but she may show something when we tell her that we have her cocaine in custody.'

James admitted, 'I am not experienced in this sort of case, but I would like to come along to see how it is done. Who do you think would do a good job, Percy? We have some talent here to choose from. I for one think you should be part of the team, Percy. Who else volunteers?'

Ken and Paul looked at each other, and Paul said, 'I think the Gray and Armstrong team are the best to do this, but because it is a woman, it should be either Kate or Alicia, to see what she does. Maybe they can prompt her.'

Ken said, 'I know Kate will be itching to be in the team. However, Alicia has a greater imagination and could outdo anything Fiona comes up with.'

'All right,' said James. 'The rest of us can be in the searching team, while Kate, Percy, and Alicia do the questioning. I have great faith in Alicia's questioning, and the other two know the methods of what and when to ask. And I agree, Ken, Kate should be in at the end. It was her case in the beginning. We will be searching while they are interviewing, so if they need help, we will be around.

'Well, that is decided. Is tomorrow good for all of you? You too, Paul. You have been in this case from the beginning, when Gerald rang me to give him an alibi. We are all involved, really, and I hope we can finish it off, including the three murders. We should have an answer on the CCTV of Fiona at the mall by tomorrow, and we will be set to go first thing, before she goes out. I would hate to miss her because she went shopping.'

They all laughed, keyed up because they wanted answers and perhaps could ferret them out. At that moment, Kate walked in the door after delivering Derek and said, 'What is so funny?' Ken explained the search and interviewing the next day, and an enormous smile from Kate showed that she was thrilled by the thought of tying up the ends of her case.

Alicia announced that she was going to do more research on the Haskell family and went off to her computer.

Percy said he wanted to do surveillance of Fiona's house to see what she does in her day. He went off to the garage to collect his car.

Ken and Kate opted to go through all the details in the file to see if they missed anything.

James was left sitting at the table, looking at the board and mentally counting their options. Had they missed something? He still did not feel comfortable with what they had. Something was missing, and he could not see what it was. Although he was sure Fiona was the one involved in the cocaine trade, he was not positive about the rest of Alicia's what-if story. He made up his mind and rang Paul Morris to say, 'While you are looking at CCTV records, could you confirm if Iris Kumah's timing is correct too?'

Paul said, 'I have no idea what Iris Kumah looks like. You had better come over and help me on this.'

'Okay, Paul, I will be right over. I do not seem to be able to settle my mind on Alicia's what-if story. It seems too constrictive in the timing, although I am not giving up on it, just looking for alternatives at the moment.'

'It is always best to think around the subject, James. Come on down, and you may see something that you consider interesting.'

He went to Alicia and asked if she had found anything yet, and when she said no, he told her he was going to look at the CCTV for the day in question. She turned to him and said, 'While you are there, check up on the boys as well to see whether they left or stayed on to talk to Fiona. We may as well have tabs on all our suspicious characters. Derek too. You never know what you will find and who is telling the truth.'

'Good thinking, Alicia. I will be a short while only.'

As he walked away, Alicia had a sudden thought. She knew there would be CCTV at the entry of the mall, but did they have it inside the area where they normally had entertainment? Now that would be good to check out.

She looked up the phone number of the mall management office and asked for the manager when the phone was answered. Soon she was speaking to a William Woodford, manager of the mall, and her question on the CCTV was answered in the affirmative. Since they had some break-ins and various bad behaviour, they had installed cameras wherever there was a walkway, all around the shopping area. They had been installed only a few days prior to Anaya's fall. Her fall was captured, as she had dropped past a camera, but it had not caught the full fall. The police had looked at it and said it was not a good enough picture to cast suspicions on anything, and they left it.

She asked, 'Did it show pictures of those people in the area of the fall, such as the coffee shop, escalator, and lift?'

His answer was 'Yes, it would show that, although the police at the time could not see anything that would tie up with the fall, so they did not go on with it.'

'Thank you, Mr Woodford. Do you still have a copy of that tape?'

'Yes, Alicia, it is stored in our office for a few more weeks. It was a new tape at the time the fall happened. You have just caught it before it is to be put in storage and archived.'

Alicia said, 'You cannot know how handy that information could be. I will ring my husband, who is looking at CCTV tapes over at the police department. I could see that it would take hours to find anyone suspicious. You may have saved us hours of work. I will get him to pick the tape up from you.'

'So you think the girl's death is suspicious, not an accident?'

'That is our reading of it at the moment, but we have to find proof. That is not easy to find. The tape will help us enormously. Thank you, Mr Woodford. You can expect my husband, James Armstrong, to call in, in the next half hour or so.'

She rang James and told him her news, and he was very pleased. He said, 'Do you know how many people go through the mall in a day? It is like looking for a needle in a haystack. Your Mr Woodford sounds like he is holding the best information yet. I will go over right away to pick it up, and leave Paul to continue here.'

He came back with the tape, and they projected it on to their backdrop and called for Kate and Ken to come and look; four pairs of eyes would do better than two. They finally found the day in question after much fiddling about by the men, and they watched as men, women, and children rushed past, through the entry and lower floor and up the escalator and even from the lift. It was a terrific angle to catch all and sundry—some smiling, some looking grumpy, children whining, children skipping to keep up with their mothers, all shapes and sizes. Alicia said, 'I could do with a tape like this to help me with my drawing. It is so fascinating watching all these people—short, tall, chubby, slim, anything you want to draw.'

Eventually, the time of day came up that they were searching for, and they all sat forward. There was no sound from the tape, just constant movement, and suddenly Alicia said, 'There is Iris Kumah, coming out of the corridor where the medical offices are. She does look ill and tired.' They watched her walk to the coffee shop and disappear inside. She came out again to sit at the table and chairs outside the shop in the mall. She was accompanied by two fresh-faced young men, and they sat together at the table.

Suddenly again, Alicia said, 'Look, there is Fiona, just coming into the mall and looking around.' They saw her go up the escalator and disappear for a few minutes. Waiting, they saw her come down again. They checked the tape's timing and then saw Fiona sitting in the chair Iris had vacated; she was talking to the young men. Alicia said, 'Iris disappeared. She moved off when the camera was turning around. Where did she go?'

The whir of the noise and movement was unbelievable as they watched people emerge from shops and walkways towards the victim. There still was not a sign of Iris, and then she was there at the bottom of the escalator, talking to Aisha as the girl came from the coffee shop towards her.

Alicia stopped the tape and turned to James. 'There. That is what Aisha said happened, not Iris. She said she met Aisha at the bottom of the escalator, coming down. It looks like Iris was the one coming from the escalator. She could be our perpetrator. I cannot believe it of her. She seemed so nice.'

James held her for a moment. 'I am sorry, Alicia, but I think you are correct. It does look as if Iris was the one after all.'

'What do we do, James? Do we still go to see Fiona tomorrow?' asked Alicia.

'Yes, we still have beef with her for the cocaine business. I am glad we have this tape to show that perhaps it was not her who pushed Anaya. We still have no proof of that, but it is still not evidence that she did not kill the boys. We have to clear up the drug dealing and blackmail of Derek.'

Alicia shook his arm excitedly. 'James, I will check what time and day Iris was dismissed from the hospital. She told us that she read about the boys' deaths from a newspaper on her last day in hospital. What if she was already dismissed on the day previous? The hospital should tell me that without a warrant. I will check it right away.'

She looked up the number for the general hospital and made the enquiries. She looked back at James and said, 'We are right. It was the day before, but she did come back to the hospital next day for one last test, accompanied by her son. She could have read the newspaper while waiting to have her test. We will have to go over her statement again to see what other possible lies she told us. Is this the Catholic nun, supposedly so gentle and kind? It is so hard to believe.'

Kate had been listening, and she remarked, 'Women will do anything to save their children. Perhaps Iris was trying to get rid of Anaya because when Derek told her to back off—as he would have sooner or later, because he was pledged to Aisha—she would have been embarrassed by the knock-back and would have turned to Jamal. By then Iris would not have liked that to happen. She had changed her mind after the nasty way Anaya had treated her. It is like the lioness protecting her cub. She knew she would not be around much longer to protect her son. It was probably an opportune moment for her when she saw Anaya on the ladder and saw Aisha move away.'

James said, 'I can see that as a motive. You could be right, Kate. You understand the mothering thing because you are a mother yourself. We still have to experience that. I agree that it was not planned, merely a moment of rage. The doctor had told her she did not have much time left, and she had been digesting that information when she was sitting outside of the coffee shop with the boys and saw Anaya on the ladder.'

'Yes, it looks that way. We will have to visit her to find out if we are right. It is a shame. I know you liked her so much.' Ken agreed. 'Never mind her for now though. We have to chase Fiona before she does any more damage.'

'Yes, she is not one to go quietly. We should not delay picking her up and searching her house and car. James, shall I ask Paul Morris to get the drug dog, Rosco, again for the morning?' asked Kate.

'That is a good idea, Kate, but I believe she will have her house clean. She has had it searched once. Try Paul and see what he says. We should not take her lightly. Derek seemed genuinely frightened of her. I am glad we have sorted things out before we charged in and started to accuse her of them. Thank you, Alicia, for your initiative to do those checks. We could have looked like fools.'

Alicia said, 'I still believe we should have Derek wear a wire on Friday night, and we should all go listen to the jazz again and hear what Fiona has to say.'

Kate said, 'It will be too late, Alicia. By then she would recognise all of us, if we are going to interview her tomorrow.'

'True, Kate, but what if Jerry Jones was the one to listen in? She is not aware of him. I agree that if we all attended the show, she would be suspicious of us. However, I believe we will miss out on some valuable information and proof by not doing it.' Alicia was persistent.

Percy had come in from his surveillance of Fiona's house and said the lady had not been at home, so there was nothing to report. He heard Alicia's comment and turned to James. 'Are you listening, James? Alicia has a point. If we do not find anything at her house, Fiona could claim lack of proof. We need as much proof as we can get. I think it is a good idea to have Derek wear a wire, and Jerry Jones can monitor it. He is on the drug squad after all.'

James sounded somewhat weary. 'Okay, Alicia, I will ask Paul Morris to liaise with Jerry Jones. They are the ones with the equipment to do that.'

'You sound tired, James. Shall I make you a cup of tea?' asked Alicia.

'That would be nice, thank you, Alicia. Yes, I am tired. I sat up late last night to read the two boys' file. There seems so many possibilities in the whole deal. My mind is in a whirl. You have all been an amazing help so far, but I still feel as if we are missing something. It all seems too easy. There is something niggling me about the photos of the dead boys. You must look at it tonight to see if you can see what I imagined I was looking at. It gave me quite a shock. The trouble is that it is such a ghastly photo that you only glance at it and cannot bear to look again, but you must hold it and look hard to see if you can see what I imagined I could see last night. I am still not sure of what I was looking at, and no one else seems to have picked it up, perhaps because it is so ghastly.' James went on. 'Perhaps I need a good night's sleep, and when I wake up, it will all fall into place. Right now it seems like a jumble to me.'

'It is almost time to go home. Perhaps if we talk things over with Granny, it will become clearer which avenue to take. We are all a bit jumbled up with so much information. We need to clear our minds,' suggested Alicia.

'That seems to be the best idea so far. We seem to have taken these cases at a run and have not slowed down to take everything in. Granny always sees the wood for the trees. We will take it to her tonight and see what she has to say.'

Percy had been listening and said, 'You are both so right. I agree with that. I will pack up the files to take home with us.'

'Take the CCTV from the shopping centre too, Percy. It would not hurt to check over what it is telling us. I suppose too that I regret that it is Iris Kumah we suspect. I really liked her, and I find it hard to believe her guilty.' James suggested, 'You must wear your strongest glasses to help me check the shots of the boys. I still cannot believe I am right and not grasping at straws, or maybe I was so tired I was imagining what I wanted to see. I meant to have everybody look at it today to give their opinion, but we were all so busy. The moment did not happen.'

CHAPTER NINE

After dinner, James set up the CCTV on a screen. While the others were cooking and setting up the table in preparation for their dinner, he made a graph showing times for whoever they could see at which particular time and where, to make sure they had everyone accounted for. They all sat down to see what he had been doing and admired his handiwork.

With paper and pen in hand, they sat around the screen. James said, 'It has bugged me that we did not really look at who was coming in and out of the lift. We concentrated more on the escalator and coffee shop area. We did not even see Derek step out of the lift with his trolley as he described to us. Let us all now look at that before mixing it in with the other parts of the lower floor.'

At eleven ten on the tape, they were looking at the entrance to the mall and the lift area, and they saw Derek enter the lift and go to the upper floor, pushing a fully loaded trolley. At twelve ten, James said, 'Stop the tape. Look who is there. Do you recognise him, Percy?'

'Vivaan Patel. He said he did not leave his office. He is a new person of interest.'

'Where are the statements? In particular, the one he gave,' said James.

'Here they are, James,' said Alicia.

He went through them until he pulled out the statement Patel had given them in his office. 'He said he went to see her on that last day. We missed it. We took it to mean that he tried to see her, but here it says

163

he went to see her. We did not expect that, and we missed a vital clue. The timing may mean that he was the last person to see Anaya alive. We will have to ask Iris why she went up the escalator about that time and if she saw Mr Patel.'

They watched further, and suddenly Percy said, 'There he is, coming out of the lift.' It was twelve eighteen. Would that have given him time to push the girl through the window? It was after the timing of Anaya's fall by three minutes. Once again, they saw Iris appearing to get off the escalator, but Granny said, 'No, she is not coming from the escalator. Run it again. I think she is coming from the arcade beside the escalator. Yes, she has a box in her hands from the nightwear and underclothing shop around that corner. They always wrap the stock up to appear as if it is a gift. It is very fancy and also a very expensive place. I have only been in there once or twice, because it is so upmarket. Iris is catching up to Patel. She looks surprised, but she hugs him in what seems like comfort. They are walking out of the centre together, chatting.'

'Yes, Granny, that would fit in. Iris was to go into the hospital in the afternoon for more tests and was going to stay awhile, so she would have bought a new nightgown or two,' said Alicia.

At twelve twenty-five, they saw Derek emerge from the lift with his trolley and go out of the mall, not looking in any particular direction, trying to balance the trolley, which was empty and wanted to jiggle about and do its own thing. It looked as if they were unaware of each other's presence, with Patel hurrying out first from the shopping centre with Iris and not looking back.

James said, 'I do not believe any of these people pushed Anaya. I think it was an accident of her own doing.'

Percy said, 'Yes, it looks to be that way, James. We will have to ask Patel about the last conversation with his daughter. We can stop worrying about it for a while and concentrate on our visit tomorrow with Fiona. We know Fiona did not push Anaya. She was sitting outside the coffee shop with the two young men at the time.'

James said, 'Remind me to ask Paul Morris before we go to Fiona's house, whether Rosco can smell any other drug or if it is just cocaine. So now we concentrate on Fiona and the two boys' case. Alicia and

Percy, I do not like to ask you to do this. It is disturbing, but I must, for confirmation of what I think I saw last night. I admit I was a bit bleary-eyed by the time I looked at the pictures last night, and I could not believe what I was looking at. So you look and see if you can confirm my finding.'

He handed the photos around. There were several of them in an internal folder. Granny said, 'May I look also? I have seen some grim scenes in my lifetime. Perhaps I can help.'

Each studied each photograph as it came around to them.

James queried, 'Anything, Percy?'

'Nothing that I have not seen before, James,' he said in a curious tone.

'Alicia? Did you see anything?'

'No, James. Can you give me a hint of what I am to look for?'

'Granny, you have an enquiring look on your face. What have you spotted?' asked James.

'In this photo, the eyes are looking to the left. In the next one, they are looking up, and the third one makes them look as if they are half closed, with the eyes peering through the lashes,' said Granny.

'Yes!' said James triumphantly. 'That is just what I saw. He seemed to be looking around the room. The room seems crowded, with the photographer, the doctor, several forensic people, and a policeman, and in such a small space. It must have smelt badly, with the blood and whatever, and everyone would have wanted to get out of there as fast as they could. Perhaps he had still been under the spell of the drug and could not move, and what with all the knife cuts, he must have been in a bad way. But at the time those photographs were taken, he was still alive.'

Percy and Alicia said, 'How could we all have missed that?' They reached for the photographs again.

Alicia said, 'Yes, I can see what you mean. The fact that he was alive would have been picked up at the coroner's office, I presume?'

Percy said, 'There is no mention of it in the file. I have read through it several times, and in each sequence, it is written "dead boys". Perhaps he did not survive the removal to the coroner.'

'I will have to leave Fiona's interview to you, Percy and Alicia, while I visit the coroner. Try to keep the conversation on the cocaine and the search of the house until I can get there to help out. If this boy is still alive, we have a living witness to his brother or partner's murder and the attempt on him. I only have to find him. If it looks to be in the negative or takes too long, we will have to leave his arrival until the courtroom.

'The other things to look for are the papers from the boys' apartment. When it was searched after the boys were removed, there was not a scrap of paper left behind to say who they were, where they were from, or what such young men were doing living in a flat together. To me, they look like brothers, perhaps they put out the story of being gay to put people off. The younger one appears to be only fourteen or so, and the older one maybe seventeen, no older than eighteen. But there is nothing to confirm it or who their parents are and where they live. It has left them quite anonymous, and no one lives so sparsely. We all have a backup of paper somewhere.'

Percy said, 'What I did notice about their photos, because they were in repose—it may not have been noticeable in life—is that the boys do not look Indian - maybe English with a touch of African, I would say, when you look at their hair.'

'Good catch, Percy. I think you are right about that,' said James, once more examining the photos. 'They both needed a haircut, by the look of these photos.'

Alicia said, 'I feel quite miffed. I did not pick up any of that.'

'Never mind, Alicia,' said James. 'You have talents in other aspects that are indispensable to us. And you, Granny'—he looked at her across the table—'you are our secret asset.'

Granny laughed. 'Any time I can be of service, James, I am happy to be here for you.'

*   *   *

James set off early next morning, to be at the coroner's office as soon as it opened to the public. He remembered coming here during their big case of the murder of an elderly man and his dog. The staff had been so nice and had found a new verdict for that one, so he was hoping they had found the older boy alive when he had arrived. The receptionist came in for the day, and because James was the first customer, he received special service. When he showed her the photos of the boys, she said, 'I remember that case. I wondered why there was never a follow-up from their relatives. You're lucky, Dr Redfern is on duty today. He helped you last time, if you can recall.'

'Indeed I do. My client won his case on that one.'

The doctor came bustling in, looking much as he did when last James and Percy had needed information. He shook James's hand like an old friend. 'It is good to see you again, James. Come through to my office, and we can try to help you out.'

James followed him into the office and took a seat and pulled out the file he held on the deaths of the boys. He held up the sheaf of photos and said, 'Here, sir, are photographs of a living man alongside his dead brother. Unfortunately, I have only recently been given the cold case, and my team and I, when looking at these photographs, thought we saw the older boy's eyes move. We would like to think he survived the trip here for an autopsy. He had been drugged first and stabbed many times. We hope you can give us some good news.'

Dr Redfern nodded and took the photos. 'I heard about this case when I arrived back from my skiing holiday in Scotland. I have to admit, by that time, it was old news in here. One case follows the other, like night comes after day. We all expect to live to a fine old age, until some nasty person says you do not deserve it and takes things into their own hands.'

He stopped and studied the photos, and he said, 'It is as obvious as the nose on my face that this boy is alive. Who called in that he was dead?' He pulled the file towards him and looked up the doctor's name and said, 'Now we are in trouble. This is the chief surgeon's son.'

He got up from his seat and went out of the room and returned with another file and sat down again to examine it. He breathed a deep sigh of relief. 'Yes, they found he was alive, but not until he was on the table, ready for the examination. He moved, probably because the metal table was so cold. He had been severely sedated before he was stabbed, and he took a long time coming out of the sedation. I suppose some of it by then had been a deep sleep. We sent him off to a private nursing hospital because the chaps looking after him by then reasoned that if someone had tried to kill him once, they may try again. It is easy to get into the general hospital, and there is more security in the private ones. Strange, there is no name on this file. Who is he?'

'We do not know that either. His private possessions were stolen by the killer, and he seemed to be leading an illusionary life with his brother. No one knows anything about him, or they know very little detail. My crew now are at the home of the person we believe committed the murder and attempted murder, and they are holding the alleged killer there until I can get to them with this information. Are you able to tell me where he is located at the moment? I would love to have him with me when I knock on the door, to see the reaction from those we are holding'

'I will give the hospital a call and ask permission—if he is still there, of course. But I think he will be. I kept up with the story for a while. He was unable to identify himself. His entire memory had gone.'

The doctor looked up the number on the phone directory and rang. He identified himself and then asked about the condition of the patient they had sent all those months ago. James could hear the woman chattering on the other end of the line and laughing, and eventually she called someone to help out while she went to ask him.

Dr Redfern said, 'The receptionist calls him D2, because no one, including him, knows his name. They have had to teach him to walk again and also to speak English. When he arrived, he spoke only a strange language, and after asking at the university for a linguist fellow to come and listen, they decided it was Bantu, from a region in Africa. Things are moving along for him, according to the doctors, and if he had somewhere to go, they could dismiss him. Physically he is very fit. However, he has no memory of his life except the Bantu part. The patient has agreed to go with you, James, but you will have to drive. He is anxious to see the person who killed his brother and made a mute out of him—his words.'

'Thank you for all your help. When I saw those photographs last night, I could imagine a body bag thrown into a van and then put in a freezer for a few days, and my heart sank. I am so happy to have you help me again. I will go and pick him up. Thank you once again for your help.'

He did not exactly speed on the way to the hospital, but he did not go slowly. As it was early, there was not a lot of traffic on the road, and he made good time. When he asked for D2, everyone laughed, including the boy, which was all he was, really, or a new adult maybe. They took a wheelchair with them, saying that it said so much to someone standing tall over him. It may help break the ice.

*   *   *

They arrived at Fiona's house a little after nine o'clock, and when Fiona opened the door, accompanied by Alicia and Percy, she stared at the boy in the wheelchair and turned very pale.

D2 stared back and said, 'Hello, Fiona.' He had been prepped by James on the journey, as the boy said he did not remember anything about Fiona. James had said, 'There is nothing for you to say after that, D2. I will prompt you. She is the one we want talking. It may have been a matter of you against her, but not any more. She is guilty of murder and many other things in addition, and it is her we want talking. You will just lead off. Do not attempt to join in the conversation afterwards. She may realise how much you cannot remember, and the conversation will die.'

James greeted Fiona by saying, 'We meet after all, Fiona. Derek seemed rather scared of you, and now we know the reason.' He helped D2 get out of the wheelchair to climb the steps. Percy assisted James in bringing up the wheelchair, and they entered the house and seated the boy back in it. Fiona remained quiet and sat down in an armchair, staring at the boy in the wheelchair as if she could not believe her eyes.

A girl, perhaps in her early twenties, flounced into the room, saying, 'Now they are searching my things.' She stopped when she saw D2 and looked at her sister and said, 'Oh. Oh, now we are in trouble.'

Ah, thought James, *so she was in on it as well.* He turned to the girl and said, 'Flora McDonald, I believe.'

The girl flushed. 'Has Derek been telling his little secrets then?'

'So you are admitting that you were the one who blamed Derek for giving you a drug and raping you, when it was entirely untrue.'

'Well. He was a wuss, and I tied him up beautifully. His silly old man was so willing to hand over the money—to keep me quiet, he said. They were both there for the taking, both so innocent of the facts of life. When I asked the old man to take me to the bank to collect the money, he could not get there fast enough. It was so easy. I have thought of having a go at Derek again, but Fiona said not until she was finished with him. So I have to wait. Never mind, there are lots of other wusses out there, just waiting to be taken.'

'Shut up, Faye. You are a silly girl,' said Fiona.

'Was it you or your sister, Faye, who drugged and stabbed the boys?' said James.

'If I had stabbed *him,*' she said, pointing at the boy in the wheelchair, 'he would be dead, just like his brother. I told Fiona to check his breathing. But no, big sister knows everything, and he has come back to bite us.'

'So you were the one that stabbed his brother then, and Fiona stabbed this boy. Who fed them the drug?' asked James.

Fiona shouted at her sister, 'I told you to keep your mouth shut! You run on like a gramophone record—on and on. I told you your blathering would get us into trouble one day. You are so full of wind we cannot make you run down.'

D2 was laughing. Faye had pushed both of the girls into the line of fire.

Fiona turned on him. 'You shut up too! You're a big, silly oaf. If you had died properly like you were supposed to, we would not be in trouble.'

That made him laugh more. Everyone else was grinning. There was no need to question these women; they were doing it to themselves.

James thought he would elevate the conversation further. 'Fiona, are you aware that we have picked up your box of cocaine from Derek's parents' house and that we have charged Derek with possession of a prohibited drug?'

Those watching thought she was going into apoplexy with the shock. She had her hands down by her side, legs straightened out, and a look of pure hate directed at James crossing her face. It was lucky she was sitting, or she would have fallen.

Faye, ever the gramophone record, said to her, 'Now tell me how to get out of that one, big sister. You are stuffed and may as well go in with Ian and Gerald. You have brought all this down on yourself.'

'We still have his stuff. That should be worth a few quid with the right people,' said Fiona, pointing at D2.

The boy sat up straighter. 'You have my things here?'

'We did not think you needed any of it any longer,' said Faye.

'Do you know how many people have been killed for that small bundle? My grandfather, my grandmother, my mother and probably my father, and now my brother and almost me. It is worth nothing to me. Just for having it in your possession, someone will kill you for it. I do not want it.' D2's memories were obviously coming back to him. He looked very strained; his whole family had been obliterated for whatever they were talking about.

'What is it? What are they after?' asked James.

'A small package of uncut diamonds. Assassins have been sent out to recover them. Time or distance will not stop them. The diamonds were awarded to my grandfather because he had helped a politician at one time. As an Indian merchant, he gave them to my mother when she married, for her dowry. He had owned a great maharaja's emporium in the centre of the capital. In time, that could be taken from him by the locals, who said it should be owned by the local people, not an Indian. He and my grandmother were killed in their home at a later period, because although my grandmother was a local, she had given up her ethnic background to marry a foreigner. We think the murders were organised by the politician who had originally presented the diamonds, because he wanted them back. He sent in people to search for them, and they tortured my grandparents to make them give them up. People were asking where the new diamond mine was, after they were killed.

It was suddenly dangerous to have them in your possession, because no one knew where the mine was or who was trying to get the diamonds back. The mine had been kept a dark secret.

'My mother was murdered by her servants in her own home. Again, the excuse heard was that it was because she had married a foreigner. The pair of killers picked up everything they could carry, and even then, they came back for more. They had chosen a day when my brother and I were late home from school. I had a chess tournament each Wednesday, and my brother had a cricket match on the same day. We were always late home. When we walked in and looked around, there was nothing inside the house except my mother's body on the kitchen table, sliced up by a machete. We called my father. He was away on-site most weekdays and came home for the weekends. He called the police, of course, but they do nothing nowadays except pick up their pay. The country has gone to wrack and ruin.

'My father believed that the servants who had been with us for fifteen years had been given drugs and ordered to do the dirty work by the politician who was looking for the diamonds. The torture of my mother was done to make her give them the hiding place. She did not know where they were hidden. My father had made the hiding place and had not told her where it was, so they would be looking for us next.

'He took us from school, and we all boarded his plane for this country. Our father is an Englishman, and he took us to his stepmother, at her home. After she listened to what had happened to us, when my father returned to his job, she found us that small flat and told us to enrol in the local school. She did not want to be in the line of fire. The only thing wrong with all this is, besides paying our rent, she left us no money. We have not heard from my father since he returned to his job, and it has now been well over a year. My brother and I thought it was a possibility that he is dead too.

'These people will not stop until they find the diamonds. They are yellow diamonds and are easily identified, as they are very rare. Their rarity, of course, means they are worth much more than the plain white diamond.'

He stopped talking for a few minutes, and they all sat and looked at him. He started laughing, an almost hysterical sound, but his eyes were not dancing. 'When it is announced in the newspapers about the killing of my brother and myself, and our real names are revealed, these assassins are going to come after those killers to get the diamonds,' he said, pointing at Fiona and Faye.

Both women said, 'But we will be in jail. They will not be able to get to us.'

D2 sat back, laughing. 'You have no idea, have you? Money can buy anything, even from jail. That politician wants to hide from the world the knowledge that he is working a diamond mine in secret. He made a mistake when he gave my grandfather the package. He had obviously picked up the wrong one by mistake and did not realise it till later.

'Their methods of torture are many, and all are horrible. I saw what they did to my mother. The memory of it will never fade from my mind.'

James interrupted the sense of doom that had fallen over the room. 'How did you become entangled with these women anyway, D2?'

The young man sat and looked backwards into his mind; it was an almost physical release of the memories of his mother's death. 'As I told you, my father arranged for his stepmother to find us a flat. He did not want anyone to realise we had left the country, and he was going straight to his worksite just four days after my mother's funeral, which is the normal mourning period allowed. We were to move into the flat using assumed names, and he left us with everything he had in his pockets, which did not go far. We had bank accounts at home, but he did not want us to use them, in case we could be chased up. We had agreed that my brother would go to school and that I would find a job. Dad had been out of this country for too long to know the system.'

He shook his head. 'It wasn't as easy as that. I had no experience in anything practical. After all, I was still a schoolboy myself. I was only fifteen, and my brother twelve years old. At home, everything had been done for us by the servants. We had never prepared a meal for ourselves, never washed dishes or clothes, and never even made our own beds.'

He paused, and it seemed as if his memory was catching up to him. After a few minutes, he said, 'I saw an advertisement for a job in the customs department—"Apply to Gerald Norman". I walked to the department for an interview, and when he saw me, he laughed. I am tall, but I still did not look older than fifteen, I suppose. Anyway, the outcome was, he could not employ me in that job. I had no social service papers or job experience. When I told him I was desperate, he thought for a bit and said, "Would you consider selling cocaine for a commission?" I had no other alternative but to say yes. And that is how it began. Gerald was nice to me. I had the feeling that life had not been easy for him as he grew up. He often bought my brother and me takeaway Indian meals. We were posing as Indian boys to hide our ethnic background, although my grandfather was a true Indian gentleman, loved by everyone who came in touch with him. The cocaine commission paid enough for takeaway meals and some clothes, because we were growing boys and quickly grew out of the clothes we brought from home.

'Things did not change much until Gerald went to jail.' He gave Fiona a derisive look. 'After she took over, she tried to cut our commission. We were still in desperate straits and could not allow it, but she had the idea of selling the stuff herself, with Faye to help her. You know it all from there.'

Faye piped up. 'Why do you keep calling him D2?'

Fiona looked at her and said dully, 'Shut up, Faye. You have done enough damage with your chatter.'

James asked the young man, 'Did you have anything to do with Derek Choudhury?'

'I saw him playing the piano on Friday nights and again on Sunday afternoons. I was a fan of his music, but no, I did not really speak to him. I did find quite a few customers for the cocaine at his recitals, but Derek never asked about it. I am sure he was unaware of much around him. He concentrated on his music.'

'Did you see Derek with Fiona at all?'

'I saw Derek trying to get away from Fiona on many occasions, and also that Patel girl. He was not interested in either of them. He lived in a world of his own.'

'Do you remember the day that Anaya Patel fell at the mall, through the showroom window?' asked Alicia.

Once again, he paused to struggle with his memory. 'That was the day Fiona asked us to meet her at the coffee shop in the mall to talk about our commission?'

'Yes, that was the day. What can you tell us about it?'

'Fiona was not at the coffee shop yet. My brother and I met Mrs Kumah when she came into the coffee shop, and she bought us each a sandwich and a cup of coffee. She was not well and was going to the hospital that day to have tests done. When she saw Fiona arrive, she said, "Here is the woman for your meeting." I was surprised because we had not said anything to her about meeting Fiona. She got up and wandered off, and Fiona sat down in her seat. I never saw her again. Is she still alive? She looked so ill that day.'

'She is still alive, we think, as we have not heard anything from her husband or son. I may take you for a visit on the way back to the hospital.'

'I would like that. She was always so kind to me and to my brother,' said D2 sadly.

Percy, Ken, and Paul Morris had come into the room some time ago and had been listening to the conversation. Paul was holding the leash of a little dog, who had sat down and gone to sleep.

'Tell us, Percy, what have you found?' said James.

Paul Morris went over to Fiona, and Ken went to Faye. They handcuffed the two women. Paul read them their rights. He said, 'You are both accused of the killing of this young man's brother and of the attempt to kill him as well. You are also both accused of selling cocaine. We have found the drug you used to get the two young men to sleep. The method you used is still to be established. Fiona, you are also accused of having knowledge of the cocaine stored by Derek Choudhury, and we have the postal receipts for its delivery to his apartment, made by you.'

Kate, who had been very quiet throughout, asked Fiona, 'Where are your children?'

Fiona answered fiercely, 'With Gerald's mother, thank God. They moved there to dodge questions at school about their father. Now there would have been more to dodge. They are far enough away not to be bullied at school over all this.'

'Did you find anything else, Percy? D2 needs his papers returned,' said Alicia.

'Yes, I have them in a box. Do you want to take them now, son? Or shall we put them in our safe at the office until you need them?'

'I would appreciate you putting them in your safe, sir. I have only a pigeonhole at the hospital, and now that my memory is coming back, I am not too sure how long they will keep me there. I have to work out a place to go. The flat would be relet by now.'

'Don't worry too much, D2,' said James. 'You have certainly had a raw deal. We will try to find a way around things for you. People in this town are very nice, and I am sure we can find a home for you somewhere.'

Tears appeared on the boy's lashes. 'Thank you, James. I appreciate all you have done.'

'Come, Alicia, with D2. We will go and visit Iris Kumah. Kate, can you fit in with Percy?' Paul Morris and Ken had taken the two women away in the police vehicle.

'Sure, she can,' said Percy. 'We will have another look around here and lock up.'

'Thanks, Percy. Job well done. Another case out of the way. Now we have a missing child to find, or Granny will be after us for it. Percy? Did you find the package of uncut diamonds?'

'Sitting on the top of Fiona's dressing table, in a bowl. She was unaware of what she had found and made no attempt to hide them. She probably thought it was a bag of rocks from the seashore.'

'What a strange story we have unearthed here, Percy. I would like to go through that young man's papers before we return them to him. It is such a tragic story from start to finish. Alicia and I will take D2 to the Kumah family home for a chat. After that, we will have a chat with Mr Patel, and I would say that these files can be closed. We will see you back at the office later.'

'Fine, James. I would like for the little dog to have a run around the downstairs rooms to see if we can find anything, then we can be on our way. We will return the dog to Paul on the way.'

James loaded the wheelchair into the boot of the office car and set off to see Iris Kumah, hoping she was still available to talk with.

*   *   *

Jamal came to the door at their knock and gave a broad smile. 'Mother will be pleased to see you. She was saying yesterday that she wanted to know how all your findings turned out.' He showed them into the beautiful sitting room and showed them to seats, saying, 'I will fetch her. She needs a wheelchair these days.'

They both came back shortly after, and when Iris saw D2, she almost burst into tears. 'Oh, my dear boy, we thought you were dead. Is your brother with you too?'

'No such luck, Mrs Kumah. He died that day. I think I survived because the killers were in such a hurry and did not check if I was still breathing. I have been in hospital since that day, and James brought me out for a few hours to confront the killers.'

'Wow,' said Jamal. 'That must have been some meeting.'

'I lost my memory after the knifing and had to relearn English and how to walk. I was disabled for such a long time, but I can tell you, today's activities have me nearly back to normal.'

James said, 'D2 has to find a new job and a place to live, Iris. He has a confession: he is not really fully Indian. That was a disguise he had to invent because he was being chased by assassins—not the ones who killed his brother, but ones he fled his own country to evade. He was not able to finish his education because of all these things, so he is going to try to catch up if he can. It is a very tragic story. I was wondering if your husband could find him a job to get him on his feet. This could be a good project for you and Jamal, helping him find somewhere to live. He tells me his best version of cooking a meal is to buy takeaway.'

'Why do you call him D2, James?' asked Jamal.

'He was unconscious in the hospital for a long time, and when he woke up, he could not speak English or remember his name. The hospital had to appeal to a university for a linguist to listen to him to find out what language he was speaking. He was speaking Bantu or Shona, an African language, even though his father was English and he had attended an English school. The part where the Indian comes in is that his grandfather was Indian, or Goan. But initially he had forgotten all that. He also had to learn to walk again, and the nurses laughingly called him D2. I never knew his name—it is not in my file—so I followed suit. He is D2 to me.'

D2 looked from one to the other of them and leaned forward and said, 'First of all, I want to thank you for your friendship. I have forgotten that you can trust some people. I have been going through life keeping my private affairs secret from everyone. The hospital put me in an induced coma to allow my body to heal. I had so many knife wounds. I was almost dead, and the drug Fiona had given me in a bottle of soda water did not help. It appeared to most people that I was dead.

'When I awoke from the coma, I was nursed by a black nurse who spoke Bantu, an old language. Firstly, I heard her crooning to me while she bathed my wounds and rebandaged them. I realised I understood her. Everyone else sounded like they were talking gibberish to me. I had really lost my memory, but the Bantu—or Shona, as it is sometimes called—took me back to my early history, when I had my own Bantu-speaking nurse. It became my first language.

'My grandparents had given a village to my mother, their only daughter, when she married my father. My grandmother's father had been, until his natural death, an elder in the village. My grandmother had inherited the whole village when he died. What that meant, really, was that she was responsible for the others in the village and their well-being. When my brother and I were still only babies, we went to live in that village until we needed to start school. Those early days—chasing chickens, patting dogs, collecting eggs, and helping dig the gardens in a very beautiful countryside, where we were loved by everyone—were my earliest memories, ones I went back to from time to time on school holidays, with my brother and my mother. It was an ideal life and was treasured by us all. In today's world, everyone is supposed to be educated, so we moved to a house in the city, once again given to my mother by her parents.

'It was a large house. Grandfather had furnished it from his emporium, which sold anything you needed. The grounds were large, and we had two permanent gardeners to look after them. The inside of the house was looked after by a married couple and a lady cook who had a young girl come in to help her on weekends.

'My mother's time was taken up by good works, which grew immensely when the people rebelled and took over the streets and farms, wiping out many white people and sending the remainder away overseas. Looting was the name of the new game, and the politicians allowed it to happen. Mother spent her days helping people who were attacked, many of them English, who had lived in the country all their lives and knew no other life.

'My father was safe because his job as an engineer on the gas pipeline was needed by the country. But it was not safe for him to travel, so his car sat in the garage. A bus dropped him home to us on Friday, and he was picked up by the same bus on Monday each week. During the week, he was safe in staff accommodation near the site of where he worked. He often said, when he was home with us, that it was time to move to the UK. But my mother argued that other countries had these bad times for a few years and that they died down after a time and things were restored to normal. She loved her country, and the bad times were yet to start happening to our own family.

'Grandfather was born in Goa, a southern Indian province, and he had done well building up his emporium. He was well liked in the community and paid for many new schools and other works with the money that the business brought in. Jealous rivals were behind his downfall my father believed, and assassins ended it, killing both grandparents in the search for the uncut diamonds. Why the politician could not have merely asked for them back, I do not know. We would have given them with alacrity. But everyone was suspicious of everyone else in the country. By then, all good manners had gone and reverted back to the primitive way of life, and they sent drugged-up assassins instead.

'My mother was murdered in the same way by our domestic staff, whom we had thought of as faithful and loved like family members. The gardeners heard the commotion and ran off instead of calling the police. By the time my brother and I returned home from school, there was a total quietness, except for the buzzing of flies.' He shuddered and went on. 'I will never forget that noise. We knew as we approached the door that we would find something grotesque, and you cannot imagine anything so gross as our mother piled up like slabs of beef on the table.' He had a look of wonder on his face at the fact that he remembered. Tears were flowing down his face, and he wiped them away with the back of his hands.

Iris said, 'That is enough for now. It may have helped you, letting it all out, but *now* we must give you some good memories to chase the bad ones away. Jamal has many friends at the university who we will pay to help you through your studies, and soon you will be even with him. How old are you now, D2?'

He laughed. 'I knew you were kind, Mrs Kumah. You were nice to me from the beginning. I am eighteen now, I think. I will have to calculate it when I see my passport again. I have lost most of a year hiding in that hospital. I am not sure what date it is any more.'

'You can work it out with Jamal. Unfortunately, I spend most of my time sleeping, with small spurts of energy in between. I am just so happy I can help you in any way I can.'

James and Alicia knew it was a hint that it was time to go, so they stood up and walked towards the door, saying farewell as they left. James said he would ring Jamal later to answer any questions he may have.

In the car again, James asked, 'Are your passports amongst the batch of papers we are to put in our safe, D2?'

'I am not sure yet, James. Little pieces of memory are coming back to me, bit by bit, as they seem to be needed. I may have more information by the end of the day. I am starting to feel jittery. I have not spoken so much in a very long time. It is like watching TV and realising you know what comes next each time anyone speaks, sort of in staccato. I was pleased that as soon as Faye opened her mouth this morning, I recognised both her and Fiona. Following what everybody was saying was hard at first, but gradually bits and pieces fell into place in my mind.'

'Do we have your permission to open the package and at least find out your name and date of birth?'

'Certainly, James.' Then in a curious voice, he said, 'It is strange that I cannot remember my own name.'

'Do not worry yourself, D2. I kind of like that name anyway. Now that you have made a start, things will keep coming back to you. You will be right up to speed soon. I will not disclose your name to anyone until I have spoken to you again and until we have spoken again about who may be looking for you. Also, we know a really good journalist who will be able to write about you and especially your later story, including both you and your brother. That will put anyone off your trail. Perhaps we will not resurrect you for the assassins to find. We will have to give you a new life.'

Alicia said, 'That is a really great idea, James. Once that gets into print, you will be safe anywhere, D2.'

'Thank you, both of you. I feel as if I have fallen amongst the good fairies.'

They dropped D2 back at the hospital, leaving him to make up his mind how much of the story he would choose to tell the nursing staff. Alicia said, 'I bet he will tell no one. He will not trust anyone for a long time. That was a fantastic idea of yours, James, to take him to see the Kumahs. They are the ideal people to help him, and he already trusts Iris.'

'I saw the look on his face when her name was mentioned. He is waking up bit by bit, and soon he will come back to normal. He trusted Iris in his earlier period, so he will allow her in. With Iris, Jamal will make headway with him too. I think they are much the same age. I thought of asking Mrs Sharma and decided that although trustworthy, she is a bit more "out there" and could frighten him with her straightforward manner.'

'He is just a boy with no family, no one backing him, and no one to turn to. He would be a dream for Granny. She could fuss over him as much as she liked. But I think Granny's age is against her taking on a new orphan to care for. We can play a part though by keeping an eye on him if he will allow it.' Alicia had been distressed for the boy when he told Iris his family history.

'We are going to see Mr Patel now—we are nearly there—to ask him about his last words to his daughter. That will finalise that case too,' said James.

'Do you realise, James, that we have had nothing to eat or drink since breakfast, not even a cup of coffee? We left the office running early this morning and did not think of bringing food.'

'We will not be long with Mr Patel, and then I will take you to a restaurant on the way back to the office for a nice lunch. Can you wait that long?' he said, smiling at her.

As he pulled into the parking bay at the tailoring business, Vivaan Patel was waiting for them. James remarked, 'Are you waiting to speak with us, Mr Patel?'

'Yes, James. Iris rang me to say you were on the way. I came to greet you rather than have you plough your way through the workshop.'

'How did Iris know we were coming? Neither your name nor our business was mentioned while we were there.'

'Since her illness, Iris has developed a sixth sense. She had it before she became ill, but it has developed much further lately.'

James introduced Alicia and said, 'We wanted to confirm your timing on the day of your daughter's fall. We saw you in the mall on the CCTV camera. Did you have time to speak to Anaya?'

'Sadly, no. She ignored me the whole time I was there. When I left, she had been standing on the top of the ladder, dancing and singing. I told her to come down, as it was too dangerous, but it was as if I was not there. She was living in a fantasy. I turned around and left her. I thought that while I was there, she would stay up on the ladder to keep from talking to me. It was so dangerous, to my daily regret. There must have been something I could have said to induce her to come down from the ladder.'

'That is basically what we thought happened. You understand that we have to confirm everything before we close the case on an accident such as that,' said James.

'I understand, James. Thank you for explaining to me. I'd like to report to you that our sons are turning out to be nice, practical boys, polite and willing to be helped. If nothing else, their sister's example has led them in the right direction.'

'Goodbye, Mr Patel. We advise that from this moment, Anaya's case is officially closed.'

CHAPTER TEN

There was a holiday spirit in the office that afternoon; everyone was walking around with a big smile. Percy and James went off to report their findings and arrests at headquarters. The others hunted through requests for outstanding jobs.

When James and Percy came back to the office, they were greeted by a 'Hip hip hooray!' and big smiles from everyone. Percy put up his hand and said, 'We have a young girl to find in our next cold case. Start studying the file. If you all look at it before going home, we will discuss it first thing in the morning.'

When the others had dispersed, James said to Percy, 'Let's look at that box of papers of D2's. I am really curious to see what type of passport the boys travelled to the UK with.'

'Right,' said Percy. 'I will collect it from the safe and bring it into your office. I did not look into it previously. I thought it needed a witness to the opening of the box.'

'Just so, Percy. I think we should have Ken in here too. We will photograph everything and make record of what we find.'

James got up and called Ken into his office, saying, 'Bring in the camera and a tape recorder. We need a visual record as we take the papers out of the box.'

The passports of the two boys were the first things they drew out of the box. Each man took a passport. James said the first one, in the name of Edward Oliveri Bowering, was an English passport, and the picture showed a child of about eleven with dark hair. His skin was not so dark. In fact, he could have passed easily as an Indian child or even a suntanned English one. The second passport, also an English one, was for Jason Lawrence Bowering, with the same colouring. It was obviously D2 in his earlier years, aged fourteen. The next passports were for the same two boys, but they were Zimbabwe ones, with the same names. So they had dual nationality, with at least one country in Africa.

An enrolment form for the local school, two years previous, was for Oliver Edwards, and the form was signed by his brother, Lawrence Edwards. Percy said they were certainly in hiding using those names. You would have to be clever to pick them up while they were using their own names but turned around, which sounded valid.

There was a rent agreement for the flat rented for them; it had been paid through a bank, so no name appeared on the receipt. There was an odd assortment of papers which did not mean anything to the team, but they were photographed and put back in the box.

James opened the British passports and thumbed through and said, 'There does not appear to be an entry for this country two years ago. That is strange.' He put them down and looked at the other passports in the box and said, 'No entry here either. These are unused passports, no exit stamps or entry stamps to be seen. How did they get into the country?'

Percy said, 'Maybe they are on a later page. I have noticed at airports that sometimes the officials open it up halfway through the book and stamp it.'

Each took a passport and opened one page after another—still no entry stamp in any of the books.

James said, 'It looks like the boys were smuggled in unofficially. How do you manage that at the last minute? D2 said they did not hang around at home but made directly for the UK. It could not have been on an airline of any nature, as all have to conform to the local laws of entry—except the air force, I suppose, but even they would have checks made of any flights entering the country from a place like Zimbabwe, for instance. I will give my earlier employment department a call and have a chat. There is a real mystery here.'

He went to his phone and rang his previous boss in Immigration and asked if a check could be made of entries into the country using the boys' proper names and dates of birth. He gave the dates he thought would be correct. He did not elaborate on who they were. That could come later when he had worked the mystery out. From experience, he knew this would not be an easy search, so when he put the phone down, he said to the team, 'I think we have done enough for today. Who is ready for home?'

Percy locked up D2's box back in the safe and said, 'Me for one.'

'Great,' said James. 'Everybody, have an early night. Tomorrow we chase up a missing girl. Oh, just a couple of phone calls for me to make before we go. I will ring the Choudhury elders and tell them of our results today. Also Derek. It will take a lot of worry from them, and the elder couple can go safely back to their own home.'

'They will be happy, James, to have that news. Tell them to talk to each other. They seemed to be at odds about several things. They should talk and clear the air. It makes for happier families,' said Percy.

James grinned at his partner. 'We are learning from each other, my friend. That was exactly what I was going to say to them.'

*　　*　　*

Later that evening, James broached the fact that D2 had entered the country illegally. James asked Granny and Alicia if they had any ideas on that.

He was surprised when Granny said, 'I have been told that before and during World War II, many flights bypassed officialdom and came in to land on private airfields. At the time, flying was still a new fun thing to do, and many of the big properties around the county had their own airfield and private planes. These airfields were owned privately, and many well-to-do young people learnt to fly and used their own airfields. They were closed down after the wars, and officialdom took over. It was all before my time and is only hearsay on my part, but I know it was true—for a short time anyway. My father used to admire the people who could afford to do these things. He was envious, as he wanted to learn to fly. It never happened for him, poor dear. I was told that he tried to join the air force, but his hearing was the thing that failed him. He was so disappointed.'

James leaned forward. 'So Granny teaches us a lesson again. Thank you, Granny. Now we have to work out which of these fields is still operating. It would have to be reasonably close to here for D2 and his brother to have ended up here. They did not have the means to travel, nor the knowledge. They were innocents, only children, from another country, but their father is British. We will do a search on Bowering in the morning and see if any landholders around here bear that name.'

'The names the boys have are telling in another way too, James,' continued Granny. 'You mentioned in your tale that the grandfather was from Goa? Would *Oliveri* have been his surname? The Goan people were ruled by the Portuguese for centuries. If I recall it correctly, *Oliveri* could have been one of their names. Is it possible for you to check out in your little box thing that you carry around, on Oliveri, Goan, anywhere in Africa, or even in England. This man appears to have been very wealthy. If they named a child after him, they may have used it without an *i* at the end, as it was a second name, and he seemed influential in his family. Perhaps he owned such an airfield somewhere around here as an escape route for if and when it was necessary. He must have seen the way his chosen country was turning, and he booked an escape route while he could. But poor man could not use it for himself, as there was a murky danger that he was unaware of, waiting for him and his wife.'

James, Alicia, and Percy looked at her with awe, and James said, 'The oracle has spoken once again. How I love you, Granny! You are always coming up with the goods for us.'

'It is because I have lived a lot longer than you, James. Local history comes into it a lot, and of course, I am a great reader,' Granny said, smiling at them.

James pulled out his laptop to do some research and then said, 'If I do it now, I will not be able to sleep, because my mind will be chasing aeroplanes all over the land tonight. No, I will deny myself until the morning, and I will have Kate do the chasing while I lead on the missing girl case.'

'A wise move, James,' said Percy, 'although another thought comes to mind. This means that there is a private aircraft registered to Bowering somewhere in the system, either here in the UK or in Zimbabwe or somewhere in Africa. I would bet that it is here in this country. Otherwise, it would have been confiscated by the ruling regime in Africa by now. Bowering is the pilot, and he used it two years ago to deliver the boys to safety. If only he had known. Every country has its own nasty lot of people.'

'This means he has the aircraft hidden, perhaps in the village D2 mentioned,' said Alicia. 'I hope the village has escaped the local danger at least. D2 talked of it with so much fondness.'

'Which begs the question: what has happened to Bowering senior? Nothing has been heard about him in two years,' added James.

Alicia remarked, 'Perhaps D2 has something still lost in his memory bank. It may surface in a day or so. We will have to speak with him again.'

Percy said, yawning widely with his hand over his mouth, 'We have opened up a new kettle of fish. Let's leave it and come back fresh for it tomorrow.'

James and Alicia nodded, and James said to Granny with a guilty look, 'Have you read the lost little girl's file yet? I left it out especially for you to have a look at it.'

Granny laughed. 'You cannot fool me, James. I saw it drop out of your briefcase yesterday as you walked out of the door. Luckily, I picked it up and had a quick look, or it would have been out in the garbage by now if Caroline had seen it first.'

'Caught. Damn, now you know me too well for me to fool you,' said James, laughing with the others, including Granny.

*　　*　　*

Next morning, Kate was assigned the search on Oliveri. She came up with a lot of information almost at once and took it to James and said, 'You were right. Douglas Oliveri was a part-Portuguese, part-Goan Indian who registered the maharaja emporium many years ago in Zambia and then moved on to Zimbabwe. Shortly after, he had emporiums all over Africa.

'All the shops were successful, and after his marriage to a local beauty queen, he made the last place his home and left a manager in the other shops. He had minor shops all over Africa which he started up and then left for local people to manage for him. He is what you would call an entrepreneur. Also, he is a philanthropist, because he gave so much of his fortune back to the people, with schools, clinics, and such. They say, with this picture of the man on the file here, that most of the country died in spirit the day Douglas Oliveri and his beautiful wife died by the hands of evil.'

'Is there any mention of the daughter? D2's mother?' asked Alicia.

'Not yet. All this came up almost right away. I haven't searched further yet.'

'You are doing great, Kate. Keep going for a while. Also, look up Bowering. We do not have a Christian name for him yet,' said James. 'Ken? Have you any idea how to search for property sales in this area— not in the town, but substantial property a little out of town that would have an airfield?'

Ken said, 'For the same man, Oliveri?'

'Yes, but try Bowering in it as well. It seems he may be the pilot. Someone brought those boys here from Africa, and D2 said his father brought him. Douglas Oliveri may have purchased a property for his son-in-law and grandchildren to escape to. But Bowering was too angry to wait until the boys were settled. I assume he went back to see if he could discover the secret diamond mine and the instigator of the killings of these special people in his family. They were special to their own country but more special to Bowering. The killing of his wife may have sent him over the edge.'

James sat thinking it over for a while and then said, 'I think I will ring my friend at London headquarters to see if an intelligence agency can chase Bowering up. In movies and television shows, there is always an agency ready to take off in the blink of an eye to rescue the "goodies". Thinking more about it, I suppose I mean mercenaries.'

'Wait, James,' said Percy, 'at least until we have finished our search, so that we can pass the information along. Wait until this afternoon at least. That will make it look as if you know what you are talking about.'

'All right, Percy. I will ring the hospital D2 is in, to see how he pulled up today. It was amazing watching his face as his life came back to him. I wonder if he has remembered more overnight.' James gave a guffaw of laughter, more at himself. 'Okay, Percy, you have convinced me. I am being a bit premature. This guy has been missing about for a year anyway. Another morning will not hurry things along.'

Ken came back with some information about a property, inland from the coastline and a near a village. 'It is in the name of Douglas Oliveri and Jason Bowering.' He said, 'This is a historic property. It was used as a landing field for aircrafts needing a quick "turnround" during the war. The aircraft would come in and refuel and take off again. Also the house was used by the army for rehabilitation of war casualties. Nothing much has been done with it since, and the large house is quite dilapidated. There is a groundsman mentioned, who looks after the property. I rang him, and he said he was employed to keep the runway and hangars in viable condition. When I asked for his employer's name, he stated that he was not in a position to give that information out. He has been employed on the property for the last five years.'

'Bingo,' said James. 'Now can I ring my friend?'

'No, James,' said Percy, offering a word of caution. 'Ring D2 as you mentioned. He may be able to tell you where Jason Bowering is, so you can pass that along with the rest of the story. Ask him about his physical health as well. I would bet that if anyone is going to look for Jason, D2 will want to go along with them. He knows the country, even if he was only a schoolboy at the time he left. He knows where his father worked, he knows the village where the aircraft may be hiding, and surely he must know some people sympathetic to his cause.'

James turned serious. 'You are right, Percy. I tend to jump the gun a bit, and I know nothing of this sort of thing. I was so shocked yesterday when D2 told his family history, and I think that has made me forget my common sense. I only want to help the poor boy, no matter what the consequences. Gathering information is the best we can do. We are not trained for this sort of adventure. The only time I have left my own country was on our Indian holiday and to visit my parents in Spain. I have not really had to deal with very bad people—not like how they sound from D2's reports. These make Haskell and Norman sound like sweet people. What sort of person could cut another up like D2 described? It must have been a real horror show for the two boys to discover their mother like that, knowing the same thing had happened to their grandparents as well.'

He rang the number for the hospital, and D2 came on the line after a few minutes. When asked how he was after the revelations yesterday, the boy said, 'I am still a little confused. I am unable to settle down and get things in sequence. It is coming out like a jumble of facts.'

'That is to be expected, D2. You have a lifetime to catch up with. Write it down as you think of a new aspect. You can sort it out later. Have you thought of your father overnight?'

'A little. He keeps hovering about on the periphery. At the time he left us, I was angry with him for leaving us. His mother—actually, it is his stepmother. His own mother died when he was in his teens, and I do not think he liked his stepmother very much. That is why he never brought us to introduce us to each other. His father is living in a nursing home somewhere, and she was plainly not interested in us and all our worries.

'I think my father was very angry about what happened to our mother and my grandparents. He had loved them as if they were his own family. He was so angry that he could not see that we—my brother and I—needed him to fill up the space in our lives. I think his idea was, he wanted to get back to find the killers and the secret diamond mine, in that order. He told us he had an idea who the top man was, who he needed to front, but he needed proof and was not going to find it here. So he dumped us and flew back. We have not heard from him since.'

'Whose idea, D2, was it for you to change your names?'

'It was his idea. He said that our name would jump out of a page if someone was looking for us. We agreed to keep our actual names and only turn them around to appear different, but if he was looking for us, he could have picked the names up immediately. It was his idea also to appear not to be brothers, as that was who the assassins would be looking for. He reminded us that the world was getting smaller. Anyone could be found anywhere in the world if they did not take precautions. I wonder if he took his own advice and changed his name. I do not think so. He was too well known as the son-in-law of the mighty emporium magnate, Douglas Oliveri.'

'It is amazing that he did not leave you more funds to help you out in your new life. Have you thought that over?'

'Yes. In the first few months, when we did not receive anything or any message from him, we decided he was in jail or dead or at least in hiding from the people who would have been chasing him. We hoped that when he went back, he went straight to our village and is in hiding there. It is quite isolated. But as time has passed and we have had no word, we decided he was dead.'

'You sound matter-of-fact about it, D2.'

'I have not had time to think about it while I have been in hospital. I could not remember anything. Little pieces of my earlier life danced around in my mind, usually when I was waking up, but they disappeared with the daylight. I was unable to link the pictures together. They did not stop around long enough for me to grab them and tie them down. It was like a kaleidoscope or jigsaw puzzle, to see these things appear and fade again before I could properly register them. Since yesterday, it is like I have made a real breakthrough, but there are still major parts missing.'

'How is your health generally, D2? Would you be able to manage your life out of the hospital?'

D2 laughed. 'I have been thinking to myself for months now that I can outrun anyone. I was always a good runner. The only thing stopping me was, I could not remember anything, even my name—neither the real one nor the one we were using—nor would I know where to go. It makes me feel quite helpless to have no memory of my life. The lessons on how to walk are no longer needed, and I build up my muscle strength every day with a visit to the hospital gym, overseen by experts. I am quite well again. The doctors have explained to me that it is because I was a healthy young person at the time of my "killing".'

'Have you seen the doctor today to explain your recovering memory, D2?'

'Yes, this morning, and I am to have some tests later today with a group of doctors, to see how far I have come. Thanks to you, James, I am halfway there, I believe.'

'Do you want to know your name, D2?' asked James with curiosity in his voice.

'Not yet, James. I am hoping it will come to me by itself. Do not give me any hints. I think when I know that, I will be cured.'

'Would you be averse to me reporting your case higher up in the police department? I have a friend in a very high position, and I would be curious to find out what he thinks of your story and if he can offer any help in some way in finding out what has happened to your father.'

D2 thought for a few minutes. 'I was thinking last night that when I am dismissed from this hospital, I may make a trip back to Africa to make enquiries about my father. Not all of my country has gone crazy, and I have been reading newspaper reports on the Internet. I was awake most of the night, looking for information on its progress, and things are finally making the change back to normal, which my mother predicted. I want to go to our village and find out if it is still "ours" or if it has got caught up in the troubles. My only problem for this is that I have no money. I thought this over all night, and I have come up with "But you do have thousands of pounds in uncut diamonds". My next thought is, how do I find out how to sell them and announce to the world that they come from a secret mine in the area where we lived, without bringing my name forward as the seller but getting back at the evil man who decimated my family?'

'Perhaps I can help with doing that research, D2. What do you think about taking your story higher?'

'If it will help, James. I am not sure yet which way to go or what to do. That will come, I suppose, but I have only the short story at the moment.'

'I will see what I can do in confidence with my friend. He is a dependable person, I have found in my dealings with him. Perhaps he can advise you on what to do, with our country's help.'

'Thank you, James, for taking an interest in me, a complete stranger to you. I appreciate all that you have done already. I have felt so alone at times since I have been in this country. Our way of life in my home country was more casual. I thought I would never leave. Now I do not know if I want to go back, to have the memories of better times and hideous times thrust at me at every turn.'

'As Iris Kumah said yesterday, you have to make some good memories to clear the bad ones away. Unfortunately, Iris will not be with us much longer. It seems as if people keep passing through for you, I suppose, but they all leave legacies behind them. They in themselves will be your good memories. You have good memories of your grandparents and your mother. Think positive about them, and it will stop you from getting despondent. Your earlier life sounds idyllic. Keep that in mind. If you need someone to talk things over with, I am always ready to help, and I will introduce you to my wife's grandmother. Nobody can be despondent after chatting with her. She keeps us all going. So there. You have a ready-made family already, to help you if you get down.'

D2's voice sounded better after that spiel, thought James. It was obvious that he had had a few bad moments through the long night. 'I will contact my friend and get back to you within a day or so with whatever they can come up with, especially the diamond sale. I am sure it is not the first time that sort of thing has come up. Goodbye for now. Remember, I am just a telephone call away if you need help.'

James finished the call feeling weak. He was not able to support the boy except for a short period; he had a job to keep up with and was not free to take on strays. He felt so sorry for the boy and wanted to help, but it would not be practical for him to drop his other responsibilities to take on full-time care of someone. He felt torn; he hoped they would be able to fix something up quickly.

He sat back in his chair and rang Jack Whistler, and in effect, Harold Griffiths—Jack's boss and the senior man. After the greeting and the telling of D2's story, there was a long silence at the end of the line. It had hit home with them, as it had with him. He could hear the clearing of throats, and Harold Griffiths came on the line and said, 'What have you promised the boy, James?'

'Nothing yet, sir, except help with selling privately the uncut diamonds to help him on his way. He has been living on commissions for selling cocaine, as it was all he could do to obtain enough money for him and his younger brother to eat.'

'Well, that vocation is over for him, since you locked up the cocaine. Congratulations on your resolution of that case, James. You have done well in a short period to finalise those cases and even find one still alive.'

'I will ask around to see if anyone knows about what is happening in most states in Africa and if we have anyone in the field who can give us an update. Do not sell the diamonds. We do not want the boy dashing off to find his father yet. Give me a couple of days to check things out. I will ask about selling the diamonds. I am sure a deal, including the fact that it is a secret mine, will bring all sorts of denials from their ministers. It could give us an advantage if Jason Bowering is still alive to be rescued. It has been a long period since he returned, so it will be a miracle if he is still alive.'

'Thank you, sir. I was hoping it would turn out like that. I was afraid my sincere sympathy for the boy was getting in the way of my common sense, something I pride myself on.'

'Where do you propose putting the boy, to keep an eye on him? We do not want him disappearing' came down the line.

'I have had contact with a mutual friend. However, she herself is terminally ill, and I do not want to worry her unduly. We have a spare bedroom in our apartment, which we use as a study. We could clean that out in the next day or so, and he could move in with us. I would not want it as a permanent solution though. We have appreciated our privacy in the apartment to date.'

'It would help out in the short term. You say that he may be dismissed from the hospital soon. Perhaps by then we will have sold his diamonds, and he will have enough money to fund his own place.'

'Yes,' said James slowly, 'I think Alicia may agree with that decision.'

'We will get back to you, James, as soon as we get an answer down the line. You understand that now the government will take over the hunt for Bowering?'

'Yes, sir. The boy wants to go and look for his father himself. At least while he is staying with us, we can monitor that and make sure he does not take off by himself.'

'You will be well paid for your work on this, James. We will make sure that the time you have spent on it and will spend on it will be worth your while.'

'Thank you, sir.'

James put the phone down and said to himself, 'That is not what I expected. Now I am to be a nursemaid until the government decides what to do. I am not sure Alicia is going to like this.'

He went to find Alicia, but she was nowhere to be seen. He asked Percy, 'What have you done with my wife? She did not tell me she was going out.'

Percy smiled. 'You took so long on the phone that Alicia and Kate have taken it into their own hands to go visit the mother of the missing girl, as that was supposed to be the case of the day. They left about an hour ago, so they should be back soon. They rang for an appointment before they left, to make sure the mother was available.'

'I am sorry, I had to sort D2 out first. He gave me permission to tell the story to Jack Whistler and Harry Griffiths, and to try to sell the uncut diamonds as well. We have made a little progress on that, except that Harry Griffiths wants me to babysit D2 until further notice, to make sure he does not try to go back to find his father by himself. They think that the place D2 came from has picked itself up after all the demonstrations a few years back. The country is poorer now than it has ever been, and there is a chronic food shortage. He thinks it may still be a better bet if they try to get Jason Bowering back politically than have a boy alone trying for it—that is, if the man is still alive. They will make enquiries, I was told.

'Meanwhile, they have asked if Alicia and I will take D2 into our apartment at the bookshop until the diamonds are sold and he can work something out for himself. It was for that reason that I was searching for Alicia. I am not sure how she will take it. They want me to make sure he does not take off for Africa by himself before they have a try at finding Bowering themselves in a diplomatic way. I think they are worried that D2 will disappear into the woodwork the same as his father. They are all British citizens after all, so we will have to await the outcome of their chances with the government involved and the games they play, on both sides.'

Percy looked at him comically. 'Well, we have the box seat to find out the facts as they happen. You have certainly brought an interesting lot of things into our mundane life until now. It will be interesting watching D2 come to life over time.'

James looked quite put out. 'What do police officers do to keep a distance from the general public, Percy? I seem to have a personality which makes them cling to me way over the time that anyone else would have put them out to graze.'

Percy laughed uproariously. 'You are right about that personality bit, James. Everyone seems to cling to you because you are so reasonable all the time. A police officer is supposed to keep his distance, but you seem unable to do that. They seem to be like limpets as soon as you appear.'

'Do they teach you about that detachment at police school, Percy?'

'It is implied from the beginning. You cannot end up with all your customers moving into your apartment with you. You are able to get people talking, James. It is a knack that policemen do not always have. You befriend them from the start, and they fall over themselves to tell you everything they know. I have watched it happen with almost every case we have taken on since the beginning of our partnership. I would not want to change your ways, James. It is wonderful to watch. They all end up best buddies with you. They trust you like they would never trust a policeman. It is the essence of our success in the business, and we have been successful. You even keep the top policemen tucked under your arm. How good is that?'

'I will have to get a bigger apartment as we go on, Percy, to house all these buddies. I am really scared to mention to Alicia that I have told the top policeman that I will take D2 under my wing. Never mind having to face up to Granny too.'

'Don't worry too much, James. I will be there to watch how you handle it. I will try very hard not to laugh when I see the look on your face after you announce it.'

'Gosh, Percy, you are helpful. Nobody could deny that.'

'Well, the best arrest I have ever seen made was Fiona and her sister Faye. I do not think anyone got a word in. They were so busy incriminating themselves. All you got to do was say "Hello, Fiona" and bring in D2 in his wheelchair, and we got to handcuff them straight away after you said "And by the way, we have your cocaine". They confessed their sins all the way to the police department. It was so incredible I had to pinch myself to make sure I was actually seeing it. That was all your doing, James. You think things through before you act. The rest of us are still trying to work it out, and you have sewn it all up.'

'It is all just common sense, Percy.'

'So you tell me each time we make an arrest. It must have been dealt out in spades to you, this common sense, and the rest of us are still lining up for our share,' Percy said, laughing.

Kate and Alicia walked into the office. Immediately, Alicia said to James, 'What have you done wrong? You look so guilty.'

'Come into my office, Alicia. I have to explain something to you,' said James, while Percy started laughing.

Alicia looked suspiciously at Percy and followed James into his office. 'I bet you are going to tell me that we are going to accommodate D2 in our spare room. We do not use it much anyway, James. We will clean it out this weekend.'

James looked back at Percy, standing with his hands spread out. 'See how well Alicia knows me, Percy? I do not have to explain anything to her.'

'I will agree as long as it is not for too long. We enjoy our privacy, James.'

'The gentlemen in London asked us to take care of D2 until they have worked out a solution for him,' said James. 'They do not want to lose sight of him until they have done their research on Jason Bowering and found out whether he is still alive.'

'Granny and I spoke about it this morning, before we came into the office, and we thought that is what they would say.'

'I was also told that we will be well paid for our care and D2's lodging—by the government, I presume. We as a team have also been congratulated for the case to date and for the arrest of Fiona and Faye. I guess you could say we have won some more brownie points. I did point out to them that the apartment is not very big and that we do like our privacy. They said they would do their best, but of course, it is not just up to them now. It has become a political duty to get Jason Bowering back to the UK, where he is still a citizen, even if he has not lived here for a long time—that is, if he is still alive.'

'Okay, James, we will do what we can. Meanwhile, Kate and I visited the mother of the missing girl. She is still missing. The stepfather has left the house too now. Kate and I thought it over on the way back to the office, and our take on the situation is that, as the girl is no longer there, the man is not interested in his bride any more This brings us to, was it his interest in the girl that made her leave? Or did he help her disappear, in a bad way?'

Kate had wandered into the office too and said, 'The stepfather moved out only four weeks after the wedding. That begs the question, was it the girl that was the interest for the man, not his new bride? Perhaps he married her to get to the young girl. It has been done before, and sometimes the girl is found dead. We have not put that to the mother yet. I think she is in denial. She is in love, she thinks, with her new husband and will not believe anyone vilifying him. We have come back to the office to do a check on him and anyone around him—at his place of work, for instance. He has been in the same job for fifteen years. Someone must know what sort of fellow he is. His new bride says he will come back to her when it is proved that he did not do away with the daughter. She is looking forward to the reunion with her husband.'

James asked, 'Did the woman give you any idea where she thinks her daughter may have gone?'

'She has no idea. We asked about the girl's father, and we were told they do not know each other. The girl was born after the mother's first marriage broke up. She has not seen her first husband since before the girl was born, and there has been no acknowledgement from the father of the daughter since she was born. She was very adamant about all this.'

'It seemed a bit odd to us,' added Alicia, 'and we decided we would do a check on the actual father. It has not been done before, as Kate was able to fish out that the woman had changed her name. When the first marriage broke up, she went back to her maiden name. We now think we will do a search of the mother's parents as well, to see if the girl went to them, for one, or has ever corresponded with them. The grandparents may have given the girl her father's details. There is no mention in the case file that these details were chased up. Perhaps when the disappearance first happened, the mother was very upset and left out a lot of detail for a follow-up to be done. The return to her maiden name was not mentioned in the file, for instance. What else did she not disclose? I think that is vital information.'

'It sounds as if the police team who did the initial interview were given the flick by the mother,' said Percy.

'Exactly, Percy. That is how we read it. And after a while, as they got nowhere with the information she gave them, they did not try too hard, thinking the girl would come back when she got hungry. Kids are so often peeved with their parents and want to do the big runaway thing and go for it until they get hungry and come home acting as if they did nothing wrong,' said Kate.

'Except this one did not come home, and it fell through the floorboards, left in the cold-case pigeonhole,' said James. 'It could have been that the newlyweds were wrapped up in each other and did not notice at first how long the girl had been gone, perhaps thinking that she must be staying with her girlfriends. A bit late then for anyone to chase any clues, like fingerprints on the window and door, and anything missing in particular that the girl may have been fond of, like a favourite doll or clothes. Some parents do not deserve to have children.'

Kate said, 'We will get on this research that we need first, and perhaps tomorrow we can chase the husband up at his place of work. I will look for the Internet information first and find out where he works. That was also not on file. We can make an appointment to meet him at lunchtime tomorrow. Do you want to do that interview, James?'

'It might not be taken so lightly if it is a bloke. Percy and I will do that one. You girls chase up any grandparents and go and talk to them tomorrow. Follow up on the girl's birth father after that if you can get the information. How long has the family lived at the last address, and where did the stepfather live before the marriage? Can you work on that this afternoon as well? Ken, it looks like you are in charge of the office tomorrow, for a while anyway.'

'That is fine with me, James. We are starting to get a backlog of our own cases. I will work on some of them and speak to people to keep them onside. We have been missing for the last two weeks with the cold cases.'

'Good on you, Ken. Yes, we have been missing. I did not mean for them to get in the way of our own clients, but in the end, we finalised more than we set out to do. Settling the cocaine from the customs office was a big bonus, and we were not aware of that when we started. It fell into our lap. Okay, lunch on us. I will go and fetch it from our own coffee shop and bakery along the mall and will be back in ten minutes, if you want to get the kettle boiling and the coffee maker working while I am away.' He went out of the door.

Alicia said, 'Did he ring up an order when we were not looking?'

Nobody had seen him ring up an order, so Alicia said, 'Then we may have to wait more than ten minutes.'

But no, he was back in the allotted time, and they all looked curiously at what the box that he brought back might give up.

James said, 'I do not have time to take you out to lunch, but you have all worked yourselves very hard the last couple of weeks. So I rang earlier and asked for a feast. I do not know what they have given me, but it smelt beautifully all the way back to the office. I hope you like it.'

It was a feast indeed, and when they had eaten all they could, James said, 'Take the rest of it home for the kids, Kate. That was so good it makes up for the fact that you did not get morning coffee yesterday and had to have a late lunch also, but we really did so well yesterday that we did not want to slow down to eat. Percy was saying earlier that it was the strangest arrest he has ever had to make. The two women, Fiona and Faye, shot themselves in the foot as soon as they saw D2. Still, I do not think it happens often that a dead man comes to life several months later to haunt and accuse you.'

*　　*　　*

Kate and Alicia went on with unearthing facts about the missing girl's mother, father, stepfather, and grandparents during the afternoon.

The mother seemed innocuous; nothing came up to grab their attention. They got the name of the girl's birth father from the mother easily enough, as well as the address for them at the time a wedding was performed. Jessica Owens married Peter Reynolds in another town further up the coast. They could not find a divorce notice for them. The girl's birth certificate announced that no father was registered, and she had been given the same surname as her mother. By that time, the mother Jessica, had moved to their own city, using her maiden name of Owens. Seven months later, the baby was born.

The parents of both first-wedding participants were still in the same city, up the coast.

The new stepfather was in their own town, working as a council employee in the planning department. He had been employed there for fifteen years, always in Planning. It all seemed so easy, but James said he and Percy would have a talk with him. James also said he wanted to find out about the birth father, the first husband. Why had he not made a stand to claim his daughter? What about the divorce? Or did the wife run away from her husband at the time? If she was not divorced, there was a problem.

James asked Percy if he would like to accompany Alicia for a nice drive up the coast to find these people. It was going to be a nice day; a drive along the coast was always pleasant. He said he would go himself, except the London people may ring back to ask for more details on D2. James would deal with the new husband. Perhaps Kate would like to go with him? It would not take too long, and they could come back to help Ken, as he would mind the office for the day. This was agreed to, so everyone went on with the work that had been piling up.

A little before five o'clock, James received a phone call from Dr Redfern from the coroner's office, saying he had just returned to his office after watching an interview with D2. There had been several doctors from around town present, including several psychologists and psychiatrists. All had interviewed D2 at some time since he had woken up from his induced coma. After they heard his history—or what he could remember of it, as there were still some gaps in his memory—it was deemed that the boy's brain had hidden from him all the truth in his life, including his own stabbing, as it was overloaded with the trauma it had been put through.

'It is as if the stabbing was the last straw for him, and the coma he was in—not the induced coma—closed his brain down. Some thought it was possible that he would retain the loss of memory, and it was your intervention, James—putting him face-to-face with the persons who attacked him—that saved him. Each medical person agreed that it was your idea that saved him, and they said you need to receive the accolades due. I put my bib in there and said that I think you and D2 have still some unfinished business and that you would not like this to go public. However, they plan to write up the case and send you a copy for your files, to show their appreciation, and until D2 allows them to go public with the case, as they need to have his permission, they will not do any more about it. They were so eager to go public with the case.

'They have plans to dismiss the boy from hospital, as he is no longer in need of medical attention. Once more, I demurred, saying you would let them know when alternative accommodation is available to him. I may have overdone it on your behalf, but you seemed like the sort of chap that would pay ongoing attention to D2 to keep him safe. Was I right in that, James? I am sorry if I have got in the way, but some of these fellows are so pompous. I could see them dismissing the boy and not following through because he is not a paying patient. That would have left him stranded on his own again.'

James laughed. 'I am going home now to clean out our study, the only space we have available, so that D2 can move into our apartment over the weekend. Alicia, Percy, and Granny have agreed with it, as long as it is not permanent. Our apartment has only two bedrooms, not large, and we do like our privacy, as any married couple does. This has been requested of me by the powers that be until they have hunted the father down in Africa. We all hope he is still alive. I will keep you updated from time to time. We do not have a date to work on, so we can only hope they get moving on it sooner rather than later. Thanks for the update. I appreciate it.'

'Before I go, James. Did you find out his name yet, or is he still D2?'

'Yes, we do know his real name, but we are leaving him as D2 for the moment, for safety reasons. We do not know yet what other dangers are in store for him. That is why I have been asked to monitor him from close up. Believe me, in our apartment, it will be close up.' James laughed. 'I guess we will manage.'

'If he needs medical assistance in the near future, I am still registered as a general practitioner, even though I work mainly in the coroner's office nowadays. Give me a ring if he needs any attention, James, rather than going to someone who is unaware of his history.'

'That is very kind of you, mate. I appreciate that. We do not know if he will have any repercussions from all that he has gone through. It could be helpful to have you on hand, as it were, to help out. I spoke at length with him after we arrested his almost murderer, and he seems to be a nice young chap. I think he will get on fine once it all sinks in—or should I say, comes out.'

'Okay, James, the offer is there. Perhaps I will see you soon. Bye for now.'

As James put the phone down, he called out to Percy and Alicia. 'We have to hurry up and get D2's room ready for him. He is going to be dismissed from the hospital on the weekend.'

All the staff crowded into his office, and Ken said, 'That is a bit early, isn't it? He still appeared uncertain yesterday when we left him.'

James said, 'We have no choice. Besides a lack of memory, there is nothing wrong with him any more. Physically, he is probably better than you and me, Ken. We only work out two evenings a week, but he works out under a trainer every day. I think he will be able to look after himself, which is good when you think about it. He will not need much guarding, and if someone comes while he is in the bookshop, he can look after Granny too.'

'Will you bring him to the office during the day, James?' asked Kate.

'I have not got that far in the planning yet, Kate. I suppose I will have to. He would be driven mad with nothing to do. Granny does not need help any more in the bookshop.'

'Good,' said Kate and Alicia together. Alicia said, 'He can be our receptionist for a while. We are starting to get backed up around here.'

They all looked around at each other, and James said, 'Any objections?'

'None,' said Percy. 'He will fit in just fine, and he can earn his board and lodging.'

'Well, that seems settled. I am glad I thought of that,' said James.

Everyone laughed, and Kate said, 'You have not had time to think about what you were going to do with him once you got him, so someone had to make the decision.'

'Actually, you are all right. It does sound like a good idea. I just have not had the time to think about it. I am still getting over the fact that it is us who are going to babysit him, and I have not got around to what his activities will be. This has all been sprung on us so quickly, with all the other things happening at the same time. He will be good as a receptionist. It will mean that we will know where he is at all times, and we can watch over him and make sure he does not do a runner to Africa. Also, things are getting so busy. We need all hands on deck this week to help clear the backlog, and having D2 here will give us the time we need. The police chief did spring those cold cases on us without any warning. We have completed them all, except the missing girl, in exceptionally good time. I am sure you are all proud of yourselves.'

Alicia said, 'Yes, James, we now think of ourselves as real detectives. However, we now need to think of a new name for D2. We cannot present him to the public like that. Has anybody got any ideas?'

Kate said, 'What about *Daniel*? It is as if he came out intact from the lion's den.'

'Yes, that sounds good,' said James. 'Has anybody else got any ideas?'

Ken said, 'I think we should stick to the Indian idea. Someone may recognise him, and we do not want to change his story too much. After all, he has been around this town for two or three years now.'

'That is true,' Percy said. 'Keeping up the idea that he is Indian is the way to play it. He is a little too brown to be called English, even with a suntan. He is a very good-looking boy. Do any of you know any Bollywood men's names?'

Nobody did, but going through the Indian names they knew, Alicia said she liked *Bharat*. She went to the computer and searched Indian boys' names. *Divit* jumped out at her, and she said, '*Divit* means "one who has conquered death" or "immortal". It also begins with a *D*, in case we forget and call him D2.'

They all liked that, so it was decided—no more D2. He was now Divit Edwards, as he was known previously from his brother's name at the school he attended. They had to bring his known surname forward, in case anyone would recognise him. A query could cause all sorts of issues in the town if people started asking questions.

Percy added, 'We will have to make sure he keeps his hair short. If not cut, it will be an afro, and then people will query him.'

James said, 'That is possibly why he has kept his hair short, although while he was in hospital, someone must have realised that and made sure he had a haircut, possibly the nurse whose language he remembered.'

'Well, we have all worked that one out. Thank you, folks, for thinking ahead. I am afraid my brain is a bit frazzled, with all that has been going on. I think it must be time to go home and retire it for a bit.'

'We all agree with that,' said Percy, and everyone nodded. It had been a very busy couple of weeks.

'Do you want help clearing the study for Divit, James?' asked Ken.

'I think we will be okay with it, Ken. There is still a bed in the room, from when we looked after Jody. The desk too can stay, and the wardrobe. We really just have to move all the books. We could do with a new bookshelf. I will have one delivered for our collection of odds and sods and personal books. We do have a small storeroom, but that is stacked with our London junk. We will have to clear that someday. We often have a go at clearance, but we end up putting things back because of the memories they evoke.'

'I have experienced that sort of clearance, James, but it came to a head when I agreed to come down here. I shut my eyes and threw everything out,' said Ken.

'Yes, Ken, that brings us back to your position here. With all this extra work we have taken on with the cold cases, you are guaranteed a permanent place with us if you still want it. Have a chat with Kate about it and let us know what you decide. We have been very happy having you here,' James said, looking at Percy, who nodded.

'Thank you, Percy and James, and you too, Alicia. I will talk it over with Kate and get back to you on it,' said Ken.

'Well, that is it for the day. I am sure you are just as tired as me. I will see you all in the morning,' James said, picking up the lost little girl's file to put into his briefcase.

CHAPTER ELEVEN

The day was sunny but breezy. Never mind, as they would be in the car most of the time, Percy thought. Alicia had suggested that he drive to where they were going, and she would drive back, to give him a break. *That is fair enough,* thought Percy. *I do get tired nowadays.*

It was a long drive, which gave them time to discuss the case. Alicia went over what was said at the interview with the mother of the missing girl. She said, 'Both Kate and I suspect something is going on with the mother. When we checked the file, it seems it was not the mother who had reported the girl missing at all. It was the girl's schoolteacher. Shelley—that is the girl's name—had not been at school for several weeks, and no information was given by the mother each time they contacted her about the girl's health and whereabouts. She shrugged it off each time, as if it was a normal thing for the girl to be away from home.

'The teacher, Sally Borman, decided to visit the girl's home, and the mother was quite rude to her, saying it was none of her business. So the young woman thought, "If she is going to be like that, I will report the missing girl to the police." And she did. Of course, the police could do no more than she had done at first. On entering the child's room with an open window, they decided it was a set-up for them. According to the teacher, Shelley had not been to school for several weeks. The window could not have been open that long. Insects get in, and the cold was enough to ensure that the window was closed each night. However, they were unable to break the mother from her statement that Shelley had run away. She maintained that she would be back when she missed her mother.

'Shelley has not come home. Our instincts were that her mother did not seem very sorry about it. She treated our conversation with her as an intrusion into her private life. It has now been six months since the girl missed her school lessons, and when we spoke to the teacher, she was very concerned for the girl. I wonder what her grandparents are like. They have not been too concerned either. No one has heard their opinions. They refused to be interviewed, saying that neither their daughter nor their granddaughter have contacted them since the first wedding. They have never seen their granddaughter and now do not want to hear anything more about her, as it is not their business after all this time.

'That is all so far, Percy. The usual notices were left everywhere. Nobody has seen her. But what amazed both Kate and me is that the stepfather also wants to be left out of the story. What is going on, do you think? Someone must know something. A child of ten is not someone that just disappears, unless they are murdered and perhaps buried in the garden. However, the police dug the garden up and checked the floorboards and came up with nothing at all.'

Percy thought it over. 'Perhaps she has shut the girl up in the coal cellar. New homes do not have a coal cellar usually, but the old homes would still have them, used now for firewood or just rubbish storage. I have seen some used for storing bicycles, others for storage of the municipal rubbish bins. One I saw was used as a kennel for a big dog. Coal fires were outlawed many years ago, somewhere in the 1950s, after the Great Smog of London in 1952. I cannot remember when they were banned elsewhere, but it was a long time ago. Prior to that, every house had a coal cellar, to store the dirty stuff outside the house and also out of the rain and snow.'

'I think the police would have checked that, Percy, unless it was nailed up. No, I think something else is afoot. Why did the newly married man leave his bride of a month? Don't you think that is strange?'

'James and Kate will have to find that out, Alicia. Our job is to look at the grandparents and the ex-husband—if, in fact, he is an ex. There was no sign of a divorce, according to Kate's search.'

'By the look of these houses we are passing, it looks like our first destination will come into sight any minute. Yes, there is a church, usually one of the first things you see. The address for the Owens is in Church Street. Go slower, Percy. There is the house, opposite the church. Would that be the rectory? It has a cross on the letterbox and another at the edge of the vestibule leading into the house. Her father must be the resident rector,' said Alicia, pointing at a large white painted house with a pretty garden at the front and a white painted garden seat under a shady tree in the centre of a manicured lawn area. The house was opposite to an art deco–style church, which was obviously well maintained and which had a services timetable on a large board facing the street.

'Well, that was not mentioned in the file. I wonder if the police visited these people?' speculated Alicia.

They parked the car at the kerb, away from the driveway, and both got out and walked up to the front door. Percy rang the bell, and they waited for a few minutes before a white-haired middle-aged lady answered, poking her head out and saying, 'The minister is not home at the moment. He is out doing house calls. Is there anything I can help with? I am his wife, Janine Owens.'

Percy spoke first. 'Hello, Mrs Owens. You are the one we have come to see. May we come in, please?'

In the way of old-fashioned hospitality, the woman opened the door and stood aside while they entered. Then she showed them into a neat room, which had obviously been set up as a study but was also an interview room.

Percy introduced Alicia and then himself, handing over a business card. Mrs Owens looked at the card, and her features did not change. 'How can I help you with your business, Mr Gray?'

Alicia said, 'We are here, Mrs Owens, to investigate and ask you if you have heard from your granddaughter recently.'

'I have never heard from my granddaughter, Mrs Armstrong. Sometimes I find it difficult to remember I have one. I did not know whether Jessica, our daughter, had a girl or a boy. I have not seen her and have had no word over the years of how she is doing. My daughter chose to move away from us and her husband when she found out she was pregnant. She has not changed her position in all that time. We had an argument when she told us that she was leaving her husband of three months. We could see she was upset about something, but she would not tell us what it was. We remonstrated with her, saying things get better in time. She is a very small woman—or, as we thought of her at the time, girl. She was barely out of her teens when she married, and she was a headstrong girl, easily upset. We thought she and her husband must have had an argument. She did not say that she was pregnant. She almost ran out of the door, and we have not heard from her since. Nearly ten or eleven years have gone by.

'We tried to find her, and eventually, six months later, someone told us that they saw her, at least six months pregnant, in a doctor's office in your town. We went there and tried to find her, but she must have changed her name. There was no record of her in the city records or any other place we looked, and of course, the doctor's office would not give out any information about her. She had always been a strange girl, my husband and I agreed. She dismissed herself from her father's congregation when she was about twelve and refused to attend any services in the church, saying that it was like five people lived in the house—the first was God, the second was Jesus, and then came our family of three. She was a silent child. She was not someone to come to us and ask about things, nor would she listen to reason from us. It was like having a stranger in our midst the whole time she was growing up. We were pleased when she decided to marry. We thought she must have found someone who understood her. So when she disappeared three months later, we were as equally shocked as her husband Peter was.

'Peter is still in this town. He is a council worker—in Planning, we believe. He has not remarried and comes to see us from time to time to see if we have heard anything about her. We did not tell him that a friend had seen a pregnant girl that she was sure was our daughter. We did not want to cause him any more pain. He was so bewildered when she disappeared, and he told us he thought they had been getting along marvellously. He could not understand why she did not come back home. He had made a delightful home for them so they could move in as soon as they were married. The wedding took place in our church, despite her unwillingness to attend services. We did not understand anything about Jessica, Mr Gray and Mrs Armstrong.

'From our counselling of our parishioners, I know it is a common cry—"You do not understand me". We honestly tried hard to understand. She is our only child. I had difficulty producing her. In those days, we were not given the choice of caesarean birth. It was only offered then in the case of emergencies. My struggles to produce Jessica did not count as an emergency. My own doctor was away at the time, and the midwife taking care of me during the birth was an arrogant woman who believed doctors were no better than her, so she refused to send me away to another town for birth by a doctor.

'I have many times wondered if some damage was done during the long hours I was in labour and if that was the reason our child was a little different. I was not able to become pregnant again after Jessica, so some damage had been done to me. We wondered all her life if Jessica was damaged. She was our beloved daughter, and until she was twelve, we believed she was normal, if a quiet child. It was when she was entering puberty that she changed and hardly spoke to us. We were terribly upset and tried not to show it to her—or, in fact, anyone in our community. We had hoped she would grow out of it. Her disappearance after three months of marriage still upsets us, though we have learnt to live with it. My husband is a caring man. He has not understood Jessica's attitude at all and grieves for her loss. I feel angry at times about the way she behaved, but I have tried to understand that this was not her fault. It was mine, for not ordering that midwife to send me to a doctor. Perhaps our sorry lives would have been explainable if we knew what had gone wrong.'

Alicia looked upset at this story. 'Mrs Owens, we are so sorry about Jessica. We can report that your daughter is alive and well, but Shelley, your granddaughter, disappeared six months ago. Your daughter insists that she ran away because Jessie got remarried to Ian Page—would you believe, another town planner in our local council office. She said Shelley was jealous of her attention to her new husband and ran away to punish her.

'It was Shelley's schoolteacher who reported her missing, and the police have been trying to find her to no avail. We have been called in as new faces and brains on the case to see what we can do about finding the little girl. You are our first interview, and we will press on until we have reached the end, whatever it may be. Is it a coincidence that Peter and Ian are employed in the same capacity? It is another strange point in a weird case. You must be thinking "Has Jessica murdered her own child?" Well, the police thought so and inspected the house and grounds, even digging up the garden to see if they would find a body. We are pleased to report that they did not. We will go on with our search. We will go and see Peter Reynolds now, to seek his view of his absent wife. We will try our best to be kind to the man.'

'Before we go, Mrs Owens,' said Percy, 'would you allow us to take a photo of you and of your home from the street? It is to be put on file to confirm that we spoke to you. The reason we are here so early in our search is that you did not show up in the file, and we wondered why not.'

'Although it has been twelve years since we have had word of our daughter, Mr Gray, I—and I am sure my husband also—will be glad to hear that Shelley is missing because she wants to be and is alive and well. I recognise Jessica's unwillingness to allow anyone into her thoughts and what she would call her own business.'

Alicia gasped. 'That is exactly what she said to me when I went to interview her. That is amazing.'

'I had a lot of time to study Jessical before she too ran away, Mrs Armstrong,' said Mrs Owens.

'For your information, Mrs Owens, Jessica has been using her Owens name all this time, and her daughter is known at her school as Shelley Owens. This is who we are looking for,' Percy said, watching her face. He saw the shock on her face. They said no more and left to drive further into the town, looking for the council offices.

When they arrived, it was to find that Peter Reynolds was not available. He was on his annual holiday and had gone to Jersey to visit some friends. He was not expected back for at least another week. As they came out of the offices, Percy's phone rang. It was Mrs Owens. She said she had spoken to her husband, and they had agreed. If Percy and Alicia were returning home, could she have a ride with them? She wanted to see Jessica. Perhaps she could find out the facts for them.

Alicia and Percy agreed, saying it would be a one-way trip, as they had work to follow up on. Mrs Owens said she would be thankful for the lift, and her husband could come and pick her up later on, after she spoke to her daughter. He was unable to take her till later because he was visiting people on the other side of the town, but he would be free to bring her back.

They agreed and called back to the rectory to pick up their passenger. Mrs Owens was silent in the back seat of Percy's car, with Alicia driving for much of the distance they had to cover. Mrs Owens seemed to be dozing, but she sat up when they were at the edge of town and followed where they were taking her, which was to the house where Kate and Alicia had interviewed Jessica the day before.

Mrs Owens seemed content with that, and they waited to see if Jessica would answer the door, before driving off to return to the office.

*　　*　　*

James had returned to the office after interviewing Ian Page and was interested in what they had to say. His comment was that Ian Page had no idea what was going on with Jessica and Shelley. He told James that Shelley had disappeared one day while he was at work, just a few weeks after his marriage to Jessica. His new wife would not comment on Shelley's whereabouts, except to say the girl had run away.

Percy said, 'Where do we go from here?'

James shrugged. 'Well, Ian Page said he is aware that people are saying he did away with the girl, but that is not true. To stop any further gossip, he returned to his mother's home, where he lived prior to the wedding. Jessica asked him to come back, but he refused, telling her he would come back when she produces Shelley. But she continued to say that Shelley is fine and that she will come home one day, with no other explanation. He said he has never been so befuddled before in his life, and at this stage, he is never going to return to his wife. He has had enough of lies from Jessica and the gossip in the community.'

Alicia said, 'Perhaps after Mrs Owens has spoken to Jessica, we will know more of what is going through Jessica's mind. Clearly, she knows what is going on, though nobody else does. Let's hope she tells her mother. Mrs Owens said she would ring us after speaking to her daughter. We will have to wait until she finishes her conversation and time with the daughter she has not seen or heard from in ten years. It may all be innocent. We must wait and see.'

'We are ready for D2, Percy,' said James. 'We cleaned out the study last night and put fresh sheets on the bed, and Alicia produced an eiderdown we have never used from our storage room. There is a bedside table with a lamp on it, and it all looks pretty good, even if I say so myself. It will do for him for the short term we expect to have him with us. We left a couple of books for him to read for a start, but as you know, there are plenty more where they came from, downstairs.'

'Alicia's grandmother surprised me last night, James, accepting D2 into the household so easily. It even appeared as if she had known it would happen.'

'Do not underrate Granny, Percy. She knew what would be offered by the government for us to act as babysitters. It was the rest of us that were in the dark on the subject.'

'Yes, I believe that, James. What a special lady,' said Percy.

'Have you heard anything today, James, while we were out? About a D2 update, I mean.'

'Nothing more for the moment. I presume we will be advised officially when they release D2. So far it is only Dr Redfern who has advised us, and that was unofficially,' answered James.

'I cannot help wondering how Mrs Owens is getting on with her daughter,' said Alicia. 'I cannot settle down until she calls or comes in. Who would like a cup of tea? I will make it while I wait.'

When they sat to have the cup of tea, Mrs Owens came in the door of the office. She was smiling, so Alicia and Percy sat up and offered her a cup of tea and asked her to sit with them. It looked as if there was good news. Mrs Owens looked happy, and while she was drinking her tea, James asked if she minded if they recorded her statement.

'Please, go ahead, Mr Armstrong. My daughter considers herself not guilty of anything other than withholding information. I personally think she has a mental condition which swings into place whenever she has to manage a conversation with more than two or three people at once. In between times, she appears quite normal. That is why the information she has given out to police and others is minimal. She told me that Shelley is staying with a friend named Maureen, whom Jessica had shared a house with for several years. Shelley and this friend are always happy in each other's company.

'Jessica stated that she had had no trouble with her daughter at all until the marriage to Ian Page drew near. Shelley was doubtful of him joining the little family. It had always been Jessica and Shelley. After the marriage had been in place for a month, Shelley asked if she could go and stay with their earlier housemate. Jessica objected, but the girl packed up her things anyway, took some money from her mother's purse, and set off. Maureen is now living in London, which is why Shelley has not been found, and Maureen was unaware that the police are looking for her.

'I have Maureen's address if I need or want to see if this is a true story. Jessica has agreed that we pass this information on to you or whomever you want to give the information to. When I asked her why she did not tell Ian Page this story, Jessica said, "He did not believe me when I said that Jessica had run away. So I decided he was not worth any trouble, and he could go too. I am sorry, but I do not tell lies. He would not believe what I was telling him, so I let him leave."'

'There has been a lot of man- and woman-power chasing up Shelley. Why did Jessica not tell someone before now where the young girl was?' said Percy.

'I said that to her,' said Mrs Owens, 'and her answer was "It is none of their business. If they want to chase their own tails, let them. I told them all that Shelley had run away, and not one of them believed me. Did I have to get down on my knees and beg them to believe me? I just shut them all out in my mind and went on as usual."

'I told you, Mr Gray, that my daughter is different. Perhaps you should ask the health system to examine her and see if she has a blankness in her head. As I said, her birth was hard, and forceps were used to pull her out by her head. I objected at the time, but I was not able to insist on very much. My exhaustion after two days of heavy labour made me oblivious to that midwife and her strategies in the end.'

A knock came at the door, and standing in the doorway was a white-haired man with a clerical collar. Mrs Owens rushed to the door and said, 'These are the wonderful people who have found Jessica for us after all these years. We have a granddaughter called Shelley, and she is the one now missing.' She turned and looked at Percy. 'Can we go and find our granddaughter? Or is it up to you?'

Percy said to them, 'If you wish to find Shelley, be our guest, but you will have to bring her into this office to introduce us, as the police department will think it most unorthodox and may chase you up instead of Shelley. We will ask for a medical test for Jessica. She has an odd way of looking at things which is itself very unorthodox and, in my opinion, needs to be looked in to. It appears it is life-changing for those around her, such as Peter Reynolds and Ian Page. It must be very uncomfortable for them. We will advise Ian Page when Shelley is brought to us, but perhaps you would be better to describe the circumstances to Peter. It seems he is the girl's father, and he has been unaware of the fact for ten years.'

'There is a lot to do. I am sorry you have been put through all this trouble,' said Mr Owens.

'This is our business, finding people. I am glad it appears to be turning out well for you. When do you think you will be following up on calling to meet Shelley?' said Percy.

'Tomorrow, as early as we can, so I can get back to work. If I am held up, I will have to elect a locum to take over for a few days,' said the man.

Alicia said, 'You may need that locum to take over for a few days. Shelley will be at school most of the day, we presume, so it will be late in the afternoon before you can catch up with her. You may need to stay in London overnight. Ring Jessica's friend Maureen to work it all out. Remember that you have to keep us up to date with what you do, or we may have to take over the arrangements for ourselves. I am sure though that Shelley would rather have you call on her than us looking all official. The girl is only ten and may not be aware of all the trouble she has made, and surely she will be pleased to meet her grandparents and perhaps her father. It will be a new world to her. When you have made the arrangements with Maureen, please let us know of your movements.'

'I think we understand those instructions. Do we, love?' the man said, turning to his wife.

Mrs Owens said, smiling, 'Yes, and thank you all for your trouble. Ours has been a lonely life as a family since Jessica disappeared.'

The team smiled as the Owenses left the office. The two older people were holding hands and looking joyful. Alicia said, 'I hope it is all they want it to be. It seems to me that the granddaughter thinks a little like her mother. I hope I am not reading it right. What do you think, Kate?'

'A bit like you, I think. The girl did not want to share her mother with a new husband, so she left home. That is not normal behaviour for a ten-year-old. We will have to wait at least until tomorrow evening to find out the grandparents' opinion. I hope we did the right thing.'

'What if you two, Kate and Alicia, go to see this Maureen tomorrow? If the girl is at school, we can make an appointment with the headmistress to call at the school to see her. The Owens seniors will not get to see the girl until later. To make sure that Jessica is telling the truth, this needs a follow-up after the way she has led everybody on,' Percy suggested. 'What do you think, James?'

'I was wondering myself, why we are letting these two elderly people do our job? It is a bizarre event, chasing up a ten-year-old who ran away from home, whose mother knew the whole time where she went, and allowed the police to believe she had killed her child. That is not normal behaviour. If you two ladies are willing, I think it a good idea to get to Maureen's house and see Shelley for yourself and get her story, before the grandparents muddy the story.' James looked perplexed. 'If Kate cannot go, I will go with Alicia. If we do it early, we should only be away for the morning.'

'I think it better if you and Alicia go,' said Percy. 'Some look at women investigators as if they mean nothing, like Jessica obviously did initially. This woman has to learn a lesson: that we mean to find her daughter and will not leave it to her mother and father. It is too bad for her if we find her daughter first. The grandparents can catch up with her later, depending on what we decide when we are there with the child. We do not know what we will find, but Jessica did not give her daughter's address to us. I for one am very cross about that.'

'Yes, Percy,' said James. 'You are right. This case has cost the police force oodles. Somehow the joy of those two older people swung us away from our job. We need to see the girl for ourselves. We do not know whether they were acting to fool us. As you point out, she could be any child brought forward for the occasion. The Owenses have never seen her. It may be someone else brought forward to fool us. Jessica has certainly fooled a lot of people up till now. I do not like this case one little bit. Yes, sorry, Kate, but I think Alicia and I should go. If we are a little late getting back, it will not matter so much. You have your children to think about.'

'It is lucky then that I wrote Maureen's address and phone number down when Mrs Owens waved it at us,' said Kate.

Alicia breathed a sigh of relief. 'Good on you, Kate. I am afraid it took me by surprise, and I did not get around to asking her for it. She did not really show us. She passed it before our eyes very quickly, as if she did not want us to know where it is.'

Percy said, 'It sounds as if we are all getting a bit tired. The weekend is coming up, and we can rest on our laurels a bit and come up fresh again on Monday.' He could see by the smiles that the team agreed to that. 'Will you drive up to London, James? Or catch the train?'

'If we leave early in the morning, we should catch Maureen before she sends Shelley to school, so we will leave early and drive. That is better than waiting around for a taxi when we get there.'

'That leaves the three of us in the office tomorrow. We should be able to get through a few of the outstanding jobs while you are gone,' said Ken.

'Thanks, Ken,' said James. 'It is good to have you guys here to help out. The way things have been lately, we would be miles behind without you.'

*   *   *

That evening, Percy, James, and Alicia, spoke about the case of the day with Granny. She liked to hear what cases they were working on, and they agreed that Granny came up with some wonderful insights into the various cases. Alicia told her about the lost little girl, the files of which Granny had teased James about losing from his briefcase. She had read the folder in the file during a quiet moment in the day and now wondered what they had come up with.

Alicia told her of the day's happenings, and Granny said, 'There was a similar thing like this that happened a few years ago. You had just gone to London, Alicia, and I think it was before you and James met. It was not in this town but further up the coast. I cannot remember all the details, but it was a church couple convicted of selling young blonde girls to the Middle East. They were jailed for a minimum period because they could not find anyone who would testify against them. The more I think about it, the more I remember the story.'

Alicia and Percy looked at each other with their mouths open. They turned to James, and Alicia said, 'What do you think of Granny now? How can we check this case out?'

James picked up his phone and called Paul Morris and filled him in on the story that Granny had told them. Then he told him of the findings of the day, including the rector and his wife, presumably Jessica's parents. He ended by saying, 'Alicia and I are leaving at five in the morning to visit Maureen, hoping to catch the woman and the girl before they go off to work and school. It now looks as if we will need you to come along to arrest them. What do you think? Also, can we get a printout of the former prosecution? It was about ten years ago, I believe—before Alicia and I met.'

'This is a clever catch, James, if they are the same people. Maybe Jessica has taken over for her parents. She would have remembered some of the contacts. Would she sell her own daughter though?'

'Mrs Owens said her daughter was strange. Maybe she had the baby to groom her for sale. The child is of a small build, like her mother, and has fair skin and blonde hair. This is shown in the only photograph Jessica produced for the police. A copy is in the file. I do not know, but perhaps a good price was given for the previous sales, and Jessica remembered and thought she would do it her way. She got married to Peter Reynolds, who I will bet is a small man, and as soon as she was pregnant, Jessica left him and has not been heard of till now. Also, it was not Jessica who reported the girl missing. It was Shelley's schoolteacher.

'It was just by chance that we looked up the grandparents. Percy said he wondered about the shock on Mrs Owens's face when we told her that Jessica had reverted to her maiden name. Of course, this may ring bells in the community when the names get out, and they would be made public. The good man Owens is still the rector of a church, which does not bode well for his future if word does appear in the news again. I would say that they are thinking very hard right now about how to stop these things from happening again. Do you think I should have a word with my London friend in the force and have a policeman stand on duty outside the house we will be visiting first thing in the morning?

'We were befuddled by the senior Owens couple into allowing them to find Shelley, their only grandchild. They made a great deal about how they would like to discover her first and how they would bring the child to us. After they left our office, we all wondered what we had just heard. Was it all real? Alicia and I decided we would set off early, like five o'clock, to catch them at home in the address in London before the older couple can get there.'

'James, make that call now. I think we should take off earlier, at four in the morning, in case of hold-ups on the road in the morning traffic. I do not remember the earlier case, but we do not always get the news from further along the coast, because we have so many cases of our own. I will ask one of the team to get on it. At least the name of Owens should be easy enough to find, even if they did not serve much time. The officer should have it by morning. They can send it to my phone, and we can compare them. I will meet you at the bookshop at four. I will park in the alleyway for safety.'

'Good, thanks, Paul. It will be good to have you along. See you in the morning, and I will make that call and book a sentry right away.'

James dialled the number he had for Jack Whistler and had the call directed to Jack's home. After James told him the full story, Jack said, 'I will order a man to be on duty right away. We do not want them slipping out at midnight, in the darkness.'

'Thanks, Jack. I am off now to get some sleep for a few hours. We have not been getting much sleep lately. We have been run off our feet, but we do seem to be making progress. I will let you know after I find out what is going on at that address. In a way, I hope it is nothing, but my gut feeling says it is a big deal. I will catch up with you tomorrow, Jack.'

When he turned back to Percy and Granny and Alicia, he said, 'I am off to bed. If we have to travel in the dark to catch these people out, I had better get to bed right away. I will not wake you up in the morning, Granny. Alicia and I will slip out quietly.'

'Goodnight, James and Alicia, and good luck for tomorrow. I believe you are making the right moves,' said Percy.

CHAPTER TWELVE

I t was very dark and cold when they left the house next morning and greeted Paul Morris in the alleyway behind the bookshop. The moon was hidden by clouds, which they hoped would be gone by the time they reached the outskirts of London, as it would make it easier for them to navigate the quiet streets in the semi-darkness. It took some time in the winding streets for them to find the house they were looking for, but eventually they spotted a police vehicle at the kerb around the corner of the street they thought must be Maureen's.

The house was still in darkness, and they watched as the lights came on in the house at six o'clock. All the house lights came on, one after the other, and they could see shadows on the blinds as someone moved around. At seven o'clock, they decided to make a move. James asked the constable to move around to the back of the house as they knocked on the front door.

While the group waited for the front door to open, a taxi pulled up at the kerb outside of the house, a stream of exhaust smoke coming from the tail of the cab. Paul Morris moved over to talk to the driver, and after a few minutes, he came back and said the driver was waiting to pick up five persons to take south, to the tunnel to France, and then on to Holland.

As Paul stepped back towards the small group at the door and told them this in a low voice, James let out his breath and said, 'It looks like we are only just in time.'

The door opened with the click of a lock on the inside and a bolt pulled across. A suitcase appeared in the doorway, then another, and another. Then a woman's voice said, 'We will only be a few minutes.' She did not look out or step out of the door but disappeared back upstairs. James and Alicia and Paul watched her go up the stairs, and they stepped into the house and closed the door and pulled the bolt shut after themselves.

The woman's voice said loudly, 'Put the bags in the car, will you? We will only be a minute for the final check, to make sure we have everything.'

Paul said, 'You will have to come back downstairs to answer a few questions, please.'

A red-headed woman looked over the balustrade at the group standing inside the door, and she said, 'Who are you? What do you want at this time of the morning? I do not have time for a survey. What are you doing here so early in the morning anyway? It is still dark outside. I have to get my children dressed quickly for our trip to France. I do not have time for you and your silly business, whatever it is. Let yourself out again, please, and go away.'

James said loudly, 'Our business is police business, Maureen. Come downstairs, or we will come up.'

'Don't be silly,' she said. 'Go away. I have four children to dress. I really do not have time for your nonsense this morning.'

'We have a warrant to search your house, Maureen. Please bring the children downstairs immediately for an interview, and some of us will begin the search of your premises.'

They listened and heard a scuttle of feet disappearing towards the rear and the sound of a door opening. Paul phoned the constable standing out the back of the house and alerted him, saying, 'A number of children are headed your way. I will come around and help you gather them up.'

He went through the kitchen to the back door and arrived in time to see the first pair of small feet coming down the ladder. 'Handcuff the first couple to the handrail, Constable. I believe there are four little girls, also a woman, about to arrive.'

Meanwhile, back in the house, James said, 'I think the first thing we must do is dismiss the taxi driver after getting his details. The address he was to deliver his passengers to will be very important in any further investigations and in court.' He went to the car outside and proceeded to talk to the waiting driver, who appeared most disappointed that such a large fare was not to be his, especially after he had got up at five o'clock to be ready in time.

After taking down all the details of the cab and cab company and the relevant numbers, James told the taxi driver he could leave. He walked to the side of the house and around the back, and he handed his handcuffs to the constable so that he could cuff Maureen, the last one down the fire ladder.

'Please come into the house, Maureen and girls,' James said. 'Which one of you is Shelley?'

One of the girls looked around at the others and held her hand up.

'What is your full name, Shelley? And I need your full address and a phone number too, if you have one.'

'Yes, sir,' said a quiet voice 'Am I the one you are looking for, sir? My name is Shelley Owens.'

'Come in, Shelley, and the rest of you, I need all your names and addresses,' said Alicia. 'Where can I find four pencils?'

Shelley stepped out of the group and went to a drawer and produced four pencils.

Maureen called out to the children, 'Remember what I told you about talking to strangers. Girls, you do not have to tell them anything about yourselves. Keep your mouths shut. Do not say anything at all.'

Alicia gave Shelley a business card and said to Shelley, 'I am Alicia Armstrong, and that man over there is my husband, James. We work for a group called Gray and Armstrong Private Investigations. The next man there is Detective Inspector Paul Morris, from our city police force, and the other gentleman is Constable Strong, from the London police force. I am about to tell these gentlemen to call for backup from the local police, and they will bring some policewomen to make sure you are safe. I believe this lady, Maureen—do you know her surname? Shorten, is it? Well, Maureen Shorten was abducting you to sell to some men in Holland. There are some men in the world who like very young blonde-haired and fair-skinned little girls. You must admit that each of you fits that description. I want you to tell me, Shelley, what were you doing here with Maureen Shorten today?'

'She told us we were going to have a holiday in Amsterdam, which is in Holland.'

'What about school, Shelley? It is not a school holiday period. How did Maureen explain that to you?'

'She says it will only be a short time, and we will not be missed because we have not been at that school long enough for the teachers to get to know us. She keeps changing our schools around. I miss the school I went to when I was at home. Miss Borman was a very good teacher, and I loved her.'

'Is that why Jessica, your mother, decided to move you here to London? Was Miss Borman getting too interested in your well-being?'

Shelley looked uncertain for a few minutes and said, 'Does that mean interested in my work? She said I was the best pupil in her class.'

'Yes, I would say that, Shelley. She reported you missing from school, and your mother was angry about it. How long have you known Maureen?'

'I suppose it is all my life, or nearly. We used to share a house, the one where Mummy is living now, until a short time ago. Then she said it was time I got to know my other sisters better. This is Shirley,' she said, pointing to a lookalike girl who was about nine years old. 'She lived with us but went to a different school than me.' She turned around. 'This is Sandra, and this is Sally. They lived with Maureen, and they too go to different schools. They are the same ages as Shirley and I are. Maureen calls us the *S* seasons. She laughs when she calls us that.'

Alicia asked, 'Have you met your grandparents, John and Janine Owens?'

'I cannot remember them, although Mummy used to say they lived in another town and did not have time to visit. I am not sure which ones are grandparents. We had a lot of people come to meet us at home, mostly men who would say we are too young yet, and they would go away again. Mummy stopped us from going to school on the days they came, and she told us to sit still all day and read our books. She made us dress up in our best clothes, and we had to sit quietly until the men left. I hated those days. I wanted to go to school to do work and learn. I think Shirley felt the same, but we were too frightened to talk about it mostly.'

'What happened to you when your mother and Ian Page got married?'

'After the wedding, Mummy made us go into her bedroom, where she and Ian had sex every day. Ian did not like us there, but Mummy insisted every day that we watch what they were doing. She called it "adding to our education". Ian left after a short while of living with us. He said it was indecent to have two young girls watch them making love. Mummy laughed and said it was "making babies". She said that is how Shirley and I were made, so we should learn how it is done so we can make babies when we are old enough.'

'What did you think of that, Shelley?'

'I was frightened. I knew Ian was angry about it, so I asked Miss Borman about it. She looked sick when I told her what Ian and Mummy did in front of us. It was soon after that Ian left, and Mummy sent us away to live with Maureen. She said to us that we make things too complicated and that she was angry at us and that it was time for us to go too.'

'Has your mother talked to you since you left to live with Maureen, Shelley?'

'No. I heard her tell Maureen about us watching her and Ian in the bedroom, and she said I made Ian leave because I did not like watching them in bed. She said he had not been back, so she was very angry with me and did not want to see me again. Then Ian may come back to her. She did not think she was pregnant yet.'

James had turned on his iPhone at the beginning of Alicia's chat with the girl and recorded Shelley's story, with a view of her face while she spoke. He looked at Alicia now and turned the phone off.

Paul Morris said, 'I think it is time we called for backup. We have enough on your phone with Shelley's chat. We will leave Maureen until we have her in the interview room. I do not think she will be as easy to chat with as Shelley. I will send a message to my office to arrest Jessica Owens and also her parents. We can interview them after cooling their heels for a day or two. I will have to ask the arresting party to allow for four young girls. They have had a lucky day missing out on a fate worse than death, I would say.'

Alicia turned to Shelley again and said to her, 'The police officers will be taking care of you, Shelley, and your sisters. They will be looking after you from now on. What your mother and Maureen had in store for you was not nice for you, Shelley. I am so glad we caught up with you before you began your trip to Amsterdam. Things may not have turned out so good for you if we had been ten minutes later. Thank you for chatting with us. It has made things easier for you and for us. Now we know what they were taking you away for. We had only guesswork until we met you.'

There was a loud knock on the door, and Jack Whistler himself came into the room. They had not expected that. He shook each person's hand and said, 'Congratulations! This was well done. Go and have some breakfast, and send us a report as soon as you are able. You have saved the lives of four little girls this morning.'

There was also a van with four policewomen, and some swept the young girls into their arms. It had been a big morning for the youngsters, and you could see it on their faces, having to face the police in uniforms. Constable Strong had been the only one wearing a uniform until now. It had made things more informal for the children. Now they looked frightened.

Alicia hugged each girl and said, 'You are in good hands now, and they will choose good homes for you to go to. I hope to see you again, looking happy in different circumstances.'

Maureen could not stop herself from having the last word. 'Shut your mouths, all four of you. Do not say anything at all. Pretend you are dumb.'

Alicia said, 'You do not have to even think about Maureen any more. She cannot get to you. She will be separated from you now, and you do not have to be frightened of her and what she will do to you.

She will go in her own van, with a police escort. You will go with these policewomen, and they will see to it that you are all okay.'

The detectives waited until the house was cleared, and they pulled the suitcases into the room. James said, 'Forensics have got it now. We are heading home. Thanks, everybody, for the backup. Nicely done. And, Constable Strong, you deserve a medal. I will send the report to you, Jack.' The three of them climbed into the company car and headed for the highway, going south.

Alicia said, 'Please stop at the first good-looking shop. I am starving, as you two must be also, and it is only ten o'clock. We have the whole day before us.'

'Way to go,' said Paul Morris. 'I believe we have your granny to bless for this case, Alicia. Everybody should have a granny like that.'

James said, 'She solves most of our jobs for us and sends us out to pick you up to arrest the nasty ones. Yes, she is a particular favourite of mine. After her granddaughter, of course.'

'I am glad you said that, James. I agree, she is a clever lady,' said Alicia. 'Now for a cup of coffee. There is a place coming up on our right. Stop there.'

'I want to have a nice big pie to go with my coffee,' said James.

'Make that two,' said Paul. 'I am starving as well. I only had a cup of tea and a slice of toast before heading to the bookshop this morning.'

'Me three,' said Alicia. 'We have earned it after that talk with Shelley. I have never heard of anything so gross as what those two women were planning for those children. I must confess, I am astonished and shocked by it all, and if the Owens grandparents are in on it, I hope they go down for a long time. But the next interview should be done by someone trained in child psychology, I think. Mainly to protect the children. The children must be traumatised by what they have had to put up with in their short lives.'

Paul said, 'I agree, Alicia. You did very well today, talking to Shelley. We could not have made an arrest without that interview, but Shelley tied up Jessica and Maureen and, in a way, eliminated Ian Page as a suspect. The poor man was also a victim.'

By this time, they were in a car bay next to a shopping centre, and James said, 'This will have to be it. It is too dangerous to pull into the parking bays at stand-alone shops. A truck could take us out at any time there.'

'This is fine, James. Let's go discover a pie shop.' Alicia linked arms with the two men.

When she sat down at a table next to a coffee shop which had a bakery, she scrolled through her phone while waiting for their order, to see if she had missed anything while they had been busy.

She saw a message from Susan Cooke. 'Thanks for the introduction to your lawyer and friend, Alec Overington. He is the best. I already have the divorce papers and am to get my house, complete without mortgage, and the car too and part of my husband's superannuation to date. That is wonderful, oh yes. Roland will be paying Alec's bill, as well as the girl Marta's wages, and he has given her an airline ticket for when she is ready to go home to her family. I have applied for two jobs and should know by next week if I made at least one of them. After a long time of putting up with misery, things are now looking up for me. Once again, Alicia, thank you.'

Alicia read this out to James and said, 'This was my first win as a detective! I am so pleased I have a happy client.'

James laughed and reached for her hand and gave it a squeeze, then he said, 'It is you who is wonderful, Alicia. You will be getting a lot more notes like that. We should print them and make a book of them.'

The pies (two for each hungry man) and coffee came, and Alicia tucked her phone away again in her bag. The pies were terrific, and the coffee very good. Alicia mused to herself, *Yes, I will start up a file of my credits. James has his credits in his CV. I think I will start mine too. Who knows what the future holds for us all?*

CHAPTER THIRTEEN

That afternoon, there was a call for James from Jack Whistler, who wanted James to update him on D2. He said, 'I did not want to take your mind away this morning while you were coping with such a mess. Harold Griffiths asked for the update when he heard I was heading out to look at that job this morning. He reminded me again when I got back to the office, so he is interested.'

'I have had my mind tied down with that case you saw this morning. Thanks for your appearance, Jack. I would have probably said "What is D2?" if you had asked. I tend to try and keep my mind on the job at hand when we have a situation like that. It can get away from you in a second if you allow your mind to drift. Yes, back to D2. I am picking him up from the hospital at eleven in the morning and bringing him back to our apartment at the bookshop. The doctors have given him the okay, health-wise, and a lot of his memory has come back. They have impressed on me not to try and hurry to close any more gaps in his memory. It will happen in time, and some things may never come back. It was late yesterday when I spoke to the administrator at the hospital, as they had not contacted me directly. The only advice I had of D2's move was from the doctor at the coroner's office, who had chased the boy up initially at my request.

'Dr Redfern recognised that the history of the boy should be kept in-house, so he probably asked the administration to wait for my call on the subject. Quite frankly, he has been great about the secrecy aspect. We plan now to bring D2 home to the bookshop. Now we have renamed him again to Divit Edwards, as he was known as Edwards prior to the incident in which his brother was killed. He does not know anything about the renaming yet. We plan to have him come into our office daily, and we will use his services as a receptionist. Would you believe? This was all dreamt up by my staff, and we will pay him while he is there, to keep his services valid and to not have nosy parkers asking questions about him. *Divit* is an Indian name, so we are keeping that for him to hide behind if anyone does ask.

'Doing things that way, we will have twenty-four-hour surveillance of anyone that approaches him. He will be living and eating with us, and also working with us. I cannot see anyone getting to him without one of us seeing it happen and intervening on his behalf, so he should be safe enough. Have you any update on how things are going at your end of the bargain?'

'Not much, James, I am afraid. The word went out to the secret service the day we learnt about D2, but I guess that is why they are called the secret service. We have not learnt anything back. Things have changed after a long time with the same man at the helm in government over in Africa, so I suppose that makes things a little slower. But in the long run, they would like to clean up their country, don't you think? We have to wait it out. The diamond sale has also been slow. We think that no one wants to touch it, because of the thought of it being confiscated by the country it came from. That would leave everybody involved without payment. That makes everyone jittery. We will have to wait a little longer. I am sorry, James.'

'I did not expect miracles, Jack. I know how slowly the wheels turn in government circles, no matter which country is involved. I will not say the diamonds do not matter. They have been paid for many times over by D2's family, right down to D2 himself. I feel that he is owed some sort of explanation though. It would make a breakthrough for him and would perhaps perform a miracle by giving him back the rest of his memory. We will make sure he is okay in the short term by letting him be with us on a daily basis. It might release him from wondering why everyone is against him, which is how I would feel if someone killed off most of my family.'

'I can understand all that, James. He is lucky he has come up with you on his side. To be released to strangers from the hospital now would have been a nerve wracking moment for him. We have not forgotten him, and we knew you would come after us if we waited too long for answers. But we are deeply involved now and will not forget him. We have to wait until the wheels of the government turn. I do not have the answer for how we can hurry them up.'

'All I can say, Jack, is that it is going to be an interesting time getting to know him. Our whole staff is embroiled in his future now, including Alicia and Granny and me. We will bring Divit—I have to remember that name—into the office on Monday, ready to do a full day's work with us. I have several reports to put together, so I will not be out of the office for a few days and can keep an eye on him. We have tied up several jobs in the last two weeks, including this morning's jaunt to London. We have had no breaks between jobs to have time to write them up, so this will be included in Divit's preliminary week under supervision.'

'Thank you, James. I appreciate all you do. So does Harry Griffith. You struck a chord with him way back when, and he thinks you are the white-haired boy. He is not far wrong. Keep up the good work, James.'

Jack's call reminded James to ring the chief of police locally and put him in the picture. They had completed all the cold cases he had given them, except for the paperwork, but if James informed him of this now, the chief may have some more cold cases sorted out for them to take over by the time the reports were submitted. James reflected. They had not been easy, any of them, but now they had finished them. He felt quite excited to think they would get more. The cases had stretched their imagination; there was no doubt about that. But the fact that they had been worked by a team when they were fresh had given them a head start, he thought. Yes, he would like some others. So he rang the head man and gave him a rundown of what they had done to date, saying that the final reports would be on their way to him within a few days.

* * *

The next morning, James left the bookshop and headed for the hospital, where he knew D2 would be waiting nervously. He also felt nervous. This was a new venture for him; it was like meeting another member of the family he had not seen in a long time. He saw movement as he pulled into the car bay and saw that D2 was accompanied by several nurses. He guessed that they were the ones who had nursed him when he was admitted with stab wounds and was comatose for so long. James presumed that would make a bond between patient and nurse.

D2 was smiling, and each nurse lined up for a big hug and a kiss, sorry to see him go but happy that he was able to leave now. James introduced himself and took the boy's small bag. He had no need for clothing most of the time that he was ill, and James made a note to go shopping on Monday to outfit D2 for the business look he must have in the office. James was asked to sign the register of D2 leaving the hospital, still using that name. The unveiling of his new name would come when he got to the office on Monday morning. At the moment, it had not been discussed with the boy, but James was sure he would readily get used to the idea. For the rest of the weekend, they would be taking things easy. They all needed a rest after the previous two weeks' work. James thought of Percy. He seemed back in charge nowadays. He had almost broken down after the nursing home job. It had taken a lot from him, but James had noticed—and Alicia had also mentioned to James—how Percy had picked up, having the extra duties with the cold cases. She also remarked that she hoped he would not overdo things.

As James and D2 neared the bookshop, he looked over at D2 and saw a big smile on his face. Apparently, the boy recognised the bookshop. That made everything easier. There was no apprehension on his face, and he looked eager. He must have come here at some time in his past. As they parked and walked to the door of the shop, D2 asked, 'Where am I going to live with you, James? In the shop?'

'Hm, sort of, D2. Not in the shop, but above the shop. That will make it safer for you. Alicia and I have been living in the apartment above the shop since we came to this town. Alicia's grandmother, whom we call Granny, lives next door, and Percy—you met him when we arrested Fiona and Faye—lives in Granny's spare room, for her safety. The business we are in has its own perils from time to time, so we have needed to make sure we are safe in all directions. You will feel safe here with us, but it is only until we find your father and you have enough money and it is safe for you to go out alone. A sort of safe house, I suppose you would call it.

'We have had to share our apartment on several occasions, and we know it works for all involved. We have our meals in Granny's house. Alicia is the main cook. You will appreciate her cooking. She is a good cook. We have to make sure she is not doing too much. She was our receptionist until the police chief gave her a promotion recently, and now she works very hard as a detective. Perhaps you can help her out occasionally, D2. We all help each other out if we can.'

The boy's face was comical. 'I am sorry, James. I do not know how to cook.'

'I did not mean that you have to cook, D2. Just help with things like peeling potatoes or making a salad. There are a lot of cookbooks in the bookshop. Perhaps you could read some. You may need to cook for yourself in your new life, D2. It is good to have the basic knowledge.'

'How long am I to stay with you, James?'

'No time has been put on it, D2, but it was suggested you stay until you have answers about your father. The political way of life has swung around again in your country, but we are still not sure you are safe. So we will accommodate you and help you until an alternative comes up. Our apartment is not large, so it was never meant as a permanent home for you. But we will ensure that you are as happy as can be while you are with us.

'We also have a job lined up for you, which will put some money in your pocket—not a lot, because you will be a complete novice when you start off. Depending on your future, you may want to continue with it until you have finished your studies. We are all new with these ideas. If you want to change anything, you must tell us. Obviously, we do not know everything about your past life, although we would like to help you in any way we can with your future life. So it is a two-way street. We will tell you if we are unhappy with anything, and you must tell us if you are unhappy with things.'

'What sort of job, James? I know you do not want me to sell cocaine any more, and I am not experienced in much of anything else.'

James laughed. 'No, it will not be selling cocaine. That is illegal, and it is only because I have taken up your case for you that you have not been arrested for it. My staff and I at Gray and Armstrong Private Investigations have all chipped in with advice and suggested that you take over Alicia's job as our receptionist.

'First of all, we plan to drop the D2 name, although I quite like it. We will call you Divit Edwards. That is all in keeping with your Indian lifestyle. *Divit* means "immortal" in Hindi, so the Indian part of our population will recognise it. We have quite a few Indian clients who pop into the office, so they will think nothing of having you there as our receptionist. It is a sort-of disguise for you.

'This means that you will live with us and work with us, and we will be able to watch out for suspicious characters who may take too much interest in you. Percy, Ken, and Kate were all police officers in the past. They know what sort of suspicious character we may encounter, so we can nip things in the bud if necessary. You can see that we have you covered so no one can get to you and so you will feel safe. The only wish I have with all this organisation, on your part, is that we hope you do not feel smothered by us. We all wish you nothing but good, so if you feel we are too much, tell us. We will back off.

'We also hope that Jamal Kumah, Iris's son, will be free to help with your education. I know that at the moment, he will be taken up with his mother's last days. They will keep him busy for a while. But after she has gone, he will be looking for something to take his mind off things, and he will contact us to find you. In fact, I will contact him and let him know where you are, for when he is free to help. Iris looked very ill when we called in to see her, so much worse than when we saw her only a few weeks previous. We will be sorry to lose her in our lives.'

'It seems that when I care for someone, they are taken from me. Take extra care around me, James. I am cursed.'

James looked at him directly and shook his head, then he said, 'No, Divit, you are lucky. These things were not done because of you. You happened to be an appendage to all the people who have died, and you have survived the carnage. You should thank God every day that you are still here to make sure that the people who did these things to your family are arrested and tried for their murders. It is up to you, with our help, to prove you are a true survivor.'

Divit was quiet for a while and then said, 'You are right, James. It is up to me, the survivor, to make sure these people are caught.'

'With our help, Divit. You must not go off by yourself to get revenge. We have already got Faye and Fiona. Now you must wait with us until it is time to strike for the others. The day will come, Divit. You are not ready enough to handle them on your own yet. Wait to see what our government can do. They will tell us when it is the time to strike.'

'You will help me, James?'

'I have no knowledge of your home country except what I read in the papers. I think I will be more hazard than help, Divit. I am sure the people I have contacted will be in a better position to help you. We will see when the time comes. At least I will be on the sidelines, helping as much as possible. Meanwhile, we will see to your education and daily learning until that day arrives.'

Divit said, 'Dr Redfern came to see me last night. He wished me luck and said that I was very lucky that you, James, have taken up my case. He said that of all the people he has come in contact with, you are the best at your job. He believes that you are the one who is best placed to protect me and that you will help me to the best of your ability. He seemed very sincere, so I believe him. He said he could not think of anyone he knows who would take me into their own home to protect me. They would be too frightened, in case they got caught up in my troubles. That is why I was so happy when you came for me this morning. I thought you might change your mind. I will do my best to do everything right, so if you think I am not doing enough, please let me know.'

James laughed and turned and held out his hand for Divit to shake, and he said, 'A pact then? You try your best, and we will try our best to keep everyone safe. Which reminds me, when we get upstairs and get settled in, I will ring that newspaper journalist I know and trust, to come to the office on Monday to write your story up for publication.'

When they had settled in upstairs after greeting Granny, Alicia, and Percy, they made themselves a sandwich, as the others had already had a sandwich and a cup of tea during a break between customers in the bookshop. Divit wanted to know what duties he would do in the office. He was worried because he had only been fifteen when his education had been interrupted, and he was not sure he could cope.

James told him not to worry. 'Ken will teach you how to use the computer to be able to look things up. Very necessary for a detective. Kate can also teach you about computers and what questions to ask when people ring in with an enquiry. On Monday, Alicia will devote the full day to you, instructing you on polite telephone use and taking messages and where everything is in the office that you might need. She will also sit at the front desk with you for a couple of days, helping with all enquiries that come in, so that you will have a good example.' He assured the boy that every one of them wanted to help and that although everyone gets first-day nerves when they start a new job, if he wanted to know anything, he should just ask the closest person.

*   *   *

On the next day, Sunday, Granny proposed that the town market would be a good distraction for them. They could have lunch at Mrs Sharma's stall and see her reaction to Divit. It may need some explanations if she recognised him in any way. It would help them prepare for future meetings in the town, where people may make assessments, so they could learn how to explain the fact that he was alive.

They all thought that was a good idea, and Granny suggested that they have another town in mind, to divert people's attention. James immediately suggested Oxford, as it had a very diverse population, with students coming from all around the world. Also, if anyone grew too interested about it, he could rescue Divit, because he knew the city so well, having lived there while he was at university. Everyone was pleased with that, and they set off for the town square.

Mrs Sharma did not recognise Divit and only asked where he came from. When he said he was visiting from Oxford, she steered the conversation in a different direction. So that was one hurdle over. It was apparent that because they thought the boy had died a year ago, no one recognised him; he had grown and thickened out with all his exercising and looked older than the boy they would have remembered. They did not expect to see him as the same boy.

James was so pleased. He had been wondering if anyone would recognise Divit, and now he did not have to worry. He decided during the week to make another trial run on the subject and rang Derek Choudhury to come into the office for a chat—to clear the table, as he expressed. Divit was seated at the receptionist desk when Derek came in. Strangely, the boy who had lost his memory recognised Derek but was not recognised in return. Each of the office staff came by to pick something up from the desk while he was standing there, and nobody noticed any sign of recognition. Later Alicia said, 'It is because he thinks the boy is dead. Now twelve months later, he does not look like the same boy but appears to be a young man, much taller and built heavier. I do not think we will worry about him being recognised now.'

James said, 'I hope anyone looking for him will make the same mistake, especially as the newspaper report mentioned both boys are dead. Divit may have a free life after all, without any worries of someone looking at him and saying he is the one. Unless, of course, they know Jason Bowering, whom Divit may look more like now as he grows into manhood.'

Percy said, 'I did not think of that. Of course, as he matures, he may look more like his father. We will have to appeal to the girls to change that in some way. We have no pictures of Jason Bowering senior to go on. We should have another look into his box of papers and passport to see if there are any photographs. I did not look hard at the rest of the stuff in the box after we found the passports.'

'There is a slight chance, Percy. We will have to ask Divit if we can look again at the box of papers in the office safe.'

Divit agreed that they look but still did not want to know what his real name was, so he told them to be the ones to look.

When they pulled the box from the safe, they went through all the papers there, but no photos were found. James said, 'If I try the immigration department for a photograph, they will have one, but I am not too sure how old it would be. It could be way out of date.'

'Perhaps not too old, James. It depends on when he had it renewed last. The ones belonging to the boys were only three years old. It is possible that he renewed his at the same time, which was just before he brought the boys to the UK. It is worth a try, and we will be pleased if it is available, rather than us being left hanging, wondering.'

'That is true, Percy. I will give it a go and call my friends in the immigration department.'

He made the call and was told it was no trouble. There was a jingle on his phone an hour later, and there they had Jason Bowering senior, who had renewed his passport at the same time as he did the boys'. Jason's eyes were blue and his hair brown, and Divit was obviously taller than his father. His mother's eyes would have been brown, from her heritage, and then again Divit's hair was dark against the straight brown of his father's.

'What do you think, Percy? Not much alike at all. Shall we show Divit this photograph? It does not say his name except further down in the message. We could put our hands over it and only show the photograph to him.'

'All right,' said Percy. 'First, we will ask him. I do not want to trigger any reaction we do not want.'

'I will put this photo on a full computer screen before showing him. Then if he wishes, we can print it out for him. What do you say?'

'Ask first, James. It could be a breakthrough in his memory bank I would hate to disturb the memory if he does not want to see the picture.'

They called Divit into James's office and put the question to him. A look of shock crossed the boy's face, and they thought he would say no. But after a few minutes of thinking about it, he nodded and said,

'I think I have been hiding from the memory of my father because he dumped us and did not come back. My younger brother was very upset about it, and I never allowed him to talk about it, because we both felt so bad about things. We were so close to starving until Gerald Norman gave me the job of selling his cocaine, and something Fiona did not know is, he gave us a good handout to start us going. Yes, I will look at the picture now. He cannot hurt us any more than he has.'

James printed the picture out so that Divit could take it away and study it privately, and he said to the boy, 'Stay here in my office until you are ready to come out. I will go and sit with Alicia for a while.'

Divit looked up at him and smiled. 'Thank you, James and Percy. Dr Redfern was right in his opinion of you. I am very thankful for your help.'

The two men, feeling emotional themselves, wandered out to where Alicia was sitting at the front desk, looking up the story of the Owens pair, who had been jailed ten years ago. Paul Morris had sent the copy to their computer, and until now, nobody had had time to look at it.

When Alicia looked at the two men, she jumped up and said, 'What is it, James? Has something happened?'

'Nothing bad, Alicia. We have just printed out a copy of Jason Bowering senior's passport photo to show Divit. I am not sure whether we did a good job or a bad one. It has evoked memories for Divit which his mind has been hiding from him. He is in my office now, having a bit of quiet time while he gathers his thoughts. Dr Redfern warned me not to press him on anything, to let the story come out in his own time, and I think I have blown it.'

'Surely it is a good thing, James. It would be terrible for the memories to come back to him at the wrong moment. Something would have triggered the memories sooner or later. This way, he has time to think things over in quiet repose rather than in public.'

'Ah, Alicia, always the voice of reason. Of course, you are right. We will just have to wait it out and hope we have not done the wrong thing.'

'Wait', said Percy, 'until he comes out. He may be happy once he realises he has made a breakthrough. We all have our bad memories. I know they are not as bad as Divit's, but each person goes through moments of pain, thinking about the past. We have to encourage Divit to face up to his bad moments and carry on. At least he is not resorting to drugs or alcohol to forget. He is a strong personality to have survived all the bad things that happened around him, and we must uphold him as we have been doing, as I think we are making headway with him. Most of the time, he is cheerful, and that is a good sign.'

'Yes, Percy. So, Alicia, what can you tell us about the Owens couple from ten years ago?'

Alicia began. 'It seems that Jessica was initially one of the girls they were going to sell. However, a bad case of measles made it impossible to sell her, so the deal they had went on without her. To me, after dealing with Jessica, I think she resented that the big moment of her sale did not go through, and she decided then and over the years that she could manage things better than her parents had. That is, of course, if they were her real parents. They had been caught, but not until after the shipment of three girls went on. We have no particulars on those three girls. They were never seen again. But in the years before they were sent off, several children had been stolen from prams and playgrounds around the country, and it was wondered if these were the girls that were sold eventually. No real evidence came up, only a single voice from Rector Owens's own church congregation that asked what had happened to the Owenses' family of four young girls. The police could not find any evidence although their house and church were scrupulously searched several times. No sign of other children living at the property was found. There was only Jessica in her hospital bed, and she was not talking. There are several comments in the file about the girl's silence.'

'So, Alicia, do you think that Jessica rang Maureen after the Owens couple visited her, and she said "Go. It is now or never"? Which is why Maureen was taking off so early in the morning in a taxi to take them to Holland?'

'Exactly, James. It all fits. If it is possible to talk to Shelley again, I could ask a lot of questions we did not have before that morning. But I know that the counsellors will not allow us to speak to the young girls. That is why I questioned them on the spot, while we had the chance.

Luckily, Jack Whistler came in then instead of earlier, or else we would have missed out on our chance altogether. It could have turned into another fiasco, like with the elderly couple ten years before. They were guilty as hell, just more organised, and they tidied up after themselves, leaving no evidence. I cannot find any evidence either about the person who pulled the pin on the Owens family ten years ago. It is possible he or she was hissed out of the community.'

As Alicia finished speaking, Divit came from James's office. There was a sad look on his face, but there was no sign of tears.

Alicia asked, 'May I have a look at your father's photo, please, Divit?'

He looked at James and said, 'You did not show her?'

'Not without your permission. It is for you to show her if you wish, not me.'

Divit handed Alicia the copy James had printed out for him, and he said, 'At least if the assassins come looking for me, they will not recognise me from that photo. I think I look more like my grandfather. He had large brown eyes. But the frizzy hair is from my grandmother, who used to wash her hair and try to straighten it on a daily basis, although it always sprang up into curls again. We would laugh at her. She was beautiful. Everyone said she was a beauty, but like everybody else, she wanted to look different.'

Alicia hugged him and said, 'I think you have taken the best of both sides. You are a very handsome boy.'

The boy blushed. 'Thank you, Alicia. It is good to hear such nice things said about me. The nurses in the hospital would try to make me blush. They said it was like watching the sun rise first thing in the morning.'

The men laughed, and James said, 'Enough of this. You will make him a namby-pamby if you keep this up. And before you ask me what that means, Divit, we will all get back to work. You have been with us two weeks now, Divit, and I am happy to say you are fitting in with us very well. I will ring my friend in London now to get an update on what is happening in your case. Do not expect much though. These things seem to happen very slowly. But if I pressure them a little, they may pressure the next in line, and one day they will say "Yes, we have found your father". Well, we can always hope. I will make that call now.'

James went back to his office and noted the damp tissues in the waste bin. He rang Jack Whistler's number and asked if there had been any movement in the case. He received the answer of 'We would have told you, James, if we had news'.

'Of course, I know that, Jack. I am only trying to keep chins up around here. Things get emotional sometimes, but I must say, he is a remarkable young man. Today I appealed to the immigration department, and my friends there sent us a picture of Jason Bowering senior. It was taken only three years ago, so it is quite up to date. We were afraid that as our young friend grew a little older, he would look like his father, which could put him in the line of more danger. He appears to be more like his grandfather though, which is not a bad thing. He is a handsome lad.'

'I would like a copy of that photo, James, in case anyone asks for a copy when the man is found, to check that he is the right person.'

'I am sending it to your phone right now, Jack. Isn't it remarkable what we can do with technology nowadays? I have another report I am sending to you. This will take a little longer. It is a copy of the file on the Owens family ten years ago. I think you will find it interesting reading. I will send it all by fax, as it is quite lengthy. Your team up in London will be doing the work on this new one. I will send our file on that too. I have only now finished my report on it, and I will also send Detective Paul Morris's report to you. Combined, the three make for a terrible tale altogether, and I hope you can break down the women, Jessica and Maureen, to get the full story. I was very disturbed first by the story a ten-year-old told us and the fact that ten years ago, we had the Owenses in our hands and allowed them to escape. To think this type of thing goes on in our community, and people close their eyes to what is going on around them, because they do not want to get involved.'

'Thanks for all that, James. Well done. I feel the same as you about that story the young girl told. To think that Jessica is her mother makes it all the more incredible and terrible for the child. We will do our best to find them guilty. We may have to call on your team to give evidence if required.'

'Anything, Jack, as long as they are sent away for a long term. I am sure they will find it uncomfortable in prison.'

James went back to the reception desk and told Divit, 'Nothing has been heard from your father yet. It is an ongoing investigation, and we will be told if anything pops up. Meanwhile, I have been thinking about this chase for your father, Divit. How would you like to find a map? I think I have a map of Africa in my old school atlas. That could be a starting point to try to pinpoint where the village you told us about is located. Also, write down the name of anybody back at home who you would trust. Perhaps give them a 1 to 10 on the trust scale. It may give a lead to the people searching. It may come to nothing. But you are the only one who can pinpoint your village, and they may find some answers there. Do you remember whether the aeroplane your father owns is stored at the village?'

Divit nodded.

'I am only pulling up questions as they occur to me here. I have read that petrol is in high demand and extremely expensive. I presume aviation fuel would be the same. I have read of huge streams of people lining up for a cupful of motor spirit. I imagine if an aeroplane was kept in hiding in a village, it would be very difficult to refuel after flying all the way from England. Another query: did your father leave his car at the village when he left for England? Was it hidden from view?'

There was another nod from the boy.

'Did he say where he was going to stay once he reached your village? You did say he was going back to work after the four days of mourning that is expected after the death of a wife. Would he have gone back to your home?'

Divit shook his head. 'I do not think he could have gone back to our house. It would have been too much, even for him.'

Alicia said, 'What do you mean, Divit, when you say "even for him"?'

'Nothing, really, Alicia. I am so angry that he dumped us here without funds to live on. We were only children. How could he have done that to us?'

'Do you not think he was trying to save all your lives? Perhaps he thought his stepmother would take you on. That was a mistake on his part, but he was not aware of it at the time. As I was saying earlier, on a different subject, how can people not help merely because they do not want to get involved? That explains his stepmother to a T. It was too late to convey that to your father. He was long gone on his own vendetta.' James continued looking at Divit as if to influence him.

'You sound as if you are on his side, James. I could not understand at the time. We had been cossetted children with a loving family, and all of a sudden, we were thrust into a strange country with nothing except a bed to sleep in—nothing to eat, no one to talk to, absolutely nothing. We were not only bereft of our loved grandparents and loving mother. We were children alone in the world who had to look after ourselves in a strange country. Yes, I was angry at him and remain so, I am sorry to say. I know you do not want me to say these things, but they have been swirling around in my brain for three years. I think that is why my mind shut down while I was so ill from the drugs and stabbing I received from Fiona.'

James looked depressed; he could not imagine the circumstances the two boys had been thrust into. He continued, asking Divit to draw a map of where he thought the village was where the aircraft was stored. He had to change the subject slightly but could not bear the picture that was being built up in his own mind, of two children left to cope for themselves. It was a hard story to hear.

Eventually he said, 'I think I need a rest. It has been an eventful day. We have not heard back from the police chief about whether he is hunting out some more cold cases for us to work on. I have finished the reports I was to write, and now I am looking for something else to occupy my mind. But it is too late in the day to start something fresh. I have only now remembered that I need to thank my Immigration friends for their helpful information. Why don't you—Percy, Alicia, and Divit—go home now? I will come after my call, and I will lock up the office when I have finished.'

'That sounds like a good idea, James. Let's go, folks,' said Alicia.

James watched as the three went out of the office, and he closed the door after them and locked it as a precaution. He went back to his office and rang his previous boss in Immigration as he said to Alicia, but after greeting him, he asked, 'Can you do facial recognition on people who apply for British passports?'

'Yes, James. What are you looking for?'

'The fellow you sent a photo of looks slightly like someone else I know. It is not a great likeness, but one that is niggling me. That fellow we asked about is Jason Bowering, but the picture made me start wondering. Did this fellow have a previous passport in this name? That particular passport stated that it is now three years old. What of his earlier passport? Did he let it expire? When did he use it last? Can someone get away with a change of name? All this has come to me since I looked at that photo, and the impression on me is not vague, only puzzling. I have not spoken of it to anyone else yet. Therefore, the question is, can your facial recognition come up with any answers for me?'

'I will call in someone to help, James. I am a little old-fashioned and do not understand the technology that well. Things in the technology field change so quickly. It is hard for a fellow my age to keep up.'

'Thanks, mate. It may only be my imagination winding me up after a busy week, but I cannot let it go. I appreciate your help.'

'I am not sure how long it will take. I will get back to you as soon as I can. Perhaps tomorrow.'

'One other thing, mate. Do not give the information to anyone but me. The story about it is, there is someone in our office who might be concerned about the answer. He has been very ill for the past twelve months, so we have to look after him.'

'No problem, James. I will call you on your mobile first.'

'Thanks. I will hear from you soon.'

He picked up the office keys and let himself out of the building, and as he locked the door, Percy's voice said, 'You picked up on the picture as well, James. I could not believe my eyes when I first looked at it, but I did not say anything while Divit was there. Then I saw through your "having to make one last call" strategy and waited to find out what you have found.'

'I cannot get much past you, Percy. But you are the one good at faces. Did you recognise someone in the Jason Bowering picture?'

'I think it may be another Haskell, a little older than Ian and Fiona. His eyes are the same, and his face is a little fuller, as older people seem to have more of a looseness about them. But I would say an older brother perhaps.'

'That is what I think as well. We have been looking at a lot of Haskell pictures in the last year or two, and this one is similar. But what of the two young boys? They do not look at all like him. In fact, they could be the sons of Oliveri and an African mother. It is something to think about. We will have a chat with Divit tonight about what he remembers about his father, mother, and grandparents. We can make it appear casual, just enquiring. I was also struck by the boy's apparent dislike of Jason Bowering. Is there more that he knows about him? Did some facts come to him while he was examining that photograph? I think we have stirred up another hornet's nest, Percy. Can you keep him talking tonight while I have a chat with Alicia upstairs to ask her opinion on the photograph? She has good recognition skills, much better than mine, so if I can see a Haskell peering out at me, she must see more. I do not get to have private chats with Alicia ever since Divit arrived, and I do miss them.'

'Sure, James. Things have changed with the boy there all the time. It is not his fault, only we cannot say too much about our cases while he is with us. I think Granny notices the change as well. She liked the after-dinner disclosures. She has become part of the team.'

*   *   *

After dinner, they tried to draw Divit out, but he was not in the mood to confide in them and excused himself to go upstairs to bed for an early night, saying he was very tired.

James and Percy looked at each other. They made sure the door was closed, and they lowered their voices. James asked Alicia, 'What did you think of the photograph of Jason Bowering, Alicia? Did he remind you of anyone?'

'The Haskell family. The same blue eyes. They are a light blue, an unusual colour. Almost but not quite grey, not quite blue. Also, the thin face, but it was not as thin as Fiona's. I would say an older brother, because of the skin texture, and if not, then a first cousin.'

'Why do we go around the question, Percy, when all we have to do is ask Alicia? She is our facial recognition champion. I have asked Immigration to check up on those features to see if there is a passport issued for the photo in another name. They will get back to me on my mobile tomorrow. Now, Alicia, who do you think Divit and his brother look like?'

'The person they call Grandfather. I would take a bet that their DNA match and Bowering's are not in the same gene pool.'

Percy grinned. 'So we have all come to the same conclusion. Good show.'

James said, 'We will have to work quietly to find out what happened. Divit is deeply disturbed already, so much so that his mind closed down for a year. Perhaps I can ask Dr Redfern to talk to him. I am afraid of returning him to no man's land again. Perhaps we can try hypnotism. I will ask Redfern his opinion on that.'

'Ring him now, James, on your mobile. We do not want the boy listening on the landline.'

James rang the number that Dr Redfern had given him, and he updated him on the story to date and asked about hypnotism.

Redfern said, 'Can you leave it with me overnight, James? I will consult with a fellow I know in another field and get his opinion. He is closer to new techniques than me. The fellows I deal with do not usually talk back when I ask them questions,' he said with a laugh.

'Thanks, mate. Can you ring me on my mobile to make sure you come directly to me?'

'We should leave it there for tonight. We are all tired, and we will have messages coming for us from all directions tomorrow,' said Percy after James ended his call.

James and Alicia crept up the stairs and could tell that Divit was asleep. They breathed a sigh of relief.

* * *

Next morning, James was kept busy on his mobile in his office with the door shut. Ken looked at the door and said, 'No open office today?' Percy answered, 'He is expecting a few calls which need his concentration, so he has asked us to field all enquiries for him and let him know if anything that comes up is important.'

Alicia called out, 'I just fielded a call from Derek Choudhury. He asked if he could make an appointment with James. He said he is not in a hurry, any day will do, but he prefers mornings, as he has lectures in the afternoons. This week or next. Shall I make it a message for James, to call Derek sometime this week?'

'I am sure the rush will be over by then, Alicia,' offered Percy.

Divit appeared a little subdued that morning, and Alicia asked if he would like to take a break or a walk to get the cobwebs from his brain. They needed milk and tea to boost their stock. Did he feel brave enough to try out his shopping skills, or would he prefer for her to go with him?

He laughed and said, 'It is time I learnt that lesson all over again, Alicia. I will give it a go.'

She asked, 'Would you like me to walk three paces behind in case you need me, Divit?'

He appeared really amused by that conversation and said, 'How about I try things out, and if I feel strange about it, I can hurry back here to my bolthole and hide my face?'

Those listening cheered, and he went from the office with a bag to carry things and some money from the petty cash and a big smile on his face.

Kate said, 'He is picking up. He is not nearly as doleful as he was last week.'

'Thank goodness,' said Alicia. 'I think his troubles are about to catch up with him. That is why James is closeted in his office. It is concern, in case Divit hears something he may not like.'

Kate was intrigued and said, 'What are you working on now, Alicia?'

'Just some more of the same, Kate. I am looking into the Haskell family history to see if I can pick up any oddities. We may have to answer some questions when we get to court with the Haskell girls. It is better to be prepared. Have you picked up any more about Douglas Oliveri?'

'Not yet. I put it away a few days ago and have not had a chance to get back to it. Do you think I should give it priority while Divit is away from the office?'

'It would be a good idea, Kate. We seem to be tiptoeing around him a bit, trying not to upset him. But we need to do follow-ups on what we have already discovered so it does not all get pushed to the bottom of the deck. We do not need to tell him what we are working on in the back offices.'

'Point taken, Alicia. I did put it away after that one mention, meaning to get back to it later. I will keep on with the search now that he has gone shopping, and I will close off if he comes into my office space.'

Alicia went on with her Haskell history search and suddenly said to Percy, 'Have a look at this.'

She had discovered that the property with the airfield had belonged to the Haskell family before and during World War II. The name of the property was listed as Bowering House. There was no mention of what had caused its decline, but the pictures of it during its heyday showed a very prosperous house and extensive grounds, including an airfield and hangar. Alicia looked up the date and noticed the photos were taken between the two world wars. Shown in a different photo was a happy family group, listing the names as mainly Haskells. There was also a group photo of some of the men wearing flying gear with helmets and goggles such as they wore in those days. The pictures were small black-and-white photos, and it was hard to find a lookalike of the modern family to match, except that they were all slim and had fair hair, like the passport photo of Jason Bowering. They appeared to be a well-to-do family; everyone in the group looked well dressed in the style of the day. Alicia copied the story and the photographs to the printer and put them in a folder on James's desk. When he came out for a drink, she explained what she had done and said, 'We shall have to open a secret file for things like this.'

Percy asked James if he had any information yet, to which he answered, 'Yes, but there is more coming. I will tell you when the opportunity arises.' He went back into his office and closed the door. Alicia could see that he had spotted Divit approaching the outer door.

She saw Kate go to the printer and pick up some sheets she had copied, and she also put them in a folder to keep them confidential. Things were moving, she thought.

Divit made the coffee and tea like a trooper, and he explained it was a skill he had picked up while in the hospital. James left his office to join them, sitting around the boardroom table while they had their morning drink of choice. Alicia casually asked the young man, 'How did you meet Fiona?'

'The first time I saw her, she was shoving papers into our apartment letter boxes, and she stopped and gave me the ones due for my box. That was the day I saw the advertisement for the customs job. It has not occurred to me before now that it may have been a fix to catch my eye.' He sat thinking about it. 'It is not possible, is it? That she had been looking for me the whole time? Why would she do that? I had never heard of her before that day.'

'Perhaps someone set you up, Divit,' suggested Kate.

'I did not know anyone, so how could they have managed that? We had only been in this town about three weeks at that time. No, I think it is only a coincidence. It is not a possibility. We had only just arrived and moved into the flat. We knew no one, and no one knew us.'

'What about your father's stepmother? She organised the flat for you,' asked Kate.

'I suppose that is a faint possibility. My brother and I had never spoken to her. Why would she send Fiona to seek me out?'

'That is a very good question, Divit,' said James as he stood up to go back to his office. They could hear his mobile ringing.

The others broke up to go to their jobs too, leaving Divit looking dazed somewhat with new thoughts. 'Damn,' he said. 'I wish I could remember more details. I feel so dumb.'

James poked his head out of his door as the boy walked past. 'Come in, Divit, and have a seat.' He waited for the boy to get settled and asked, 'Can you remember your father's stepmother's surname, Divit?'

The boy thought for a while and answered, 'I think it was Haskell or something like that. As I said, after meeting us, she wanted to have nothing more to do with my brother and me, so it is a hazy memory.'

'Did you know that Fiona and Faye's surname was Haskell before Fiona married Gerald Norman? And I presume Faye Haskell is still Faye's name,' said James.

A look of complete shock came over Divit's face. 'You mean I am related to Fiona and Faye?'

'I presume that is a correct statement, Divit, but we have not worked out the nitty-gritty yet.'

'If we are related, why did she try to kill me? Faye certainly killed my brother. I saw it but was unable to move to save him.' He looked with appeal at James and said, 'How did you find this out, James? Is it true? Or are you trying to trigger my memories by giving me shocks?'

'Unfortunately, Divit, it is true. But we have yet to work out the whys of it. We also have to know more about your father. We think his real name is Haskell, and he has taken the name of a property once owned by the Haskell clan. The property is named Bowering House. We are still looking for the connection. Do you have anything in your memory, of the Bowering name?'

'I think we landed our aircraft at a place that had a sign at the gate saying 'Bowering House'. We did not stay there. A man arrived with an SUV and brought us here. My brother and I moved into the flat, and my father and the man drove off again in the SUV. It did not take any more of my father's time than ten minutes all up, from the time we hit the city streets.' He looked up with wonder. 'That is a new memory. I have been hovering over the question "How did we get here?" since I woke up in hospital, and that is it. I know that when I tried to remember this, I would get very angry and would want to cry, and now I have it. I remember thinking at first, "How come it was called Bowering House? Do we own it?" These thoughts have worried me for three years. Do we own it?'

'Your grandfather, Douglas Oliveri, and Jason Bowering purchased the old house and the lands about four years ago in joint names. At the moment, seeing as your grandfather is dead, the property is owned by Jason Bowering, except we think Jason Bowering is really Jason Haskell, Fiona's older brother. I have been trying to follow the trail all morning but have got no further than that. Can you comment any further, Divit, to help me out?'

The boy appeared shocked by the revelations of his possible name and was almost incoherent, trying to understand. James thought, *It is a shock to me, finding all this information. If the boy had no inkling previously, he is going to go on with the shocks as the revelations come, and they are coming thick and fast.*

He had heard back from Immigration this morning that Jason Bowering had previously held a passport many years ago as Jason Haskell. It was the same man in the attached passport photographs. He was originally listed as being an assistant to Douglas Oliveri, and then as a warehouse manager. In his latter passport, he was listed as a private secretary to Douglas Oliveri. James had also worked out that it was not possible that Divit was Jason Bowering's son. The man had still been in England fifteen years prior. Divit was eighteen, they now knew, from the boy's passport.

James was thinking of the possibility that the boy's father was Douglas Oliveri himself. Both boys looked like him. And there was the crinkly hair; the mother must have been African. Was it possible that the mother was from the village where Divit said he had spent his first years? Oliveri may have spread himself around and spawned two children. With boys being the most valuable in most countries, perhaps he had wanted to acknowledge them and give them an education, so he asked Jason Bowering to take on his—Oliveri's—only daughter and claim they were his. This was all a puzzle, and there was no one alive now for a DNA test.

James rang Dr Redfern again. He was fast becoming his medical guide. After James described what he had come up with, he asked if there was any way to identify any DNA now that the principal people were deceased. James was advised to ask if Divit had anything of his mother or grandfather in his possession; they may be able to pick up something from those items. The boy's own DNA would prove whether he was the son of an English person. If he could produce something worth testing, he should drop it off at the coroner's office, and Dr Redfern would see what he could do. They would have to have the boy's own permission to do a test.

James sought Divit out again and asked the questions, and at first the boy said, 'No, I do not think I have anything.'

James was dejected now, being near yet still so far from a resolution, but he said, 'What if we go through the box we have in the safe? There may be something there you have forgotten about.'

Divit said, 'I have no idea what is in the box. I have been told it was all picked up from Fiona's house. Is that correct?'

James nodded. 'Nothing has been thrown away. We only looked for passports, and the rest is intact. I guess Fiona was told by her brother not to leave a paper trail.'

Percy produced the safe key to bring the box to James's office. They checked each piece of paper, mostly check-out slips. Then at the bottom of the box, they saw an amulet wrapped in a piece of felt, in an envelope that was unsealed.

It was a small amulet, and Divit remarked that it had belonged to his grandfather. His mother had given it to the boy after his grandfather's death, as a memento. His grandfather had always worn it around his neck; Divit was not sure what it was. He had worn it himself at times since he had been in this country, because it made him feel closer to his grandfather.

James and Percy agreed. This was the only possibility for testing; the remainder were only rubbish that Fiona had picked up to do as her brother instructed. James said, 'Do you realise that Jason—whatever you want to call him—must have been in touch with Fiona to be able to issue those instructions? So he is not dead, just missing for the time being. Divit, can you remember if Jason went to the village at all?'

'Only to check the aircraft, James. He did not like the village. He said it was like going back in time to visit there. We went mainly with our grandparents or with our mother while Jason was at work.'

'What is the work you think Jason did on a daily basis, Divit?'

'He told us boys he was an engineer on the gas pipeline. We had no reason to question it.'

'In his various passports over the time he has been out of Britain, he described himself as a warehouse manager or a private secretary to your grandfather, which was the last claim. Can you imagine him in those roles?'

'I know he was close to my grandfather. When the family came to dinner, either at their house or ours, they would sit and talk for hours, while Grandmother and Mother would sit outside on the lawn and watch my brother and me play cricket or kick the football around. We liked those times. We thought of it as family fun.'

'Did your mother and father get on well together, Divit?'

'I supposed so. To be really honest, when you are a kid, you take your parents for granted a lot. My father did not shout or yell. He used to say that only barbarians raised their voices. He never hit us, and if we did something wrong, he would send us to be chastised by our grandfather. Now that you have made me think about growing up, our father was hardly ever there, and if we asked, Mother would say he was working. He was away all week anyway, so we did not see much of him even then, because we had our sports and I had my chess club that I liked to go to on the weekends. When he was with us, he did not give us much attention. He was always reading a book or playing on his tablet, often playing games, I noticed once.'

'Did you have the opinion that your father loved you, Divit?'

'I do not think he did. We always seemed part of the chattels. He never talked to us like I saw other fathers talk to their sons at school. Even when he told us to get ready to go on the plane and pack a small bag, he did not say where we were going. It was "just do it". I know he was angry, but so were we. We were only children. I am still angry when I think of it.'

'What did he tell you about the diamonds—to hide them?'

'Actually, I have been thinking about them this week. I think he dropped them, unnoticed, while getting out of the plane when we arrived. I remember picking them up and shoving them in my pocket, not realising what they were at the time, and he did not notice. He told us to hurry up and get into the vehicle. At the time, I did not know what they were. They looked like any stone you can pick up. Dad used to collect stones. I think he liked to look at them. He had quite a collection, kept in a long glass vase on our dining table as a decoration. It was only later that I remembered my father and grandfather talking about them. I was doing my homework in the study, the room next to the dining room. When I put two and two together, I realised it was that package they were talking about. Grandfather said he should find a better hiding place for them. I did not say anything to my father about them being in my pocket, mainly because he was in such a hurry to get away from us that I did not have a chance to bring it up.

'Now I think that he was planning the whole time to have Fiona kill us. He needed to get us away where we were not known. I even think he had my mother killed, and if this is all true, my grandparents as well. So if we had been killed, it would have been two too many, and there would have been suspicions aimed at him. I have not thought of a motive yet, but I will get there. I have also been wondering how he explained our disappearance from our home. I am sure someone would have asked. My grandfather was a popular man and often boasted in his club about us grandkids.

'My grandfather was very wealthy. Everyone knew that, even us boys. He was always giving money to schools and clinics and anything he thought was worthy. We always had the best of everything. I know *he* loved us. He showed us in every way he could. I am not so sure now when I look back at our family sitting around at home. I do not remember him talking much to my mother. It was like she was angry at him. But being kids, we were never told the reason, and we just accepted it. Grandmother was the one who talked to Mother mainly and seemed to be the go-between for them. It is strange how these pictures pop out at me. I have tried so hard all year to remember even the basics of life, and suddenly I am having these flashes of family life that I did not see clearly as I lived them. Now they are standing out to me, like a movie I am living in.'

'You are doing very well, Divit. You are helping me see this movie as well. If I am right, it was a complete family circle—grandparents, parents, and you two lads in a happy home. You had servants to do the work, you did not have the need to cook or clean for yourselves, and your grandparents visited often, maybe once a week on weekends. Am I right?'

The young man sat looking inwards at James's picture of them and said slowly, 'No, we were not a complete happy family circle. There was Grandfather not talking to Mother. No, it was Mother not talking to Grandfather. I am sure that is right. There was Dad not talking to us boys. He seemed only to put up with us. It was like a circle all involved with each other but strained somehow. I cannot say any more about it. Somehow the picture is hurting me, and I can feel my brother being aware of it and being extra nice to me. He was always sensitive to other people's feelings, so I guess he could feel the strain too.'

'Divit, stop trying to think about it for a while. I can see it is upsetting you, and I do not want you to be unhappy with us. We care for you, Divit. We may seem like strangers to you, but we have your well-being at heart. I want to take you to visit with Dr Redfern. He has offered to check you over and do a DNA test. We do not believe that Jason Bowering Haskell is your father. You needed a birth certificate to get a passport, and we think the one he supplied was a fake. We want to prove it with the DNA test. While we are there, we will have the people look at that amulet we found. It may have your grandfather's DNA on it, and also proof of your family roots. If we had something of your mother's, we could also test her DNA. Are you sure you do not have anything?'

'I remember that when we received our passports, my brother and I, Dad, and Mother all looked at them. Mother was especially pleased to have a passport to use if necessary, as the country was going from bad to worse. Having the passports meant freedom for us, as we also had the aircraft with which to escape if it became necessary. I remember her holding on to those passports as if she did not want them out of her sight, in case they got lost or stolen or if we had to go suddenly. At that time, robberies were an everyday occurrence too, another hazard. We had the two gardeners to look out for us, although when they were really needed, they ran away. But what I mean is, Mother carried those passports around for many days before she worked out that they were safe enough in the house. Could her DNA be on those passports?'

'I do not know, Divit, but we will take them with us when we visit Dr Redfern. He may be able to tell us more. We can trust Dr Redfern. He works at the coroner's department, but he has suggested we see him rather than any other doctor, because he knows your history from the time of your stabbing and will not tell anyone else your story without your permission. Like now, he will look into your DNA but will not tell anyone the results except you and me. We have to trust him. I do. He has shown to me that he is trustworthy.'

'Okay, James. I understand that if I want to get to the bottom of my history, I'll have to trust someone sometime. We have had to keep ourselves private while we have been here in this country, and it became a habit.'

'Our appointment is for four o'clock. We shall have lunch now and try to do a little more work, and then it will be time to leave. By the way, you do realise that our staff here are also trustworthy. Nothing goes out about you unless you okay it first.'

'I have never doubted it, James. I am grateful to have such friends.'

The time for the appointment came quickly. Alicia had to remind them to hurry, or they would keep Dr Redfern waiting.

* * *

After their usual greeting, James handed the bag with the passports and the amulet over the desk and said, 'This is all we were able to find at the moment. I have only just had the thought that Divit may have something in his bag, although Fiona and Faye did do a good job of swiping all they could get. Is that bag back at the apartment the one that you brought with you to Britain, Divit?'

'Yes, it is. We were only allowed one small bag each because of the weight for the flight. One held my clothes, and also my brother had one. I do not think they were ever emptied, because the room in the flat was so small. The wardrobe was tiny, like a broom cupboard, so we stored most of the stuff in our bags. We held to the unkempt look because we did not have an iron and everything came out creased. We stored the bags under the bed because there was no room elsewhere, so Fiona would have missed it when she went digging, because we had been lying on the beds. The bags were returned to the hospital when I was admitted, and no one bothered to look into them. They seemed the same as we had them previously, so when I left the hospital, I put in the few things the hospital supplied, which was not much. You will find one bag inside the other. I have learnt to be minimal.' He looked at the two men and said, 'Do you think there may be something in the bags that could be important?'

James said, 'It is a possibility, Divit. While you wait here for an examination by Dr Redfern, I will go home and bring those two bags back. It should not take long.'

'They are in the base of the wardrobe, James, easy to find, and I have not used much of the stuff I brought from the hospital because you bought me new clothes at the first opportunity.'

'Righto. I will be back as fast as I can.'

He was back in twenty minutes and said with a laugh, 'How is that for a superman trip? Granny was wondering what I was up to, and I had to say "I will tell you tonight". How are you getting on here?'

Dr Redfern said, 'I have given this young man all the usual examinations I can remember from my days as a GP, and he seems to be a fit specimen. His eyes are good, hearing is fine. Now for the DNA test, which is a simple one, unlike the one we will have done on the amulet and anything in the bag and also the passports. I have to pass them on to a colleague, as I do not have the skills or apparatus to do the testing, but we should have the results back within a few days. I am pleased to say he has passed all the tests.'

Divit looked relieved, and James said, 'It is my own opinion too. I agree with you. Besides being a little slow at some of the things we have asked of him—which we expected anyway, as he is still recovering his skills—he is doing fine, and his memory is coming back in bits and pieces. We hope to be able to fit all the pieces together very soon. I think having the DNA test will answer many questions. Thank you for your time, mate. We look forward to those answers.'

They left the office and went home. The rest of the family were having a cup of tea, so they poured their own. James told them all about what they had been doing.

Granny, when told of the Haskell element, gave a sigh and said, 'It is amazing how they keep coming into focus for you, over and over. This is a story for our journalist friend when you find all the answers. He will make a year's salary out of this one story. Mark my words.'

They all laughed. So many of Granny's words had already come true. No one would dismiss her as an old woman who knew nothing. Not in that house.

CHAPTER FOURTEEN

I t was two days later that Dr Redfern rang back with some results. He said he would like to bring them to the office himself to explain what they found. 'Would four this afternoon be all right for everybody, or would Divit like the results first, to look over and think about them?' James said he thought the boy should see them first.

When asked, Divit said, 'This is a community now. You all know the story. I do not mind you knowing the rest. I do not want secrets held back. You have all been such wonderful people. I feel as if you are all part of my family. I will go and buy a cake and make some tea for our meeting with Dr Redfern. I have just been paid my first honest wage in my life. It is time to celebrate.'

The team cheered, and Percy said, 'I am happy to be part of your family circle, Divit, if you are going to be so generous to us.' This brought another cheer as Divit went off to buy the cake.

*   *   *

The news did not appear to be sombre as Dr Redfern stuck his cheery face in the door of the office at four o'clock and called 'Hello!' in a loud voice. He was shown into the boardroom, and the others crowded in too, anxious to hear the news. Percy had gone to pick up Granny to help celebrate Divit's first pay packet and the promised cake. As they arrived and took a seat at the table, Redfern began.

He was sombre as he spoke. 'Jason Haskell Bowering is not Divit's father. It is still a mystery who his father is, but the test shows that Haskell is not possible, because Divit's DNA is 50 per cent Indian, with African and Portuguese about equal in the balance of the DNA test. No British at all. We are no further with who his father could be. At the moment, in the testing office, there is a bet that Oliveri is his father, not his grandfather. Could that be possible, Divit?' he asked, facing the boy.

The look on the boy's face as he looked at Dr Redfern showed that he was stunned by the result. He did not say anything for several minutes, and the team waited patiently.

At last, the young man said, 'I suppose it is possible. He was the only one in the family who ever showed my brother and me any love or concern. I know my mother loved me, but when I think hard about it, it was more a sister's love, not a mother's. She would listen to what we had to say and would hug us to make us feel better if we hurt ourselves, but she never clung to us as I saw with other mothers when their children fell over. I remember that because I often wondered if she loved me, after watching other children with their parents. She seemed to have more affection for my brother than me, but not a lot more even for him. Is it possible she was not my mother but a sister? We looked similar, I never doubted that, but how could it be that we were being brought up by our sister? And why was she married to Jason Bowering?'

James said slowly, 'Think of it this way, Divit. What if your grandfather was having an affair with another woman and had two children by her. Perhaps it was in another country, where he must have visited the emporiums he built from time to time. Perhaps it was another part Indian/African woman. He would have been attracted to her because of their shared heritage. Maybe—this is all conjecture, you must understand—your father's daughter visited with him at some time and found out about the two little boys, or something happened to the woman, the mother of the boys. Perhaps she died in childbirth, and that is why your sister/mother was closest to your brother. It was virtually from his birth, and you would have been two or three at that time. Oliveri wanted to bring the children back to where he could keep his eye on them. To do so, he would have had to admit that they were his children. Those societies can be very moral, and he would not have wanted people to look down on him because he had cheated on his wife. He was a man on the up and up all over the place, and he was supposed to appear a clean, honest person. So somehow he married his daughter to his private secretary—at considerable cost, I would imagine—and you were kept away from the capital, in the village, as you remember, until it was thought safe to return to the city as man and wife with two sons to set up in school after their sojourn in the countryside.'

Each staff member and the visitor sat looking at James and then burst out in applause.

Granny said, 'That is very imaginative, James.'

James was looking at Divit and saw the belief come over his face. The young man said, 'I think you are right. It has all fallen into place for me. Why we lived in the village for so long, for instance. I remember that it was mainly my mother and brother, myself also, and my grandparents came often to visit. My father was not there at all until we needed to go to the city because of my schooling, and we moved into the house that Grandfather had got ready for us. My father was already living there, and I remember being shy around him because he was white. I had only seen black or brown faces before seeing him. I was intrigued and kept looking at him, and he got very annoyed with me. I remember that scene distinctly. He never liked me looking at him, and he would tell me to run along to my room. I remember that expression so well. I heard it often enough.'

Granny asked, 'What could he have done to get the girl to marry an Englishman and look after her own brothers? That is the unbelievable part.'

Divit said, 'I think I know. I listened once to what the servants were talking about. The city ones did not know I understood Bantu—or Shona, as it is called now. It is mainly spoken in the villages. English is used mainly in the cities. They were chatting with their friends once when Mother was off doing a lecture at the university. They were saying that she had gone to South Africa for university and had got into a bad crowd there and was locked up in jail for smoking pot. There had been a wild party, and she had been in the middle of it. This, of course, was not what a well-brought-up girl would do, and there was a lot of money changing hands to keep it quiet and to restore her reputation, which had been bandied around the city at home, and not in a nice way. I did not understand at the time all the innuendoes of this conversation, but I expect Grandfather said he would disown her if she did anything like it again. He could be quite stern with her at times. Now I understand why.'

Kate asked, 'Is this enough to make a girl settle down with a strange man and look after two children as if they are her own?'

Granny answered, 'This is fifteen years ago at least. Women have been suppressed in many of those countries, and the alternative, if she was turned out and stranded from her luxurious home, may have been offensive to her. At least she would be free once the boys were grown.'

James said, 'It still does not explain why she and her parents were killed, and also why Divit narrowly escaped being killed and his brother lost his life. I am still sure it has something to do with the uncut diamonds. Do you realise that the last man standing after all this is Jason Haskell Bowering?'

'Except that Divit escaped. Now I think Jason Haskell will return to the UK if he learns that Fiona did not kill him. He needs to finish the job. We did the wrong thing when we had that newspaper report published. We have fallen right into Haskell's hands. Now the authorities in his own country will believe both boys are dead, and the wash-up is, all of Oliveri's wealth, including diamond mines, will go to Jason Bowering, the Johnny on the spot.

'Remember that Oliveri was a wealthy man. He had businesses in quite a few capital cities. When one country had a revolution, he was still backed up by the other properties in safe cities. I would say Haskell has worked all this out and thinks he can take over the fortune all by himself, with no one left to fight him for it—except for Fiona's little mistake of not making sure Divit was dead.'

Dr Redfern said, 'To think all this out must have taken Haskell all those years, planning for the moment. Even with Oliveri alive, he would have had to be careful about what he was planning. But you do not get that wealthy by being a dumb man. Oliveri must have made him show his hand. Perhaps the uncut diamonds started it, which caused the slaughter of him and his wife. Then Haskell went on to finish the job and got rid of his own wife. Next he had to get the two boys out of the country where they were known, so he could get rid of them without it being carried back to Africa.'

'I can see all those things, James, but how will Haskell deal with things now that Fiona and Faye are in jail?' said Ken.

'Watch this space. First of all, we have Divit covered in the short term. Haskell will want to affirm the newspaper story, so he will have to make the journey back here to speak to Fiona. He will find out she is in jail. After she tells him Divit is alive and with us, he will see what he can do to find him. Perhaps his stepmother knows. If she lives here in town, she would have heard all the gossip. This time he will have to do the job himself. The rest of the family is in jail, except for his stepmother, so she will have to help him once and for all, to get rid of the pesky stepson. Hmm. Do we know anything about the stepmother? Has anyone done a search on her?'

Alicia said, 'No, we did not have her on our shortlist for anything but neglect. We will have to take the search home to our laptops for some homework, or perhaps we can put Divit on the job in the morning for his first computer search. One of us can guide him through it.'

'Now that is a good idea, Alicia,' said Percy. 'A little training never hurt anyone.'

They saw Divit's face light up, and he said, 'I remember what she looks like. You guys are making this story work for me. I can remember much more than last week, for instance. I think I would recognise her if I saw her or even a picture of her.'

'The first thing I must do before I go home is to ring Jack Whistler and let him in on this story to date,' said James. 'It changes the whole story of why we want to find Jason Bowering. He is not the cowed sick man we had in mind at all. If he has seen the story published last week, he will be hurrying back to verify it so he can finalise changes in the empire of Douglas Oliveri, as he will think that at last he is the last man standing to win the prizes.'

Dr Redfern said, 'I am astonished by how far this has gone, James. I am sorry that I have to leave now. My wife will be expecting me, and I have been here much longer than I thought I would be. Please let me in on anything further you come up with. So far I did not believe I would be so astonished by the revelations. Now I would hate to miss an episode. Thanks for the coffee and cake, Divit. I feel privileged to be here to help you celebrate your first pay packet.'

Kate and Ken also left for their home, and James, Alicia, Granny, Percy, and Divit were left sitting at the table.

James said, 'First of all, everybody, you do not have to rush home to cook dinner. We have an appointment at our favourite Indian restaurant. This is mainly to celebrate Divit's first pay packet, but also, I do not want to let go of this story yet. My mind is churning with all the possibilities, and I want all of you to concentrate and think of what might happen next. We could be in the middle of an international incident if we let our guard down. Haskell has not finished his murderous round yet. He must be planning something, and quick. I do not believe we will have long to wait to feel it.'

'What about Bowering House, James? It has been his way of getting into the country unseen. He may have the aviation fuel by now. Even if it is stupendous in price, he has the means to pay for it,' Percy offered.

'We must alert Jack Whistler, and he can arrange for a watch on it. It is an advantage for Haskell to be able to enter the country without anyone knowing. However, like most airports, if a radar is placed on it somehow, they would have to come in really low to avoid it. That means flying low over a built-up area, and there are plane watchers who can be asked to report anything unusual.'

'Do we have an address for the stepmother, James?' asked Alicia.

'Not yet, but Divit will find it in the morning. We will be able to handle her if she is here, and this does appear to be where the family are all domiciled.'

Granny asked, 'Does anyone have knowledge of how well Bowering House is looked after? Does the caretaker live there or close by? Are there any other staff, or is the place really rundown and not liveable?

Haskell will have to stay somewhere. Do you have someone who is able to check hotels?'

'All good questions, Granny,' said James. 'Everyone is doing well. We will keep it in mind while we are having dinner, and if anything comes to mind, speak up. Any little thing can make this blow up. I have written all those notes down so I can go over them again tomorrow.'

As they were packing up, the phone in James's pocket vibrated. He pulled it out and looked at the caller's name, then answered. DI Paul Morris said, 'Hi, James, thought you might be interested. I have had the local watch pass by Fiona's house on a regular basis since we picked her up, not really thinking we would score anything, but I just now had a call that a light has come on in what may be the kitchen area in the house. What do you want to do about it?'

'Can you have a permanent watch stand by to see if someone comes or goes? Also, is there a vehicle standing there that was not seen previously? If there is movement out, is it possible for a tail to be arranged? A photograph of the person would also be of help. We now think Jason Haskell Bowering is coming to call any day. Perhaps he is looking for the diamonds. We made no mention of them in our newspaper story. I will bring you up to date tomorrow morning on all the happenings and revelations we have come up with in the last day or so.

'If the person in the house is a woman, could you have her arrested on a charge of breaking and entering? That would do to hold her until we can have a chat with her. We believe she would be Haskell's stepmother. If it is a man, it will be Haskell himself, newly arrived, so he will sleep well tonight after a trip from Africa.

'The other plan could be to dispatch a team at first light to Bowering House to investigate if an aircraft is in the hangar there. There is a man who looks after the grounds and hangar area. You could take him in for questioning as well.

'It sounds as if our newspaper article got to Haskell. He must have seen the story printed in a British newspaper. As an expat, he would buy newspapers to find out what is going on back home. He is back because he called and spoke to Fiona in jail, I would put a bet on that. I will ring Jack Whistler now and tell him what we have learnt today and to back you up. We think we have discovered that Jason Haskell Bowering is a very bad man, and we must not let him leave the country if it is him in the house.

'This is not a matter of international business. This is a matter of an Englishman committing murder, murder, and murder, and an attempt to take over a wealthy man's spot in many countries in Africa. In fact, if he had not had our young guest's brother killed and had not made an attempt on Divit also, we would not be able to hold him, except for unauthorised entry to the UK. If Fiona will not talk, you will not be able to stop young Faye from spilling the beans on him. I do not think we could touch him, otherwise. But he overstepped the mark here by coming back.'

'Okay, James, I think I have all that. I am going out this evening on a date, so I possibly will not speak to you until the morning. But I will organise the sentries before I leave the office. I will catch up with you tomorrow.'

James apologised to his waiting family and guests, and they went on to have their dinner, a little late but welcomed anyway by the restaurant staff. As James sat down, he noticed Derek and Aisha Choudhury sitting at a corner table for two. They raised their glasses to him and went on chatting with each other.

When the Choudhury couple got up to leave, they stopped as they passed James's table, and Derek said, 'You are a hard man to catch, James. I wanted to come and see you, but you have been busy, I believe.'

'Sorry, Derek, I have had my hands full for a while. I will be busy tomorrow too. How about next Monday? I should be free by then. Is it urgent?'

'Not at all, James. Monday will do fine.'

As they turned to leave, the building they were in was shaken by a blast. They all ran outside to see if they could pinpoint the area of the source, and Granny said, 'It looks as if it is in the bookshop area. Can you take me there, please, James?'

Percy paid the restaurant, and they ran to their vehicle. Followed by Derek and Aisha in theirs, they hurried towards where they could see plumes of smoke in the air.

James rang Paul Morris and said, 'Stop what you are doing and come as quickly as you can to the bookshop. I think someone has blown it up.'

As they got closer, they could hear sirens and fire engines as they flashed past them. They followed them to what had been an apartment and bookshop with a house next door, which looked like a charnel house and shop. Books and paper were fluttering all around as flames, getting hold of the books, spread along the street. It was difficult to see what had happened, until they heard a fireman's voice calling to another. 'There is a vehicle stuck in the doorway of the shop. It looks like an SUV. There are two bodies, a man and a woman, in the front of the car. Both are dead and burning. Back up, everybody, and let us have some room to see if we can get some water going on here, although it is too late to save these two. We should look for more bodies inside if we can get in. Call for a tow to get this SUV out of the way.'

James and Percy and Divit jumped out of the vehicle and dashed forward to a fireman, and James said, 'We are the occupants of the apartment upstairs, and it looks as if our decision to eat at a restaurant tonight was lucky for us. My wife's grandmother and our associate would have been in the house next door, and luckily, they are both with us here.'

'It is lucky you were not home and asleep, or you would be fighting this pair on the way to the pearly gates to see who gets in first. Buy a lottery ticket, son. This is your lucky day. Stand by for a while, will you, and keep clear until we are able to clear the way. I think you may have to go to a hotel for the night. We will need to take a statement from you about this.'

James gave the fireman a business card and said, 'I called the police as soon as I could see where the smoke was coming from, and I think I will have the names of the two in the SUV for you, although they will have to be identified by our young friend here, whom they were trying to find.'

The fireman looked with interest at Divit and said, 'I think I have seen you before, son, haven't I?'

'I do not think so, sir, but James will sort us all out. We will not leave until you say we can. We have nowhere to go yet.'

James patted Divit on the back and said, 'Granny is our concern now, Divit. She has lived here all her life. This is a sad moment for her.' They went back some distance to where the car was parked, away from the smoke.

Derek chose that moment to come forward, and he said, 'I am sorry, James. My father has an apartment next to our workshop, big enough for the five of you. Please be our guests for as long as you need accommodation. What you have done for us as a family is too valuable to calculate. I am sure my father will see it the same way.' He wrote down an address and pulled a key from his key ring and handed it to James, then he walked back to his car and drove away.

Percy gave a wry grin and said to James, 'This buddy system you have seems to work both ways.'

James said, 'Let us go and see if Granny and Alicia are all right. This is a terrific shock to both of them, especially Granny. Her whole life's history is going up in smoke. I hope it does not give her a heart attack.'

When they went back to the car, where the two women sat holding each other tightly, Granny looked up with a smile and said, 'Thank you, Divit, for the invitation out today, and to you, James, for the dinner invitation. Otherwise, I would not be sitting here with you now. The thing I am sorry for is, I should have packed a bag before coming out to meet you. I will have nothing to wear tomorrow.'

As she had calculated, everybody thought that very funny and broke into smiles.

'Derek has offered us accommodation for as long as we need it. Not in his penthouse, which only has two bedrooms, but in a large apartment next to his father's workshop. That should do us while we work things out,' advised James.

Divit said, 'I am so sorry, Granny, that my troubles have followed me here and that you should lose your home and the bookshop, and you too, James and Alicia and Percy.'

'We did not foresee anything like this, Divit, but you cannot blame yourself. The invitation for you to stay was from all of us. We are glad to have you with us, safe and sound,' said Granny.

'Yes, Divit,' agreed Alicia. 'We would have never lived with the fact that someone else got to you while you were alone in the world.'

DI Morris pulled up next to them in his vehicle and said, 'I can offer you a cell for the night if nothing else comes up, James. Unfortunately, our sentry outside Fiona's house was blindsided. There must have been two of them. He was knocked unconscious and was not able to call in the movement for fifteen minutes and was incoherent even then, and by the time anyone could understand what he was saying, I got the call from you. He could not give a description, as they approached him from behind.'

'It looks like a man and a woman in an SUV stuck in the doorway of the bookshop, Paul. They are both dead and burned beyond recognition. To me, it looks like they tried to ram the door, and sparks caught the leaking petrol from the collision of the heavyweight door and vehicle. I picked out the number plate before the car was totally engulfed, so we can confirm the vehicle but nothing much else.

'We might find a few more clues in Fiona's house. I presume it was them, and it is the only place we have to look—other than the Bowering House, to see if an aircraft is parked there. What would you say, Paul, about going right now, with an escort, to that landing field? It may be light by the time we find it. It may be the caretaker here in the car. The only way to find out is to find an aircraft parked there.'

Divit said from the back seat, 'I want to come too, James. Remember, I am Jason Bowering too. That aircraft may be mine now, also Bowering House, and I have the right to be there if someone pulls us up and disallows us entry.'

James and Paul looked at each other, and James said, 'Legally, he has a point. We will pick up his passport in our office before we leave. Luckily, we had it in our office today for DNA testing. Otherwise, it would have gone up in smoke too.'

Percy said, 'Do not leave me out. I want to see that property. I have lived in this area all my life and never heard of it until this case. Now I am anxious to find out more about it and why it is dilapidated.'

'I think we will have to take an aviation expert with us too. What about your friend, James? Freddy White, the ex–air force flyer. He may know something about it,' said Paul.

'Good one, Paul. How did you remember him?'

'I think he is about to become my brother-in-law. My sister has been seeing him since we all had dinner in your apartment last year.'

Alicia, who had been listening, said, 'Yippee! So I matched up one pair.'

Everyone laughed. James said, 'It sounds as if we will have a veritable convoy by the time we get to this house. You can be my driver, Percy. I do not know that neck of the woods. I am from out of town. Divit can come with us to show his credentials if there is anyone there. Alicia, we will take you to the Choudhury apartment and leave you with a car to do some shopping tomorrow with Granny. We all have only what we are standing in. Also, we will need food, I imagine. We will keep in touch if we can get a line to you. We do not know if there is service in the area.' He stopped and thought for a few seconds and said, 'There must be some signals somewhere, to advise when an aircraft is coming in. We will have to check that out when we get there.'

Paul asked, 'Do you think it may be necessary to take a couple of coppers with us to make an arrest if necessary? What about young Tony Walton and one other? Tony seems to think you are the man of the moment—any moment in time.' He laughed.

James laughed too. 'Yes, Tony is a valuable chap to have around. He has helped out in a few of our cases and has always done a good job. He thinks ahead. I like that in an assistant.'

'Okay, I will organise that. Give me a few minutes. It looks like that fireman is looking for you.'

There was the fireman, waiting for Paul to move aside. 'James Armstrong?' he asked.

'Yes, that is me. This is Valerie Newton, grandmother to Alicia and therefore to me, and this is Percy, another resident. You have already met Divit Edwards, our tenant. We have been offered an apartment to help us out, by someone who we were talking to in the restaurant where we were having dinner when we heard that enormous crash and whoosh and followed the smoke signal here to arrive about the same time as you did.

'Well, then I guess we have your statement. That is all we need to know at the moment. But we will have to come and see you to take your written statement sometime soon, and we need an explanation of who those people in the SUV might be.'

'We hope to have an answer to that question sometime tomorrow. We do not know for sure who they are. As you can see on our business card, we are detectives, and we believe someone involved in a current case did this damage. We knew they were dangerous, but we did not expect this destruction. Everything we own has gone up in smoke. Thank God for credit cards. At least we will be able to have new clothes tomorrow.'

'All right, sir, I will hear from you soon. Take care that there are no others waiting for you.'

'Believe me, Joe,' James said, picking up the name from the tag on the fireman's uniform, 'my family and I will be very careful until someone is locked away for this evening's work—that is, if they are not in that vehicle in the doorway.'

They looked back at the bookshop and house with flames still licking around them and high into the air. James felt the anger rise, and he said, 'Someone has to pay for this, so if they are still alive, I will be chasing them. They will not get away with it.'

'Take it from me, James. It is better to let the anger go. Concentrate on other things. It will save your blood pressure from rising.'

'It is not just me, Joe. My wife's grandmother was brought up in this house. It has been her life, that and the bookshop. Now she has nothing left.'

'I have seen it before, James, believe me. She will not worry about it half as much as you will, so take it easy and go on with life to the best of your ability. The insurance company will pay for a new house, but your blood pressure is going to be your main worry.'

'Thank you, Joe. I will keep that in mind.'

CHAPTER FIFTEEN

They drove first to the office to pick up Divit's passport and then to the address that Derek had given them. They found a very nice, quite large apartment with four bedrooms and two bathrooms, a nice living area, and a kitchen/dining room. Granny, always the one to cheer anybody up, said, 'This is wonderful! We will manage well in this apartment until we can find an alternative. It is very nice of your friend, James, to let us have this.'

'We are leaving you here, Granny and Alicia, so have a good sleep. We will see you sometime in the morning. I will be in touch, at least when we arrive back, to let you know what is happening.' He kissed the ladies and went back to the car and sat in the passenger seat.

He said, 'Okay, Percy, time to go. We will have to stop for breakfast somewhere along the way. Try to sleep, Divit. We might need your eyes to guide us when we get close to the property.'

Percy drove first to the police station, while Paul changed from his personal car to a police division vehicle and picked up the constables, Tony and Jack. He had called Freddy White earlier and waited until he joined them, and he sat in the passenger seat. Freddy, known in the army when he served in Afghanistan, was named Freddy the Friendly Flyer because he had saved so many by arriving when the battles had been fierce and managing to knock out the enemy.

They took off in convoy, with the GPS set for the numbers on the map that James had given to Paul as a guide. So Paul was the first in line, with Percy following. Percy's car was too old for a GPS, and he had not needed one until now, as he knew the city well. They stopped at the outskirts of the city, at a service station for Percy to top up on fuel, and they had coffee and warm rolls, in case they would not be able to stop again for a while. They had no idea what they were going to encounter. Percy said, 'It is like flying blind.'

*　　*　　*

After two hours on the road, Divit said, 'This looks familiar. Turn off at the next side road. I think we are about to arrive.'

They went silently down the road, hoping that if there was anyone at the property, they would not hear the vehicles. Suddenly they saw some great gates with a sign across the top saying 'Bowering House'. The gates were locked by a chain and padlock, and Paul said to Tony, 'Do your best, Tony. The bolt cutters are in the boot.' With little effort, the gates swung open. Paul said, 'The locals probably are not aware of the aircraft hangar. It is quite a distance to the next property. Houses are sparse along this road although I notice on the map there is a village a short distance away.'

Freddy said, 'The hangar will be at the back of the house so the aircraft can take off towards the ocean and not cause a lot of noise to those locals.'

By now, the second car came alongside them, and James said quietly, 'I think we should leave these cars in a line in front of the gate so nobody will be able to get past if there is anyone here. Fancy a walk, boys?'

They lined the vehicles up so that no one could drive through, and they set off towards the rear of the house. After ten minutes, in the near-dawn light, the ground levelled out, and Freddy said, 'We are on the start of the runway. We should see the hangar any time soon. The ground is very flat around here. You cannot see the house now. There is a small hill hiding it, and trees, which appear to be fairly newly planted, maybe three or four years ago. They will grow quite tall eventually.'

Just then James was glad they had chosen Freddy to accompany them. He seemed to know what to look for. They might have wandered around for an hour, looking for a place to start. It was a large property.

Ahead, he saw the glow of early-light sunshine on the side of a grey building and said, 'Bingo, boys, we have found it. Should we fan out to approach from different directions towards the doorway?'

'A good idea, I think,' said Freddy. 'I cannot hear any noises. Perhaps there is no one here, or perhaps the caretaker is asleep.'

Divit said, 'That is possible. He has a small flat at the back end of the hangar.'

James said, 'I have not seen too many hangars, and none up close. I think, Paul, you should lead the way towards the door with Divit, in case you have to announce yourselves. Percy and I will come in from the left, and Tony, you, Jack, and Freddy come in from the right. If we all arrive simultaneously, whoever is in there will not know what to expect, and he cannot shoot us all down if we are divided.'

Paul said, 'Have you done this sort of thing before, James?'

James said, 'Only the orienteering games we played at university. They were all fun and games, not a threat at all, although they were very competitive.'

Paul said, 'It sounds like a good idea. Has anyone got a better one?' No one spoke, so he said, 'Okay, chaps, let's do it. By the way, Tony, Jack, and I all have weapons, so if things get rough, stand away from us.'

They followed the plan, and all ended up going through to the back of the hangar, at the door to the flat, which was unlocked and empty. Freddy looked into the aircraft parked in the hangar and said, 'It is a Lear jet 45, a very expensive aircraft.' He walked around for an inspection and found the fuel gravity access panel and announced, 'The aircraft has already been refuelled for a quick take-off. Shall I let the tyres down? He will not get far if I do that.'

'Go for it, Freddy. When you have done that, we shall all go and look at the house. Has anyone got anything to open old-fashioned doors?' James asked.

'Look in the boot when we get back to the cars, Tony. I put various keys to open just about anything that opens and shuts. Divit can have the pleasure of using them. It will be his property after all, in time,' said Paul.

Divit grinned. 'My pleasure, gentlemen.'

They were able to access the house without too much trouble, and Paul again said, 'I will lead the search. Jack and Tony can follow me in case someone comes out toting a gun.'

They were all interested in the house. It looked dilapidated on the outside, but walking inside was amazing. It made them all hold their breaths as they looked around. The house had been repaired and painted, and the furnishings were all art deco and wonderful. It looked as if it may have been in its heyday of the earlier century, perhaps 1920s, and smartly so. Someone had spent time and money here, doing the old house up, and presumably left the outside looking worn because they did not want visitors.

The men came to the bedroom section, and suddenly they were alert. Someone was living here. The beds were made up; women's clothing was in one of the rooms and a bathroom. Another room showed that someone visited, as there were only warm-weather men's clothes in the wardrobes, as if they may come in winter, and men's cologne and soaps in another of the bathrooms. All the bathrooms had been renovated, and quite recently, by the look of it. They did not find the occupants.

*　　*　　*

At nine o'clock, there was a horn toot from a car at the gates. The team had been having a cup of tea and toast from a toaster they had found in a kitchen cupboard. Divit said to encourage them, 'This house is in my name, which is Jason Bowering, according to my passport. Please be my guests. It is breakfast time.' They had needed no other persuasion and had sat down to eat.

They filed out of the house to greet the newcomer, who introduced himself as Thomas Bastian, the caretaker of the property. He asked to see every man's credentials, and when he came to Divit, he said, 'I have seen you before, haven't I?'

'Three years ago, as a boy of fifteen. You have a good memory, Mr Bastian. My name is Jason Bowering.' He held out the British passport in that name, which showed him as a much younger person. 'Where is my father, Mr Bastian?'

'He arrived yesterday, very early in the morning, and he and Mrs Haskell went into the city in the SUV.'

'Could you tell us what the registration number on that vehicle is, sir?' asked Paul.

The number Thomas Bastian gave to them was the same as that of the SUV they saw burning in the doorway of the bookshop.

'Has Mrs Haskell been living here in the house?' asked James.

'Yes, she turned up about the same time you arrived with your father, young man, and she has been renovating the house ever since.'

'Was Jason Bowering here often in that time?' asked James.

'He comes once or twice a year and only stays a week at a time. Mrs Haskell and Mr Bowering do not appear to like each other much. This is the first time I have known them to go away together. It is Mrs Haskell's vehicle, I believe, but I do not question either of them about things except for anything required for the grounds and the hangar. I have a job which I enjoy and have free rein on what time I appear and leave, so I do not want to interfere in any way which would make them terminate me from my job.'

'All right, Thomas, we will clear the gate so you can get in. If either of your bosses appears, I want you to immediately call this office,' Paul said, handing over a card. 'Tell the person answering the phone that it is urgent, top priority, and to contact me. However, I do not believe you will see either person again, and you may soon have this young man as your boss.'

Bastian looked confused. 'All right, sir. I do not understand what this is all about, but no doubt you will tell me in time.'

'In time, Thomas. But before we leave, we are going to hunt through this house for evidence. You are welcome to go about your duties.'

Freddy said, 'We have disabled the aircraft, Mr Bastian. Please do not change what we have done. It is very important for international purposes that this aircraft does not leave the hangar without our permission.'

The already confused man turned white. 'Am I free to leave the property now? I do not want to be swept up in international incidents.'

'We think you will not be worried again, Mr Bastian, and we prefer for you to stay to warn us if the couple return here,' said Paul.

Thomas Bastian went on towards the hangar, and the others started a search of the house. No area was left at peace. They found a box in which to put all the papers and anything they thought could be of use, to carry to the police car. Around ten o'clock, they reasoned they would not find much more, and they would have forensics come to have another look the next day.

Freddy said, 'Would you give me a few minutes? I have only just thought about it after this search. Most pilots have what they call a nav bag that they do not fly without. Occasionally, the electronics in an aircraft goes haywire, and the screen goes blank. Every pilot carries navigation instruments in his bag, hence *nav bag*, and an assortment of papers necessary—in this case, perhaps a passport. We have not found a bag in the house or in that small flat, but maybe Bowering kept his bag in the aircraft, behind his seat. I will pop over now and have a look.'

'Take Tony with you, Freddy, just as a precaution. We do not trust anybody nowadays.'

Fifteen minutes later, the pair returned, with Freddy carrying a black bag and giving a victory sign. They tooted as they left the gates and headed for the city.

Freddy went with James and Percy, as they knew where he lived. As they neared the city, Freddy said, 'Thank you, James. That was a very interesting sojourn. I am happy to be of help.'

'We will let you know, Freddy, what we come up with. It looks like the woman in the burning car was Mrs Haskell, and the man her stepson, Jason Haskell Bowering, who is Divit's stepfather. We will tell you the rest over dinner one night soon, but it will not be in the bookshop apartment. That is gone forever, unfortunately.'

James called Alicia and explained what they had found. He asked if she wanted to come into the office and help look through the box of items from Bowering House. She excused herself, saying she thought she should stay with Granny today. Could she look tomorrow? She was very interested, but it had been a hard night for both her and Granny to get through.

James said, 'Ask Granny. She may be interested in coming here, and it will take both your minds away from the bookshop.'

Alicia turned and asked her grandmother and turned back to the phone and said, 'We are both coming. You are right. We will only grow more morose if we stay here alone, thinking about the bookshop.'

'I will order in for the office lunch. We have not had our regular meals, and we are all hungry. Paul and the two policemen are still here with us, and Ken and Kate did a great job opening up the office. We did not let them know what and where it was all happening, but they heard of the fire this morning on the radio news and came into the office via the bookshop route. They said there are police screens around both the house and bookshop areas, and it still seemed to be smouldering, although they could not see much. They were huddled in the office, hoping we had not been caught up in the fire, as they had heard nothing from us.'

James and Percy laid the contents of the big box picked up from Bowering House on to the boardroom table. Percy said, 'We will have two piles which we want sorted: interesting and not interesting. Do not put anything in the bins. We will go over it again later. The first up is the nav bag. I think this is the place we will find things, because Jason left things in the aircraft instead of taking it to the house. Perhaps he did not want his stepmother's inquisitive nature to take over and disclose what he held secret in the bag.'

First out of the bag was Jason's passport and a chequebook. They looked at the stubs in the chequebook, and Percy said, 'He kept this for the big stuff. It looks like he paid for the renovations to the house, and the wages and costs were paid from this account. Big numbers written in here. He did not stint on the decorating of the house. Maybe it was to be his home base when it was finished.'

James flicked through the stubs and looked at the name of the bank. No African business could trace it through the cheque stubs, and he said, 'This appears to be a local account that he used, so nobody else had access to it or knew what he was doing. I would be interested to know how much is being held in the account. We were right about the timing of the renovations. It started after he dropped the two boys and abandoned them. There are payments to his stepmother too. I would bet she was blackmailing him about the boys. She seems to be his contact here in this country. I suppose because Jason had been gone so long, he had no contacts left to watch out for him. Is there anything in his history to say what he did before he left this country?'

He went on after a minute's thought. 'We will have to check that out. I get the feeling that he might have been a mining engineer. He had a close interest in stones. Divit said he kept a large vase full of stones as decoration on a table. Then again, there are the uncut diamonds. What if he was the one mining the diamonds, and he was blackmailing Oliveri because the secret mine was on his lease?

'Also, Divit told us that Jason went off on a bus each Monday and returned on the bus on Friday. That is not an office worker's routine. I have this feeling that those diamonds are involved in the whole story, and not because some politician gave them to Oliveri. I think Jason took the diamonds after he killed Oliveri. I am almost sure that was a story put out by Jason after he killed Oliveri and his wife, and it also served him to blame them for his wife's death too. He hurried back after ridding himself of the two boys here, to cover up the diamond mine, I would bet.'

At that moment, Alicia and Granny came in and greeted everyone, and Granny said, 'What have you found?'

'Not a lot yet. We were waiting for you. How would you like to go through the passport, Alicia? Your keen eye will be able to note how often he moved his base,' said James.

James explained to the two newcomers what they had found in the cheque stubs, and Granny's retort was 'At least a lot of this stuff was bought locally to keep the town going. I see your friend Chamberlain sold a lot of furniture to him, James.'

'I missed that, Granny,' he said, picking up the chequebook again and looking at the stubs. 'You are right. He purchased most of that art deco furniture from Chamberlain's luxury import-and-export business. Again, he used a local painter and wallpapering company. The town will miss him. Also, carpets and mats are from a local firm, and here too are window treatments. His stepmother was very busy, but I notice it was Jason who paid the bills. I presume we will find the invoices in the box.'

'All this from item number one,' said Percy. 'What else is in that bag?'

James pulled out a notebook/diary which had a page for each day. 'Here you are, Kate. Study that and make an itemised account of what he has been doing. Wait, there is another one here. One for last year too. He liked to keep up with things, to carry these around wherever he went. He must have had his finger on the pulse.

'A cardigan to keep him warm. That is about it. You may pick up some interesting things in that diary. Can you help Kate with it, Ken? We will go through the box. I expect that most of this stuff will be his stepmother's paperwork. Actually, I will leave it to you all for a moment. I have been putting off calling Jack Whistler, hoping we would come up with something more concrete, but I think I have put it off long enough. I will go to my office and make a call.'

When James made the connection to Jack Whistler and told him of the burning of the house and bookshop and the bodies in the SUV and the follow-up visit to Bowering House, he could hear the distress in Jack's voice that it had come to this.

James said, 'I believe it was Jason Bowering and his stepmother in the SUV. We checked the number plate. What we do not know is why it happened that way. Was Jason making a last-ditch stand to kill Divit, his stepson? Or was he trying to knock all of us out of testifying against Fiona and Faye at their trial? Or both? I think it was both. Divit had to be knocked out for good. They found out that Divit was living with us. Therefore, we had to go too, we knew too much for his safety.

'It was the stepmother's vehicle, but we have no evidence if it was Jason in the passenger seat, except that the aircraft is in the hangar at Bowering House. There is no sign of him anywhere else. It seems a botched job altogether for someone who had achieved so much by murdering Divit's whole family.'

Jack said, 'Perhaps the woman insisted that she drive her own vehicle. People do get possessive about their vehicles. Not knowing you installed heavy doors, she expected to break through, but circumstances were against them with the heaviness of those doors.'

'That is what we think happened. So do the firemen that attended to the fire. It does mean that at the moment, we have no proof it was Jason Bowering. I think it may be time to call off the search for him, Jack. He has arrived in the UK. His aircraft is at Bowering House. The groundsman/caretaker there said he does not have another vehicle, and he has not returned to the house—yet anyway. We will wait for a few days to see if any DNA can be taken from the bodies found at the scene.

'Can you find out what the international search team have come up with? We have our own ideas on it, but once again, no proof. It would be good to hear someone else's opinion. What is for sure is that we are not looking for a broken man mourning the loss of his family. We threw that version out of the window since Divit got most of his memory back and told us about his earlier life in Africa. If we are searching for Jason, we are looking for a triple murderer, thief, and con man.'

'I will ask, James, and get back to you after I have delivered your version. What are you going to do now that your dwellings have been taken from you?'

'We have not had a chance to even think of it, Jack. We went off in the middle of the night to search Bowering House. We have disabled the aircraft. I had a friend help out there who knows about aircraft. We searched the house and hangar, and we have a pile of paperwork to go through to help us find something we can hang on Bowering. So far, we have not slept or eaten very much, so we will be too tired to think about it by this evening.

'A client of ours has loaned us a large apartment to use for as long as we need it. I feel a little like I too am dead at the moment. I will get back to you tomorrow. We will be smartly dressed in brand-new clothes and refreshed enough to give everything a fresh look. That is what I am hoping. Sorry, Jack, having just stopped to talk to you, I am suddenly overwhelmed. Percy, Alicia, and Granny must feel the same. So as soon as possible, we will lock up and go to our new beds and sleep.'

James sat in his office for a few minutes, feeling numb and too tired to continue, but he knew he must. He joined the others around the boardroom table to see what they had found. One pile seemed to be mainly related to the decoration of the house, all the receipts made out to Jason Bowering. The smaller bundle had photographs and memorabilia of the family. At the bottom of the box, there was a coffee-table book filled with photos dating back to 1900 at least, perhaps further. The women were dressed in long dresses, hats, and feather boas around their shoulders. There was no mistaking the Haskell look. They all looked very well-to-do and fashionable. What had the ancestors done to reduce them to murderers and con men and women? That was the only description he could give for the whole current family.

Paul said, 'Besides what we found in the nav bag, James, there is not much here that can help us. What if we call it a day and go to our respective abodes and meet again tomorrow morning?'

James laughed. 'Nicely put, Paul. Yes, I am beginning to feel as if I could sleep for a week.'

Percy said, 'We are with you there, James. A lot has happened in the last two days. It is time to rest so we can take things in if we do find something. There has to be a story here somewhere.'

Ken said, 'Why don't you all go off to, as Paul puts it, your abodes? Kate and I will continue here with these day-to-day scribblings of Jason's, and if we have time, we will try to find if he was a mining engineer.'

'Call that last idea in to the force office, Ken, if you run out of time. They will come up with an answer so that we will have all the facts tomorrow morning,' said Paul.

'Thanks, everyone, for what you have done today. It is greatly appreciated, but Paul is right. We have been overstretched today, especially Percy and me, having had to see our abodes go up in smoke. Emotionally, I feel quite unstable right now.' James did look a bit wonky, they all thought.

Alicia took his arm and said, 'Come, Percy and James. You too, Divit. Granny and I have at least had the benefit of some sleep. We will take you to our new abode, for you both to catch up. Thanks, everybody, for today, and to you, Ken and Kate, for carrying on.'

*   *   *

The apartment was very nice, James thought when he walked in. He needed a shower. He felt so grubby and smelt like smoke. He lay down after showering and was immediately asleep. Percy too did the same. Divit sat with Alicia and Granny for a while and said, 'I do not know how to thank you for all you have done for me and continue to do for me.'

Granny said, 'You are as tired and upset as the rest of us, Divit. I have shown you your room. Go and sleep too. We will all feel better in the morning.'

CHAPTER SIXTEEN

After a good night's sleep, they all felt a little better, and over breakfast, Granny said, 'I have been keeping something from you for a while now.'

'What is it, Granny? Are you ill?' asked Alicia, looking concerned.

'No, dear. I am quite well. What I have been holding back is, the council officers have approached me several times to discuss the bookshop and house. The plan is to repossess both sites for planning a future cruise centre and shopping area. They showed me what they have in mind, and now, I think, is the right time to contact them to say we will not be rebuilding on the site and to go ahead with the plan they showed me. We will be paid quite a nice sum, I think, but I will ask around to see if the consideration is enough. We will also have the insurance money for both the house and the bookshop, so we will be well off.'

'The plan they showed you is gone in the fire, I presume, Granny?' asked Alicia.

'Yes, Alicia, but it was only a provisional plan at best. Once they have my permission, they will draw up a positive plan. Their idea then is to call on other houses in the street to see if they will consent. In the long run, we do not have a leg to stand on, and I think it was very nice of them to ask me politely first. If they get enough owners to agree, the price they quoted to me, I think, is very fair. I think others will agree. They plan to make a cruise liner office and a shopping centre with apartments above it. We will be amongst the first to be offered an apartment. We can buy an apartment, or even two, because we had the bookshop as well as the house.

'As you know, I have given the idea of selling the place a lot of thought over the past ten years. I am getting too old to manage the bookshop, and really, it is because of Rob Gooding, who gave us the bookshop, that I have not gone ahead with it. But Rob is in poor health now, and they do not expect him to survive another winter. He has so much pain from his arthritis and is now permanently in a wheelchair to get around. When he hears about the fire, I am sure he will say *sell*.'

'And you have kept this to yourself, Granny. Why didn't you share this with us?' asked James.

'We have all been very happy, James, since you came to live here. The office is walking distance, and we were so cosy. I really did not want to change things. But the fire has changed everything. We have to relocate anyway. I think we should contact the council and give our okay on the deal and take the two apartments. Even if we do not live in them, they will be a good investment, and if we have first pick, we can take the ones on the end over the cruise terminal, which will be quieter in the long run, opposite the wharf and walking distance to the town. It has been a great position to live all these years.'

'Where do you consider we will live, Granny? Have you worked that out as well?' asked Alicia.

Granny laughed, pleased now that the moment of telling was over. 'No, Alicia, we will have to look around and decide together It has all happened too quick for an answer so soon.'

Percy said, 'Am I permitted to help choose a new spot?'

All laughed at his comment, and Granny said, 'Of course, Percy, you are part of our family too. We cannot manage without you.'

Looking at Divit, she added, 'We will include you too, Divit, if you wish. We do not want to exclude you now, but I think you would be happier with a younger group. We do not have to decide yet. We need money to do anything, so until the insurance company has done their investigation, we will stay here, as Derek was so kind as to allow us an indefinite stay.'

'I think Jamal Kumah would welcome you, Divit, when his mother is gone,' said Alicia. 'He will be overcome when she goes. He is an only child, and as a result the family is very close. So he will welcome your company. By then, we will know where you are situated both financially. You will appreciate the younger company, and you will decide what you want to do, like maybe go back to Africa. But it is early days, and you are welcome to stay with us as long as you want.'

'Meanwhile, Divit, you have your job as receptionist for as long as you want it,' said James. 'Which reminds me, we are expected at the office. We had better get a move on. Are you coming too, Granny? We will give you a space in the office too, a change from the bookshop. Have you contacted Caroline yet?'

'Yes, James. I rang her early yesterday to save her from coming in to find a fire burning up our livelihood. I told her we will pay her till the end of the month because there is no longer a bookshop.'

'Okay. Percy, we will have to take both vehicles. Everybody in the cars in fifteen minutes, and we will be off to work for the day,' said James, rising and walking to the bedroom to get dressed.

*   *   *

When they arrived at the office, Ken and Kate had already unlocked the doors and turned on the lights, and they were working at the computers. Kate said, 'We are still following up on Jason Haskell Bowering. There are so many different ways he has used his name. It is like a puzzle, following the story. You were right, James. He studied as a mining engineer at university. The only one of the Haskells who went to university, he is the eldest in the family and was a good scholar and received his degree with honours. His first employment was in South Africa, where he fulfilled a two-year apprenticeship, mostly in diamond mines. He seemed to have made a name for himself, as he was offered work in other parts of Africa. We had to progress from there by checking dates in his passport, but he was never out of work and moved around a lot, from job to job. At one stage, we thought he was very unsettled, jumping from one job to another, perhaps without a wife or somewhere nice to live. We do not know. No reason was given, but he certainly was able to pick and choose his jobs in those first years in Africa.

'His longer employment started with Oliveri, after he had been in Africa about eight years. And of his marriage, if he took part in one, we could not find confirmation. It just started talking about Jason and his wife, the daughter of magnate Douglas Oliveri. It was mentioned first when Divit started school. Previous to that, his addresses had been at mining sites, and it suddenly changed to a city address. That is about where we could not find what he was doing. His passport said he was personal secretary to Douglas Oliveri, but it does not give a description of what he was actually doing. In those last few years, he was flying in and out of other African countries a lot, but the reason is never mentioned. It just states "work-related".'

James said, 'Divit, if we can get no further and Jason does not turn up, I think we should find a lawyer and someone who knows their way around those countries, and you should go back to your home and make a statement that you want to take up where your grandfather left off. Your heritage is in those countries, and you have a Zimbabwe passport for a start, as well as a British one. If you do not fill the void where your stepfather left off, you will miss out on the wealth your grandfather generated. You are the last of his family. It should all come to you. If Jason has interfered, it does not matter. You would be his heir, as there is no one else to take it up. If you do not do this as soon as possible, it will all be lost to the relevant countries. They will close over the gaps left from when Jason left the country to come to the UK, and take it all into general revenue. Tomorrow we will ask for help from our government officials in the countries concerned, to help you out. But choose well. Even your clever grandfather was taken in by a con man.'

Granny said, 'That is very good advice, Divit. Do you remember any names of friends of your grandfather's that could be trusted?'

'I am still trying to get my memory back, Granny. That is stretching things a bit far. Can I think about it for a while?'

'Of course, Divit. I keep forgetting that you lost your memory. You seem so bright. How about you and I get a desk in a quiet corner, and we will go back in history to see if you can think of anyone? We can do a real mind search, going from day to day until we strike gold and find that certain person. There must have been someone your grandfather trusted. Come on. We will make a start while these others are milling about.'

She took Divit into James's office, and when he raised his eyebrows at it, she said, 'It is important, James. A day could make all the difference when facing up to government officials.'

James said, 'Well, we have enough to do in the boardroom. I do not need my office.' He laughed at being bossed around by Granny.

Derek Choudhury came into the office and said, 'I am sorry to be a nuisance, James, but I have been asked to work on Monday and thought I would pop in now. I will not take up much of your time.'

Janes smiled. 'I am sorry to have to talk to you in the reception area. Granny has taken over my office for the morning, and I am left floundering somewhat. What can we do for you?'

'I wanted to thank you, James, for pursuing Faye Haskell—or Flora McDonald, as I knew her. I do not plan to sue her. I think it would be a waste of time and money. But it has restored my father's faith in me. Last time we spoke casually, you said that one day you would like to visit your sister in Australia. I have been thinking of what we can do to reward you for all you have done for me, and I have two open-ended tickets for you to travel business class to Australia as a start, to have a holiday.'

'Derek, that is very generous of you, but not necessary. Your loaning us your business apartment is a blessing to us. We are absolutely devastated that we have lost everything we owned in the fire. We will recover, given a little time, and having the apartment to house us is a great beginning for us.'

'I understand all that, James, but my father and I would like to do more for you. You have restored our family, and believe me, that is the most wonderful gift you could give anyone. We would like to help you through this crisis in your life, including your wife and her grandmother and Percy Gray. Give us a chance, James, to help you. Money is of no object to us. I told you I inherited my grandmother's family fortune, and it is very extensive. So what else can we do to help?'

James looked overwhelmed and Percy came in and said, 'What is it, James?'

'I am out of my depth, Percy. I do not know what to do.'

Percy looked at Derek and said, 'What caused this, Derek? I have never heard James say anything like that before.'

'I offered him help. I think at the moment, he is befuddled, with all that has been going on. Really, he needs a break to give him time to come to terms with everything,' said Derek.

'Well,' said Percy, 'I can understand that. Things have got out of hand. We all feel that way at the moment.'

'So let me help. What can I do?'

Percy said, 'James is not used to asking for help from someone for himself. He has always been the helper. Come with me, Derek. There may be a way you can help with our particular problem at the moment. To be quite honest, we are way out of our comfort zone on this case.'

He took Derek to James's office and announced to Granny and Divit and James, who had followed them into the room, 'Derek is a respected member of the university, where he is studying business and mathematics. Look past the mathematics for a moment. As I said, he is studying business. He is in a better position than us to understand our problem—how to help Divit in the business world in Africa to take up the reins of the multiple businesses that his grandfather built up.

'Derek, would you be able to build up a team to go to Africa with Divit, comprised of your university associates? Firstly, a lawyer would be needed to make a claim for the businesses. Secondly, a business specialist, including a person who could work out the finances. Thirdly, he would need a bodyguard. What else, Granny, can you think of?

'Of course, he would need some of these people to be African, if possible, to understand the local politics. Are there such people studying at your university? If successful, money will be of no consideration, because there could be massive wealth at stake—enough that Divit's stepfather murdered four of Divit's family and almost Divit himself to take over the fortune.'

'Wow,' said Derek. 'No wonder James looks fazed. That is a massive mission. Tell me the rest of the story, please, and I will go and have a meeting with my professors at the university to get a team together to travel with Divit. I for one could look into business and finance. That is my speciality. Although if we can get another person to help as well, it would be better. Two minds are better than one, especially in a foreign country. Do they speak English there, Divit?'

'Yes, Derek, it is counted as the language of my country and is taught at schools from kindergarten. I will have to look up the other African countries where my grandfather built up his businesses. But as he spoke only English and the language from his early years was Indian—and Portuguese as well, I suppose—he would not have understood the local dialects. All his business would have been conducted in English.'

Derek looked again at Divit and said, 'I have met you before, haven't I?'

That comment seemed to break the ice and tension in the room. Everybody laughed, and James explained the circumstances where they had met previously. Derek looked amazed and said, 'We all thought you were dead. I am sorry, Divit, to seem so nonplussed, but I am. I, like the rest of the people around me, thought you were gone, and here you are, sitting before me with this incredible story. This is truly amazing.

'I will contact my university professors today and explain all the details and see what they say about forming a team to investigate in Africa alongside you, Divit. I think we would need a police protection group with us too, James, as a precaution. Would you come with us?'

James shook his head 'I am sorry, everybody. This is way out of my league. If it were in this country, I would be in it like a shot, but in Africa, I would be useless. You need someone who knows their way around and speaks the local dialects, to know what is going on behind your back. Ask around. A former inhabitant would be the best to look for. So many people were evicted from Zimbabwe, for instance. There must be someone who would like to return. I will ask my contacts in the police force to shop around. They would surely be in touch with some of them.'

'This is going to be a very expensive move, James,' said Granny.

James said, 'It will be explained that if Divit is successful in his mission, he will cover expenses. It is a gamble everyone will have to make. There is a possibility of ongoing work after he is established, for anyone who wants to stay on. Meanwhile, he will pay expenses with help from Derek along the way. He can pay Derek back if successful. The others will have their expenses paid while they are on the job and may have to say "Too bad" if things do not go Divit's way. It needs to be done quickly—no pussyfooting around—before the countries are aware that Jason Bowering is not coming back. That knowledge will give you the upper hand for a while. The governments will ponder what is happening. You could call it a coup, I suppose. But it has to be fast. It has nothing to do with governments if an heir turns up to take over Oliveri's heritage, but if things go slow, they will look for reasons they should have it all themselves. All those countries are struggling. They would welcome a windfall.' This was a long speech by James; he worked things out in his own head as it went along.

'What do you think, Derek, now that you have heard the story?' asked Percy.

'Excited' was the first word out of Derek's mouth. 'I have been dodging going to work under my father. I know I will have to walk in his footsteps sooner or later, and I have been trying to put it off. It is stultifying to think I will have to make clothes and sell them for a living for the rest of my life. I will not buck the system if I can have an adventure like this first. Then I will get married and settle down.'

'Bravo, Derek,' said Granny. She turned to face the young man beside her and continued, 'Divit, Derek will lead the way at first, and then you must brace yourself to take over and govern yourself. You are made from stern stuff. Your family has paid a steep price. Do not let it go for nothing. There will be a lot of individuals along the way who will try to stop you. But again, you may find someone who will want to help you because of your grandfather's memory. He was a popular figure and is missed, according to the report of his death that we found. Just remember your grandparents and do not give in.'

Divit hugged Granny and said, 'I am glad to have had you in my life, even though it has only been a short time. I love you all and want to be like you and have a family like you. I know I will not have it if I stay here. My history is behind me, and I have to let it catch me up and go forward. Thank you, all of you, and especially James. I want to be just like you, James. You are my true hero—wise, compassionate, lovable, and strong, especially in your strength at the loss of your homes, caused by my pursuers. You have not said one word to me about how it was my fault. I will promise now that if our mission is successful, you will not have the want of a home again. That is my firm promise to you all.'

James said firmly, 'It is not your fault, Divit. Never think for a moment that any of us have laid any blame on you. We want only for your future to be assured. Go with Derek. He has the sort of mind that is able to bypass anything that gets in the way. That is who you need beside you to keep you focused. You will be confused at first, but let Derek lead you until you are ready to take over your destiny.

'You could sit in our office for months, but it will never satisfy you. It is for you to fight for your future now that you have reached an age where you are looked at as an adult in this country. We look forward to hearing from you to see how successful you will be.

'Thank you, Derek. You have been a wonderful help also when things were looking so low for us. We will use these airline tickets, close up the office for a while, have a holiday in Australia, and come back refreshed, ready to start again.'

Alicia had come into the room sometime before and now called out, 'Hooray! Percy will have to come too and look up his son. Of course, Granny must come too, to make a party of it. We all need a holiday. We have worked hard this year.'

Printed in Great Britain
by Amazon

21407810R00174